'With *The Housemate*, Sarah Bailey expertly plays with memory, guilt and grief to build a tension-filled, vivid world, where there are many ways to be haunted by the ghosts of our past. You'll be right there with the fascinating, flawed Oli Groves as her professional investigation of the Housemate Homicide increasingly veers toward personal obsession. Each new twist in the story skilfully balances bombshell revelations and believability, in a crime that feels achingly familiar, yet shocking at the same time. Much like Oli, I couldn't stop until I knew the truth, too.'

Jacqueline Bublitz, author of *Before You Knew My Name*

'The plot is brilliant, the pace is relentless . . . Oli Groves is a brilliant protagonist: brave and fragile, kick-arse and compassionate—and so very human. *The Housemate* is a book of great emotional power and depth—Bailey's best yet.'

Chris Hammer, author of *Scrublands* and *The Seven*

'An enormously immersive story with Bailey's trademark gordian knot plotting, true to life characters and twists galore. This is Australian crime at its best and *The Housemate* is destined to summit the bestseller charts.'

J.P. Pomare, author of *Call Me Evie* and *The Last Guests*

'I'm as obsessed with Bailey's protagonist, Oli Groves, as Groves is with the story she is chasing. Clever, ambitious, prickly: she's the perfect journo to lead us through this clever and ambitious thriller. Loved the deep dive into the rotten underworld of secrets and corruption, and Bailey's wry take on the changing face of journalism. *The Housemate* is addictive reading in the very best of ways. Sarah Bailey knows her stuff.'

Kate Mildenhall, author of *The Mother Fault*

'*The Dark Lake* is a thrilling psychological police procedural as well as a leap into the mind of a woman engulfed with guilt.'

New York Journal of Books

'*The Dark Lake* hooked me from page one! Sarah Bailey combines the very best elements in this stunning debut thriller—a troubled detective still trying to find her way as a female investigator, a small town haunted by secrets both past and present, and a beautiful victim whose unsettling allure appears to be her biggest asset and largest downfall. With clever twists and all-too-human characters, this book will keep you racing toward the end.'

Lisa Gardner, #1 *New York Times* bestselling author of *Right Behind You* and *Find Her*

'This polished debut is a winner from the first page.'

Daily Telegraph

'I read *The Dark Lake* in one sitting, it's that good. A crime thriller that seizes you from the first page and slowly draws you into a web of deception and long buried secrets. Beautifully written, compulsively readable, and highly recommended.'

Douglas Preston, #1 *New York Times* bestselling author of *The Lost City of the Monkey God* and co-author of the bestselling Pendergast series

'Debut author Sarah Bailey depicts both the landscape and Gemma's state of mind vividly, bringing into focus the intensity of Gemma's physical and emotional pain and her increasing discontent. *The Dark Lake* adds to the trend of haunting, rural Australian crime fiction, and provides a welcome addition to the genre for those left bereft after finishing Jane Harper's *The Dry*.'

Books + Publishing

Sarah Bailey is a Melbourne-based writer with a background in advertising and communications. She has three sons and is currently the managing director of the Melbourne and Sydney offices of advertising agency VMLY&R. Her internationally award-winning Gemma Woodstock series includes *The Dark Lake*, published in 2017 and winner of the Ned Kelly Award for Best First Fiction and the Davitt Award for Best Debut, followed by *Into the Night* in 2018, and *Where the Dead Go* in 2019. *Body of Lies* is the fourth book in the series. Sarah has also published the bestselling *The Housemate* and Audible original *Final Act* in 2021.

BODY OF LIES

SARAH BAILEY

ALLEN&UNWIN

SYDNEY • MELBOURNE • AUCKLAND • LONDON

First published in 2024

Allen & Unwin
Cammeraygal Country
83 Alexander Street
Crows Nest NSW 2065
Australia
Phone: (61 2) 8425 0100
Email: info@allenandunwin.com
Web: www.allenandunwin.com

Allen & Unwin acknowledges the Traditional Owners of the Country on which we live and work. We pay our respects to all Aboriginal and Torres Strait Islander Elders, past and present.

A catalogue record for this book is available from the National Library of Australia

ISBN 978 1 76106 917 8

Set in 13/17 pt Garamond Premier Pro by Bookhouse, Sydney
Printed and bound in Australia by the Opus Group

10 9 8 7 6 5 4 3 2 1

FOR NICK,
WHO IS THE MAIN REASON IT TOOK ME SO LONG
TO WRITE THIS BOOK

PROLOGUE

SUNDAY, 18 SEPTEMBER, 7.37 PM

Bob Dalgliesh pummels his meaty hands on the steering wheel of his Nissan Patrol like it's a drum kit and clips the dashboard with his index finger for good measure. 'And meeee,' he croons along to the Counting Crows, then adds in an exaggerated falsetto, '*Lucky* me!' There are two hundred and four dollars in his wallet that weren't there this morning—and he wasn't even supposed to go to the pub this afternoon. Bloody lucky he did.

Bob exhales through a beery burp. He rounds the bend and levels the car out into the straight stretch of road that leads to the farmhouse. Stars freckle the milky sky, an almost full moon on display. Cows congregate in small groups along the fence lines on either side of the road, their long faces eerie in the moonlight.

Queen comes on the radio, and Bob turns up the volume. His off-key singing is interrupted by text messages landing on his phone. Steadying the wheel, he peers at the screen. It's not Janet, as he suspected, but one of his mates, McCorkle—something about a fight at the pub. He's sent a video message attachment. Bob tosses

1

the phone aside. He can't bloody do two things at once, and he doesn't want to tempt fate after his win.

Lights appear in his rear-view mirror. A station wagon approaches quickly, then overtakes him, rattling past like a bat out of hell. He sees the profile of a female driver, thick dark hair, a pale face.

'Hold your horses, lady.' Bob watches the car zoom ahead.

Moments later another set of lights appears in his rear-view mirror, belonging to some kind of four-wheel drive. It swerves wildly into the adjacent lane as it careers past, then reverts to the correct side of the road, engine revving.

'Prick,' Bob mutters, flustered.

The station wagon is already fifty metres away; it must be going at least a hundred and thirty k's per hour. Bob watches the other car approach it, going equally fast.

The two sets of brakelights get closer to each other—too close.

'What the hell?'

The four-wheel drive blocks his view of the other car, then jerks sideways, accelerating to level beside it. The vehicles drive in parallel for a few nerve-racking moments. Bob doesn't hear the music anymore, watching dumbly as the two cars briefly become one before dramatically breaking apart.

Bob feels like a character in an action movie—Bruce Willis comes to mind—as he brings the truck to a dramatic halt. 'Yippee-ki-yay,' he murmurs, swinging open his car door.

The station wagon becomes airborne. It twists and turns, head-lights drawing chaotic trails on the dark landscape, providing flashes of saggy wire fences and oversized gum trees.

Bob has an impulse to keep everything moving—himself, the other car. Janet's always saying that take-offs and landings are the most dangerous parts of any journey.

Trying to ignore the pain of the stitch in his side, he holds out his hands as if he can somehow prevent the inevitable horror. *Please don't land, please don't land, please don't land.*

When the car nosedives into a tree, Bob swears he can see the impact ripple out across the paddocks. His knees buckle, his insides churning, as an odd little noise escapes his mouth. He screams out for help, but he's alone. The four-wheel drive is gone.

———

Red and blue lights slice across the shadowy farmland, the ambulance siren screaming into the darkness. Fred nods in time to the music, some electronic rubbish Ash has put on. Out of the corner of his eye he notices a flash of silver. He flicks glitter from a crease in his wrist; his daughter's fairy party this morning only went for three hours, but it felt like ten. His back aches, and his gut still feels slippery from the onslaught of soft drink, cake and lollies.

As he presses his foot against the accelerator, Ash gives him a look. Fred pretends not to notice and drives even faster. It's all right for Ash—he doesn't spend every five seconds at home getting jumped on or yelled at. Ash just goes for beers, watches TV and does whatever he likes. Fred enjoys driving the bus now more than ever; it feels like freedom, and he's going to damn well enjoy it.

'We're close,' says Ash, as they fly past the turn-off to the Montgomery farmhouse. He fidgets in his seat and snaps his gum. 'Despatch said it's just before the Staffords' joint.'

Fred thinks Ash seems particularly jumpy tonight. He doesn't know him that well, considering how much time they spend together, but Ash has definitely been more skittish lately. Fred just has too much on his plate to be bothered asking what's up.

Behind them, the road is empty. 'No sign of the blues,' he comments. He always feels childishly smug when they beat the cops to a scene.

'They'll be tied up at the pub,' Ash replies in a monotone.

'What's happening at the pub?'

'Some guy lost his shit and punched someone. A massive barney broke out. My mate reckons Henno jumped on the bar and rang the gong to break it up.'

Fred snorts. 'I'm impressed Henno was sober enough.' God, he misses nights at the pub, with Henno serving him and his mates half-price beers until they were blind drunk. He even misses the ferocious hangovers. 'Was anyone crook enough for a bus?'

'Charlie and Rowena attended, but I don't think it was a blood-bath or anything.'

'Sounds better than what we've got lumped with,' Fred says.

'No shit,' replies Ash. 'I was all set to head home. I'm knackered.'

Fred glances at him. He does seem tired. He has purple rings around his eyes, and he keeps taking sips from his stupid Mickey Mouse drink bottle.

'Same,' Fred says. 'Let's wrap this up as quick as we can.'

Up ahead a white pick-up truck is parked at the side of the road, headlights blasting into the paddocks, the driver door wide open. An overweight man in jeans and a flannel shirt walks into the light, waving like he's air traffic control. Ash thinks he recognises him from around town—old mates with his uncle, maybe.

'Showtime.' Fred pulls over and turns off the engine.

'Thank god you're here,' huffs the man.

'Hey, mate,' Ash says confidently. 'You called in a car accident?'

The man nods distractedly before his old-fashioned manners override his obvious distress. He turns back to shake first Ash's hand, then Fred's. 'Sorry. Sorry. Bob's the name, Bob Dalgliesh. I'm a bit shook up. She's over there.' He points beyond the vehicles.

Ash makes out a faint glint of metal several metres from the road.

'She hit the tree. I saw it happen. I was coming along behind her, but there was nothing I could do—too far away. It's not good, not good at all. I didn't want to move her and make it worse.'

'Thanks, Bob,' Fred says calmly. 'We'll take it from here, but I'm sure the cops will want a chat, so just wait in your truck, okay?'

'Sure, yep.' Bob wipes his large nostrils. 'I have girls myself. Just makes you think, doesn't it?'

'Got a jacket, Bob?' Fred asks.

The man nods.

'Might be a good idea to put it on. We'll be back with you in a tick.'

Fred grabs the portable stretcher, while Ash shoulders the triage bag. A cluster of cows watches from behind a wire fence as they navigate roadside shrubs and tall grass before reaching the mangled mess of an old Subaru. There's no music, no ticking engine, no crying—no signs of life.

Ash doesn't break stride, but his heart executes the hollow thump it always does just before he reaches a crash scene. Despite his extensive training, there's a split second of disbelief that he has to deal with whatever horrible thing the universe has served up, a moment where he expects a grown-up to push him out of the way and step in. He's only been a paramedic for three years, but he's seen a lot during that time: heart attacks, strokes, accidents, suicides, two murders. Although farm accidents score first place for the most gruesome, it's the invisible injuries he finds the most stressful—the damage he can't see. The things he might miss, especially when his thoughts are all over the shop.

When they reach the car, Ash's vision blurs. He forces himself to focus. *Get it together. Concentrate.*

The bonnet has disappeared into the trunk of an ancient gum, the right headlight reduced to a feeble glow against the wood.

A woman is slumped over the wheel. She's slim, probably around forty, a brunette with ivory skin, casually dressed. There's no telltale stench of booze, but these days it's just as likely to be drugs. Her head is split open just above her right eyebrow. He's pretty sure she's not breathing.

He steps closer. There's no movement. He turns to shake his head at Fred, who shrugs, clearly in no rush to do the honours.

The next few hours play out in Ash's mind. Cops will arrive and usher them out of the way. They'll wait around before being grilled about whether they might have compromised the crime scene. Fred will bitch and moan until they're dragged back in to extract the woman and cart her off to the morgue. A tedious process at the best of times, it's far from ideal tonight. Ash should have refused to come.

After giving himself another mental kick, he clears his throat and reaches toward the woman's neck. He takes in the pout of her lips, the dried blood lining her collarbone. Sensing something, he pulls back a beat before her eyes flutter. She moans quietly.

His breath catches in his throat as his heart goes bananas. He pictures her as a toddler. As a girl in a school uniform. As a teenager wearing make-up and laughing with her friends. Now she's fully grown, broken and dying on the side of the road.

How did you end up here? Ash's head spins.

'Come on, mate. Move.' Fred elbows past with the stretcher. 'Let's get her to church and see if one of the gods can work a miracle.'

CHAPTER ONE

SUNDAY, 18 SEPTEMBER, 9.47 PM

My left leg has gone numb, and I wince as pins and needles take hold. Scarlett is heavy in the baby carrier against my chest, her breath hot on my neck. Careful not to wake her, I stretch out my calves and wriggle my toes.

'You don't have to stay, you know,' says Dad.

I smile. 'I know, but I want to. *We* want to.'

He laughs. 'I don't think Scarlett has a strong opinion on the matter, Gem.'

I peer down at her sleeping face. 'Well, either way, I just wish she would sleep like this at night.'

'Ha!' Dad uses the silver triangle above the hospital bed to pull himself upright. 'You barely ever slept when you were a baby, day *or* night. Your mother and I were beside ourselves. It was horrendous.'

I run my hand over Scarlett's head; her downy hair is starting to thicken. 'I'm sorry.'

He waves my apology away. 'Little did we know you would be way worse later on.'

'The medication is obviously making you confused.'

Dad grins and is about to respond when a nurse strides in. She positions herself authoritatively at the end of his bed. 'Good evening! I'm Beth.' She beams at me.

I nod hello and introduce myself.

Beth yanks Dad's bedclothes straight and moves the portable table out of the way. After expertly fixing a blood-pressure cuff around his arm, she presses a button on the device next to the bed. 'Feeling good, Ned?'

'Very good, thank you.'

As the cuff inflates, she cranes her neck to glimpse Scarlett's face. 'How old is she?'

'Almost nine months,' I reply.

'How precious.' The machine beeps, and Beth reviews the results, nods and rips off the velcro. 'Very good, Ned. You have the blood pressure of a much younger man.'

'And?' Dad prompts.

'That's it,' Beth chirps. 'Everything else seems age appropriate, including your sense of humour.' She wheels the table back in place. 'Keep up your fluids, and I'll see you tomorrow.' When she leaves through the curtain, I see the elderly man in the bed opposite, his beady eyes fixed on his TV as he eats yoghurt from a plastic tub.

'You do seem well, Dad,' I say. And I mean it: he's a little paler than usual, but he looks a hell of a lot better than he did a few days ago.

'I told you, Gemma, nothing to worry about.'

'That's not quite true, Dad, and you know it.'

I'm still recovering from Rebecca's phone call last Sunday morning that had me deciphering her panicked words through a fog of exhaustion. Eventually I worked out that Dad was on the way to Smithson Hospital in an ambulance, with a suspected heart attack.

'I think your heart attack almost gave Rebecca and me one,' I add wryly.

I'm being flippant to hide how worried I've been. Dad's good health has been a constant in my life, and in the hours after Rebecca's call I imagined the worst. My mind generated a grim sequence of possible outcomes, none of which saw me casually chatting with him a week later.

'Well, all's well that ends well,' he insists. 'Honestly, Gemma, I really feel okay.'

I press my lips together and nod slightly. 'Okay.'

'Enough about me. What about you? How is Mac?'

'He's good,' I say, equally relieved to change the topic. 'He's been asked to present as part of a university syllabus later this year, which I think he's happy about.'

Dad cocks his head. 'Will he need to be in Sydney for that?'

Women's laughter erupts just outside Dad's room, followed by an enthusiastic conversation. We turn toward the noise, letting his question hang between us. He's hesitant about interfering in my life, but I'm sure he wants to ask if we've decided to stay in Smithson.

'I'm not across the details,' I say, before adding brightly, 'He's also working on a cold case.'

Dad clears his throat. 'Is that local?'

'No . . . Brisbane, I think he said. But he can do the work from here.' As I'm saying it, I realise I'm not actually sure if it's true. 'Anyway, it's keeping him busy.'

'That's good. And you? When did you say you're meeting with Jonesy?'

'Tomorrow,' I reply.

'Are you nervous?'

I snort dismissively. 'Of course not. I'm just keen to know what he wants to talk to me about.'

Dad sips his water and smiles, though I can sense his caution. 'I assume he wants you back at work.'

I can't tell whether the flutter in my stomach is dread or excitement. My former boss sounded odd when he called to ask me to come and see him at the office. Jonesy is always gruff, but this time I got the sense there was something wrong. 'I doubt it. He knows I'm still thinking things through and Scarlett's not even a year old. He probably just wants to complain about new policies being rolled out—you know how much he hates red tape.'

'Maybe he wants your advice on something. He trusts your judgement, Gemma.'

'Maybe.' But I'm worried that Jonesy will ask me to come back early or at the very least want to know what my plans are. Conversations I've been avoiding for months will need to be had. I catch my expression sliding and force a smile. 'I'm looking forward to seeing him.'

'Ben was very chatty when he came in yesterday,' Dad ventures. 'It was nice to spend time with him.'

I don't tell Dad how reluctant Ben was about visiting him in hospital. My ex, Ben's father Scott, died here from cancer just over a year ago, so his grandfather being unwell in the same place has really rocked him. 'He was worried about you—and he's relieved you seem okay.'

'You heard the nurse! I'm fit as a fiddle.'

Optimism aside, Dad is clearly starting to tire. And I've barely had more than three hours sleep in a row for days. 'I think we'll head off, Dad,' I say softly. 'We all need a decent sleep.'

Dad yawns and nods.

Scarlett is still fast asleep, but I know there's close to zero chance of getting her into the car and then into her cot without waking her up. I'll likely spend the next few hours settling her. Last week

I fell asleep on the floor of her bedroom, one hand on her stomach through the bars of the cot. Ben took an unflattering photo of me with my face mashed into the sheepskin rug before he covered me with a blanket.

Bracing myself for the tediousness ahead, I locate the nappy bag and check my phone: two missed calls from an unknown number, plus a voice message from my friend Candy and one from Mac.

'I'll call you tomorrow morning, Dad, and try to come by after school with Ben.'

'Sounds good, Gem.' He removes his glasses and shimmies into the bedsheets.

Cradling the warm curve of Scarlett's body, I tense my muscles to stand up.

Before I can, there's a flurry of white noise, like all the sound in the room is being sucked out. Dad and I lock eyes before we're plunged into darkness.

CHAPTER TWO

There's a moment of absolutely nothing except Scarlett's heartbeat against mine. Then the reassuringly repetitive beeping of machines threads through the void as the back-up generators kick in. Lights flicker on, but they're not as bright as before, casting the room in a weak yolk-coloured glow.

'Gem . . . ?' Dad says uncertainly. 'What's going on?'

I'm on my feet, heels digging into the floor and legs bent slightly at the knees, ready to ward off whatever danger might have been hiding in the dark. I run my hands along Scarlett's back, then trace down her legs to grip her toes. 'It's okay, Dad.' I peer around the curtain. 'Let me see what I can find out.'

'Please, Gemma, just wait here.'

'I won't be long.'

The elderly man opposite is still clutching his yoghurt and spoon, but now his eyes are fixed on the door.

'Are you okay?' I ask him.

'What was all that about?' he says loudly. 'Did you see the lights went out?'

'I'm not sure,' I say, just as a screech starts blasting us from every direction.

Scarlett's eyes spring open. She scrunches up her face, swiftly working her way to a full-body bawl.

'Shhh, shhh.' I pat her back in a futile attempt to calm her.

'Gemma!'

Ignoring Dad, I step out into the corridor. Two nurses run past.

'Excuse me,' I say. 'Excuse me! Hey!'

'Everything's fine,' one calls over her shoulder. 'Just stay where you are, please.'

They disappear through a set of doors further down the hall.

Scarlett's cries merge with the whoops of the siren that I assume is a fire alarm. An emergency light flashes red on the ceiling near the nurse station. I look in both directions—no visible smoke and no smell, but of course a fire could be on another floor. The hospital had a new wing built last year and now boasts sixty beds; it's one of the biggest buildings in Smithson.

I pat Scarlett's back and grope around for her dummy, easing it into her mouth. She glares at me as she sucks, aware she's being silenced. I cup my hands over her ears to mute the sound.

An elderly lady, hunched over a walker, makes her way to the room adjacent to Dad's. Remnants of food stain the collar of her peach dressing-gown. 'What's that awful noise?' She blinks in a way that suggests she normally wears glasses.

'It's an alarm,' I tell her. 'But I think everything is okay.'

'It woke me up!' she says indignantly.

'It's very loud,' I agree. 'But I'm sure it's just a false alarm.'

I smile at her reassuringly and walk confidently to the double doors further along the corridor. The red light on the security panel is off: it must have been disabled by the alarm.

I push through and make my way down the dim corridor. I can feel Scarlett sucking her dummy against my chest, but I can't hear anything except the alarm needling my brain. Maybe someone threatened a patient—it's happened before. My throat tightens, and I wonder if I should ditch my fact-finding mission and get Dad and Scarlett the hell out of here.

Up ahead is the security door that leads to the main reception. Again, I push straight through and enter the large, poorly lit space. Two nurses and three grim-faced security guards huddle near the main desk, talking animatedly to each other and ignoring me.

Beyond them, a police car pulls up outside the front entrance. A man and a woman get out and rush through the open automatic doors. I recognise Julian Everett in a tailored suit, his brown hair slicked back from his face. The woman, a constable in uniform, has a thick braid and heavy dark brows, and is almost as tall as Everett. I don't recognise her; she must be new.

'Excuse me,' I say to the hospital staff as Everett and his partner make their way over to us—then louder, 'Excuse me!'

The alarm stops, and my words echo around the room. Abashed, I clear my throat, suddenly unsure how to introduce myself.

'Is that a patient?' the constable mutters to Everett, curious eyes on me.

'She's a cop,' he replies, 'on maternity leave. Good evening, detective.' He nods at me politely and turns so his broad shoulders face away. 'Right, everyone, I'm Detective Sergeant Julian Everett and this is Constable Natasha Holdsworth. The fire brigade is circling the building and will be checking every part of the premises due to the emergency alarm being activated. Can someone tell me what happened, please?' It's clear he wants it known that he is calling the shots.

I only worked with Everett for a few months when he moved here from Melbourne last year, but that was long enough to know he's desperate to prove himself—and thinks the best way to do that is to be a cocky know-it-all prick.

'I'm Detective Sergeant Gemma Woodstock,' I pipe up, painfully aware of my make-up free face, unwashed hair, unflattering outfit, and Scarlett in my arms. 'I was visiting my father, a patient here. Do we know what caused the blackout? Everything shut down a few moments before the alarm went off.'

'What is it? An electrical fault?' a deep voice booms from behind me.

I spin around, causing the dummy to fall out of Scarlett's mouth. She promptly starts to bawl.

My chest aches. I'm only breastfeeding her once a day, and it's been almost twenty-four hours, so her panicked wail is like a trigger for my milk to surge. I attempt to soothe her while keeping my focus on the approaching man: Roger Kirk, the CEO of the hospital. Unshaven in a fashionable way, he wears dark jeans with a suit jacket hastily thrown on over a snow-white polo. We've had various interactions over the years, mainly when I've needed access to patients for witness statements or interviews. Plus, I went to school with his cousins Franklin and Mauve Kirk.

One of the security guards responds to Roger. 'We can't locate a fire or any kind of damage, and none of our guys called anything in. We think someone accidentally set the alarm off internally. Either that or it's just gone off the boil.'

'Has someone called the maintenance people?' Roger's face is flushed, and a soft tic pulses in his jaw. I'd bet money he's come straight from a boozy dinner.

'I'll do it.' A woman whose name tag reads *Jessie* springs into action and rushes to the front desk. She wakes up the computer and frantically types in a password, not even bothering to sit down.

Roger's phone rings. 'Journos,' he murmurs. 'Great.' He rejects the call and turns to me. His eyebrows dip in recognition, but I can tell he hasn't joined the dots to remember I'm a detective.

Scarlett continues to suck furiously on her dummy, and I sway from side to side, jiggling her gently.

'Excuse me,' says Everett, looking from Roger to the staff members. He seems annoyed, perhaps at the lack of response to his earlier request for the sequence of events. 'Who is best placed to talk me through what happened?'

I survey the group, an odd feeling coming over me. I'm used to being in control of this type of situation, used to being able to ask questions and demand answers. Now I feel like an impostor or a faded version of my former self. Half of me wishes I could teleport back to Dad's room and slink out of here like a normal visitor; the other half is determined to figure out what's going on.

Another security guard enters the room from one of the wards. 'I've just come across from emergency,' he announces. 'It's all clear.'

'We'll do a routine check of every floor,' says the guard who spoke initially. *Rufus Toohey* is printed on his lanyard above a photo that's at least a decade old. He turns to Everett. 'I can take you through our emergency sequence if you like.'

Roger bites the skin around his thumbnail, dark eyes darting left and right. 'Do the sweep first,' he says to Rufus. 'I want every part of this place checked. I'm not issuing a statement until I'm confident everything is fine.'

'The fire team will need to do a sweep as well,' Everett reiterates. His fists are balled at his hips.

Scarlett gurgles and everyone turns to look at her. As I run my hands along her body, I become aware of an unpleasant smell—she needs to be changed. 'I'd better get back to my dad,' I say quietly.

Everett tries to cover his smirk with an exaggerated cough, while Constable Holdsworth watches me with interest. Smiling politely at her, I tuck stray hairs behind my ears and square my aching shoulders. Embarrassed as I feel about my appearance, at least I don't need to worry about the inevitable late night and admin facing Everett, Holdsworth and the hospital staff.

Everyone seems mildly fractious as they process the redundant rush of adrenaline. I dip my head forward in an awkward goodbye, then head toward the double doors—just as they burst open, revealing a security guard and a petite blonde woman in a tailored suit. They move toward us, eyes frantic and chests heaving.

At the front desk, Jessie stops typing and stares at them, her lipstick-painted mouth forming an O.

'What now?' Roger says.

The pair come to a halt, and the woman brings a hand to her chest. She stammers, 'Someone's stolen a body from the morgue.'

CHAPTER THREE

I change Scarlett's nappy in the disabled toilet. My kneecaps grind against the scuffed lino as I listen to the commotion on the other side of the door. The tiny room is lit by my iPhone torch because the light switch was unresponsive—to do with the blackout, I assume, or maybe the general upkeep here is as poor as it is at the police station.

'Come on, come on,' I mutter to myself. I yank a new nappy out of the change bag and hurriedly dispose of the mess.

Alongside my haste to get back out there, there's a tightness in my stomach, a mix of dread and anticipation I haven't experienced since before Scarlett was born.

The blonde woman in the suit who made the announcement about the missing corpse is Sophie McCallister, the hospital manager. She told us the body is that of a young woman from a single-vehicle car crash just outside of Smithson earlier this evening; the woman died in emergency and couldn't be identified. As I smooth down the tabs of the nappy and button Scarlett back into her outfit, one question beats through my mind: why on earth would anyone want to steal a corpse?

Scarlett's eyes are red, a telltale sign of exhaustion. I shove the dummy back in her mouth, rearrange my shirt and jumper, then strap her into the carrier. After washing my hands, I slick back my hair and pinch my pale cheeks. It doesn't help.

I return to the foyer, where Constable Holdsworth is talking to two security guards, while Everett is nowhere to be seen. I grimace. I don't trust him—he needs supervising or, at the very least, frequent reminders he's not god's gift to policing.

Sophie McCallister stands near the lifts, a mobile phone against her ear. She bites her lip and shoots nervous glances across the room at Roger, who yells a question at me from the reception desk: 'Do you have anything yet?'

Jessie has returned to her frantic typing, her manicured fingers flying across the keyboard.

'Me?' I reply.

He nods. 'You're a detective.'

'Yes, but I'm on leave at the moment. My father is—'

Roger snorts, scanning the room for someone else to hassle.

Jessie adjusts her headset and murmurs something to him.

'Christ's sake.' He scowls and leans over, his face close to hers. She subtly shifts sideways as he jabs a finger at the screen. 'Try them instead,' he barks.

'Do we know if anything else is missing?' I ask. No one seems to hear me, so I raise my voice. 'Have you checked that nothing else is missing? Equipment, cash, drugs, patients . . . ?'

Everyone pauses at my outburst.

Rufus, the veteran security guard, sniffs defensively and says, 'We're getting to all that now,' suggesting that in fact this line of investigation hasn't been considered.

'You think it's an inside job?' Roger asks me.

I shrug. 'Maybe. The lights went off only a minute or so before the fire alarm was activated. That might mean there was a level of coordination from someone who knows your systems and protocols.' I notice Everett returning with another security guard, and I turn to Sophie McCallister before he can say anything. 'What else do we know about the missing corpse?'

Sophie looks at Roger, who nods permission for her to answer. I think I hear Everett mutter under his breath.

'Basically nothing,' Sophie says. 'She wasn't carrying ID. There was no bag or wallet, nothing in her pockets. The paramedic I spoke to during the transfer said cops were at the scene when they left to bring her in, so I'm sure you'll be able to link her to the car from the crash, but we didn't have any info at the time of death.'

Everett clears his throat. 'A forensic team are at the crash site now.' He angles himself between me and Sophie. 'They'll contact me with any relevant info.'

Scarlett kicks and lets out a wail. All the men take a step backwards.

'What time was she brought in?' I ask Sophie.

'Just over three hours ago.'

'It was a single-car crash,' Everett adds. 'Probably just a suicide.'

I shake my head in frustration. 'Has someone called the ambos?'

'It's a bit late for that, Gemma,' says Everett. 'Unless you think she came back from the dead and walked out of here.' He laughs at his own joke and scores a few blokey smiles from the security guards.

'The woman was alive at the scene,' I say as calmly as I can manage. 'It's possible she said something we can use to ID her. Plus, the ambos probably got a good look at her, and at this point it seems that's all we have to work with. Someone has taken her corpse and we need to find out why.'

The smug grin disappears from Everett's face. He turns to Holdsworth. 'See if you can track down the paramedics,' he snaps.

'And anyone from emergency who worked on the woman,' I add. 'There's a chance someone wanted her in that morgue so they could dispose of her.'

Holdsworth nods obediently.

'Is Jonesy coming?' I ask Everett.

'No. He's not on call tonight.'

'He'd want to know about this,' I say.

'I'll brief him tomorrow,' he replies firmly.

Roger's mobile starts ringing again. He marches to the front entrance to take the call outside.

'I'd like to see the morgue,' I say to Sophie, then turn to Rufus. 'And I'd like you to come.'

Everett insists on coming, too, and we engage in a silent stand-off before he breaks eye contact. We all follow Rufus down the fire escape. The air is dry and musty, and even though we're descending, I realise how unfit I've become.

Rufus's deep voice echoes around the enclosed space. 'Third kid was born last Easter. She was a month early and gave us a shock, let me tell you—three girls, lord help me.'

'And how long have you worked at the hospital, Sophie?' I ask.

'Sixteen years.' Her high heels click unevenly against the concrete stairs.

'That's a long stint.'

'Not as long as me.' Rufus turns to grin at both of us. 'Coming up for twenty years this Christmas.'

'The hospital has changed a lot in that time,' I say.

'So has Smithson,' he replies. 'Feels like every man and his dog wants to live here these days. The house prices are out of control. Did you see what that old place up on the hill went for last week? You'd think it was bloody Sydney the way people are carrying on.'

I don't reply, even though his comments echo conversations Mac and I have been having over the past few months. The recent surge of interest in local real estate isn't helping us decide where to settle down.

When our group reaches the bottom floor, we put on the surgical gloves and booties that I asked Sophie to find for us. My calves burn as I loop the material around my shoes, and the front of my shirt is damp where Scarlett is pressed against me. I feel completely wired now.

Rufus leads us through a heavy grey door into a large sparse room. On the right, two metal tables on wheels are pushed together, hard up against an expansive sink area fitted with extendable taps that hang from the ceiling. On the opposite side of the room there's another table, and next to it is a cluster of bins and a stack of cardboard boxes. The smell of disinfectant isn't as strong as it is in most morgues. An industrial fan is built into the exterior wall, exposed blades turning slightly in the night breeze.

Sophie gestures to the rows of metal drawers along the back wall. 'The fridges run off the back-up generator, but they're all empty now. The missing body was the only one here today.'

The others watch as I do a slow spin, taking in the details. My brain is running at a million miles an hour. I point to the door we just came through. 'Who has access?'

'My security team,' says Rufus.

'And some select senior hospital staff,' adds Sophie.

'How many people are we talking about?'

Her mouth twitches. 'Fifteen, maybe twenty.'

'You should ensure no one on staff leaves tonight before being interviewed.'

'We've already organised that,' Everett snaps. 'Standard procedure.'

We lock eyes briefly. He smiles at me but lifts his jaw, the message clear. I get that he wants to run his own show, but we don't have time to lose, and I'm worried his cockiness will get in the way of good decision-making.

'What about those?' I point to a set of double doors underneath the fan.

'They only open from the inside,' Sophie replies, gesturing to another security panel.

'Where do they lead to?'

Everett's suddenly preoccupied with his phone, his brow furrowing as he types out a message.

'It's the pick-up point,' says Sophie primly.

'Pick-up point,' I repeat, wondering what could be more important to Everett right now than understanding the crime scene. Maybe the woman's body has been found. 'You mean for the corpses?'

'Yes. It's a discreet area that the funeral homes use to execute the transfers.'

'Show me.'

Rufus pushes open the doors. They give way with a satisfying click, and I step onto a concrete ledge. Below is a narrow two-lane driveway and, beyond that, a tall wooden fence. Further down on the left, closer to the main entrance, is another concrete platform and a set of doors. 'What's that for?' I ask. 'Is there another morgue?'

Sophie joins me. 'That's the goods drop-off and pick-up—you know, medical supplies, food, sanitary items, that kind of thing.'

'Biscuits to the left and bodies to the right,' I say.

Rufus chuckles, while Sophie's expression doesn't change.

Everett comes out onto the ledge, too, and leans close to me, whispering, 'It looks like the woman was run off the road.' He has the good grace to look sheepish.

My eyes widen. 'Deliberately?'

'It's unclear at this stage but the other driver didn't stop.'

I let this information sink in. Had someone planned to kill the woman in the crash and steal her body from the scene? Or had they wanted to ensure her body made its way to the hospital morgue all along? Surely an attempt on her life must be linked to her corpse going missing mere hours later.

I'm freshly annoyed at Everett's earlier dismissiveness of the car crash. 'If she was a target earlier tonight then it changes things,' I murmur.

Everett grimaces in reluctant agreement, his eyes back on his phone.

I refocus on my surroundings. The only thing to our right is a tight turning circle. I step out further on the platform and spin to face the building. A cobwebbed CCTV camera is fixed to the brick-work, pointing out toward the street. 'Does that work?' I indicate the camera and raise my eyebrows at Rufus. 'We need to get our hands on the footage asap.'

Rufus squints up at it, red blotches appearing on his neck. 'Ah, I'll check on that for you. I can't say I remember seeing footage from down this side of the building.'

Sophie huffs, nostrils flaring.

'How did you know a body was missing?' I ask her.

'I was informed by a security guard.'

'Was that the one you were with when you told us the corpse was missing?' I ask, remembering a tall young man with thick eyebrows and a dumbfounded expression.

'Yep,' confirms Rufus. 'Lenny Tisdale's a good kid. He's been with us for about three years.'

'How did he know the corpse was missing?'

Rufus and Sophie exchange glances before she says, 'He didn't, but he was checking this section of the hospital after the alarm went off and saw that the external door was open. He alerted me, and because I'd been across the situation with the Jane Doe, I checked the drawer and realised she was gone.'

'Why did you check the drawer?' Everett asks Sophie.

'I assumed if the door was open it meant someone had been in the morgue. I don't know—she was the only person in here, so I just checked it.'

I step back inside and the others follow.

'Hang on,' I say, coming to an abrupt halt and turning around. 'The external door was open . . . ? It wasn't when we came down here.'

'I asked Lenny to close it,' says Sophie defensively. 'I didn't want to leave an external door wide open after what had happened.'

I exhale slowly, trying not to let my frustration show. 'Can you secure the external doors from the outside?'

Rufus shakes his head. 'Only from this side.'

I survey the morgue again. The external door being left open points to a solo operator—if two or more people were working together, then surely one would have remained in the hospital to shut the door, hoping to conceal the theft for as long as possible. Or it could mean that whoever was involved, they were in such a rush to move the body they didn't worry about closing the door. Of course, it's also possible that Lenny Tisdale is lying and helped remove the corpse, leaving the door open to give himself a reason to alert Sophie and secure an alibi.

'How easy is it to move a body out of here and into a car?' I ask. 'Could I do it?'

'Yep, definitely,' Rufus says. He goes to the wall of drawers and pulls one open. 'See, everything is on wheels. Once you extend them all the way, the base lifts, then you just wheel it over there like a stretcher and slide it into the hearse.' He demonstrates how the metal insert automatically extends to waist height and then can be manoeuvred as easily as a shopping trolley.

I ask, 'Is the metal stretcher part missing from the drawer our corpse was in?'

Sophie nods.

I go over to the external doors, where the lip of concrete ends at what I assume is the standard car height. 'Do you need a special car?'

'Only if you care about protecting the body,' says Rufus. 'Hearses have fitted runners to keep the stretchers secure, but if you're not fussed what happens to it, you can wheel it straight into a boot. Pop down the back seats like it's a surfboard. She was fresh, and it's not a warm night, so she's not going to start smelling for a few hours yet.'

Wrinkling my nose at his comment, I turn to address Sophie. 'Do all the funeral homes know the process of coming here and collecting the bodies?'

'Yes.' She brings her hands together. 'After a patient passes away, the family often spend time with their loved one in a private room up on one of the wards. Once they have said their goodbyes and nominated a funeral provider, we bring the body here until it is collected. There are only four funeral homes in town, all very familiar with the process.'

I think about Dad upstairs and try to stop my mind wandering to an alternative version of reality. I'm not sure what happened when my ex died, but I suppose he was brought to this room; his wife, Jodie, organised the mysterious logistics of death. I force my mind away from the grim memories. 'But this body was going to be collected for an autopsy, right?'

'Yes,' Sophie replies. 'Occasionally a body will need to be transferred to the Smithson Morgue, if the cause of death needs to be determined prior to being released to the family or if there's a criminal investigation.'

'Or if it's a Jane Doe,' I say.

Sophie nods primly. 'That's right.'

'Has there ever been a fire here before?' Everett asks.

'No, never,' Sophie replies. 'Although obviously we do regular drills. We get bomb threats occasionally, and we had a gas leak early last year—had to evacuate the building. There was an incident with a husband trying to discharge his wife and physically threatening several staff members, but that was about seven years ago. Apart from the gas leak, there's been no major incidents since the renovation.'

I was on duty the night that man tried to remove his unconscious wife from the emergency ward; he was worried about their visa status being discovered by the authorities. I think I dealt with Sophie at the time. I look around the room, fighting the fact that I'm losing steam. *Come on, think, think.* Then I notice the red security light on the panel next to the door.

'When the fire alarm goes off, all the security doors are disabled, right?' I ask, suddenly realising something.

'It's a safety precaution,' she says. 'If there's a fire, the last thing we want is someone being trapped inside.'

I remember the sudden darkness followed by the piercing screech of the alarm—the odd sensation of the hospital breathing out, its defences down.

'Including these doors, right?' I point to the morgue pick-up area.

Everett's eyes bulge in realisation and Rufus lets out a low whistle. We all look at the double doors.

'Do you think someone hacked the computer system?' Sophie turns to Rufus. 'My brother is a tech genius. He works in Sydney, but I can call him and see if he can help us work out what happened.'

'Someone probably just set off the fire alarm the old-fashioned way,' I say. 'But it's definitely worth doing a review to see if there's been a hack.'

'I'll get on to head office,' mumbles Rufus.

'Are the woman's personal effects here?' I ask Sophie.

'I'm not sure.' She seems flustered as she uses a gloved hand to check a sign-in book and some lockers. 'It doesn't appear so. Everything she had with her should have been tagged and ready for the medical examiner, but I can't see anything registered. The body may still have had clothing on—we'll check with the medical team.'

'Please keep us posted,' I say.

'A forensic team is on their way here,' announces Everett.

'And you'll need to speak to Lenny Tisdale as soon as possible,' I tell him.

'Cheers, Woodstock.' He brushes past me. I sense he's reached the end of his tether with me.

We're making our way back upstairs when a member of Rufus's team calls to say they've found the fire alarm unit that was set off. A few minutes later, we're standing next to the broken emergency panel in the empty day-procedure ward.

'I assume this part of the hospital is always sealed off at night?' Everett asks Sophie.

'Yes, it shuts at seven.'

Scarlett stirs in her carrier; I almost forgot about her. I stifle a yawn. 'Get the forensics in here, too,' I say to Everett, then to Sophie and Rufus, 'We'll need every minute of CCTV you have from this evening.'

The four of us return to the main entrance.

'Where the fuck have you been?' Roger says. He pounces on Sophie. 'I've been calling you. A bunch of journos are here, and they want a statement. I'm getting questions about the research centre, so I have to get my ducks in a row.'

'We need to start taking statements,' Everett tells him. 'Can you find a space for us to use?'

Roger clicks his fingers in Sophie's direction. 'Soph, get that sorted? I've got to deal with the bloody media.'

'I'll work with you on a statement,' she says quickly, seemingly unfazed by the multiple requests Roger has fired at her. She turns to Everett. 'The staffroom on level one is probably best for the interviews. Rufus, can you set it up, then help arrange whatever they need in terms of speaking with your team and the staff?'

The security guard nods and heads to the stairwell. Roger remains, his obnoxious ringtone blaring for a few shrill notes before he hangs up on call after call, muttering under his breath.

'This must have been coordinated,' I say to Everett quietly. 'I just don't buy that someone stole a corpse on a whim—it doesn't make sense. Maybe she was a drug mule and her dealer realised she'd ended up here. That might explain the lack of ID. Or maybe she'd committed a crime, her body was carrying DNA from the scene, and whomever she was working with couldn't risk an autopsy uncovering evidence.'

'No doubt we'll explore all those possibilities. But it's getting late, and we have a long night ahead of us.' He gives me a pointed look. 'Why don't you head off, and we can update you tomorrow when we have more information.' His voice is friendly but firm.

I falter. He's right. I should get Scarlett home. *I* should get home.

'Hopefully the ambos will shed some light on things,' I say. 'When are you speaking to them?'

Everett's nostrils flare as he shows Holdsworth something on his screen. 'Goodnight, Gemma,' he says with finality.

———

I pull the front door shut, kick off my shoes and drop the nappy bag on the hall table. Switching on the kitchen light, I take in the pleasant jumble of mess before going to the bedroom and peering into the dark. I can just make out Mac lying in bed. Our home feels slightly surreal after the chaos at the hospital. I used to feel this way after trawling through bloody crime-scene photos before picking Ben up from day care—like my world was split in half. Or that I was existing in two different universes.

'Is everything okay?' Mac's voice is thick with sleep. 'I tried to call you.'

'I know. I'm sorry. Something happened at the hospital.'

He props himself up on his elbows. 'Your dad?'

'No, no, Dad's fine. Someone stole a corpse from the hospital morgue.'

'What?'

'Yeah. A Jane Doe. No ID.'

Mac sinks back against the pillow. 'How bizarre.'

'Very. But we can talk about it tomorrow. Go back to sleep. I'm going to try getting Scar down.'

'Okay.' He yawns. 'Call me if you need me.'

I gently wrestle Scarlett into a clean onesie while she grabs at my hair. As she feeds, I sit in the dark lounge room and stare into the yard, thinking about the evening's events. In her bedroom, her eyelids droop as I pull the blind down, dim my phone and sit rubbing her chest.

The text blurs as I read the short breaking news piece. There's no mention of the car crash or the stolen corpse, just that emergency services were called to the hospital after a security scare. Despite my exhaustion, thoughts crowd my mind. The woman was in the car alone and died in emergency. She had no ID, so there was no one to call. How many people even knew she was there?

Standing next to Scarlett's cot, I stare at the wall as I bounce theories around—until I realise she's asleep and I am patting the mattress, not her body.

I check on Ben, who is twisted in his sheets with a book fanned open next to his head. Then I quickly brush my teeth before slipping out of my clothes and sliding into bed next to Mac, succumbing to sleep the moment my head hits the pillow.

In my dream, faceless bodies rise from a row of steel tables. They stagger naked and bleeding down a narrow corridor, cornering me against a locked door as I scream for help.

CHAPTER FOUR

MONDAY, 19 SEPTEMBER, 7.34 AM

I'm woken by the pop of our toaster. The fridge opens and closes, then a knife scrapes against crisp bread. Ben has never liked anything on his toast except butter and is increasingly liberal with its application. He's going through a Milo phase, and I wait for the slosh of milk followed by the quiet slurping from his *Mario Kart* mug in between bites of toast. Overdue a haircut, he'll be intermittently hooking wayward dark strands behind his left ear. I love that I know my son's quirks, his emerging routines; that I'm able to predict his expressions a beat before they appear on his face, and how he'll phrase a sentence before he speaks. I feel closer to him than I ever have, even though he's on the cusp of the mysterious teenage phase everyone has warned me about.

When I was pregnant with Scarlett, I worried her arrival would create distance between us. Scott had only just died—a sudden, horrible death we were all reeling from—and I'd come back to Smithson after four years away, with Mac in tow. I was aware it was already a lot for Ben to adjust to without the disruption of a sibling. But I needn't have worried. There are a lot of things I regret in my life, but my relationship with Ben isn't one of them. Despite everything he's been through, he's a great kid. He's still hurting—Scott was his hero—but the four of us have found our own groove, and Ben is as besotted with Scarlett as Mac and I are.

Yawning, I roll onto my back. Mac's side of the bed is empty. I vaguely remember Scarlett crying out earlier and him saying the magic words: 'I'll get her, you keep sleeping.' Gratitude catapulted me into a deep slumber—but now, instead of feeling rested, I'm groggy and sluggish.

I roll over to peer at the cuckoo clock on the wall, one of the few things of my mother's I've kept. The spring broke several years ago, so the garishly painted bird doesn't do its hourly routine anymore, permanently jutting out of the little wooden doorway instead. When I was little Mum would hold me up to watch the bird burst out and announce the new hour, and I screamed in delight every time.

I entertain the idea of more sleep, but it's almost eight. I need a shower, and then I should run Ben to school so Mac doesn't have to. Sometimes the only thing that gets me through the day is anticipating the reprieve at the end of it.

In the shower I stare at the aqua tiles as I play back scenes from last night. I picture the hospital like a blueprint, all parts visible at the same time. I'm on the third level with Dad when someone cuts the power, allowing them to sneak onto the day ward and set off the alarm. Did they then leave the hospital and bring the car around to the morgue, or did they contact their accomplice—or accomplices—and meet them from the inside? Possibilities churn in my mind until I shake my head and turn off the tap.

I twist my hair, forcing the water out, as I notice how much grime has accumulated in the grout. God, this place needs a decent clean. How will I manage going back to work when I can't get on top of things now?

I pat myself dry and pull on my robe, wrap a towel around my head and rub a circle into the mirror fog. My skin glows pink, and my lashes clump together in thick spikes. Thank god I don't look as tired as I feel.

When I come out of the bathroom, I almost collide with Mac.

'It's Candy,' he says wryly, handing me my mobile. 'I've made you breakfast,' he adds, 'muesli and fruit.'

I squeeze his hand. 'Thank you.'

'I've got to jump on a call. Ben's watching Scarlett.'

I nod and smile. 'No worries. I'll run him to school.'

'Are you okay? Last night sounded intense.' Mac's pale eyes bore into mine.

This is the deal we made: to show up and pay attention, to be present every single day.

'I'm good.' I grip his hand again and flash him a smile to show I mean it. Then I shove the phone inside my towel turban. 'Hey.'

'Jesus Christ, Gemma, I'd kill for your luck!' Candy is beside herself. 'I can't believe you were *there*. I didn't hear a peep about it until this morning. Tell me absolutely everything.'

'You mean at the hospital?'

'No, on the spaceship,' she says witheringly. 'I want everything you have on the body-snatcher situation. My network is shot to shit, and I've got nothing.'

Candy Fyfe is my best friend. She's also a journalist who was made redundant from her role as editor-in-chief of the local newspaper while on maternity leave. Her little girl, Lola, is six months older than Scarlett, and in that time Candy worked her way through blazing fury, a fleeting depression and several nights of drunkenly plotting revenge against her former employer. Throughout this emotional roller-coaster, she developed a comprehensive business plan and launched a news website—*The Long & Short*—that is slowly gaining traction.

I switch the phone to speaker and rummage through my wardrobe. 'I can't tell you much, Candy. It's an active investigation. And officially I have nothing to do with it—I'm on leave.'

'Officially.' She dismisses the word as if it has something wrong with it.

'I was visiting Dad.'

'Oh, right. How is he?'

I roll my eyes. 'He's fine, thanks.'

'Okay,' Candy says, working her way up to a negotiation, 'at least tell me about the stolen corpse. A woman, right?'

'Yes, it is, but with no ID. As of last night, none of the New South Wales missing person reports were a match—but that might have changed in the last eight hours.'

'And there was an emergency at the hospital as well . . . ? I'm hearing there was a bomb threat . . . ?'

'I don't know about that.' I'm growing frustrated. 'The fire alarm was activated, but it might have been unrelated to the other incident.'

'It's all pretty fucking weird.'

'Clearly.' I remove the towel and run a brush through my hair.

'Surely it's all linked?'

'I would assume so, but like I said, I'm not working the case.' I grab my denim jacket before deciding on a navy blazer. 'You're doing a story, I gather?'

'Of course. Some weirdo gets off in the middle of the night with a corpse . . . I mean, the headlines write themselves.'

'Well, don't quote me.'

'I know the drill!' Candy says dramatically. 'When are you going back to work? I'm sick of you not feeding me secret information.'

'Candy,' I warn.

'Yeah, yeah, you would never do that, I know, I know . . . Shit, I've got to go. I've got an interview lined up with Henno. He was at the pub when it all went pear-shaped there last night. Talk to you later, Gem.'

The call cuts off before I can ask what she's talking about.

I quickly finish getting ready and make a token attempt to neaten up the room.

Our house is a rental. It's shaped like a shallow U and hugs a dusty but decent-sized backyard. There are three bedrooms, a bathroom and a study, plus an extra toilet off the kitchen. The décor is as old as me, but the kitchen appliances are new and the front garden is full of flowering natives.

A high-school teacher and his pastry chef girlfriend rent Mac's small but stylish apartment in Mosman and cat-sit Arthur, his ten-year-old Burmese. They are keen to stay another year, while our lease is up in just over two months. We really need to decide what we're going to do. I don't own any property, and the majority of Scott's life-insurance payout went to his wife, Jodie. Mac lost a lot of money in his divorce, so he still has a sizeable loan on the apartment. We're okay, but things are tight, especially with Mac freelancing. I think it would be nice to use our savings to put down some proper roots, but I'm not willing to press the issue. As to whether Smithson is the right place for us, I'm not sure. My feelings toward my home town remain complicated.

In the lounge I drop a kiss on Ben's head and get down on my knees to kiss Scarlett. Her blue eyes fix on me, and she frog-kicks aggressively. The heart shape of her face is the same as mine, but her fair colouring is all Mac.

Ben polishes off the last of his Milo. 'How was Grandad last night?'

'He's doing well,' I say. 'He really appreciated you visiting him the other day.'

'I'm still worried about him.'

'Same,' I admit. 'But I think he's going to be okay.'

Ben and I tend to navigate optimism and hope carefully—once bitten, forever wary, I guess. And from where I sit, it's better to expect the worst and be pleasantly surprised rather than the other way around. It seems Ben is the same.

I add, 'The doctors think he'll be home on the weekend.'

'Really?'

I take his chin in my hand. 'Really. Now come on, grab your stuff. You've got school, and I've got a meeting.'

'You're working today?' There's a hint of alarm in Ben's voice.

'Not work, just a catch-up with Jonesy.'

Ben pulls his schoolbag onto his narrow shoulders. 'Okay.'

Ever since Scott died, Ben has worried about me being a cop. A few of his friends have given him grief, no doubt passing on comments overheard from their parents about the dangers of my profession. It rattles him. And because of what happened to us last year, when I was working a murder case in a town up north, I can't exactly blame him for worrying. We were lucky to avoid serious harm or worse during a terrifying confrontation with a ruthless killer. Ben and I don't talk about it much, but he still sees a counsellor once a week; I'm sure he discusses it with her, along with his grief over losing his dad.

I sigh. 'You know I've got to go back to work eventually, Ben. I *want* to.'

But even as I say it, I wonder if it's true. The pull is undoubtedly there at times—it was certainly present last night—but how much of that is habit versus desire? And how am I supposed to tell the difference?

'Ben?' I press. 'You understand, right?'

'Yeah.'

I run my fingers through his hair. 'It will be fine. I'll be fine.'

'*Okay.*' He ducks his head, clearly not in a mood to talk about it.

'Good,' I mutter. I'm annoyed at myself for not knowing how to reassure him—at the same time, I don't want to give him false hope that things will be different in the future. I've been a cop his whole life. It's not just a job: it's part of my personality. I have no idea what would happen if I gave it up.

I check the time. 'Hey, we've got to go.'

'I'm ready.' Ben nods and straightens his shirt. He's so like his dad, so solid and reliable, and I feel a sharp jolt of sadness that Scott isn't here.

I stuff the nappy bag full of the various things we'll need today and locate my handbag, making sure I have my wallet and keys. After I lift Scarlett from the playmat, I pad down the corridor to say goodbye to Mac. The study door is closed, so I twist the handle and stick my head inside.

Mac is staring intently at his phone. On the desk behind him, an autopsy report is loaded on his laptop screen. His sandy hair catches the morning sun, and a smile plays on his lips as he types a text message. All those late nights we worked together come flooding back—moments before we were a couple and then all the ones after. We had a connection akin to telepathy. Was that only eighteen months ago? I feel like we're completely different people now. Or maybe we're the same but just in a completely different environment.

'We're off,' I say.

Mac snaps his laptop shut, puts his phone down and hastily gets to his feet. 'I didn't realise it had gotten so late.' He kisses me and then Scarlett. 'Have a good day, you two. Let me know how you go with Jonesy.'

'I will.' My eyes trail from the phone to Mac's face. 'How was your call?'

'Fine.' He doesn't meet my gaze but tickles Scarlett's foot.

'Okay, well, bye.' I pull the door shut and press my lips against Scarlett's downy head, an odd little chill creeping up my spine.

CHAPTER FIVE

When I found out I was pregnant with Scarlett, Mac and I made a deal. If we were going to have a baby, we needed to be all in—no specifics, not too many absolutes, just a baseline agreement that we would be a team. We would make decisions together and trust each other, talk to each other. We agreed to feel our way through the first year, to prioritise Ben's mental health, and go from there. The problem now is that we're on the cusp of the next stage, and I don't feel any clearer than I did a year ago as to what should happen next.

But somehow, despite existing in limbo, I'm happier than I've been in years. I've enjoyed Scarlett more than I ever enjoyed Ben as a baby. I have found joy in the bracing early mornings, the lazy afternoons, and the intimate minutes we've shared in the dead of night. The terror of having a daughter has morphed into a feeling that the final piece of a puzzle is slotting into place. For the first time in my life, I've stopped willing time to pass.

A few months before Scarlett was born, Mac and I packed up our lives in Sydney and moved to Smithson. I stuffed my guilt about tearing him away from his life somewhere so deep it barely registered, but lately it's bubbling up. I know he turned down a lecturing offer in July—he didn't mention it to me, but I stumbled upon one of his emails when I was searching for an old power bill. He cited family reasons, saying travel was near impossible these days. I didn't ask him about it, conscious he hadn't raised it with me.

As I approach the primary school, I slow the car. Students file into the main gate, while parents clog the footpath. Among them, I notice my old mothers' group friend Carol. Her hands fly around her face as she tells a story to another school mother, her perfect blonde hair shaking from side to side. I haven't spoken to Carol in ages—the few old friends I had have left the baby phase long behind them. Thank god I have Candy.

'Bye, Mum!' says Ben.

'Bye, honey.'

He jogs into the schoolyard, his long hair flying. He greets a group of boys with similar haircuts, and they move in a pack toward the basketball court. Ben amicably cuffs a kid on the shoulder and lifts his jaw skyward, causing me to inhale sharply; sometimes he seems a lot older than ten.

Scarlett stares at me in the rear-view mirror, her blue eyes solemn.

'At least you're still little,' I say.

She kicks and grins.

I pull away from the kerb and wait impatiently behind the queue of cars. Maybe Mac was acting oddly because of the cold case he's working on. I should just ask him about it. We used to talk about his cases all the time, but I can't remember discussing one with him properly since Scarlett was a newborn.

Finally I escape the school traffic. There are barely any cars in the main shopping strip, so it takes less than ten minutes to get to Smithson Police Station, where I park in my old spot. The building somehow looks more modern than it did when it was built twenty-five years ago. The pale brick structure has grown into its environment, or rather the trees have grown around it, softening its edges.

I smile at the faded red mark next to Jonesy's car park. When Warren Main had his bucks party at The Toad pub about seven years ago, his crew insisted on taking photos of him clad in an op-shop wedding dress in front of the police station. A love heart was sprayed on the wall during the impromptu photoshoot, but no one could remember who the graffiti artist was, seeing as the whole group was blind drunk.

God, I've spent some time here, long days and long nights. But it's been several months since I set foot inside. I've avoided visiting, instead meeting Jonesy at a cafe. I've been keen to put some distance between this world and my new family.

Constable Mina 'Minnie' Wilson is on the front desk, and her face lights up when she sees us. Within moments she's towering over me and making silly faces at Scarlett. 'Oh my god, Gemma, she's divine. I've seen photos, but she's grown heaps already.' She exclaims brightly to Scarlett, 'You're so big!'

Minnie's above average height made her nickname inescapable. The daughter of a high-profile detective in regional Queensland, she has had to navigate an extra dose of scepticism regarding nepotism on top of the standard dollop served out to female recruits. She's been a constable for less than a year, having joined the force just after I moved back to Smithson. She has good intuition and attention to detail—and unlike Julian Everett, she's warm and genuine.

'Hang on a tick, Gemma.' Minnie pushes back through the doors, answers the switch and talks patiently to the caller about a lost wallet. Once she's recorded the details, she hangs up and beams at us. She has a smile that lights up her whole face, flecks of light permanently caught in her dark eyes. 'Sorry about that!' Then, 'When are you coming back to work?'

'That's kind of why I'm here,' I say lightly, dodging the question.

Her tone shifts. 'To see Jonesy?'

I nod. 'Yep. He's already in, I assume?'

'In his office—I heard him swearing to himself before.' Her laugh seems forced. 'Just go through, it's fine. I'll sign you in.'

'Is everything okay, Minnie?'

'Yes, of course. Gosh, it would be great to have you back—get some variety into the place. I'm sick of being asked what to buy the wives for their birthdays.'

She wants an ally here, I realise: someone who knows the ropes and how to avoid the burn, someone else to soak up the casual sexism and blokey jokes.

'A fancy bottle of bubbles and some White Musk body lotion every time,' I say with a wink. 'They can add a candle if the budget stretches that far. It works equally well for wives, daughters, sisters and mothers, and it's basic enough that they could have come up with it themselves. It's also not a terrible gift to receive. Can't go wrong.'

'White Musk, huh. I wondered why everyone smells the same at staff barbecues.' Her smile doesn't quite reach her eyes.

'Mystery solved.'

'I'd better get back to this.' She gestures to a pile of paperwork on the desk. 'It's really good to see you, Gemma. And you, Scarlett!'

Minnie scans me into the open-plan office area. I'm always surprised by how little it changes, reminiscent of a childhood bedroom that a parent is reluctant to redecorate. I walk past the same shitty scuffed desks, the same cheap chairs guaranteed to cause long-term back problems, and the same array of unreliable office supplies. The corner desk Jonesy gave me last year must belong to someone else now, judging by the shrivelled cactus and overflowing in-tray.

The meeting room I once preferred for private conversations has signs of being used for a case: a portable pin-board is blocking the internal window, and a nest of tables has been pushed to one side of the room, making space for a row of chairs.

In the middle of the main room, three uniforms are standing around one of the desks. Unsure if I've met them before, I smile politely without stopping as I make my way to Jonesy's office. His muffled voice calls out a yes in response to my knocking.

'Morning,' I say, stepping inside.

Jonesy stands and brings his hands together. He looks better than when I last saw him; his ruddy skin has a healthy glow, and he's leaner. 'Lucy has me eating some vegetable rubbish,' he says, seeming to read my mind. He waves at his stubbornly rotund midsection, then clears his throat and wipes his hands on his suit pants before holding them out to me. 'Well, come on, hand her over.'

When I pass Scarlett across the wide desk, she makes a happy gurgle.

'Did you hear that?' He holds her awkwardly. 'She's pleased to see me.'

I sink into the chair opposite, enjoying being free of her weight. My left hip hurts, so I twist at the waist, trying to loosen the muscles. 'She must sense a kindred spirit.'

Jonesy smiles at Scarlett but talks to me. 'I hear you were both at the hospital last night when all hell broke loose.'

I nod. 'I actually thought you might postpone our catch-up.'

'No need—I have uniforms out there. I'm trying to let go a bit, focus on things here.' He gestures to the piles of folders in front of him. 'It's just a shame that bloody Roger Kirk is involved in the whole saga.'

'You know him?'

'A little,' Jonesy says. 'I'm familiar with his uncle, Carlyle Kirk. Smug prick.'

'I went to primary school with Carlyle's kids, but I never met him. He's a doctor, right?'

'And a wanker, among other things.'

I smile. 'How do you know him?'

'We used to play cricket together. The man always thought he was god's gift to this town and everyone in it. Used to keep tabs on our team's stats and read them out at the end of every game, along with helpful tips. Drove me up the wall.'

Picturing Jonesy as an indignant teenager, I hide another smile. A detail I've filed away about Carlyle Kirk hovers on the edges of my memory but I can't nail it down.

'What about Roger?' I ask.

'He shares his uncle's cocky attitude but appears to keep the hospital in order.'

'Until now,' I say.

'It's too early to say whether any staff were involved.'

I keep my thoughts to myself—even though the more I've considered it the more I think it must be an inside job.

'It was weird not being there in an official capacity last night,' I admit.

'Sounds like you asserted yourself pretty well,' Jonesy says wryly.

'You spoke to Everett.'

'He spoke to me,' my boss corrects. 'I think he felt a little upstaged.'

'Well, I was *there*,' I say defensively. 'And he was missing things.'

Jonesy looks at me in the way he always does: straight through the middle. 'You can be intimidating, Gemma. Everett wasn't expecting to have someone as experienced as you there passing judgement, so give him a break.'

I cross my arms, ignoring both the reprimand and his backhanded compliment. 'Have you learned anything more about the car crash?'

'A little. You know Bob Dalgliesh?'

I conjure a sketchy mental image of an older farmer with crinkly blue eyes and a non-ironic Akubra. 'I think so.'

'He witnessed the crash, saw the woman get run off the road.'

'Deliberately?'

'Dalgliesh reckons so, but it was dark, and he was a fair distance off.' Jonesy adjusts Scarlett's weight against his chest. 'His version stacks up, though, seeing as the other driver didn't stop.'

'Did he get any details? Rego?'

Jonesy shakes his head. 'He thinks it was a dark four-wheel drive, but he's not certain.'

'Did he recognise either driver?'

'No.'

'Is it possible he's lying to cover up his own involvement? Remember we had that case a while back where the witness was the perp—'

'We don't think so. Bob's a good sort and seems genuinely shaken up. And there's no evidence his car was involved. But the forensic team are still reviewing the vehicles and the scene, so we'll know more this arvo.'

My mind is ticking through all the things to cover off. 'Have we crosschecked all missing person reports across the country, not just New South Wales? And has anyone from the hospital come forward with more information? I think more than one person was involved, based on the sequence of events. I think it's possible someone tried to kill her and then when she survived the crash, they had to finish the job and make plans to take her body for whatever reason. Have the emergency staff who treated the woman been interviewed yet?'

'Steady on, Woodstock. I'm starting to sweat, and you're not even on duty. Let's talk about last night later—I haven't even asked you how you are.'

I realise my hands are gripping the edges of the chair. Taking a deep breath, I force myself to relax. 'I'm good. Tired. Her sleeping is still erratic.'

'What, this little princess? I don't believe it.' He presses his forefinger against Scarlett's nose, making her laugh.

'What about you?' I ask. 'How are you?'

'I'm fine.' He pauses, and the silence goes for a beat too long to be comfortable. His expression is serious, and my stomach lurches nervously. 'Gemma, I'm retiring.'

If I wasn't already sitting down, I would be now. Goose bumps prickle my limbs, and my pulse flutters. Of course I've always known this would happen eventually. Jonesy must be at least sixty. He's been the chief inspector here for almost fifteen years. He and Lucy have never travelled much, and I remember her telling me she wants to go on a cruise, to see the world. But somehow it still feels shocking, perhaps because Jonesy is so linked to my identity of being a detective in Smithson, so much a part of my world here. I assumed he would be my boss when I returned from mat leave.

Scarlett emits a sharp cry, and Jonesy swiftly passes her back to me. She thrusts her fingers into my hair and pulls hard.

He clears his throat a couple of times. 'Well, that's my big news.'

I slip a dummy into Scarlett's mouth, then uncurl her fingers from my hair. 'It's definitely big,' I say quietly. 'Lucy must be happy.'

'If being in a frenzy of holiday planning is happy, then yes, she's delighted.'

'When will this happen?'

'I've discussed a six-month exit strategy with the chief. Apparently I'm spending April in Bali.'

'How horrible.'

Jonesy hikes up his pants. 'I guess I had better get used to it. Lucy has one of those giant maps and is using it like a holiday-planning dartboard. God knows where we'll end up next.' He attempts a laugh.

I nod as I fight to keep the tears at bay.

'This isn't common knowledge around here yet, so I'd appreciate it if—'

'Not my news to tell.'

'I've obviously had to think seriously about a succession plan.'

My nerves implode. I want him to say it's me; I don't want him to say it's me.

'It's important we think about the future of this place,' he continues. 'Especially with Smithson going through so much change. In a decade, it will be completely different.'

There's a knock at the door, and a young constable enters. 'Sorry to interrupt, sir, but we just got a call.'

'And?' Jonesy asks impatiently.

The constable's Adam's apple bulges, his eyes drifting to Scarlett. 'Sir, there's a baby.'

Jonesy's eyes go to her, too. 'Yes?'

'No.' The constable shakes his head and tries again. 'Someone has left a newborn at the lake.'

CHAPTER SIX

Smithson locals know that Sonny Lake is divided into zones with invisible boundaries. There's the playground for little kids watched by their lycra-clad mothers, the square of grass where older children play soccer, the north running track used by fit young professionals who enjoy its challenging steep sections, and the flatter southern offering, generally occupied by Smithson's senior citizens enjoying a picnic or light exercise.

Further along, there's the old shot tower where teenagers smoke cigarettes and drink booze—although this has happened less since the local council spruced it up, installing historical information plaques and compact CCTV units. My high-school boyfriend jumped to his death from the shot tower in our final year, splintering whatever resilience I'd hung on to following my mother's death. This was also where Rosalind Ryan, an old classmate of mine, was found dead several years ago, triggering a series of events that culminated with my leaving Smithson. Suffice to say, Sonny Lake is not a place I frequent, even as a sleep-deprived second-time mother in need of fresh air and exercise.

I slam the car door shut and quickly strap Scarlett into the carrier, holding her head steady as I rush after Jonesy and two other officers. I wonder if they're thinking what I am: there's a good chance this abandoned baby is linked to the hit-and-run victim.

The four of us navigate the steep steps from the car park to the gravel path that circles the lake. The water is still, marked only by symmetrical silver trails the ducks create. Through the dense bushland ahead, I make out an ambulance parked roughly on the grass. A paramedic is loading equipment back into the bus. Her movements are assured, but her eyes are wide, her face pale.

'Rowena,' says Jonesy, 'what can you tell us?'

'Hello, sir. Hello.' She nods at the rest of us, her voice solemn.

'How is the baby?'

'She's dehydrated but stable. Charlie is giving her fluids now. There are no obvious injuries, thank goodness.'

'How old is she?' I ask, peering into the back of the ambulance where a male paramedic is monitoring a tiny infant. I grip Scarlett tighter, remembering how defenceless and dependent she was as a newborn.

Rowena turns to me, giving Scarlett a look of confusion as she tries to work out where I fit in. 'Young . . . I'd guess no more than a week.'

'Jesus,' Jonesy mutters.

Rowena swallows and nods. 'I know. The woman that found her is over there—Helen Chester. She's pretty upset.' Rowena hands Jonesy a sealed plastic bag. 'This was the blanket the baby was wrapped in. We both wore gloves.'

The blanket is grey and generic, the type of material used in a hospital or childcare centre.

Jonesy clears the phlegm from his throat with trademark gusto, and Rowena flinches. 'Thanks,' he says. 'We'll see what we can find here and catch up with you at the hospital.'

'No problem.' She secures the back doors and climbs into the driver's seat.

'Excuse me,' I call out to her, 'did you attend the car crash last night? The woman who died in emergency . . . ?'

'No, sorry, that was my colleagues.' She pulls her door shut, and the ambulance departs in a swirl of artificial sound and light.

After Jonesy gives me an exasperated look, he starts firing questions at the uniform who first arrived on the scene. I walk along the cordoned-off area where the baby was found. It boasts thick trees, ferns and grass. A crumpled Coke can is half hidden under some bracken, along with a water-logged plastic bag and two torn cigarette packets. Faded words are carved into one of the trees along the path: *This is a time machine.*

I wonder how long the baby lay here before she was spotted. I think about Scarlett's newborn cries, impossible to ignore in the confines of our home but easily lost out here in the middle of the night with no one around.

'Hello! Hello!' The woman Rowena pointed out jumps up from the bench and raises a bony hand toward me. Her grey hair is cut into a blunt bob, and her white sneakers are so new they almost reflect the light. 'I'm Helen, Helen Chester, Smithson local. Are you a cop? I'm the witness.'

Jonesy is still talking to the uniform so I introduce myself and one of the constables, and Helen launches into a manic account of what happened. She is clearly an avid watcher of crime shows and very worked up. 'It turns out I've got weak bones. I had no idea until the doctor told me just over a fortnight ago. Anyway, the doc put me on some special tablets and told me I'm supposed to be walking as much as I can, which is what I've been doing. I've been coming here every morning since the diagnosis, apart from two days when it was raining. I still walk when it's just a sprinkle but not when it buckets down—it's just too unpleasant. So, I was walking along this morning and then I just saw it, lying there on the grass.' A tear slides out of Helen's left eye. 'I thought I was going mad, seeing things. Then I thought it was a doll. But it was a baby—all by itself! My instincts kicked in, and I picked up the darling thing. I hope I haven't compromised the DNA evidence, but I didn't even think! It was breathing, but it wasn't crying, and the poor little thing wouldn't open its eyes—and that's never a good sign.' Her chin wobbles dangerously. 'Is it?' She absently reaches forward and grabs Scarlett's outstretched fingers.

'The ambulance officers are taking care of her,' I respond soothingly, unable to provide specific medical details.

'It's a little girl?' says Helen, blinking out another tear.

'I believe so.'

'I didn't make a big scene,' she says softly. 'I just called triple zero and then I called my friend. I sat here—' she points to the bench behind us '—and I held the baby, watching to make sure she kept breathing. I prayed like a madwoman.'

'It sounds like you managed everything perfectly.'

Jonesy joins us just as his phone rings, a jarring noise against the gentle chorus of birds in the surrounding trees. His expression is grim, his eyes sliding to meet mine, and he steps away from us to take the call. I hope it's not bad news about the baby.

I ask Helen a few more questions, but it's clear she has nothing helpful to tell me.

Jonesy returns, shaking his head to communicate there's no update on the infant's condition. I wonder what the call was about.

I take Helen's details, and she confirms that her neighbour will pick her up and spend the day with her.

Two forensic technicians arrive to search the area. Leaving Jonesy and the others with them, I head over to the playground, where a group of mothers I noticed earlier is watching the scene unfold. The three play rugs spread out between them are dotted with tanbark and leaves, indicating they've been here for a while. A little boy stares at me from the top of the slide, not breaking eye contact as he glides to the bottom, his mother catching him neatly in a hug and spinning him around.

I smile at the women, hoping Scarlett creates some common ground. 'Hello, hi.' Why do I suddenly feel so bad at this? Even though I haven't worn a uniform in over a decade, I yearn for the authority it offers. Standing in front of these perky young mothers, I feel inferior. 'Mind if I ask you a few questions? There's been an incident here this morning, and I'd like to know if you saw anything that can help us.'

They appraise me with a collective sweep, before shifting their gaze back to a woman with jet-black cropped hair and no make-up. It's clear she's the group spokesperson.

'I'm a detective—Detective Sergeant Woodstock.' I show them my police ID. 'This was supposed to be my day off.' I gesture to Scarlett, which elicits a few understanding nods.

'We'll help if we can,' Jet-Black says. A baby with a matching head of hair is strapped to her chest in a complicated knot of material. 'I heard someone say a kid was injured. Is that why the ambulance was here?' Her pale grey eyes bore into mine. Then, without turning her head, she hisses, 'Billy, stop that.'

A toddler a few metres away immediately drops the stick he was holding and turns his attention to a plastic spade in the sandpit.

'I can't confirm any details at this stage, but we are investigating a serious incident involving a child.'

The women's eyes widen. I have their full attention now.

'Is the child all right?' asks Jet-Black. 'The ambulance had the siren on.'

I ignore her question and smile encouragingly at the broader group. 'How long have you all been here this morning?'

Jet-Black holds out her arms to Billy as he runs up to her, wielding the plastic spade. A water bottle and a container of chopped fruit magically appear. 'We all got here around eight. We meet every Monday morning.'

This is promising: people in a routine are more likely to notice something unusual.

'Did you see anything out of the ordinary?'

They shake their heads as if it's a move in a choreographed dance routine.

'Hear anything?'

Another synchronised headshake.

One woman raises her hand. 'This might not be relevant, but my husband was here last night, and he said he saw something kind of odd.'

'Nothing is irrelevant,' I say. 'What did he see?'

'Well—' Her face scrunches up, and she pushes her auburn hair away from her eyes '—I was half asleep on the couch when he came home. He said something about almost being knocked over by someone running through the car park. They didn't apologise—they just kept running. He thought maybe they were on drugs.'

I get out my phone and load the notes page. 'Which car park?'

'Um, probably that one.' She points to the road. 'I don't think he'd use the tower car park if he was coming from work. His office is on the main street. But I'm not sure.'

'Was the person male or female?'

'He didn't say, but I assume it was a man.'

'Do you know what time this happened?'

She wrinkles her nose. 'Around seven-thirty?'

I think about the possibility that the baby was alone here all night. It wasn't freezing, but it was cold. And a dog or a fox could easily have got to her.

'I'll need your husband's contact details,' I say, and the redhead obliges.

Jet-Black pipes up. 'There were a lot of people here yesterday evening, though.'

'Why was that?' I ask.

She combs her long fingers through her hair, which falls in perfect waves around her elfin face. 'There was a fundraiser for the primary school. My neighbour went and said there was a good turnout—they sold out of sausages.' She gestures to the barbecue area, where there are two overflowing bins and several crows playing tug of war with sauce-stained paper plates.

'Thanks,' I say. 'That's helpful.'

'Can you tell us what happened now?' Jet-Black asks in a voice that suggests she's used to getting what she wants.

'I'm sure it will be on the news later.'

As I walk back down to the lake, I wipe Scarlett's drool off my shirt. The scene has grown crowded and lost its low-key vibe. Rubbernecking runners lunge on the spot, and gawking mothers shade their eyes as they whisper to each other. The press has arrived—including Candy, who has positioned herself at the opposite end of the scrum to her old boss, Nate Lyman. A photographer walks backwards, trying to get the perfect shot of the gathering townsfolk, and almost falls into the lake. I duck under the police tape, hoping Candy doesn't notice me.

Jonesy is on the phone again, so I join the constable standing guard for the forensic team; I worked with him briefly before I went on mat leave. 'Anything turn up yet?'

'Not so far.' His breath is minty from gum.

Fighting the urge to follow it up myself, I tell him about the wayward runner and give him the phone number of the woman's husband to call and follow up. 'No one has reported a missing infant . . . ?'

He shakes his head.

I consider this. There is no ambiguity about an abandoned baby: if she hasn't been reported missing by now, it's because her guardians think she's safe in the care of someone else, or they dumped her here themselves, or they're not in a state to call it in. A custody battle, a secret pregnancy, an overwhelmed mother? Or something more sinister? I close my eyes and send a wish to the universe that the mother is safe.

Jonesy ambles toward us, still talking on the phone. 'All right, we'll meet you there,' he says, ending the call.

Scarlett is growing heavy, the carrier straps digging into my shoulders. I really need to sit down.

'That was Everett,' Jonesy says, snapping me back to attention. 'He's just received the debrief from the crash site. The car the deceased woman was driving was reported stolen from a farm a few years ago. There's nothing concrete on the other vehicle yet, but the tyre marks and damage to the vehicle back up Dalgliesh's story—there were two cars involved.'

The other case thunders back into my thoughts as Scarlett fidgets. 'I assume there isn't any CCTV along the highway?'

'There's bloody nothing. We're pulling everything we can from the streets around the hospital to see if we can locate the vehicle that collected the body.'

'And the cameras in and out of town,' I say.

'Yep. Not that we have the manpower to review it all.'

'Maybe the woman's prints or DNA will show up in our system, or even be a match in one of the genealogy sites, although I know that will take ages,' I say, trying to be positive. 'I assume her blood is all over the car.'

'Let's hope so, otherwise we're staring down the barrel of a crazy goose chase.' Jonesy glowers at the crowd. 'Bloody hell, don't these people have better things to do? Christ, I'm hungry. Do they still have that cafeteria there, Woodstock, with the schnitzel sandwiches?'

'Where?'

'At the hospital.'

'I'm sure they do. I believe they even have a salad bar now.'

'Jesus Christ, Woodstock.'

'Just looking out for you, boss.' Sadness grips me as I recall our earlier conversation. I've worked with some good people over the years, but Jonesy is one of a kind. I can't imagine reporting to someone else here in Smithson.

'Come on then, Woodstock. Let's go.' He starts walking back toward the car park.

I rush after him. 'Hang on, you want me to come to the hospital with you?'

'Of course you're bloody coming,' he yells over his shoulder. 'Hurry the hell up.'

CHAPTER SEVEN

I call Rebecca from the Sonny Lake car park and ask if she can mind Scarlett. Luckily she says yes. I drive to Dad's, singing to Scarlett, who is starting to grizzle. Half of their front fence is snow white, while the other half is a faded beige. It was Dad's latest project in a long line of home improvements. He's a mostly retired handyman, and in recent years he's turned his skills to an upgrade of the house he shares with Rebecca. His craftsmanship is impressive, although the style is rather eclectic—Mac describes it as 'misguided bachelor meets country bed and breakfast with a generous dash of austerity'.

Rebecca bursts out of the front door, wearing a ridiculous yellow sunhat and a huge smile. 'Hi, Gemma!'

'Hi.' My back twinges as I struggle with the buckle on Scarlett's car seat, the nappy bag threatening to strangle me.

My phone rings: Candy, no doubt wanting intel about the baby.

'Gemma, just leave everything with me and you go. It's fine.' Rebecca hoists Scarlett onto her hip and swings the bag over her shoulder, her silver-streaked blonde hair framing her round face.

'I won't be too long,' I say. 'I'm just helping Jonesy with something.'

'Like I said, it's no problem. Focusing on this little lady will keep me from worrying about Ned.'

We exchange tentative smiles. Rebecca and I aren't close, but I appreciate how much she cares about Dad. Since I moved back to Smithson, we've established a respectful relationship anchored by her good cooking and Dad's determination that everyone gets along. Scarlett helps.

Rebecca adds, 'I thought I'd send Ben a message and see if he wants to walk here after school for some afternoon tea with me. I made a cake.'

'I'm not sure I'll be that long.' Her face drops, and I quickly add, 'But I'm sure he would love that.'

She beams. 'I'm going to sneak some dinner to Ned at the hospital tonight, something decent, but I'm not planning on leaving until after five, so take your time.'

'I'm actually going to check on him shortly.'

'You're going to the hospital?'

'That's where I'm meeting Jonesy, so I'll pop in briefly and say hi.'

Rebecca chews on her lip. No doubt she's seen the news about last night's security incident, and she knows Dad worries about my police work. She probably thinks she should step in and represent his fatherly concern while he's incapacitated. 'Please just make sure you're careful,' she says uncertainly.

'Of course! Thanks for minding Scarlett.'

'I'm always happy to look after her, Gemma, you know that.'

As I pull away from the kerb, I wave to them. I should ask Mac to help me finish painting the fence on the weekend—Dad won't be up to doing it for ages, and it's the kind of thing Scott would have done without asking. Dad and my ex were very close, and I know Dad misses him a lot. Although he has forged a solid relationship with Mac, it's not the same: Scott was like the son he never had.

I press at a sore spot on my collarbone. I probably should have told Jonesy I couldn't come to the hospital, but the pull of the two cases is strong. And I have to admit, the thought of making Everett aware that Jonesy wants me involved is appealing.

I turn into the main drag. Driving past The Toad, I notice three cops standing near the front entrance with Henno: Archie Henderson, the publican. I vaguely recall Candy mentioning a fight there last night. It must have been serious for an investigation to be spilling over to the following day, but I doubt Henno will press charges—he's too lazy to deal with the paperwork.

Jonesy calls, and I put it through the car speaker, asking, 'Any news on the baby?'

'She's serious but stable,' he says. 'Dehydrated. Are you almost here, Woodstock?'

'Yes. Hey, what's going on at the pub?'

'Just another pain in my arse.'

'Heard there was a fight there last night.'

'I thought you were on leave?'

I laugh. 'Only when it suits you. So what happened? Henno's there with a bunch of—'

'One crime at a time, Woodstock. Now hurry up.'

'See you in five.'

Grumbling, he ends the call.

I try to stay focused as I navigate a huge yawn. My head has felt woolly these past few months, but right now it just feels full. Jonesy's retirement bombshell bubbles to the top of the mental load. His news, in conjunction with Dad's heart attack, feels like an extra reminder of everyone's mortality.

'God.' I grip the steering wheel and take deep breaths, trying to ward off the anxiety that threatens to crash over me. I force my thoughts back to the baby and the missing woman.

After sailing through the roundabout, I slow the car as I pass the shopping strip. Out of the corner of my eye, a familiar figure grabs my attention: Mac. I feel a ripple of pleasure at being able to observe him without his knowledge. His rugged blond look is reminiscent of an ageing movie star, and there's something intrinsically reassuring about the way he carries himself. He grounds me in a way no one else ever has.

Mac walks briskly, his eyes hidden behind sunglasses. He's on the phone, with something wedged under his arm. I slow the car further, even though no one is in front of me. It's an A3 courier envelope, its contents causing the packaging to bulge.

The sinking feeling from this morning returns. But I can sense the driver behind me is about to beep their horn, so I switch my foot to the accelerator and reluctantly move forward. In the rear-view mirror, Mac surveys the street, ducks his head and disappears into the post office.

CHAPTER EIGHT

The sun is obnoxiously high in the sky, the glare bouncing off the glass exterior of the hospital, as I pull into the car park. Journos have started migrating from the lake to set up camp here; I automatically straighten my shirt and tuck it into my jeans, but no one tries to talk to me as I self-consciously walk past the small group. I'm so used to having Scarlett with me that my arms swing awkwardly by my sides before I dig them into my pockets.

It's not just the absence of Scarlett that has me off kilter: it's whatever is going on with Mac. Now that I think about it, he's been acting oddly for at least a fortnight. Nothing so obvious that I've thought to ask him what's wrong, but he's definitely been more distracted and less present. When exactly did it start? Was it when he began working on this cold case, or earlier? I was unwell for a few days before Dad's heart attack, and Scarlett was teething, so I was up and down during the night and napping a lot during the day. It's all a bit of a blur.

The reality of what I'm skating around hits me. Have I been so distracted and dull that Mac's sought stimulation elsewhere? Surely not. My chest seizes. God, the grief and shame would be almost unbearable.

As I walk through the hospital, the sight of Jonesy's bulky profile further along the corridor calms me—even though he's kicking the vending machine. 'How the heck does this bloody thing work?' He sees me approaching and calls out, 'Woodstock, what am I doing wrong here?'

I scoop the rejected coins out of the plastic tray and read the instructions. 'The machine doesn't accept five and ten cent pieces. Do you have anything bigger?'

'Do I look like a bloody bank?'

I retrieve two dollars from my wallet and put it in the slot. 'Cheese and onion, right?'

'Always.'

The bright yellow chip packet drops from its ledge, and I hand it to him.

He opens the chips and quickly demolishes half the bag. 'Want one?' Yellow flavouring glistens on his fingers.

'Definitely no.'

'Suit yourself.' He shrugs. 'Everett's around here somewhere.'

'Everett's here?' I say, pretending to be surprised.

'Come on, Woodstock. It's his case, and he's a decent cop. The two of you would make a good team if you bothered to stop squabbling.'

'Maybe.' I swallow past my dislike. 'Nothing new has come through on the baby . . . ?'

'Nothing. Everett will brief the press downstairs at two, so hopefully we'll get some bites.'

I'm annoyed that Everett's briefing the press, something Jonesy would normally do.

'What about any pregnant women at high risk of family violence?'
I ask. 'The mother might have given birth and tried to take the baby
somewhere she thought it would be safe.'

'Good point,' he says. 'I'll make sure Everett adds that to the
call-out.'

Over his shoulder I see Sophie McCallister at the front desk
with Roger Kirk. It's clear they're having a disagreement: Sophie's
stance is defensive as she talks animatedly, waving her hands, while
Roger is engrossed in something on the computer, making a point of
ignoring her. She notices me watching, drops her hands and clamps
her mouth shut.

'A high-speed car crash, a stolen corpse and an abandoned baby,'
I muse. 'It's certainly been an action-packed twenty-four hours in
Smithson.'

'You think the baby belonged to the dead woman?' Jonesy asks.

'I don't think anything yet.'

His mouth curves into a wry smile before it drops back into its
default grimace. 'Come on,' he says, putting his hand on the small
of my back and leading me toward Everett and Holdsworth. 'And
try to be nice.'

Outside, camera crews are setting up tripods, and reporters are
brushing their hair and angling for the best position. I can see Candy
directing her employee Sam as he shuffles back and forth with his
camera on his shoulder.

Everett lifts his hand to the crowd and ambles over to us as if
we're at a barbecue. 'I'm about ready to roll with this presser, sir,'
he says, ignoring me.

Holdsworth at least has the good grace to offer me a smile.

'I've got a few points to catch you up on before you kick off,'
Jonesy says to Everett, who nods good-naturedly.

'Sounds like a plan.'

'Hello,' I say pointedly. 'Jonesy said the car driven by the missing woman is a stolen vehicle. Do you have any details?'

'Yes, that's right.' Everett fixes his gaze on me as if he's just noticed I'm here. 'It was reported stolen six and a half years ago, from a farm about an hour past Gowran, over two hundred k's away. We've spoken to the owner, but there's no known link to anyone from Smithson.'

'Did you speak to the ambos yet?'

He sighs. 'We spoke to Fred Katz this morning.'

'And?'

'And not much. Initially he and the other ambo thought the driver was dead, but she came around momentarily, so they brought her in hoping she could be saved. She died in ED less than five minutes after arrival.'

'Did she say anything when she came around?'

Everett shakes his head. 'Nope—barely conscious, apparently.'

My face is heating up. 'Did he remember anything that will help us get an ID?'

'Just that she was a brunette, very pale and very skinny. He reckons she was at least thirty-five, but said it was hard to tell.'

I scuff the floor with my foot, frustrated that I can't gather this case up—like I usually would—and examine all of its parts. 'What about the other ambo?'

'Haven't got to him yet, but it'll be the same deal as Fred. It's not like the woman was reeling off her key stats, Woodstock.'

'Was Fred the driver last night?'

'Yes . . . So?'

'We definitely need to talk to the other ambo then. What is his name?'

'Ashley Amato.'

I don't think I know him. 'We need to speak to him as soon as possible,' I say.

'We've tried, but he was out doing a transfer this morning.' Everett scowls. 'What's the rush, Woodstock?'

I try to curb my impatience. 'If Amato was the one in the back of the ambulance with the victim, he'll probably be able to tell us more about her than the driver can.'

Everett sucks in his cheeks. 'Sure, yeah. Maybe they struck up a friendship, and she told him her name and her favourite ice-cream flavour.'

My fists curl. 'Seeing as he spent about ten times longer with the patient than Fred did, I'd say it's more likely he'll remember a distinguishing feature. As far as I can tell, we've got no useful information about this woman, so any lead should be a priority.'

'All right.' Jonesy balls up his chip packet and holds it between us like he's umpiring a sports game. 'Everett, let's get this presser out of the way, then Woodstock and I will speak with the other paramedic. Later we'll regroup and see where we're at.' He throws the packet at a bin and misses. 'Preferably after I find a decent coffee.'

CHAPTER NINE

Jonesy and I have arranged to meet Ashley Amato in the staff tearoom inside the ambulance headquarters, a small building adjacent to the hospital on the opposite side to the morgue. Through the window I can see the media crowd has thinned out following the frenzied excitement of the presser. I've got to admit that Everett did a good job—he must have had media training. Concise without being clinical, he had good rapport with the few journos he took questions from.

An ambulance screeches into the emergency department, a blur of lights through the dirty windows. I think about my dad arriving here like that just over a week ago; hopefully whoever is in there today will be as lucky as he was.

Ashley is watching the action outside, so he doesn't notice us until we're right in front of him. He's young, at least ten years younger than me. I briefly think how unsettled I would feel if my family had an emergency and he turned up to save the day—but I'm sure that's what a lot of people used to think when I fronted up to a crime scene. Unfortunately, these days there's no fear of me being mistaken for a rookie.

The ambo seems apprehensive, even though he must be fairly used to questions from cops. Perhaps he's just a naturally nervous person. His brown eyes are unusually round, and he has short dark hair and a clean-shaven face. He takes me in the way a child might, unashamedly scanning my features one by one. I don't recognise him, but we probably crossed paths last year because cops frequently interact with ambos. I got to know a few by name in Sydney and Melbourne, and I once knew all the paramedics in Smithson.

Ashley abruptly looks away from me. He stands and offers his hand to Jonesy. 'Hi. Um, hi. I'm Ashley Amato. Ash.'

We introduce ourselves, and I take a seat. Jonesy plucks a chair from a nearby table and positions it next to me, elbowing my rib cage in the process. 'Sorry, Woodstock,' he mutters. He spreads his legs and leans his hairy forearms on the table. 'Sit down, kid,' he says to Ash.

The ambo sinks back into the chair and plays with a leather band looped around his wrist. A tattoo peeks out from his shirtsleeve.

I feel some of my old confidence surge. 'Ash, you attended the scene of a car crash last night with Fred Katz—is that right?'

'Yeah, sorry I missed the phone calls—I went straight home to bed. We were supposed to clock off just before we got the call about the crash.' He pauses. 'Look, the cops spoke to Fred . . . I'm not sure I'm going to be any more help than he was.'

I smile. 'It all helps. Was the woman conscious at all while you were with her?'

His forehead creases. 'Only briefly. She came to just before we moved her into the bus and then again when we arrived here. Her eyes fluttered a few times, and she was moaning and muttering, but she never spoke.'

'Where was the crash?' I deliberately don't ask what the victim looked like yet; I want him focusing on the impersonal first. It's the same with witness statements: get them setting the scene, then sort out the specifics. Jonesy taught me that. 'Ash?' I prompt. He's staring at me again, and I cough, trying to short-circuit the power of his gaze.

'Along the highway about six k's out of town, right near the Stafford farmhouse.'

'And she'd crashed into a tree?'

'Yeah, hard into a giant gum.'

'The car was a . . . ?'

'Station wagon, Toyota, dark coloured.'

'Did you recognise the woman?'

He blinks a few times. 'No.'

I fumble for my water bottle to force a pause. I can't seem to get into the right rhythm; Ash must sense it, because he can't seem to relax. I ask, 'What was she wearing?'

'Jeans and a plain T-shirt.'

I nod. 'What colour was her shirt?'

'Dark? Black, I think.'

'What about her hair? Short? Long?'

He closes his eyes. 'Medium length.'

'Colour?'

'Brown. I don't think it was dyed, because it was all the one colour, even at the scalp. I noticed that when I fitted the oxygen mask on her.'

'That's great,' I say, nodding encouragingly. 'What about freckles or moles?'

He shakes his head. 'I'm not sure, sorry. Nothing I can remember.'

'Any tattoos?' People with tattoos tend to notice them on others and can have remarkably accurate recall for specific designs.

'Not that I saw.' Now he shakes his head vigorously. 'Her skin was very pale, all over. And there was a lot of blood on her. She had a serious head injury from the steering wheel.' He swallows. 'I'm pretty sure her right leg was broken.'

I grimace sympathetically. He seems delicate, and I wonder if this job is the right one for him. Just like a cop, a paramedic needs to navigate despair and hope simultaneously. Not everyone is cut out for it.

'No obvious tan lines?' I ask.

'No.'

'Anything else? Jewellery, scars, piercings?'

'She had a bruise,' he says. 'On her head.' He points to his left temple. 'And a few on the top of her left arm. They weren't from the crash.'

I write this down. 'Underwear?'

He blinks. 'Her bra was plain . . . like, cotton, I think. Black.'

'Cheap.'

He opens his mouth, closes it. 'I guess so.'

'Was there anything you saw that made you think she'd recently given birth?'

He frowns and moves his head from side to side. 'No, she was very thin.'

'Did she remind you of anyone?' Jonesy asks.

Ash's dark eyes shine, and he stammers, 'Like who?'

It's as if he's worried he'll say the wrong thing, and I wonder if we're giving the impression we know more than we do. 'If she resembles someone,' I say, 'it can help us build a likeness and narrow down our options. We really want to work out who this woman was, so we can tell her loved ones what happened.'

'Of course,' he murmurs.

'Does anyone come to mind?' I press. 'A celebrity is fine if that's easier.' I'm finding my feet, motivated by the satisfaction that comes with the teasing out of information.

'Um, maybe Winona Ryder? But because she had her eyes closed, it's hard to say.'

I know what he means—I often find it difficult to match a dead or unconscious body to footage of a living, breathing person. So much of how we look is in our eyes and our expressions; in death we become more similar, morphing into a generic human clay.

'If you think of anything else, give us a shout,' says Jonesy. 'And we'll do the same. We're running some tests, so hopefully something will turn up. With any luck our girl's on the system.' He pushes away from the small table, eyes already on his phone.

'There was one thing . . .' Ash says.

'What?' Jonesy and I say in unison.

'Her feet were covered in bleeding cuts, but I don't think they were from the crash.'

'You took her shoes off?' I ask.

'She wasn't wearing any.'

CHAPTER TEN

Jonesy and I have a hurried conversation about what the woman's lack of shoes and cut-up feet might mean.

'An escapee?' I suggest. 'She was abducted and then got away. That would explain her being chased—how Bob Dalgliesh described the crash.'

'Maybe she gave birth and then fled from an abusive partner,' Jonesy says. 'But no shoes might mean poor mental health or intoxication. She might not even have realised she wasn't wearing them.'

I nod, trying to organise my thoughts. 'Maybe she was trying to get rid of evidence on her shoes and ditched them . . . Blood?'

'Could be.'

'We should get an alert out about the woman being barefoot to all the police stations, hospitals and medical centres in the region. And let's get Ash to brief a sketch artist. Until we ID this woman, it's going to be a tough one to solve.'

'Good idea.'

I can't shake the feeling Ash is not telling us something important.

'Spit it out, Woodstock,' Jonesy barks.

'I feel like he was holding back. I want to talk to him again.'

'I'm not sure what more he can tell us, but I'm happy for you to give it another shot if you think it's important.'

I feel a throb of nostalgia, thinking of the hundreds of times Jonesy has said this to me.

Leaving him to back brief Everett, I head upstairs to visit Dad. He's sitting up in the chair next to the bed, doing a crossword.

'I just thought I'd come and check on you,' I say. 'But I can't stay—I have a meeting.'

'A meeting,' he repeats.

'Yes. Jonesy's here. He says to say hello.'

Dad's blue eyes lock on mine. 'Is this about what happened last night? I watch the news, you know. You're involved in that now? What about your leave?'

'Dad—'

'Gemma,' he returns.

'I'm just helping Jonesy out. It's not a big deal.' I lean down to kiss his forehead. 'There's been another incident today,' I add, figuring I may as well tell him now.

'What kind of incident?' He seems uncharacteristically vulnerable, and I wonder if he's been more shaken by his health scare than he has let on.

'Someone left a baby at the lake, a newborn. She's here in critical care.'

Dad removes his glasses. 'Will she be all right?'

'We think so. She's stable.'

'God, how awful. But at least she was found before something even worse happened to her.'

'Yes.' I watch as he buffs his glasses with a tissue. 'And you're feeling okay, Dad? I want you to tell me if anything doesn't feel right.'

'I'd say I'm the least of your problems right now, Gem.'

My thoughts flicker to Mac and Jonesy, and I think he might have a point—but all I say is, 'Everything is fine, really. I was at the police station when the news about the baby was called in, so Jonesy asked me to tag along. It's not a permanent arrangement.'

'Not yet,' Dad comments wryly.

I ignore this.

'Please be careful, Gemma.' I sense he's going to add something, but he just resets his hold on the pen and asks, 'What's another word for "fashionable"?'

'You know I'm rubbish at those things.' I hold his papery hand. 'Rebecca said she'll be here after five. Don't eat too much! She's bringing you food.'

'God love her,' says Dad.

I decide to check on the baby, so I take the lift down to the next floor. Protected by medical staff and police officers, her tiny body lies in a perspex crib, chest rising and falling in time with mechanical beeps. She's only wearing a nappy, which accentuates how fragile she is. Even though she's getting the best possible care, I'm sad she's not having the opportunity to bond with a parent. I remember the life-affirming skin-on-skin contact and round-the-clock feeding in those early weeks, the relentless eye contact I had with Ben and Scarlett.

Switching to detective mode, I start writing observations in my mind. The infant has a dusting of light brown hair and seems to be white. Considering the demographic profile of Smithson, this doesn't provide many clues about her origin. The only things at the lake with her were the grey blanket and her plain white onesie.

The DNA test results will take at least forty-eight hours to come in, so for all I know the baby could be related to the victim of the crash. There was no car seat or baby paraphernalia at the scene, but the woman might have dumped the girl before she gained access to the car. Was it possible she thought the baby was safer at the lake? Perhaps the woman intended to return soon, but why risk the baby being found by a passer-by and taken to the authorities? Anyway, a public building or even a random front porch would have been a safer bet. Maybe the location was a predetermined drop-off point, with the baby left there in exchange for something—money or drugs? Was the woman being blackmailed? Could she have cut her feet at the lake?

My thoughts are interrupted by a woman sidling up to me. She introduces herself as Dr Nolan and enthusiastically launches into a rundown of her day, including getting called in to review the abandoned infant. 'This just put it all in perspective, you know—I was yelling at my own two kids about the state of their bedrooms and then I thought, *Whatever, make a mess. Who cares?*' Dr Nolan tells me the baby is likely to be fine but that the next few days are critical because she's so young. 'We just need to get some nutrients into her and pray no infections creep in, then hopefully we can get her home.' The doctor's bright white smile wavers for a beat. 'Hopefully her mother will turn up.'

I don't offer false promises. 'I hope so, too.'

The baby startles, her limbs jerking skyward, features crinkling as if she's having a vivid dream.

'Poor little thing,' murmurs Dr Nolan. 'All alone.'

Downstairs I find Jonesy on the phone and Sophie McCallister talking to Holdsworth. I don't know where Everett is. I stand nearby, feeling out of place.

Jonesy finishes his call. 'Right, where's Everett?' he says. 'We need to go over a few things.'

'Right here.' Everett comes around the corner, taking obnoxiously long strides.

'Let's go to my office . . . ?' Sophie looks nervous, her eyes darting around. 'Mr Kirk is in there, waiting for an update.'

Jonesy makes an annoyed sound.

'Why is he in your office?' I ask.

'People aren't looking for him there,' Sophie replies.

As we enter, Roger Kirk springs up from behind the desk, greeting us with solid handshakes and an expectant expression. I assume his office is more impressive than Sophie's, a small room with zero personality, which seems odd for someone who has worked here for sixteen years. The only photo is a group shot of several staff members gathered at the main reception area. Roger is all smiles for the camera as he hands something to a child in a wheelchair, with Sophie and her colleagues watching on and clapping. There's also a framed Bob Dylan quote on the shelves behind her desk, but otherwise the visible spaces are filled with folders and paperwork.

Roger gestures for us to take a seat, even though there are only two chairs free. Sophie leaves and returns a minute later, red-faced and struggling with two more chairs. Her boss doesn't offer to help, so I assist her to manoeuvre them through the narrow door before she goes to fetch one for herself. She puts it down with a thud, then closes the door.

'We've opened an official investigation into last night's incident,' Jonesy begins. 'Everett and Holdsworth will lead and be your key contacts, and I'll be overseeing the case personally.'

'Yes, I'd expect as much,' replies Roger. 'The hospital is important to Smithson and this issue needs to be resolved as quickly as possible.'

I suddenly remember the detail I couldn't recall earlier about Roger's uncle, Carlyle Kirk. He was in the news several years ago when the aged care home he developed on the outskirts of Smithson was plagued by complaints. I was living in Melbourne at the time and therefore didn't closely follow the story, but I vaguely recall headlines about withheld meals, abusive behaviour and doctors not being alerted when residents were sick. I'm pretty sure the claims were dismissed in court.

Roger hooks his leg out to the side and rests his foot on the opposite knee. 'What do you have so far? It's impossible to do my job with the press vultures circling, plus it's terrible timing with the fundraising drive. I've got investors up my arse, and I need it to be squeaky clean.'

I'm almost certain I hear Jonesy mumble something under his breath, but when I look at him his face is completely still.

Sophie pipes up. 'We had the security company in today. They've reprogrammed the system so the morgue door can only be opened by senior management and everyone's pass is uni—'

Roger cuts in. 'Christ, Sophie, I hardly think this is likely to happen again. Surely we're not in the midst of a body-snatching spree?'

Sophie looks at the floor and raises her heels, her hands pushing against her kneecaps. 'Of course not,' she murmurs.

'I mean,' Roger continues, 'someone must have been after this woman specifically. Perhaps a loopy family member or ex-partner. No one on staff would do something like that—it's sick.'

'Our investigation is in the very early stages,' Holdsworth offers. 'The one thing we can be sure of right now is that we can't be sure of anything.'

'Well, that's helpful,' Roger mutters, rolling his eyes. It's almost as if he's drunk: he's flushed and seems unable to look anyone in the eye.

Everett, on the other hand, remains surprisingly calm. 'All we mean is that we're exploring various angles. I agree it seems most likely that this was a targeted crime, but we're not ruling anything out—especially considering only a handful of people knew the woman was here, and most of them were hospital staff.'

I chime in, wanting to respond to Roger's earlier point. 'And while it's unlikely stealing the corpse was premeditated because the outcome of the car crash was impossible to predict, the perpetrator was obviously familiar with the hospital and your systems and could quickly make a plan. So, unless the woman is related to someone working here, I'd say a family member is unlikely.'

Turning to Jonesy, Roger jerks a thumb at me. 'What's her role in all this?'

'Detective Woodstock is an experienced member of our team,' Jonesy replies without missing a beat. 'Her perspective on this situation is invaluable.'

I can feel Everett's gaze on me, and my cheeks burn.

Roger glowers. 'What happens next? We're in damage control, in case you haven't noticed. It would be good to have something to give the media that doesn't make me look like an idiot.'

'It will take as long as it takes.' Jonesy laces his thick fingers together. 'We're building on all aspects of our case and will need your ongoing cooperation. We continue to require full access to your staff, including security. Possibly current patients, too.'

'Didn't you speak to everyone you needed to already?' asks Sophie.

'Not yet,' says Holdsworth, 'but we're working through it. And we're still waiting on the bulk of the CCTV footage. When can we expect it?'

'Rufus and the team are sorting it out,' Sophie says. 'There are multiple cameras and hours of footage.'

'Bloody big job pulling all that,' Roger says.

'Bloody serious crime,' I retort, then tell Sophie, 'Footage by the end of the day would be helpful. And if there's anything that comes to mind, please contact us immediately—even if it's just a little niggle about staff members or patients.'

A thought strikes me as I remember Dad telling me that a lot of the nurses and other staff members are casual workers, picking up shifts at multiple hospitals and clinics to earn as much as possible. Could there be a black market for bodies? The rising cost of living pressures are steep; maybe a nurse or a cleaner has been tempted to supplement their income by selling body parts.

'Does your hospital have an arrangement with an educational institution?' I blurt out. 'I know bodies are sometimes donated for science . . . Does that happen from here? And is there ever a payment made in exchange for a corpse or body parts?'

Roger shakes his head vigorously. 'No way.'

'I've never known a financial exchange to take place,' says Sophie. 'Organs are donated occasionally, but I can only remember one instance when a body was donated for scientific purposes, and that was arranged with a medical centre in the city. It's quite time sensitive, you see, which presents a challenge for us. I doubt any of our staff would be involved in anything illegal, and even if they were, I don't know who would purchase a body illegally around here.'

'When the research centre opens, we'll certainly be encouraging more medical science donations,' says Roger, 'but it's limited at the moment, which is fairly typical in regional areas.'

'Thanks, Gemma,' Everett says briskly, spreading his legs and steepling his fingers as if to imply his words carry more weight than mine. He addresses Roger and Sophie. 'As you can tell, we've got a lot to do. We'll keep you both across our movements.'

'Thanks so much,' says Roger drily. His phone beeps several times in quick succession, and he swears as he starts replying to the messages.

Jonesy asks, 'Where were you last night prior to the incident, Mr Kirk?'

Roger whips his head up. 'Me? I was at a dinner.'

'Who else was there?' Jonesy presses.

Tension courses through the room. I try to work out what my boss is getting at.

Roger throws his hands around like a teenager who can't believe his dad is grilling him about his whereabouts. 'I was with family.'

'Your wife?'

'My uncle, at his place—my wife is away with the kids.'

Nodding, Jonesy asks, 'Was it just you and your uncle having dinner?'

'Yes, but we had a call with a few business partners at around six pm. A lot of the investors are based overseas so the meetings take place around the clock.'

'And you were unaware that the woman was brought to the hospital?'

Roger splutters. 'Of course! I'm not advised about individual patients. Until her corpse went missing, she was completely unremarkable to me. Frankly, she still is, except for the media shitstorm she's created.'

His insensitivity lingers in the air. Everett makes a note in his book, and I'm glad for the scratch of his pen, as if it's recording Roger's lack of empathy.

Jonesy turns to Sophie. 'And you, Ms McCallister? Where were you last night?'

She blinks, surprised. 'I was working here all of yesterday.'

'Is that typical for a Sunday?' I ask.

'My official hours are Monday to Friday,' she stammers, 'but I'm often here on weekends, catching up on paperwork if I need to get on top of things.'

I strongly suspect Roger is the type of boss whose leadership style means Sophie is always having to get on top of things.

'What were you doing when the power went out?' I ask.

'I was on level two, speaking to a nurse about a patient transfer we were organising. After the blackout I went immediately to find Rufus at the security office, but he wasn't there, so I went downstairs. That's when I bumped into Lenny Tisdale, the security guard who alerted me that the morgue door was open. All the staff can vouch for me.'

'Thanks,' I say. 'We'll check that.'

Her mobile rings, and she fumbles to answer it. As she listens, her mouth puckers. 'Okay, send her in.' Then Sophie tells Roger, 'The PR consultant is here.'

'We'll get out of your hair.' Jonesy smooths down his own sparse strands. 'But we'll have more questions for both of you over the coming twenty-four hours or so. The faster you can assist us with securing information the quicker this gets sorted. Understood?'

Roger channels a petulant child again, clearly not used to receiving orders.

When Jonesy stands, Everett, Holdsworth and I do the same. We file out. Waiting at the door to Sophie's office is a petite woman with an asymmetrical haircut. An expensive satchel hangs from her shoulder, and her fitted linen dress makes me worry about sweat.

Everett answers his phone self-importantly, walking over to the window and propping his hand against the frame as if he's posing for a corporate stock shot.

In contrast, Jonesy seems distracted. He peers at his phone. 'Seven bloody calls since we were in there. For the love of god, it never stops.'

I check my own phone—nothing. It used to ring and chime every couple of minutes with updates, questions and emergencies, but these days it is conspicuously silent. I'm not sure which mode I prefer.

'What's the deal with the research centre?' I ask Jonesy. 'I heard about it when I first came home, and I've lost track of the status.' I don't consume news and current affairs the way I used to and I'm starting to feel totally out of the loop.

'Bloody stupid waste of money,' says Jonesy. 'As far as I know, the construction kicks off next week, and it'll be cloning sheep and god knows what else by next Christmas.'

'Roger mentioned fundraising?'

'It'll be the most expensive building in the region. Hundreds of millions have been poured in already, and they're trying to raise more for specific features. Roger's going to run it.'

'On top of running the hospital?'

'Apparently he'll step aside from here and focus on the centre. There's been some chat about that—a lot of people in the community aren't happy he's choosing the centre over the hospital.'

'And his uncle? How is he involved?'

Jonesy's pants have slipped past his waist, and he tugs them into place. 'Carlyle gets to add to his millions. He's been pitching the idea for years, thinks he's bloody Einstein.'

'Isn't it being built somewhere around here?' I ask, trying to remember the details from the article I read.

'Initially it was going to be built there—' he points to the left side of the hospital parking lot '—on top of the existing car park, but there were multiple complaints about the plans and the impact on the hospital, so it was relocated to The Lyle complex where Carlyle's other businesses are—you know, the old folks' home and whatever else he's set up out there. The designs look like a bloody spaceship.'

I try to picture it. Growing up, I would never have imagined something like that operating here in Smithson. I wonder if the missing body could have anything to do with the new centre, but I can't think how, seeing as it doesn't exist yet.

'Do you think Roger's involved in what happened last night?' I ask quietly.

'Probably not. But I'm happy to see that smug little prick sweat a bit.'

Before I can ask him more about Carlyle, Everett joins us. 'I need you for a minute, boss.'

I check my watch, surprised to see it's almost four-thirty. I have to pick up the kids.

'Hang on,' Jonesy says to Everett, 'I've got to have a quick word with Woodstock.'

'Sure.' I can tell he's annoyed, but he gives us some space.

As I watch him walk away, I suddenly feel exhausted. We have significantly more questions than answers, and I can't help thinking this might be my last chance to stake my claim on this case. But I'm not sure how realistic that is, or if I even want to stick my neck out.

Jonesy says, 'Woodstock—'

'Why did you want me to tag along?'

'Because I knew you wanted to.'

I swallow. It's not the answer I was hoping for, but I don't want him to say things to boost my ego. Changing tack, I say, 'About what you told me this morning, I'm just not sure whether—'

'Go home, Woodstock. You've got some thinking to do. If you decide you want to apply for the position, you will have my support, but you're not the only candidate—and the decision won't just be mine to make.'

'Of course,' I murmur, feeling more stung than I probably should. It's not like I can expect a role like that to be served to me on a platter.

'Off you go,' he says gruffly. 'I'll let you know if there are any developments here.'

'Thanks, I'd like that.' I fish my keys out of my pocket, give him a tight smile and turn toward the exit.

'Woodstock?'

I turn back. 'What?'

He shoves his hands in his pockets and clears his throat, triggering a jolt of déjà vu. 'It was nice having you back.'

CHAPTER ELEVEN

When I pull up, Rebecca and Ben are playing soccer in the front yard. Scarlett is propped up like a queen in a highchair on the porch, watching them and mashing a banana between her hands. Ben laughs at something Rebecca says and calls out to her, teasing, as she tries unsuccessfully to return his kick. I notice her handbag and a large plastic food container next to the front door, ready for her hospital visit.

Laughing again, Ben expertly kicks the ball before he sees me and jogs over. Rebecca picks up the ball and joins us, looping an arm over Ben's shoulders and smiling hello to me. 'Thank god you're here, Gemma. I was starting to really embarrass myself.'

She's good with them, I acknowledge, fighting the mild irritation that comes with the admission. I guess I'll always wish it were my mother playing soccer with my son, but I have no idea if she would have been that kind of grandmother. She died just before I turned fourteen, and we never talked about me having children. Looking back now, it feels like we never spoke about anything important. Mum was slender and tall, and very reserved—nothing like Rebecca, who is short, round and loud. One of my strongest childhood memo-ries is of Mum's cool hand against my forehead as she checked to see if I had a fever. I remember her serious expression as she called out for Dad to get the thermometer, her voice low and soothing. I also liked listening to her talk on the phone, and I think I can remember her singing to me when I was very young.

After I thank Rebecca and tell her that Dad is excited to see her, I load the kids into the car. On the short drive home, Ben is in a great mood and chats unprompted about his day at school. The events of the past twenty-four hours are whirling through my mind as I try to follow everything he tells me. It feels like a week since this morning.

While extracting Scarlett from her seat, I smack my head on the ceiling of the car. 'Ow! Shit.'

Scarlett laughs. Ben is already halfway up the driveway, key in hand. He throws me a look that implies I need to calm down. I grab my bag and Scarlett's, then slam the car door shut. Ben disappears inside, and I start after him before pivoting to the letterbox. I forget to check it most days—barely anyone has our rental address, and most of our bills are digital. I'm surprised to find three envelopes.

Tugging my hair, Scarlett babbles something that sounds close to 'Mum', and I laugh even though my head hurts. 'Come on, no, don't do that, Scar. You're hurting Mum.'

She makes the sound again, sending a shot of dopamine directly to my heart.

Mac appears in the doorway, clad in jeans and a T-shirt, his feet bare. His hair, damp from the shower, curls slightly at the ends. 'Gemma, do you need a hand?'

'Hey.' I squeeze past the car and the wattle tree, careful not to let the wayward branches scratch Scarlett. 'I think she just said "Mum".'

Mac's smile is wide. 'That's my clever girl.' Reaching out for her, he nuzzles her nose until she giggles uncontrollably. He smiles at me over her head, then steps forward to kiss me.

There's a reassuring surge of attraction. Mac is my person, and we're a team. The only thing that's going to get in the way of that is me. I think back to seeing him in town this morning—he was probably just sending something to his daughter, Molly, who lives in Sydney. Cursing my suspicious mind, I vow to make the time to connect like we used to.

As I follow him inside, I notice that the lounge room is spotless. Through the archway I can see the kitchen bench has been cleared and cleaned. 'Did you do all this?' I ask Mac dramatically.

'I figure you've been doing the lion's share of housework lately. And my meeting was cancelled.'

'How is it all going? I feel like we haven't spoken about it properly.'

'Not much to talk about. Things are moving slowly. I sense there's some politics regarding my involvement.' His glasses reflect the last of the sunlight streaming through the window, making it difficult for me to read his expression.

'You're probably making some poor small-town hot shot feel inferior.'

He chuckles. 'Maybe. How was your day?'

I'm bursting to tell him everything, but equally I want to take my time. Unpacking the events of our days has always been one of my favourite parts of our relationship. 'I'll tell you later.' I reach out to take Scarlett. 'First I need to change this little lady.'

'I'll do it.' Mac sidesteps me and heads up the hallway.

I pull out a chair and sink into it, hooking the nappy bag over the back and tossing the mail on the table. I load the local news website on my laptop. The abandoned baby is the lead story, and there's no update on her condition or where she came from. The hospital security breach coverage has evolved into an unconfirmed report that a corpse was misplaced during a transfer to the morgue because of an admin mix-up. I'm not sure where they're getting their info, but Roger will be ropeable. Reading on, I see that the article includes a generic quote from him espousing the quality-control standards of the hospital and his personal commitment to ensuring the matter is sorted out as soon as possible. Just like us, the journos have nothing.

I scroll down to click on a story about the brawl at The Toad. Instantly I understand why Jonesy didn't want to talk about it. The article alleges that Lee Blight, the son of local retired Senior Sergeant Marty Blight, threw a jug of beer across the room before up-ending a table where a trio of men were sitting, triggering a violent brawl. Lee fled upstairs to one of the hotel rooms, barricading himself in with furniture until the cops burst in and arrested him.

I know Marty Blight a little—or I used to, anyway. I was paired with him on a few of my early cases, and I met Lee a couple of times; he would have been around Ben's age, a skinny kid with a crew cut and freckles. I vaguely remember hearing via Dad that Lee got himself in trouble at some point over the past few years—something about stolen property . . . or was it drugs? Marty retired last year, just before I went on maternity leave, which is probably a good thing. Having your kid arrested when you're still on the force isn't an easy thing to deal with, especially for a judgemental bastard like Marty Blight, who always thought he was beyond reproach.

Some of Mac's silly one-sided conversation with Scarlett travels down the hallway to my ears, making me smile.

Ben lopes across the kitchen and yanks open the fridge. 'What's for dinner?'

'I'm not sure.' My phone rings from the depths of my bag. I answer it. 'Hi, Candy.'

Ben groans. He knows how much Candy likes to talk.

'Gemma, holy shit, what a day! But I don't need to tell you that, do I? I saw you at the lake this morning. I hope you're back on the police payroll, Nancy Drew.'

'You know I'm not.' I absently pick up the mail with my spare hand. 'I was at the station visiting Jonesy and ended up just getting swept up in it all.' One of the envelopes is from an energy company, another from the local council. The third is handwritten and addressed to Mac.

Candy grumbles. 'I bloody wish I would get swept up in things the way you do.'

The stamp has a Victorian postcode, but there's no clue as to the sender. Who from Victoria would send Mac mail here? And handwritten? Nothing logical comes to mind.

'Gemma, are you listening to me?'

'No,' I reply honestly. 'Sorry, what did you say?'

Candy speaks like a radio announcer. 'My source tells me that the fight at the pub was not what it seems.'

'What does it seem like?'

'Like some troubled kid losing his shit.'

'Is your source Henno?'

She sniffs defensively. 'It might be.'

I smother a laugh. Candy went on an ill-advised date with Henno, the publican at The Toad, about five years ago—and hated every minute of it. He has been madly in love with her ever since and jumps at any opportunity to impress her. 'It's a fair exchange,' Candy has been known to reason. 'I let him stare at my tits, and he gives me the lowdown on Smithson's best and brightest.'

Now I ask her, 'And what is Henno's theory?'

'Henno reckons something was off about the three guys Lee Blight attacked.'

I keep switching between focusing on what she's saying and on the mail addressed to Mac. The handwriting looks like a woman's.

'Gemma?'

'Candy, I'm not for a minute suggesting I know what happened at the pub last night, but I do know Lee has form. A pub brawl doesn't seem entirely out of character.'

'I've heard otherwise. Apparently he'd straightened himself out and was doing well. He'd applied to study in Melbourne next year and was off the drugs. Plus, he's never been violent before.'

'Maybe this is a relapse . . . ? They do happen, you know.'

'But why, Gemma? Why would he just walk up to three strangers and start threatening them, get involved in a serious punch-up and then run away *upstairs*?'

'Possibly because he was blind drunk. Henno's not known for being an avid enforcer of the alcohol-serving guidelines.'

'Gemma, you need to trust me on this one.'

I'd forgotten how persistent Candy is, how irritating she can be. We haven't always been friends—in fact, for a while we were downright enemies. These days I love her to death, but she still gets under my skin from time to time. 'I'm just saying you'll need more to convince me there's more to the story. It all sounds fairly cut and dried so far.'

'Come on, Gemma, where's your sense of mystery?'

'I think it's having a lie-down.'

'Well, wake it up.'

'I'll try.' I yawn.

'I'm heading down there tonight. I want to do some more digging. Plus, I need a steak and a free drink.'

Mac brings Scarlett back from her room. 'Right,' he says enthusiastically, 'there's some chicken in the freezer, and I can probably cobble together a salad.'

I push the envelope toward the middle of the table, hoping he'll notice it. Maybe he'll dismiss it as nothing or reveal it's completely innocuous. Or maybe he'll refuse to open it in front of me and then I'll know something is going on.

But he just sails past the table and goes to the fridge. 'Gem, what do you think? Chicken and a scrappy salad . . . ?'

'Gemma?' Candy bleats at me through the phone. 'Are you still there?'

Ben is on the couch, slumped so low his head is almost level with his arse.

'Let's go to the pub for dinner,' I say.

CHAPTER TWELVE

MONDAY, 19 SEPTEMBER, 6.59 PM

Mac points to the left of The Toad's dimly lit dining room. 'There she is.'

Candy's chosen our table strategically: from where she's sitting, she can see both entrances, the entirety of the dining room and the bar. 'Well, if it isn't the whole modern family.' She reaches out to hug us all hello. She's at least a head taller than I am, and her dark athletic body is encased in a tight sapphire T-shirt and white jeans. Gold medallions dangle from her earlobes. Her black hair is pulled back sleek from her oval face. She looks like a supermodel.

Mac greets her warmly. 'Hey, Candy.' He's always really liked her, and the feeling is mutual. Ever since she helped us navigate the months following Scott's death, she frequently reminds me of how wonderful Mac is.

Candy kisses Scarlett's forehead and smacks Ben's open palm in a noisy high five before she aggressively summons a waiter. The young girl pauses mid-stride and looks nervous as she takes our drink orders, her face half hidden by her coppery hair.

'Can we get a highchair here, please?' Candy asks, making it sound like we've been waiting for hours.

'Of course.' The girl shoves her notebook in her pocket and darts off.

'Where's Lola?' I ask Candy, rounding up Scarlett's dinner things: a bowl, a container of food, her bottle.

'With her father,' Candy replies dismissively. She has very little interest in Philip beyond his ability to take care of Lola from time to time. If Candy is a tornado, then Philip is a dead-still day. I'm not sure she ever particularly liked him, but he gave her Lola, and he doesn't make her life difficult. Overall I think things have worked out well for both of them.

'How's business?' Mac asks Candy.

'A bloody nightmare,' she says, swigging her beer. 'The journalism part is okay—it's the making-money part that's a problem.' She leans forward conspiratorially. 'But I might be close to inking a deal with Murphy's. If I can lock them in, it'll be smooth sailing until Christmas at least.'

'Murphy's?' Mac says. 'What kind of deal?'

Murphy's is the latest chain store to open its doors in Smithson, a business determined to appeal to young families putting down roots. It sells groceries and furniture, whitegoods, plants and hardware, and booze—pretty much everything people can be convinced they need.

'I pitched them an idea,' Candy says proudly. 'They run an exclusive daily discount with my short morning story and another offer with my long afternoon story. But they both only last until midnight on the same day.'

'And,' Mac says, 'people have to visit your website twice a day to be valid for both.'

'Exactly. There are email code thingies people can download. I don't really understand the details—I got some tech whiz-kid to work out how to do it.'

Mac nods his approval. 'Guaranteed to get eyeballs on your site so you can sell more ads. Very smart.'

Candy beams. 'Thank you.'

She's determined to prove her business can work. She'd rather die than admit defeat to her former employer, not after she told him to go fuck himself.

The highchair arrives, and I manoeuvre Scarlett into it and strap a bib around her neck. Another waiter brings our drinks and we order our food. I take a sip of my beer, savouring the sensation of cold liquid running down my throat. Mac and Candy talk enthusiastically about her business as I coax the food I brought from home into Scarlett's mouth.

Between her mouthfuls I take in the crowd. It's a mix of families, teens and couples. I spy Henno at the bar, chatting with two old men who appear to have melted into their stools. Every few minutes, he shoots a look in our direction. I can hardly blame him—Candy stands out like a colourful butterfly in the mainly white, very conservative crowd.

I recognise two of Ben's schoolmates dining with their parents and siblings. It used to be impossible for me to go out in Smithson and not see people I know, but it's becoming less common. The town has changed so much in the past couple of years; there are new faces everywhere, not to mention the new venues popping up all over town. While there are things about Smithson I dislike, I prefer the familiar haunts and their quirks to the modern bars and restaurants with their big-city trends and mass-produced décor.

A hard energy radiates from a group of male teenagers near the bar. They laugh obnoxiously and slap each other on the shoulders, their mouths wide as they gulp back beers. Maybe they're dangerous, maybe not.

An older couple enter from the stairs and survey the room before marching confidently toward the bar, holding hands. The woman's long skirt flares as she walks, revealing tan high-heeled boots with the toes cut out.

I remember Jonesy once admitting to me that Smithson is his town and that it's his job to protect it. 'It's cheesy,' he said, 'but I feel like I'm one of those country cops in an American movie presiding over my jurisdiction, and I think I've felt that way since I first put on my badge.'

I scrape mashed vegetables from Scarlett's cheek with a spoon and redirect it into her mouth. I'm not sure I feel the same way as Jonesy, because my relationship with Smithson is more complicated than his. The town smothered me until I felt I had no choice but to escape, and while Smithson will always be the place I grew up, leaving was undoubtedly one of the best things I ever did. Of course, I want it to be a safe place for my friends and family, and for them to live here happily, but I don't feel an innate instinct to protect it. Does this mean I can't do Jonesy's job?

'Don't you think, Gemma?'

I blink at Candy's question. 'Sorry, what?'

She and Mac exchange a knowing look.

'What?' I repeat, trying to curb my irritation.

'I was just saying you must be really missing work right now, especially after the little taste you've had over the past few days.'

Our meals arrive suspiciously quickly and Candy's comment is forgotten. The conversation turns to the state of the world, our useless politicians and the myriad problems they're failing to address.

The Toad isn't known for its food—it's not really known for anything except intoxicated patrons and being open until one am—but I thought Henno might have felt compelled to revamp the menu, considering all the new patrons in town. Obviously not. I don't really care, though: I'm simply excited to eat a meal that won't lead to dishes I need to wash.

'Can I go talk to Jack?' Ben is pushing back his chair, wiping his mouth. Jack is a schoolfriend; I've met his mum a few times, and she seems nice enough.

'Not until you're finished,' I say, just as I see that his plate is clean. He raises his eyebrows at me and darts off.

'What are you working on?' Candy asks Mac, chomping on a chip. 'Have any juicy cold cases for me to write about?' I watch as her eyes slide around the room—she is always on high alert.

Scarlett bangs her tiny fists on the plastic tray, demanding more food. I feed her as I listen to their conversation, feeling uncharacteristically detached from them.

Mac says, 'I'm working on a couple of jobs, but nothing I can talk about, I'm afraid.'

'You're worse than Gemma,' Candy grumbles. 'She never bloody tells me anything either.'

Mac laughs good-naturedly and winks at me. 'I'm doing a bit of online teaching over the next few months. And it's likely there'll be some consulting opportunities with my old crew in Sydney.'

Scarlett lets out a sharp screech.

'All right. All right.' I offer her another spoonful, which she angrily pushes away. I feel stung that Mac didn't tell me about the consulting opportunities . . . or maybe he did, and I've forgotten. My thoughts are so cloudy. Perhaps I'm not even ready to consider putting my hand up for Jonesy's job.

I finish my meal and clean Scarlett's face, then extract her from the highchair and hug her close. There's loud chatter at the bar. A young man in double denim, hair slicked back, makes his way across the room toward a pair of women, ignoring a chorus of catcalls from his mates.

Mac finds my hand under the table and talks into my ear. 'I'll take the kids home. You stay.'

'Are you sure?'

He kisses the side of my face. 'Positive. Have a drink, catch up with Candy.'

'Okay. Thanks.' I try to push the doubts from my mind.

He takes Scarlett and bends to kiss Candy's cheek.

'Fuck off, you're leaving?' She pouts like a child and grabs my hand.

'*I'm* leaving with the kids,' Mac corrects. 'Gemma is staying.'

'Gosh, I love you, Mac,' she says. 'Your only downside is that you don't have a hot and incredibly intelligent, extremely wealthy single brother.'

He laughs. 'I apologise profusely for my shortcomings.' His face is flushed, his eyes sparkle, and I remember all the times I wanted him before I knew he liked me. Our connection is so strong—surely I have nothing to worry about . . . ? 'Have fun, ladies.' He heads over to collect Ben.

Candy watches them leave. 'God, he's the best, Gemma. I don't know how you bear it. He almost makes me reconsider writing off all men for the rest of eternity.'

'No need to be so hasty,' I joke.

She raises an eyebrow at me.

'No, I mean Mac's great obviously.' I don't want her to catch on that something is wrong. 'But he's rare.'

She drinks a large gulp of wine. 'True.' But she gives me another look.

'What?'

'Nothing. So you said you met with Jonesy this morning. How was that?'

I tell her about my meeting but leave out the part about him retiring.

Candy's eyes twinkle. 'And there really aren't any leads on the baby? Or the missing woman?'

'Not that I know of. But remember, I'm not officially on either case.'

'It's cute that Jonesy let you tag along. He must be dying for you to come back to work.' She leans even closer. 'So . . . how is he?'

'Who, Jonesy?'

Her eyes are suddenly on the table, her glass—anywhere but me. She must know. Secrets in this town are like dandelion seeds: they take flight and turn up all over the place.

'He seems fine,' I reply lightly. We're tiptoeing around the guts of it, but I don't have the energy to unpack it with her just yet. I want to be sure of my own thoughts first.

Candy nods. 'That's good.' She fingers the stem of her wineglass. 'It's just that . . .' She shakes her head before she brightens, switching gears. 'Now your dependants are out of the way, let's find out what really happened here last night. Let's find Henno. And if he's a dead end then we'll find someone else to talk to.' Candy has cultivated a ragbag of people, her eyes and ears on the ground. I used to have a similar network, but I'm out of the loop, having been away for so long. She stands and flicks her long hair over her shoulder before frowning at me.

'What, I need to get up?'

'Yes, Gemma, the news isn't coming to us.' She saunters off, hips swaying like a pendulum.

I roll my eyes, grab my handbag and follow her to the bar. The music is louder on this side of the room, and I'm jostled from all sides. I'm not claustrophobic, but it's been a while since I was in such close proximity to so many people—clammy skin against mine, their breath on my face, voices in my ears. Candy ploughs through the group, pulling me behind her. We've seriously jumped the queue, but no one seems to mind. She holds two fingers in the air and nods brusquely at Henno. He blows her a kiss, but her expression remains neutral. I don't know where his optimism comes from.

'What are you getting me?' I shout into the back of her hair. My face is mashed against a muscular shoulder encased in a flannel shirt; I can smell grass, beer and sweat.

'A G&T,' she yells over her shoulder.

Moments later, Candy hands me a large glass with a wedge of lemon jammed into its side. She indicates that she wants to talk to Henno, and he acquiesces, shuffling closer to us and leaning across the bar, grinning at her. I push past damp limbs to stand next to her.

He smiles at me. 'Hey, Woodstock. Nice seeing you out and about.'

'Thanks.' I sip my drink. 'Nice to see you, too.'

Henno's front tooth is charmingly crooked, and two faint scars follow his left hairline, the legacy of a legendary fall from a tractor when he was a kid. He's had a haircut recently, and it suits him. I think he's lost some weight as well. I really have been in quite the bubble.

'How can I be of service to you this evening, my lady?' Henno trills.

Candy drums her white lacquered nails impatiently against the bar. 'We want the dirt on the bust-up last night. All of it.'

'Anything for you, my sweet.' He beams at her and winks at me. 'Lee Blight was just sitting at the end of the bar, minding his own business, and then out of nowhere he lost his shit at a table of tradies. It went from a quiet Sunday night to total chaos. He flipped a table, and there was glass everywhere. The guys he went off at retaliated—one threw a plate that shattered all over the upturned table and then it was on. About fifteen minutes later the cops arrived, broke the whole thing up and we all had to answer a shitload of questions. The tradies were fine, just scored a few cuts and bruises. It was two other kids that got their heads knocked around. They were spoiling for a fight and jumped in, and Blight went at them as well. There was blood everywhere, but it looked worse than it was. They've scored some impressive shiners but they're totally fine. I didn't get to bed until three—I'm shattered today.'

'And Blight?'

'He wasn't in a great way. Had blood all over him when he came back downstairs, and his hand was a mess. But I reckon it's his mental health that's the main issue. He needs help, losing it like that.'

'Why did Blight go upstairs?' Candy presses. 'Why didn't he just leave?'

'Dunno. 'Cause he was high as a kite?'

'Did he seem high?' I ask.

'He seemed fine until he went bananas. Then he was ranting and raving about all kinds of things—none of it made any sense that I could tell.'

'Did he know the other group?' I ask. 'Maybe they said something to set him off . . . ?'

'Not that I heard, but I was working the bar so wasn't close enough to say for sure.'

'Is Blight in here a lot?' Candy asks.

'He used to be. I reckon about two years ago he was in here almost every other night, but last night was the first time I'd seen him in yonks.'

I jump in with a question. 'Did you talk to him when he used to come here? Do you know much about him?'

'Not really,' Henno replies. 'He's a weird one, always has been. Got himself into some bad situations over the years. One of his big brothers was into sport, and the other one was smart, good at school and that. But I don't think Blight was much good at anything, and it didn't help that his dad was a cop—that kind of pushed him the other way, if you ask me. He was always getting himself into trouble.'

A waitress interrupts to ask Henno a question. She's very pretty with a heart-shaped face and wavy white-blonde hair. Candy bristles beside me, and I hide a smile. Henno steps away from the bar with her as they discuss a booking.

'We're off,' Candy announces, tugging me along before I can say goodbye to Henno.

'Whoa, hey,' I complain.

But she's on a mission, pulling me to the end of the bar. I catch Candy glancing back at Henno, who is still in deep conversation with the waitress.

Candy loudly orders us more drinks and then says huffily, 'He's so flaky. We were in the middle of an interview.'

'He *is* working,' I say in Henno's defence.

'His work can wait,' she declares, unlocking her phone and scrolling through her impressive contacts list. 'Mine can't.'

I'm enjoying being Candy's sidekick and having a break from Scarlett. The other cases try to force their way into my mind but I sip my drink and think instead about what Henno told us, trying to picture the scene. Pub fights are not uncommon in Smithson but it's usually a booze-fuelled brawl between mates over something trivial. Often they're resolved before the cops arrive, although things might have changed with the influx of new residents. I'm just about to ask Candy what she wants to do next when Henno ambles over.

'Thought you'd left, my love,' he says good-naturedly.

'Do you have anything else to tell us?' Candy says rudely. 'I have other sources I can speak to.'

Henno seems pleased she's annoyed. 'Before Jazzy interrupted us, I was about to tell you that I did see Blight the previous evening.'

Candy shoots daggers at Jazzy, who is serving a group of attractive young men further along the bar. She juts out a hip. 'Where did you see him?'

'At the petrol station. It's ironic now but at the time I thought to myself that he seemed solid, like he had his shit together. He said things were going well when I asked. He looked good, too, better than he did before he left Smithson.'

'Do you know if he has a job?' I ask.

'I'm not sure about that.'

'Did he say what was going well?' Candy asks.

'Nope. But like I said he was in a good mood, friendly and all that.'

I can tell Candy is getting frustrated.

I give her arm a reassuring pat and ask, 'Did you recognise the tradies he went off at?'

'They were cocky bastards, I can tell you that much. They were giving Blight shit when the cops brought his arse back downstairs. They work for Bilson, the big construction company, on contracts I'd guess—you know, fly-in fly-out and where's my big pay cheque thanks very much. They won't be welcome back here again. The cops spoke to them for ages and seemed to think they were clear, so I'm guessing they don't have records or anything. Surely you can look all that up on your bat phone, Gemma.'

Scott used to complain about the out-of-towners taking the larger building projects and all the best jobs in exchange for unrealistic working conditions.

I ignore his dig and ask, 'Maybe Blight was pissed about them taking local jobs . . . ?'

'Maybe.' Henno lifts his hand to greet a patron behind us. 'Or maybe he's a bit loopy from all the hippy bullshit.'

'Hippy bullshit?' I ask, my eyes flicking to Candy's.

'Yeah, you know, breathe in and think about your aura and all that shite.'

'Henno, don't be cryptic,' Candy snaps. 'We're both too sleep deprived for riddles.'

'All I'm saying is that you probably need to visit The Retreat. Apparently that's where Blight's been holed up these past few years.'

CHAPTER THIRTEEN

I'm only thirty-eight, but I feel like I've lived a lot of lives. There were the fourteen years before Mum died, when everything was normal. Then there was the horror of losing her, followed by the roller-coaster of falling in love with Jacob and the numbing shock of his suicide. The years after were a blur of grief and displacement that felt like it lasted forever. Eventually I attempted to settle into adult life in Smithson, and for a while I had everyone fooled, including myself. I became a detective, met Scott and had Ben—but my attempt at normality proved to be short-lived when I blew everything up by having an affair with a colleague. All my demons came tumbling out, and I hit rock bottom. I left Scott and Ben to embark on a soul-searching stint in Melbourne, followed by several more constructive years in Sydney where I met Mac.

And now I'm right back where I started. Is this the life I'm supposed to be living? Would I ever have come back here if Scott was alive and well? My desire to run away has all but disappeared, but I remember its allure. I wonder if Lee Blight felt the same. Maybe going to The Retreat was his way to start over, to go off-grid and decide who he wanted to be away from the temptations and expectations of his life.

Before I was born, The Retreat was an infamous religious cult run by a disgraced business owner, Randall Goggin. In the mid-sixties he declared bankruptcy, but then his parents died in a plane crash and left him the family farm. He quickly convinced several members of his former company, as well as members of his local Catholic Church, to move to the property with him. Over the next decade he built a small but passionate community centred around extreme religious beliefs. Like all cult leaders he was charismatic and compelling, and at one point there was thought to be over two hundred people living on the property. In town there were rumours of abuse, incest and rape, but nothing was ever reported.

The cult fizzled out in the late seventies when Goggin drowned in the dam during a drug-fuelled animal sacrifice. Sheep and goats were frequently sacrificed and offered to god, and as part of the ritual the cult members were expected to enter the dam and hold their breath for as long as possible. After Goggin's death, The Retreat shut down completely. A decade later it was reopened by one of his nephews as a place for people seeking an alternate lifestyle, and it's been that way ever since. The residents live off the land, homeschool their kids—and, as far as I know, keep to themselves.

I can't recall any issues with The Retreat since I've been a cop, but after Henno mentioned it last night I've been wondering if there's a chance the woman from the crash was being kept there against her will and escaped. That might explain why she wasn't wearing shoes, why her feet were cut up, and how she ended up in a car that was stolen several years earlier. It's a long shot but probably worth checking out.

My thoughts tick over as I watch Mac stumble against the wardrobe, losing his balance while pulling on a pair of jeans in the dark. I didn't feel great when I got up at three-thirty am to feed Scarlett, but I feel worse now. An ache clutches my head, and there's a nasty throbbing above my eyebrows. When I have a rare drink these days, I pay for it.

'What time is it?' I mumble.

'Go back to sleep,' Mac says. 'It's still early.'

'What are you doing?'

'Going into Gowran—I'm trying to track down an old witness, and a retired journo has offered to meet with me before he starts work.'

The crisp earthy scent of Mac's aftershave hangs in the air. He doesn't offer any further explanation, and I watch him finish getting ready in silence. It sounds entirely plausible, but I think about the envelope addressed to him, which was nowhere to be seen when I stumbled into the house at midnight after playing sleuth and drinking with Candy.

'Is everything okay?' I ask him.

Sitting on the bed, he pats my leg. 'I'm just working through the red tape. You know how it is.'

'Red tape is my middle name,' I quip. 'Are you planning on taking the car?'

His expression turns sheepish. 'Is that okay? I said I'd drop Ben off at Jack's on the way—they want to play soccer before school anyway, so then you don't need to worry about driving him. Can you do without the car until I'm back this afternoon? I can pick Ben up from school, no problem.'

I turn over and stare at the ceiling still feeling uncharacteristically suspicious. 'It's fine. I can always borrow Dad's car.'

'Okay, great.' Mac kisses me. 'Hopefully your day is a bit calmer than yesterday . . . Although, knowing you, you probably won't like that.' He grins and pushes loose strands of hair from my face.

I want to pull him back under the covers and make him stay with me all day, shut everything else out and get him to talk to me, touch me. Mac's been my rock since we met, unwavering in his certainty that we can make things work. His confidence gives me confidence. We understand each other; we know better than anyone that our work takes us to strange, dark places that can make everything else seem like a simulation. I shift my head, inviting another kiss. Is that what's happening? Is he deep in a case and struggling to connect to the everyday world? To connect to me?

'Did you have fun last night?' he asks, his mouth close to mine.

'I did. But I have a feeling I'm going to pay for it today.'

His kiss is intense and passionate, but it carries something else: an apology, a question, guilt? What the hell is going on?

'I've got to go.' He stands but keeps holding my hand.

I almost say something—I almost ask why he feels so far away. But I can't make the words form in my mouth. I'm scared to acknowledge that I'm worried; I'm scared of what he might say. 'Let's talk later,' I say instead. 'Love you.'

With a nod, he drops my hand. 'Same. There's a Gatorade in the fridge if you need it.' He picks up his bag and leaves the room. He's wearing a good shirt—and the aftershave.

I sink back against the pillows, trying to stay calm. Surely not. Not Mac.

Ben sticks his head into the room to say goodbye. I summon a smile and tell him I hope he has a good day. The front door shuts behind them. The rumble of the car fades away. For a few moments the house is quiet, and I am alone with my thoughts.

Then Scarlett starts to wail.

CHAPTER FOURTEEN

Candy picks me and Scarlett up, and we go to Reggie's, one of the cafes that has survived the influx of mainstream franchises offering cheap coffee and loyalty cards. I used to come here all the time with my partner, Detective Felix McKinnon, who was also my lover when I was with Scott. Recalling our secret coffee dates makes me worry even more about Mac. Is he in a cafe somewhere with another woman? I know how blurry the line can seem and how easy it is to find yourself in too deep.

My head pounds from the G&Ts, not helped by the anxiety swirling in my gut, and I distract myself by tuning in to the conversations around us. Two women on my left are talking about the medical status of the abandoned baby; to my right, an elderly couple are engaged in an animated conversation about what kind of woman gives up her own child. Further along, a muscular brunette robotically bounces a toddler on her lap while she reads an article on the front page of the local paper by Candy's old boss about the new research centre, speculating if it will be plagued by the cost-cutting that the hospital has allegedly endured under Roger's stewardship.

'It's busy here today,' I say to Candy as brightly as I can manage. Small talk feels the safest, considering my stubborn hangover and increasing paranoia.

'Everywhere is bloody busy around here these days.' Candy is speed-texting someone. I can tell she's pissed about Nate's article—he never authored pieces when she worked with him, and she thinks he does it to spite her.

'I guess Smithson being busy is good for your business,' I say, trying to be encouraging.

She grunts, still texting. She's hungover, too, but her determination to land a lead on one of the stories is winning out over her headache. When our food arrives, she puts her phone down, applies a liberal dose of salt to her scrambled eggs and takes a giant slurp of coffee. I sip my own coffee and feed Scarlett some of my eggs. The older couple make faces at her, and she bangs noisily on the highchair tray, revelling in the attention.

'There's absolutely no need for that, sweetheart,' Candy says, wincing.

She gently grabs Scarlett's hands, encouraging her to stop, but my daughter thinks it's a game and adds shrill giggling to the banging.

'I'm glad Lola is in day care today,' Candy says. 'God love her.'

'One is better than two today,' I agree.

'Last night was fun, though,' she ventures.

'It was.'

Leaning forward, she says in her best newsreader voice, 'I've heard that everyone at The Retreat wears the same clothes, like a uniform. And that they regularly make the kids drink animal blood.'

'Gross. Who's in charge?'

'That's the type of thing my investigation would uncover, Gemma.'

'Of course.'

'I think we should pay a visit, find out more about what Lee was doing there.'

I sigh. 'I know you do.'

'Don't *you*?'

'I do, but for different reasons. I'm interested in finding the mother of the baby, not getting to the bottom of whatever weird diet a group of anti-vaxxers follows.'

'Two birds one stone,' says Candy hopefully.

'Maybe,' I reply noncommittally. 'The Retreat would be an easy place to conceal a birth or hide someone. Let me talk to Jonesy about it.'

Candy pouts. 'I was going to do a story on that place anyway. I was!' She holds up her hands at my sceptical expression. 'Now it seems I need to get my arse out there or someone might beat me to it—and by someone, I mean Nate. If the cops start sniffing around, he'll be right behind them. I swear he bugs the police station.'

As Candy keeps talking, another thought forms in my mind. From memory The Retreat is situated on a huge piece of mostly uncultivated land: a good place to hide a corpse.

'It's supposed to just be families, isn't it?' Candy asks.

'Sorry, what?'

'The Retreat—I always thought it was just hippy families. So why would Lee have been staying there?'

'Guess they've expanded their demographic. No one can afford to be choosy these days.'

Her eyes light up. 'Maybe Lee will agree to an interview and give me some scandalous details. *That* would generate clicks. Everyone loves an insight into cult life.'

'He could cover off cult life and prison life,' I say wryly.

'Yes, Gemma, you're catching on!' Candy claps her hands at me. 'That would make an incredible piece.'

'I don't think his dad would be too keen. In all seriousness, I think we need to be careful,' I say, even though trying to come between Candy and a story is like trying to stop a thunderstorm.

'I don't need to be anything of the sort,' she retorts. 'I'm a free agent.'

I can't help but smile—her enthusiasm is contagious. 'You're forgetting that I'm not.'

She crosses her arms. 'About that . . . what *are* you, exactly?'

I point to Scarlett, who is fishing mashed vegetables out of her bib and examining them studiously. 'A parent.'

'Are you going to go back to work? Are you going to stay in Smithson?'

Candy's blunt questions feel like punches. I take a bite of my cold toast. 'I don't know,' I reply truthfully.

'You're a cop, Gemma—a good one,' Candy says firmly. 'You always will be.'

Her words cause pleasure to ripple through me, but my head interjects with a soft protest. Is being a cop all I am, all I can be?

I try to explain. 'It feels different this time, like I still want to be a cop, but I just can't quite picture it. I can't see myself being a detective *and* a parent *and* a partner to Mac. I don't know why.' I force a smile. 'Anyway, luckily I have a bit more time to think about it.'

'Not much. Not unless you're happy to report to some shit-for-brains dinosaur who thinks the only things you're good for are petty crimes and death knocks.'

My heart sinks. The genie is already out of the bottle. I was hoping to mull over the situation for a few weeks and give myself a chance to process Jonesy's news without having to define my feelings. 'You know about Jonesy.'

'What can I say? I make it a point to speak to wives in the supermarket, help them with things they can't reach from the top shelves.'

I picture Candy towering over Jonesy's wife, Lucy, at the supermarket, passing down products in exchange for intel.

'Come on, Gemma. You have to throw your hat in the ring for the gig. It's what you've always wanted.'

I stare into the dregs of my coffee. 'I guess.'

She looks disappointed. 'Isn't it?'

'I'm just not sure it's the right time.'

'As if that has ever stopped you before.'

Lifting Scarlett from the highchair, I clean her hands and face. 'I've got a lot on my plate. And I wasn't a good mother when Ben was this age. I want to be better with her.'

'Gemma, you're being silly. Ben has to be the most well-adjusted kid in this town, and that's a credit to both you and Scott. You might not be a perfect parent, but he's a great kid.'

'In spite of me,' I say, hot tears forming behind my eyes.

Candy grows unusually serious. 'Where is this all coming from? I know the crushing weight of mother guilt can descend unexpectedly, but I thought you were immune.'

'I'm definitely not.' I think back to all those lonely nights in Melbourne and in Sydney, when I cried myself to sleep missing Ben and wondering what I was doing with my life.

'Mac the Miracle Man seems well.' It's a statement that carries a question.

I busy myself with my meal. 'Yes, he's good.'

'He seems happy working from here,' she presses. 'Seems happy here in general.'

'I think so. He's still getting a lot of work offers.' My heart is racing, and I try to think of how to change the subject. I'm not ready to talk about the suspicions lurking in my mind about Mac, not even with Candy.

She arches a dark eyebrow and opens her mouth, but her obnoxious ringtone cuts her off. 'This is Candy Fyfe.'

I pry a teaspoon out of Scarlett's hand, swapping it with a serviette that she promptly puts in her mouth. Kissing the top of her head, I try to shake the stress that Candy's questions set off in my core.

'What?' she blurts, then, 'Are you sure? Holy shit.' Her eyes widen, and she blinks several times in quick succession. Something is terribly wrong.

'What is it?'

She doesn't respond to me, just fires questions at the caller. 'When? How? Who told you?' Her silver earrings jangle as she nods. 'Of course I'm coming. I'll meet you there.'

'Candy, what is it?'

She grabs her bag and shoves her chair so hard it tips over, crashing into the tiled floor. 'Roger Kirk's been murdered.'

CHAPTER FIFTEEN

When we turn into Emerald Drive, the first person I recognise is Everett. His left palm is pressed against a tree as he talks on the phone and kicks his right foot repeatedly into a tuft of native grass. He's wearing a dark tailored suit and tie, and his hair is slicked back from his forehead. He's scowling, but his face is drawn. I feel an unexpected jolt of empathy. Smithson has its fair share of tragedy and violence, but murder isn't a frequent occurrence, and it's not easy having to shoulder the collective fear and grief of a small town. Plus from what Candy said, this sounds especially nasty.

She made me drive her car from the cafe so she could upload news alerts to her website on the way here. Her fingers fly across her keyboard as she hotspots to her phone. Up ahead, her incredibly patient part-time cameraman gestures wildly, and I edge along the street toward him, careful not to run over anyone in the small crowd. Cops, journos and neighbours stand in distinct groups, eyes fixed on the imposing double-storey house. Sam moves onto the nature strip so I can guide the car into a narrow space he's saved for us between an Audi and an unmarked police car.

Candy jams her laptop into her bag. She thrusts the door open and starts talking Sam's ear off.

I catch Scarlett drifting into sleep, so I quickly get out of the car and slide her into the carrier. She breathes softly against my chest as I study the crowd: a sea of pale faces, many with their hands over their mouths in shock. Eyes follow Everett as he walks from one side of the front yard to the other, his mobile still fixed to his ear. I hate to admit it, but he looks like he's in charge.

Candy gestures at me impatiently and stalks across the road, ushering Sam and his camera gear along with her. I follow them, moving my hand in a slow circle on Scarlett's back. When Everett spots me, he doesn't even try to hide his irritation, while Holdsworth offers me a tentative smile.

Ash Amato is leaning against an ambulance, talking to another paramedic. I draw closer and try to get his attention—I still want to talk to him more about the woman from the crash, arrange for him to brief a sketch artist and push him on what he noticed that night. But he abruptly disappears around the other side of the ambulance.

'Woodstock!' Jonesy booms as he steps out of Roger Kirk's house, causing me to jump and Scarlett to startle. 'Fancy seeing you here.'

I stay where I am, forcing him to come to me.

He sidles up, red-faced and out of breath. Several journos attempt to get nearer to him, calling out his name, but are warned off by baby-faced constables.

'Good grief, what a circus,' he huffs, steadying himself on a parked car.

'You all right?'

'Of course I'm bloody all right,' he snaps. 'I was just about to call you, Woodstock, but you're clearly one step ahead. I hope that doesn't mean we need to add you to the suspect list.'

'I was having coffee with Candy when someone tipped her off.'

Jonesy snorts. He likes Candy but dislikes all journalists on principle, so for consistency he pretends to find her unbearable.

'What the hell happened to Roger?' I say quietly. 'I mean, we saw him yesterday.'

'God knows. Someone's gone and butchered the poor prick.'

Roger was so alive, so smug—full of nervous energy, yes, but not worried for his life.

I ask, 'Do we know if he was killed this morning or last night?'

Before Jonesy can answer, a boxy Mercedes with tinted windows turns into the street. The crowd murmurs.

'Carlyle Kirk.' Jonesy scowls. 'Just what we need. Come on.' He hustles me toward the house, weaving us through a throng of first responders. Over half of the Smithson police force must be here. Amid the blue uniforms, I spot Minnie towering over her fellow officers. I try to catch her eye as we walk past, but she's facing the other way.

Roger's house is devoid of all character, unless having zero personality can be considered a character trait. It's painfully modern, two grey blocks on top of each other. I recall my dad, who takes an avid interest in Smithson real estate, talking several years ago about the concrete eyesore Roger was building. 'Looks like a prison for rich people!' Dad said at the time—which, considering it now, is a very accurate description.

We find Everett on the concrete front porch, deep in conversation with a tall man in a dark suit. Everett stops talking as we approach and says to Jonesy, 'Sir, this is Jack Barnes. Mr Barnes, this is Chief Inspector Ken Jones.'

They shake hands. I take in the man's striking silver hair and piercing blue eyes. Jack Barnes looks like a lawyer. It's impossible to imagine him wearing anything other than a suit and tie. I guess he's in his mid-fifties, but his skin is artificially tanned and his expensive suit hangs well on his athletic frame.

'Yes,' Jonesy says flatly. 'We've met before.'

Barnes nods. 'Yes, that's right. Good to see you, mate.' He turns to me and offers his hand. 'I'm a lawyer. I represent the Kirks.'

'Detective Gemma Woodstock.'

'Very good, that's good.' He rocks on his heels, eyes glazing over.

'Jack was the one who found Roger this morning,' Everett explains, with just a touch of a warning note. I don't know him well enough yet to understand the hint. Does he want us to go easy on Barnes or help press him for clues?

'I've been assisting the Kirks for years,' Barnes says. 'Since Roger was a teenager . . .' He runs his eyes along the side of the house to a balcony where a striped towel flaps in the breeze. 'This is very upsetting. What I saw in there . . . I might be in shock.' He chews his lip and looks past us again, his head bobbing as his eyes fill with tears. For a moment it seems like he might succumb to his emotions, before he rallies, squaring his shoulders and tossing his head as if to dismiss the ugly images playing in his mind.

'What time did you arrive here?' I ask.

'Just after nine am. Roger and I had arranged a business meeting. You're obviously aware of what transpired at the hospital earlier this week. Rog wanted my advice on a few aspects of the incident, so we planned to have a working breakfast.' He gestures to a rumpled paper bag and a little cardboard tray with two takeaway coffee cups just inside the front door. 'I brought those.'

Jonesy clears his throat and jerks his thumb at the house. 'The door was open?'

'No,' says Barnes. 'I knocked and rang the doorbell, but there was no answer. I remember I stepped back down there.' He points to the gravel driveway and what I assume is his car, a sleek black convertible.

'I thought maybe Rog was upstairs, in the shower or something, so I called out. But there was no reply. I called his phone, too, but, well . . .' He drops his hands to his sides, looking utterly forlorn.

'How did you get inside?' I ask.

'I have keys, so after a while I let myself in—and straight away I knew something was wrong. I could just sense it. I put all the food down, not sure why I did that, and then I went inside and that's when I saw him.'

'Why do you have keys to the house?' asks Everett.

Over his shoulder I see an older man, also dressed in a suit, arguing with a constable and being corralled into a car by two others.

'I've had a set of keys for years,' Barnes replies. 'I used to feed their dog whenever they went away, but it died at the start of the year. I never got around to asking if they wanted the keys back.'

'Tell us what happened next, step by step,' I say.

Everett opens his mouth to interrupt, but Jonesy holds out a hand.

Barnes swallows thickly. 'I saw his legs first. And then the rug. It was bad. There was so much blood, I knew he was dead. I was almost sick.'

'Did you touch him to check he was deceased?' I ask.

'I don't think I did, but I'm not sure. No, I didn't.' His hands go to the back of his skull, clutching either side, and he grimaces, straining his jaw.

I think these movements are likely the same ones he made when he discovered Roger's body. Witnesses often make similar gestures when they relive trauma and backtrack through emotions.

'I got close to him. I could tell he wasn't breathing, and he wasn't moving. There was so much blood.'

Barnes's shock seems real, but lawyers are good actors and finding a corpse automatically puts anyone under suspicion, especially if they knew the deceased.

I jiggle Scarlett absently, recalling what Roger said at the hospital yesterday. 'Roger mentioned his family are away. Do you know where they are?'

'Dominique and the kids spent the weekend in Sydney. They're due back today. She and Roger have been having some issues lately, and I was helping with that, too. It's very amicable,' he adds quickly, 'and nothing concrete had been agreed. Roger just wanted to explore his options.'

Everett steps in front of me. 'We'll need to get some prints and a swab, then ask you a few more questions. If you head over to Constable Holdsworth, she'll help get you sorted and also make sure you don't need any medical attention.'

'I'm fine, I don't need anything. I just . . . I mean *we* just need to know who did this. He was *attacked* in his home, for god's sake. Why?' A touch of mania has crept into his voice. 'I need to make some calls, and I need to speak to Carlyle.'

'First we need to get a few things sorted here.' Everett places a hand on the lawyer's suit-clad shoulder and steers him over to Holdsworth. Returning, he smiles tightly at me. 'Well, here we all are again.'

'Thoughts on Barnes?' I say, ignoring his tone.

Everett shrugs. 'I don't like to play guessing games so early in proceedings, but for what it's worth I believe him. It is interesting, though, that he said he was advising Roger on the hospital incident.'

'Why is that?' I ask.

'Because,' Everett replies, not even looking at me, 'Roger gave us the details of another law firm that's handling the matter.'

'Maybe he just wanted his friend's professional opinion,' I suggest.

'Maybe. But Barnes was vague on the purpose of their meeting this morning.'

'Shock?' I suggest.

'Could be. Anyway, that aside, the guy was distraught when I got here; he seems genuinely traumatised.'

'How bad is it in there?' asks Jonesy.

'Up there with the worst I've seen.' For once I appreciate that Everett doesn't mince his words. There's nothing worse than being wishy-washy at a murder scene.

Candy calls out to me from the street and I turn the other way to face the house. She should know better than to hassle me in front of my colleagues.

I appraise the entrance of the house. Plastic covering has been laid across the threshold and disappears into the hallway past Jack Barnes's discarded breakfast treats. 'Forensics are inside?' I ask. 'What about the ME?'

Everett nods. 'The whole crew's here. They will be all day, I reckon. It's a mess.'

Curiosity pulses through every nerve in my body. I've never been one to shy away from a crime scene. Some cops find them confronting, and others find them to be a distraction, but I like to know what I'm dealing with, no matter how gruesome. When prompted I can recall almost every scene I've attended, with snapshots of misery filed away in my mind. I've learned that a scene is a treasure trove of critical information. Clues lie in wait, begging to be found. Plus, I've always felt that bearing witness to someone's last minutes, getting as close as I can to the moment they died, bonds me to both victim and perpetrator in a way that feels important. It's as if once I've seen the destruction firsthand, my resolve to seek justice becomes personal. It lights a fire in me that needs to be extinguished, and the only way that can happen is with a resolution.

That's why I want to see inside Roger Kirk's house. 'Can I go in?' I feel awkward having to ask, but because it's not my case I can't just waltz in like I normally would. Everett might be a pain in the arse, but I owe him at least a little respect.

He glances at Jonesy and shrugs. 'Just be careful. We don't need any stuff-ups.'

The tips of my ears burn. 'Of course,' I reply, summoning all the self-control I can to avoid telling him to get fucked. I turn to Jonesy. 'Do you want to come?'

He grimaces as he checks his phone. 'I have a call to make. Boss wants another update.'

Jonesy's boss, Superintendent Melissa O'Connell, is new in the role and has lots to prove. Her leadership style is constant communication, something he finds unnecessarily time-consuming. I wonder how I would manage her, whether I could deal with the scrutiny. Jonesy is rough around the edges, but he's always run the station by the book and is great at galvanising big teams. Although I'm more poised, my impatience gets in the way of both politics and procedure.

Since we arrived, the crowd has doubled in size and the vibe has shifted from shock to fear. Anger will be next. People don't like the sense of their safety being threatened, and the police are generally blamed when it happens.

The technician at the front door hands me a large forensic suit and booties. I step carefully into the gauzy material, zipping it closed around a sleeping Scarlett before leaning against the house to pull the booties over my shoes. I run my hand across her forehead, swallowing a sharp feeling of guilt. I suddenly feel uncertain about placing my child in the presence of such overt evil. Even though she won't understand, I can't help wondering whether the horror might somehow infiltrate her innocent soul.

'Everything okay?' the technician asks, watching me.

'Yep, all good. I'm just about to go in.'

'Little girl?'

I nod.

'She's fast asleep,' he says, matter-of-fact. 'And if she wakes up, it's not like our vic is going to know.'

He busies himself, bending down to forage through a bag, and gratitude flows through my system. 'Thanks.' My eyes well with tears. He's right. Scarlett will never know about this, and I feel compelled to see the scene for myself.

'No worries. I just hope you're not a fainter—it's a total bloodbath in there.'

CHAPTER SIXTEEN

A huge bird's nest hangs from the hallway ceiling—or that's what I think it is, until I spot a light globe nestled in the centre. At the first doorway I pause and scan the room: a minimalist desk, an almost empty bookshelf and an uncomfortable-looking chair that appears to be held together by a few leather straps. Not for the first time, I wonder why people with money are obsessed with owning such impractical items.

I continue along the plastic floor covering, pulling the material from the forensic suit aside to check that Scarlett is still asleep. Her eyes are buttoned closed, feathery lashes splayed out across her cheekbones. I kiss the top of her head as we pass two bedrooms and an ornate bathroom.

When I reach the kitchen, I introduce myself to a technician busily photographing the items on the bench. A solo frame is propped on the sleek sideboard, featuring Roger and a pretty woman standing side by side, three young children lined up in front of them. This is the only indication of who lives in the house. The kids are wearing tailored outfits that I'm sure cost more than Ben's entire wardrobe. I think about my domestic existence with Mac, Ben and Scarlett—the narrow spaces and messy rooms, our belongings in a happy chaotic jumble. This environment could not be more different; it feels unlived in.

I enter the lounge. Pacing in a circle at the foot of a staircase and talking on his mobile is the local medical examiner, Boyd Mattingly. His lanky frame is encased in a forensic suit and his scruffy dark hair is contained by a bright blue hairnet making him look even goofier than normal. He raises his bushy eyebrows at my Scarlett shaped bulge before he steps into an adjacent room to continue his conversation. 'Well, what time can you fit me in? No, it's for three teeth.' I can't tell if he's talking to a forensics lab or making a dental appointment.

Taking a deep breath, I prepare myself for the scene on the other side of the room.

I notice the blood first but almost simultaneously process the dramatic rust-coloured artworks adorning the main wall: life imitating art. A large aqua lamp protrudes from the corner to the middle of the room, and a clock above the fireplace has words instead of numbers, crudely marking the passage of time with loud, obnoxious ticks. Roger lies on his side at the foot of a plush grey chair. Beneath him, the rug is snow white except for the uneven circle of blood that pools near his torso. His eyes are closed, but his mouth is open, exposing his flaccid pink tongue. I process several things at once: Roger is dressed in jeans, a polo and socks; today's newspaper is open on the side table, next to a glass of water; he's been stabbed with neat slices, not bashed. This violence was calculated.

As I catch my reflection in a mirror hanging on the other side of the room, I wonder if Roger looked at himself in the same glass earlier this morning.

Boyd returns. 'Not pretty, is it?'

'It seems incredibly aggressive.'

'Almost frenzied.' Boyd rolls the z on his tongue. He points at my bulging suit. 'I heard you have a little one. Congratulations.'

'Thank you. This is Scarlett. Fortunately, she's asleep. I'm not officially back at work yet—I was just sort of here today.' I put my hands on my hips, not sure if I've adequately explained my being here. I'm aware it's odd to be having a casual conversation in the presence of a dead body, but Boyd and I are used to death being a part of life.

'Well, it's nice to see you anyway. No doubt they'll be keen to have you back. I hear there's a bit of an exodus looming.'

'What do you mean?'

He rubs his face and pinches the skin between his eyebrows. His broad shoulders are slightly hunched. 'I heard that Kingston and McCabe are retiring at the end of the year.' He pauses. 'Alongside a few other changes.' I assume he's referring to Jonesy and wonder if my boss realises quite a few people know his supposed secret.

'Change is the only constant,' I say neutrally, hoping to deter further discussion.

'Change, death and taxes—the foundation of all life on planet Earth.'

I smile. 'Wise as always.'

Boyd laughs. 'It helps that people are so predictable.'

'Thankfully not so predictable that we're out of a job.' Returning my attention to Roger's corpse, I'm shocked by the blood-smeared wounds all over again. 'He was sitting there . . . ?' I point to the chair next to the side table.

'Seems so. Didn't even get a chance to take his vitamins.' Boyd shows me two white tablets next to the water cup. 'Of course, they might not be vitamins. We'll check that.'

I recall Roger's slightly erratic behaviour at our meeting. 'Is there any indication he *was* on drugs or meds?'

'There doesn't seem to be anything out of the ordinary in his bathroom cupboard or bedside table. No prescription meds apart from some out-of-date Valium.'

'Any immediate thoughts you're happy to share?'

Boyd walks to the edge of the blood-soaked rug. 'Well, I can tell you he wasn't stabbed in the back. All the injuries are on his chest, abdomen and hands. He also appears to have a broken finger.'

'So he knew it was coming?'

'I'd say so.'

'Did he fight back?'

'A little, but not for long. The cuts are deep. I suspect he bled out quickly.'

I peer at Roger's lacerated hands and try to picture it—a conversation that led to an argument . . . ? But then where did the knife come from? Maybe as they fought, the attacker went to the kitchen and returned with a knife. It's more likely that almost as soon as the perpetrator entered the house, they attacked Roger.

I shiver as I channel the terror paired with the hope that must have coursed through Roger's system in his final moments—fight, flight, freeze and pray.

'Where's the weapon?' I ask Boyd.

'Not here, or not that we've found. There's some blood spatter that the teams will be excited to dig into.' I follow his pointed finger to where a trail of red spots leads from the rug onto the marbled concrete floor. 'It could be that the knife was dripping until it was contained somehow.'

'Any chance of finding DNA here?'

'A chance, sure. Whether it will be useful to your case or not, who knows?'

'Do you think—?' I'm interrupted by a piercing scream from the front yard, followed by anguished cries and other voices. 'I'd better go.'

He nods. 'It doesn't sound fun out there. Much nicer in here.'

But to me, the scene seems to be getting uglier. The blood is more shocking, and Roger's twisted limbs seem more tragic. Wanting to disrupt my grim thoughts, I say, 'It was nice to see you despite the circumstances.'

A shrill voice snakes from the front yard down the hallway. 'Roger, *Roger*! Let me see him!'

'Anytime,' Boyd says. 'Good to have you back on board, Gemma.'

I return along the hallway. The voice carries the tone of someone who has been told something so awful they refuse to believe it. 'No, no, you let me see him!'

I step into the sunlight just in time to see a trio of officers trying to console a distraught woman. I recognise Dominique Kirk from the photo in the kitchen. After removing my suit and booties, I go to stand on the lawn near Everett and his crew. I can't see Jonesy.

'Let me inside! It's *my* house.' Dominique is crying, a snotty affair. Holdsworth leans close to talk to her. After a few moments, she sinks to the ground in shock. Her wavy rose-gold hair frames her heart-shaped face. Large eyes sit over prominent cheekbones and a small sharp nose. Her skin is almost translucent, except for her blotchy cheeks. She reminds me of a doll. 'My babies,' she weeps. 'I can't. No.'

The older man with the silver hair joins her and envelopes her in a hug: Carlyle Kirk.

I spot Jonesy getting out of the passenger seat of a police car, gripping his mobile like a stress ball. 'Woodstock!' he barks as he ambles over to us. 'How was it?'

'Brutal—and my gut says premeditated. If it had just been someone lashing out, I think the impact of the first wound would have shocked them enough to stop.'

Everett's jaw clenches.

'Apparently Roger wasn't short of enemies,' says Jonesy. 'So I imagine we'll have several suspects to play with. There are already nasty comments on the news alerts.'

I think about the expensive furniture as I take in the manicured lawn and the fancy car in the drive. What a waste—Roger had it all and now has absolutely nothing. I wonder how many people he screwed over to achieve his superior lifestyle.

'Do we think this is linked to what happened at the hospital?' I ask.

Everett lifts his shoulders and sniffs. Jonesy doesn't say anything.

'Whether it is or not, I need to keep moving,' says Everett. 'We've got a lot to do.'

Scarlett seems to take this as a cue to jerk awake and start crying. She needs a feed and a nappy change.

'I better go,' I mumble. 'Jonesy, I'll talk to you later.'

He's on his phone and doesn't reply—I don't think he even heard me.

'Bye, Woodstock,' says Everett pointedly.

I notice Ash standing on his own at the end of the driveway and make a beeline for him, hoping we can arrange a time to talk. I'm a few metres away when he pulls his phone out and starts talking, walking briskly in the opposite direction. I come to a halt. Has he just faked a phone call? While he appears deep in conversation, he keeps glancing in my direction. I can't work it out—have I upset him somehow?

Flummoxed, I whisper soothingly to Scarlett and look around for

Candy, even though I'll need to make my own way home—there's no way she'll want to leave yet.

On my way to the front gate, I pass Carlyle and Dominique Kirk. Carlyle's jaw is set in a hard line, his arm wrapped protectively around his nephew's wife as she sobs into his chest.

CHAPTER SEVENTEEN

In the back seat of Candy's car, I change Scarlett's nappy, mix some formula, then feed her as I watch the crowd grow. The mysteries beat through my brain like a chant: the car crash, the stolen corpse, an abandoned baby, a dead millionaire. What the hell is going on? The timing and proximity link the incidents, but I know from experience that while patterns and connections are important, forcing cases together can be a mistake. Each one deserves to be investigated on its own merits, and the victims need as much objectivity from us as we can summon—they don't tend to get it from anyone else. But the reality is that puzzles often overlap; when they do, it's critical to find where they join.

I pull Scarlett's onesie back on. It's covered in tiny pumpkins in honour of her favourite food. Mac bought it for her.

I push thoughts of Mac aside and think about cases I've worked where there was an abandoned child or infant. Every one of them was left by a young mother who felt she'd run out of options, a female between sixteen and twenty-five with no tertiary education and either earning a low income or unemployed. Drugs were usually involved, as was mental illness, and the mother usually had a sense the baby was better off without her. At least whoever left the baby at the lake didn't decide she was better off dead; I've worked several of those cases, too, and there is no light to be found in that darkness. I still think there's a chance the baby belonged to the woman from the car crash, although the interviews with Ash, Freddie and the medical team don't indicate she recently gave birth. But if the baby does belong to the dead woman, it might provide a motive for stealing her corpse—a way to buy some time before she could be linked to the baby. But why would that be important, seeing as the little girl was dumped at the lake?

I tap my finger on Scarlett's bottle, which is almost empty. Now Roger is dead. Could he be the baby's father? Maybe he was having an affair.

I feel a wave of frustration. We need the DNA reports from all of the victims as well as the tox and forensic reports from the car crash asap—and knowing how long they can take, I just hope Everett has a good relationship with the lab.

Sitting Scarlett upright, I burp her as she tries to pull my hair.

'Who knows what's going on, hey?' I say as I nuzzle her cheek. 'It doesn't make any sense.'

'Gah!' she cries, pointing at the people on the street.

The driver's door swings open, and Candy sticks her head in. 'Hey, ladies.' She rubs her hands together. 'This story is *wild*. I can't believe it! Roger was already newsworthy, and this just makes him more interesting.'

'Please don't ever consider switching to a career in life coaching.'

'You know what I mean. It's a massive story! Sad, obviously, but undeniably massive.'

We turn in response to a rise in volume from the crowd. Dominique has reappeared on the street, and people hiss at each other to make room as she staggers past. Carlyle follows, calling her name, his handsome face ashen.

'See,' murmurs Candy, craning her neck. 'It's a cracker.'

I can tell she's thinking about headlines and copy, how to package up the shock and grief and deploy it as soon as possible to her growing readership.

'I saw you go inside,' she says. 'How was it?'

'Unpleasant.'

She nods, and I can tell she's dying to ask for details but realises I won't give her any.

'Tell me what you know about Roger's uncle,' I say. 'I know he's a doctor. And he owns a retirement home. And he's extremely wealthy . . .'

'Tick, tick, tick. The consensus is that Carlyle is a genius. Before he turned eighteen, he studied medicine at some fancy university—in Switzerland, I think—and came back with top honours in psychiatry. Years ago he invested in pharma companies and made a killing. That's how he got the cash to set up his psych clinic and Lyle Lodge, the state-of-the-art retirement home, and buy all that property. His next big bet is the research centre. He's got the mayor in his pocket—you should hear her talk about it, you'd think NASA was setting up in Smithson.'

I remember what Jonesy said. 'To be fair, I've been advised that the designs do give off convincing spaceship vibes.'

'I'm not knocking it,' Candy says. 'It's going to be great for business.'

'You mean your business?'

'Yes, of course! It will give us access to some of the country's top scientists. Science sells these days, especially anything to do with mental health and reversing the ageing process, two things the new centre is planning to focus on. I've had some initial conversations with Carlyle's people about establishing a media partnership.'

'Which has nothing to do with getting revenge on Nate,' I say, teasing.

'Absolutely nothing. I love science, always have.'

I laugh. Candy loves making money and winning.

'But why is Carlyle staying in Smithson?' I ask. 'He's obviously extremely talented, so why wouldn't he move overseas?'

'No idea. He's environmentally conscious and lives in a huge eco lodge outside town, so maybe he just wants a quiet lifestyle. He's crazy wealthy, but I don't think he's very showy. His daughter Mauve is his lead comms person, and she's already made it clear that if we do a deal, the media coverage is to be focused on clinical trials and patient outcomes rather than Carlyle himself.'

In primary school Mauve was a confident, showy kid. Franklin was more reserved but, even then, I knew they were wealthy.

'Where did Roger go to school? He wasn't at Smithson Primary like his cousins.'

'In Sydney, I think. His dad was a successful businessman and I think they left Smithson when Roger was a baby. He's always been close to his uncle. I think Carlyle sees, I mean *saw*, Roger as his successor. Mauve's ambitious and highly competent, but she's not interested in science.'

'Franklin was a nice kid, from what I remember.'

'Yeah, it was sad what happened to him.'

'He's a quadriplegic?'

'I don't think he ever woke up after the accident.'

I can vaguely remember the news coverage. I was eighteen and dealing with the fallout of my boyfriend's suicide, a tragedy that left me with no capacity to absorb a story so similar. Franklin, back in Smithson after his final year at boarding school, was camping with friends near Tyson Falls. They claimed that while he was in good spirits at the camp site when they went for a walk, he was nowhere to be found when they returned. He'd suffered depression on and off throughout secondary school, so speculation was rife that he'd jumped. Tyson Falls was a known suicide spot. A frantic search was conducted, and Franklin was found the following day on a ledge a few metres down the cliff face. He had a serious head injury and spinal damage and was flown to Sydney for emergency surgery but remained in a vegetative state. I remember hearing something about him receiving experimental treatment overseas. While the prognosis is clearly grim, I can understand someone with a science background like Carlyle wanting to do everything in his power to save his son.

'You should check out Carlyle's website.' Candy scrolls on her phone as she talks. 'He has a cult following in the psych world—he's all over TikTok and Instagram. And since he built the nursing home, he's always being asked to comment on aged care issues.'

'Wasn't there a lawsuit against Lyle Lodge few years ago? What happened?'

'Alleged neglect. But Carlyle wasn't charged in the end.'

'So the claims were bogus?'

'I'm not sure,' she says. 'I spoke to a lot of people at the time, and it sounds like there were some pretty bizarre things happening out there.'

'Like what?'

'Like patients claiming they were being denied certain foods despite there being no medical reason for it. And stories of them being left alone for periods of time or being forced to listen to certain music.'

'Music?' I repeat.

'Yeah.' Candy wrinkles her nose. 'One woman told me her mother swore the nurse put on aggressive rock music when she cleaned the room and didn't turn it off when she left. The old woman complained, but the nurse refused to do anything about it and left it on all night. The patient was very upset.'

'Maybe the residents were confused. Wouldn't a lot of them have had dementia?'

'Maybe. The lawyers did struggle to get coherent witness statements. Plus there were a lot of people coming out in support of the place. It's very popular.'

'Other residents, you mean?'

'Yes, and their families,' she says. 'There was a lot of community support, too. It's not like there are that many options to ship your folks off to around here, and it employs a lot of people. And the staff accused of wrongdoing swore black and blue that nothing untoward was going on.'

'What was your take?'

'All the residents and families I spoke to seemed genuine, and they had no reason to lie. It did sound like some unusual things were going on, but maybe there were just a few staff members trying to push their views about food and exercise onto their patients. Even though Carlyle was in the clear, he promised to overhaul the staff and review all the policies and procedures.'

'Did he . . . ?' I pause as another news van turns into the street. These aren't local journos: Roger's murder has attracted the heavy hitters.

Candy scowls at a woman sashaying past in a sleek pantsuit, her blonde bob stiff with hairspray. I recognise her from Sydney news bulletins. 'Bloody thinks she's Lois Lane or something,' Candy hisses.

I smile. I've always enjoyed Candy's public displays of jealousy. 'Where's Sam?' I ask.

'Hopefully climbing Roger Kirk's back fence and getting some decent snaps of his backyard.'

I roll my eyes. 'Okay, well, I'm going to head off.'

Her fingers hover above her phone. 'Is something wrong?'

'No.' I gather my things. 'I'm just not on duty.'

'As if Jonesy cares. He wants you here, you know that.'

'I've got to get her home.' I pull Scarlett back into the carrier.

Candy looks stricken. 'I can't leave now.'

'It's fine—I'm going to walk.'

Her phone rings, and I take the opportunity to exit the car. I swing the nappy bag over my shoulder and wave goodbye, but she's already lost in conversation. Making my way to the back of the crowd, I edge past the Kirk residence again. I can't see any CCTV on the house or in the front yard, but some of the opulent houses closer to the corner have external security cameras. None of them appear to be angled at the Kirk residence, but I make a mental note to ask Jonesy about pulling everything we can get our hands on.

'It's just unbelievable,' a woman mutters to the man next to her as I walk past. 'I saw him yesterday.'

Another woman stands with her hand over her mouth, her head shaking from side to side. 'God, it's just awful, those poor kids. And Dom—did you see her? A total mess.'

Further along, two women are propped on each side of a boxy brick letterbox, their heads bent close. 'Surely Dom will move to Sydney now,' one of them is saying.

I slide my sunglasses on and pause next to them, hoping they didn't see me with the cops. 'This is so awful,' I say. 'Did you know him well? I can't imagine how his wife must be feeling.'

They exchange glances. 'She might be his ex-wife, actually,' the one with the dyed red hair says conspiratorially. 'I'm pretty sure they just split.'

'Gosh,' I say. 'That's complicated.'

The blonde sniffs. 'Yes, well, Dom doesn't mind a bit of drama—not that she would want anything like this to happen, of course,' she adds hastily.

'You live here?'

They nod.

'All my life,' replies the blonde. 'My parents left me this house.'

I flick a look at the grand double-storey dwelling and its manicured garden. I can't imagine living somewhere so perfect. 'It's lovely.'

'Not so lovely today,' says the redhead darkly. 'I can't believe someone was murdered less than fifty metres from my bedroom.'

'Did they fight a lot?' I ask.

'Not lately,' says the redhead. 'But I assume that's because they finally called it quits.'

'Last Christmas, on the other hand, was a doozy,' adds the blonde. 'There was screaming in the street, which was embarrassing—especially because I had guests over. Dom took the kids and didn't come back for a week. She's been away with the children a lot ever since.'

Two more police cars turn into Emerald Drive, serious young faces behind the tinted glass as they inch their way through the human traffic.

I ask, 'I wonder what Roger and Dom were fighting about . . . ?'

The woman swats a fly away with a manicured hand and purses her inflated lips. 'Something about him lying to her again. He was obviously cheating on her, the arsehole.'

CHAPTER EIGHTEEN

The evening settles across the backyard, tucking itself around the edges of the shed and the tips of the trees until it is completely dark. I throw diced onion and garlic into the oiled frypan and give it a prod before turning my attention to the rest of the vegetables. I'm listening to a podcast interview Carlyle Kirk did at the beginning of last year, in which he talks about his ambition for the research centre. It's a great interview, and his answers are thoughtful and passionate.

Ben is at the kitchen table, his eyebrows dipping in concentration as he works on an assignment, something about the ethics of time travel. Scarlett is on her playmat, cooing loudly at a plush koala. She lies on her stomach, her position of choice these days, and I notice how strong her legs have grown as she tries to propel herself forward. She'll be crawling soon—and walking before we know it. I can barely remember Ben at the same age. When I try to work my way through the timeline of his childhood, it's as if he went from baby to school age in an instant.

I add chicken strips to the pan, along with diced carrot, broccoli and capsicum. *We know so little about the human brain,* Carlyle is saying to the journalist, *especially when it comes to addiction and age. We will welcome curious minds from all over the world to come and join our learning journey. We want to partner with people in all fields of research. Science is much too secretive, with everyone doing their own thing and staying in their own lanes, but it's my view that the future is open source. Sharing data is the only way we'll all make progress, and we must make progress if we want our species to survive.*

The sizzle of the meal blends with Scarlett's cooing and Ben's typing, and my mind returns to the case. There's no denying I want in on this investigation. The seed was planted when I followed Rufus to the hospital morgue on Sunday night. I don't know what's feasible, but I don't want to watch from the sidelines or hear things second-hand: I want to be properly involved, follow the threads, and work out how the pieces go together. This is the problem with being a detective: cases drop with no warning and zero consideration of existing commitments. As Jonesy often says, death is inconvenient— and never more so than when he wants to watch a major sports event. Clues don't wait. Evidence washes away, witness accounts fade and the truth morphs. Timing is everything, and getting into the right rhythm as soon as possible is critical. It's something I've always been good at. I have a knack for establishing a cadence quickly and bringing my colleagues on the journey. Leading a case is like conducting an orchestra and when you get the arrangement right, harmony is achieved, but the investigation into Roger's death is still discordant. We don't have much to go on, so it's difficult to know where to start. We don't even know how many cases we're working.

'Mum?' Ben sounds impatient.

'Sorry, what did you say?'

'I asked what's for dinner.' He has abandoned his assignment and is crouched on the floor next to Scarlett, teasing her by holding a toy just out of her reach.

'A chicken stir-fry, is that okay?'

'Yep. I might just have a quick shower first.'

'Okay. Can you please tell Mac dinner will be ready in about fifteen minutes?'

'Sure.' He heads down the hall toward the main bathroom.

As he departs, Scarlett lets out a shriek, then starts to cry.

'Hey, hey,' I say, as she works herself into a frenzy. 'He'll be back. Come on.' I lift her up and return to the kitchen.

Tears trail down her cheeks, and she reaches out to the frypan.

'No, that's not a good idea.' Twisting my body away from the hotplate, I plant little kisses all over her face until she smiles.

'You should have called me to look after her.' Mac appears next to me and takes Scarlett, swinging her around and kissing her cheeks just like I did. 'She's not exactly the best sous-chef.'

'She's been fine. I only just picked her up.' I check on the rice. 'She's about to crawl.'

'Lord help us,' he says, beaming at her. 'It's about time, though—she's nine months next week. How old was Ben when he started crawling?'

I scrunch up my face. 'About eight months, I think. I was back at work . . .'

A hazy memory snares in my thoughts: Scott down on hands and knees, cheering Ben on as he crawled clumsily across the lounge; me, exhausted and watching from the kitchen where I was trawling through case files. I missed so many of Ben's early milestones, and it's horribly unfair that Scott will miss all the ones yet to come.

'What about your kids?' I ask, swallowing past the sadness. 'Were they early crawlers?'

'They were—I remember we had to baby-proof everything earlier than we thought we'd need to.' He laughs and returns to lifting Scarlett into the air.

'Have you been in touch with the kids lately?' I ask casually.

'Ah, not really. Just a message here and there. I figure they're both busy.'

Mac's children from his first marriage are in their twenties, navigating busy lives and successful careers. Neither of them is wild about me, but it's not a major issue, and the few times we've met we got along fine.

'Maybe you should send them something,' I say. 'Let them know you're thinking about them.'

'Like what?'

I start to dish up the food, my heart thumping. 'I don't know, something easy to post. It's always nice to get something in the mail, don't you think?'

'I guess so,' he replies uncertainly.

My stomach drops. It's clear that the package I saw Mac with wasn't for his kids. I call out to Ben that dinner is ready. Mac carries Scarlett to her highchair, pretending to land her like a plane before strapping her in. I place the steaming plates in front of us, and for a moment it's just the sounds of us eating and the birds in the yard singing, the news turned down low in the background.

'How's your case going?' I ask Mac as I wrestle with my suspicions. 'I feel like I don't know anything about it.'

'It's going well,' he says brightly. 'I finally got on to the man who worked with the victim, so that was helpful.'

'Tell me the details again.'

Mac slides his eyes in Ben's direction, indicating it's something I won't want him to hear.

'Just the gist,' I say.

'A priest was murdered in Queensland in the seventies, but no one was ever convicted. Some new information has come to light, linking it to another murder, and there's a chance the coroner will agree to an inquest.'

'Why did they want you on it?'

'The victim had connections to Smithson, and seeing as I'm a local, I got the call.' He wiggles his eyebrows at me, but his tone is strange; the humour seems forced.

'I would never kill a priest,' says Ben. 'You wouldn't be able to go to heaven.'

Mac and I laugh.

'I like your logic,' says Mac. 'Although I think any murder you commit is likely to make acceptance into heaven a challenge.'

'What's the new evidence?' I ask.

'Just some witness statements.' Clearly he doesn't want to elaborate in front of Ben.

'Do you think the inquest will happen?'

'There's a good chance.' Mac stares into the kitchen. 'But you know how hard these old cases can be. Witnesses are deceased, and the paper trail is sketchy.'

'Can I please be excused?' Ben asks, placing his cutlery across his clean plate.

'Sure, honey,' I say. 'Have you done all your homework?'

He moves his head in the affirmative. 'Can I play online for a bit?'

'Just for a bit,' I say. Once he's left the room, I ask Mac, 'How was the priest murdered?'

The news bulletin about Roger's murder flashes onto the screen, and Mac turns up the volume. I appear—I'm coming out of the front gate on Emerald Drive with Scarlett in the carrier. Mac turns to me, eyebrow cocked.

'I was obviously going to tell you! I was with Candy this morning when she got the call, so I tagged along. As you can imagine, she's beside herself with excitement.'

'The woman is a tragedy vampire,' Mac says affectionately.

'That she is,' I say, then add, 'It was pretty bad. I saw his body.'

'His family are well known around here, I gather?'

I nod. 'And we need to work out if there's a link to the missing corpse and the abandoned baby.'

'We?'

I shoot him a look, wondering if he's teasing me, but his expression is serious.

'Are you working this case, Gemma?'

'I'm still on leave.'

'I'd want to work on it,' Mac says.

'I can't stop thinking about it.'

'You could go back early. Jonesy would be thrilled to have you back.'

'Possibly,' I say, feeling overwhelmed by Mac's encouragement. 'I'd have to ask him.'

'I'm sure Rebecca will help with the kids, when I can't look after them.'

'Thank you.' My throat is tight with gratitude.

As he clears the plates, he drops a kiss on my forehead. 'No need to thank me, Gemma. We're a team, you know that.'

'I'm going to call Jonesy and see what he thinks. And then I'll get Scarlett sorted.'

Mac starts rinsing the plates. 'I have to call an ex-cult member in about thirty minutes, so that sounds perfect.'

I laugh, and he shoos me out of the room. After closing the door to the study, I dial Jonesy's mobile.

'Hi, Gemma.'

'Lucy,' I say, surprised—I can't remember Jonesy's wife answering his phone before. 'How are you?'

'I'm well, thank you. Tell me, how is that adorable baby of yours?'

'She's doing great.' I've pivoted clunkily from career mode to small talk. 'I'll have to come and visit soon so you can see how much she's grown.'

'Yes, I'd love to see her.'

I haven't seen Lucy in months, and Jonesy's retirement news hangs between us. She's always been his anchor. Even though they are very different people, they have one of the best relationships I've ever known. Unlike Jonesy, Lucy is immaculately groomed. Even at this time of day, her petite frame is surely clad in a tailored shirt and cashmere jumper, her nails and hair perfect.

'Is Jonesy there, Lucy? I need to speak with him about something.'

Her voice drops. 'We're just in the middle of something right now, Gemma. Can I have him call you back tomorrow?'

'It won't take long. Just a quick question.'

'It really would be best if—'

'Lucy? Are you still there?'

'Hang on, Gemma.' Her voice is cool, nothing like her typical bubbly tone. There's a muffled sound, then I hear her say, 'Ken, I was just trying to—'

This is followed by a brief silence as the phone is muted before Jonesy comes on the line. 'Detective Woodstock, good evening.'

'Is everything all right?'

'Right as rain. Marty's here, and Lucy was trying not to interrupt our *Law & Order* buddy watch.'

'This won't take long,' I say, refraining from commenting on Marty Blight being at his house. I know they're old friends, but Marty is such a jerk. I was always irritated by their closeness.

'Spit it out, Gemma,' he says.

'I want in on the case.'

'I would never have guessed.'

Irritation flares—I'm not sure if it's at him or at myself for being so predictable. 'I want to know if it's a possibility.'

'Sure it is.'

I sink into a chair; tension I hadn't realised I was cooking shifts from boiling to a simmer. 'Okay, good. How do you want it to work?'

'What are you going to do with the kid?'

My heartbeat picks up. 'Don't worry, I'll work it out with Mac. I'm sure Rebecca will help.'

'I can't put you in charge of the case, Woodstock.'

My jaw clenches, although I expected as much. 'That's fine.'

'Have you really thought it through? I don't want my news causing you to make rash decisions.'

Is that what I'm doing? Am I trying to prove to him that I'm ready to do his job?

'Scarlett won't be a baby for much longer,' he adds. 'Maybe it's worth waiting until the new year like you planned.'

'Will you even be around by then?'

'You'd better not be coming back just to spend time with me, Woodstock.'

'I'm not.' It comes out as a whisper. 'That's not what this is about.'

For a moment, neither of us speaks. Maybe he's right: I guess I do see this as my last chance to work with him. I think about our conversations over the years, of all the times he forced me to confront something about myself or to see something from a different angle—to believe in myself. God, I'm going to miss him.

But all I say next is, 'I just want to help. I think I can.'

Jonesy's laugh is kind. 'I have no doubt. And we could do with extra support. A blind man can see we're short-staffed.'

'Lucky I called then.'

He snorts. 'All right, Woodstock. Let's agree to some ground rules.'

'Okay.'

'You're not the lead.'

'You said that already.'

'I'm just making sure you registered it,' he says wryly.

'I'm not reporting to Everett, though.'

'Not officially,' he agrees.

'So, how will it work, exactly?'

He exhales noisily. 'You do whatever you need to do. You can work in parallel with the team—but share your info with Everett and respect him as case lead.'

'I want access to everything,' I prompt.

'You'll get full access,' he confirms. 'But go via Everett. And try not to piss everyone off.'

'I'll try.'

'Bloody hell,' he mutters.

'Jonesy?'

'What?'

'Thanks for this.'

'You're all right,' he says. 'A pain in the arse, but all right.'

I laugh softly. 'I'll take that as a compliment.'

There's a significant pause. I rise onto my tiptoes to stretch my calves, using my free hand to fan out a suite of A4-sized photos that Mac's left on the desk. A dozen people lie in a row on the ground near a bonfire; they're wearing elaborate headdresses above tribal markings painted on their faces. A little boy looks dead, staring blankly at the sky. Goose bumps form on my arms. The photos are confronting. I wonder at Mac's state of mind working a case like this. I know I can become distant when I'm dealing with disturbing content; maybe trawling through this old evidence is causing him to feel disconnected from our happy family bubble.

'I'd better go. Tell Lucy I said goodbye,' I say, recalling our awkward conversation earlier.

'Will do. Make sure you get some beauty sleep before tomorrow morning.'

'Tomorrow morning . . . ?'

'Roger Kirk's autopsy. Welcome back, Woodstock.'

CHAPTER NINETEEN

WEDNESDAY, 21 SEPTEMBER, 6.12 AM

My eyelids are like weights. I moan and roll over, burying my head in the pillow and praying it's earlier than I suspect it is. I feel like I could sleep for another ten hours and still be tired.

'Don't get up yet.' Mac moves closer, and I fold myself into the warmth of his body. He runs his hand up and down my rib cage before dropping it to the curve of my thigh.

'Maybe I don't want to go back to work after all,' I say.

'I think you do. But maybe not for at least fifteen minutes.'

'What's happening in the next fifteen minutes?'

He presses his lips against mine—gently at first, then more firmly in his familiar unrelenting way. This intensity is one of the things I loved about Mac from the start. He is always so focused, and when he focuses on me, it's like he is consuming me. He removes my T-shirt, and I give myself up to the moment, pushing my exhaustion, the kids and work from my mind. For a few minutes all I register is what he is doing to me. Then I lie across him as our heartbeats slow to their normal pace and our sweat cools on my skin.

I check the time. 'Just five more minutes,' I say, trying to summon the energy to get up and face the day. Lying here with Mac feels special, and I don't want to break the spell. Technically I don't have to be in early, but after my conversation with Jonesy I sense I should front up and meet the team, get everyone used to the new arrangement and prove I'm serious. Plus, I want to drop Ben at school and tell him about my going back to work.

I idly massage Mac's scalp.

'You have my permission to do that all day,' he says, closing his eyes.

We lie like this for another minute, my fingers pulling through his hair.

'I really should get up,' I say.

When he reaches out to me as I heave myself up, I'm tempted to slip back under the covers.

'You got up for Scarlett twice last night?' he asks.

I rub my eyes. 'I think so.'

Yawning, he props his pillow against the headboard and watches me find clothes. I hang them over the chair in the corner and head into the ensuite. The water burns cold, then hot. I drink straight from the shower stream and start to feel more awake.

'You're very beautiful, Gem.' Mac is staring at me through the open bedroom door.

I move further into the shower out of his eyeline, self-conscious about how my body must look in the stark light.

'You are,' he insists. 'Stunning. I think it all the time, but I don't say it often and I should.'

'You're fine,' I say, embarrassed at his praise. I can't help but wonder if his compliments are coming from a place of guilt.

'Are you sure you don't mind me going back to work early?' I step out of the shower and quickly wrap myself in a towel. 'It's not what we agreed.'

'You're not a force I'm keen to get in the way of. I understand you want to lean into these cases, and I don't blame you—they're interesting. And if you're happy, I'm happy.'

'Likewise,' I say, and we smile at each other. I feel like I'm going mad, shifting between feeling like everything is fine between us and then worrying that he's keeping things from me.

I apply make-up and blow-dry my hair. In the shower, Mac sings a song I don't recognise. It reminds me of when our lives were interwoven in his tiny apartment. After such a long time on my own, I craved the intimacy he demanded of me. Then Scott's illness interrupted our trajectory, whatever it was going to be—and suddenly, we were apart. Now we're reunited, but our lives are more spaced out. We're no longer working together, and we have Scarlett and Ben to consider, but it's the environment, too: the house is bigger, the streets are wider, our lives are more fragmented, and so we intersect less. Maybe we just need to try to do this more, to be close.

I kiss him as he steps out of the shower.

'I'd do more than kiss you again,' he says, 'but I'm all wet.'

I duck away from his outstretched hands, pass him a towel and grab my jacket. 'I have to go anyway.'

I can hear Ben in the kitchen and Scarlett cooing in her cot. I go to her, my steps light.

Forty-five minutes later, I'm less relaxed after Ben forgot his lunchbox and we had to go back to get it. I arrive at the station and head straight to Reggie's for a takeaway coffee. It's not even nine, and I feel like I've run a marathon.

Everett is standing in the station foyer when I return, looking like he's had a million hours of sleep. 'Good morning, Gemma. Nice outfit, very formal. I'm about to do a coffee run, but I can see you already have one.'

'Yep.'

We stand in an uncomfortable silence. I want to nod politely and break away, but I don't have a security pass—and there's no way I'm asking him to scan me in. 'I'll come with you,' I say brightly.

He raises his eyebrows. 'Why not? I could do with an extra pair of hands to carry the coffees.'

As we walk back through the car park, I squint into the sun and start to branch off toward Reggie's.

Everett heads in the opposite direction and says, 'Coffee's better at The Maple.'

'I doubt that.'

'Humour me.'

The Maple smells like burnt bacon. Everett reels off a substantial coffee order, then stands with his legs apart and flicks through the newspaper, checking his phone every few seconds. I read the news on my phone until the waiter returns with two cardboard trays laden with coffees.

'Grab the door for me, Woodstock?'

'No problem,' I mutter.

'Ta.' He sails through and then hands me a tray, holding the other one like he's a waiter.

'Roger's autopsy is scheduled for ten, right?' I rush to keep up with him.

'Correct. Don't worry, I'm aware you're attending.'

'Did you get any useful information out of Carlyle or Dominique Kirk yesterday?'

'Not really, just a lot of bullshit about privacy and respect for their grief.'

'I want to talk to Dominique,' I say. 'Their marriage was on the rocks, and I think Roger might have been cheating on her.'

Everett stops walking. 'Okay, look, Woodstock, I'm not going to be a dick about you being added to the team, but I'm not going to pretend I like it either. It's messy, and I don't like messy.'

'Neither do I.'

'And yet here you are,' he retorts.

'I just want to help.'

Plastering on a smile, he nods hello to a uniform I don't recognise. 'Sure you do. And maybe you also want to position yourself.'

'I don't know what you mean.'

He presses his lips together and takes a brisk sip of coffee. 'I'll be the bigger person. I'll play nice, and I have no doubt you can help. I've never said you're not a good detective—and I can't get a decent team locked in on this for trying.'

'I'm not reporting to you.'

With a smirk, he starts walking again. 'Don't worry, the boss made that part very clear.'

I hurry after him. 'I already have some ideas that I want to follow up, but I'm happy to let you know what I'm planning so we don't trip over each other.'

'Very generous.' He gestures for me to open the station door for him.

'I expect the same back,' I say, pulling it open.

He ignores me. 'Morning, Minnie,' he says, placing one of the coffees on her desk.

'Thanks, Ev!' She takes a big slurp. 'God, I needed that. Gemma! You're back!'

'Woodstock's doing some work experience.' Everett winks as if we're in on a joke.

'I'm just helping out on the case,' I tell Minnie, refusing to acknowledge him.

'That's great!' She does seem pleased, but something is lingering behind her eyes—caution? Perhaps I make her nervous. She adds, 'The others are in the Banksia Room.'

After dropping the dregs of my cold coffee in the bin, I follow Everett into the office. Holdsworth and seven cops I don't recognise are assembled in the biggest meeting room. I'm surprised the large case pin-board has been fixed—it's been broken for as long as I can remember. A photo of Roger is pinned at the top. Next to it are two sheets of paper with text reading *Missing corpse—female* and *Sonny Lake baby*. Several names and details are written underneath. As far as I can see, there is no timeline, no blueprint of the hospital, and no map of the lake or the streets surrounding Roger Kirk's house.

'I think you all know Gemma.' Everett hands out coffees and doesn't wait for a reply. 'As per my email this morning, she is going to follow up a few bits and pieces to help ease the load. We'll make sure we don't trip over each other.' He stands at the whiteboard. 'Right. Let's do a recap.'

'Should we wait for Jonesy?' I ask stiffly. I'm annoyed at him using my own words against me.

'He's sick today,' Everett says. 'Okay, starting with the Kirk homicide, please.'

I can't recall Jonesy taking a sick day for as long as I've known him, but he did seem a bit off yesterday, so he must have been coming down with something. Maybe that's why Lucy was being so protective last night: she's worried he's overdoing it.

'We've received the initial forensic report from the scene,' says Holdsworth. 'The only fingerprints detected belong to the family and the lawyer. Barnes's version of events checks out.'

'Any sign of the weapon?' I ask.

Holdsworth shakes her head.

'And no knives were missing from the kitchen?'

'Correct,' Everett interjects. 'We're assuming the weapon was brought to the house and that the killer took it with them.'

'After reviewing the scene, it's certainly my view that the attack was premeditated.'

'Glad we're keeping you happy, Woodstock,' Everett replies breezily, before he asks the group, 'Did the neighbours have anything useful to say?'

'Some of the houses in the street have security cameras,' I add. 'We should request the footage if we haven't already.'

'We're obviously pulling all of the CCTV,' Everett says. 'Minnie's managing that.'

At the back of the room, Minnie moistens her lips and nods.

'Has the CCTV from the hospital and the lake come through yet?' I ask, turning to her. Out of the corner of my eye, I see Everett throwing his hands in the air.

'Some has,' says Minnie, coming to the front of the room. 'We received this.' She pins a printout of a video frame to the board: a shot of the paramedics wheeling a stretcher into the emergency department. A dark-haired woman lies on the stretcher; her arms and legs are visible, but her face is obscured by Ash Amato's frame. 'There's less than thirty seconds of footage, and we'll struggle to get an ID from this. Unfortunately, there's not a clear view of her face.'

I nod. 'I'm going to speak to the paramedic about briefing a sketch artist, too. I think that's our best bet for an ID, unless we luck out with the DNA.'

'Great,' says Everett. 'But can we get back to Kirk, please?'

I understand that Kirk's murder is high profile, but I don't like the way he is deprioritising the missing woman. Someone ran her off the road and then went to the trouble of stealing her corpse and we need to find out why. I'm worried that other women might be in danger.

A uniform says, 'Some of the neighbours mentioned that Kirk's relationship with his wife was volatile.'

'One told me that Kirk was cheating on his wife,' I add.

'There's no evidence of that,' replies Everett, 'based on the initial review of his phone and email accounts.'

I'm annoyed he didn't mention this to me earlier. 'He might have been involved with someone at the hospital,' I suggest. 'That way there wouldn't necessarily be a paper trail. They might have communicated in person.'

'I don't think Roger Kirk was killed by a woman, Woodstock, so I'm not sure it's relevant.'

'Maybe he was involved with someone who was married and their spouse found out,' I counter. 'Or maybe Dominique paid someone to attack him when she discovered he was cheating. Or maybe he was cheating on her with a man.'

Everett sighs, and I'm aware that the tension between us is probably making everyone feel uncomfortable. 'Based on his various business dealings, it's more likely he screwed someone over. Apparently, Roger was big on promises but less big on keeping them.'

'What kind of promises?' I ask, trying to sound reasonable.

'He had several mates with manufacturing businesses—hospital equipment, medical devices, all high-end stuff often worth over a million bucks per unit. We've been hearing that Roger got them contracts at the hospital here and flogged a bunch of the equipment to other hospitals in the state via his network. But there have been issues with the performance of several of the units, and it turns out the insurance underwriting these entities wasn't vetted properly, which has led to the hospitals being significantly out of pocket. Roger's been conspicuously hands-off when questioned, and because most of these deals should have been competitive tenders from the get-go, the situation is problematic from a legal point of view. Bottom line is that he has pissed off a lot of powerful people.'

None of this is particularly surprising to me. Roger exuded a type of energy I've seen before in men addicted to doing deals, men who see every scenario as an opportunity and a competition to win or lose. Typically they're in finance or real estate, but it makes sense that these characteristics have infiltrated the increasingly competitive health industry.

'Plus,' Everett continues, 'he's heavily involved in raising capital for the research centre, and it seems he's put a few expensive noses out of joint on that front as well.'

'You think someone is angry enough over a botched business deal to kill him like that?'

'People have killed for a lot less. We're talking about multimillion-dollar deals.'

I tap my pen against my teeth. Despite my irritation at Everett, I'm enjoying the rush that comes with trying to fit all the pieces together. Maybe the woman was linked to one of the medical companies or had dirt on Roger. But even if that explains why she was run off the road, it doesn't explain why someone stole her body. I keep coming back to that. Why take her corpse? Does it have something to do with the abandoned baby?

I ask, 'Have the initial tox reports from the blood in the car come back yet? Do we know if the woman had drugs or alcohol in her system?'

'Turnaround times aren't great at the moment,' Everett tells me.

'Have you hassled them?'

'It's under control, Woodstock,' he snaps.

I refrain from saying anything further in front of the group, mindful that if he kicks up a real fuss Jonesy might reconsider our arrangement.

Everett continues, 'Carlyle Kirk, the victim's uncle, ID'd the body last night and the autopsy is scheduled for this morning.' He glances at his watch. 'Holdsworth will be present, and Woodstock will be attending, too.' His eyes flicker to me.

'And,' I say, 'I'm going to speak to Dominique Kirk later this afternoon, if she's up to it.'

I wonder why Dominique didn't ID her husband's body and mentally add that to the list of questions to ask her.

'Woodstock will speak to Dominique Kirk—again.' He makes it sound like a complete waste of time. 'I want to divide up Roger's business contacts, then speak to as many of them as possible today and tomorrow and confirm their alibis. Plus, I want a deep dive into all the standard stuff: bank accounts, emails, insurance policies, assets, property—his will. Let's serve up the lot and see what tastes good.'

Everyone seems comfortable with Everett's showy style, engaged even. I wonder how they would react to my more traditional approach.

'Did anyone follow up with the man who was running at the lake the night before the baby was found?'

A constable raises his hand. 'Yes, I did. The man confirmed someone almost ran into him near the car park but the person was wearing a hoodie and it was dark so there's nothing to go on apart from the individual being tall.'

'Thank you,' I say. 'Let's continue to review any footage from the area, okay? And ensure we ask other witnesses if they saw this individual. They might hold the clue to the identity of the infant.' Several constables nod.

Encouraged, I ask, 'And what about the security guard who alerted Sophie to the morgue door being open at the hospital? Lenny Tisdale?'

'We interviewed him on Sunday night, Gemma,' replies Everett, 'and his version of events matches Sophie's.'

'But did he—'

Everett interjects, 'Write down any other ideas you have on the board, and let's aim to meet back here at the end of the day, trade info and plan out tomorrow.' He writes *5 pm* on the whiteboard and draws a circle around it. 'I'll see your pretty faces then.' As everyone starts filing out of the room, he claps like a sports coach.

Frustrated but determined not to let Everett get to me, I home in on Minnie, who is writing madly in her notebook. 'Was there any CCTV footage of the morgue pick-up point?' I ask her. 'I saw a camera there.'

'It's broken,' Everett replies before she has a chance to answer. 'We're in the process of reviewing the vehicles that came in and out of the car park and the side street on Sunday evening. But someone could have accessed the morgue pick-up point direct from the road, so I'm not confident we'll find anything.'

'That's convenient,' I say.

'We're still waiting for some files to come through,' Minnie says uncertainly. 'From the wards and the lift areas.'

'Let me know when it's in, okay?'

'No problem.' She smiles at me, but then her gaze slides to Everett. Is she scared of him? Or is she simply unsure of the chain of command now I'm here?

'It has to be an inside job,' I say to them forcefully. 'Unless the person who ran her off the road was certain she would be taken to the hospital and planned to steal her body from there the whole time, which I think is highly unlikely, the only people who knew she was there and are familiar enough with the building layout are medical staff.'

'Or security staff,' says Everett, scanning his phone.

'Or ambulance staff,' I add, thinking about how cagey Ash was at Roger's house.

'I'll make sure they're all on the list,' says Minnie, taking notes.

'In terms of next steps on the baby,' I say, 'I was thinking we should pull all recent family violence claims involving pregnant women. And we need that bloody DNA report—we need to rule Roger out as a link.'

'You really think the baby could be his?' Minnie asks.

'If he got someone pregnant it would certainly provide a motive for his death.'

Everett clicks his tongue. 'Nothing stopping you from adding your ideas to the board, Woodstock.'

'Well, I do think we should put together a list of properties to search along the highway and outside town. Based on what we know there's a good chance our crash victim was kept somewhere and then escaped. There could be other women being held against their will.'

His jaw tenses. 'Roger Kirk's murder is the priority, Gemma. You've seen the size of the team. There's no way I can spare a dozen uniforms to randomly search properties on the off-chance a woman was being imprisoned. I'd rather focus on trying to determine her identity and go from there.'

'I get that it's a time suck, but the fact she was barefoot and pursued has convinced me that she was an escapee. If I'm right, maybe the person or people who imprisoned her felt like they owned her, and that's why they stole her corpse.'

'I'm not saying you're wrong but I need a bit more than a maybe to go on, Gemma.'

My nostrils flare with frustration, even though it's true that checking properties is a huge task and would take out most of the team for weeks. And all the evidence may have been cleaned up by now.

I puff out my cheeks and slowly expel the air. 'Do we have a timeline of all the events written up anywhere?'

'Sure do. Right there.' Everett points to the scant information along the bottom of the board. 'But if it's not up to your standard, feel free to get out your Sharpie.'

He exits the room, leaving me with Minnie.

'Is he always like that?' I ask.

'I guess so.' She flushes. 'Sorry, I've got another meeting now. See you later?'

'Sure,' I say as she rushes out.

From the doorway I watch my colleagues answer phones, collect papers from the printers and check files on computer screens. I'm not even sure where I should sit. After putting my satchel on an empty desk near reception, I fetch a glass of water from the kitchen. I hunt around for something to eat, but the fruit bowl is empty and the biscuits in the cupboard expired three months ago.

Rinsing my glass, I realise it's just past nine-thirty. We need to head to the morgue, so I gather my things. Through the window I see Everett and Holdsworth getting into one of the squad cars. I rush outside and reach the car just as Everett starts the engine. He winds down the front window, aviators shielding his eyes. 'Meet you there, Gemma.'

CHAPTER TWENTY

A fragrant cocktail of strawberry and sanitiser lingers in the morgue waiting room. Somehow I've beaten Everett here, and I wonder if he's gone a different way just to fuck with me. I used to come here regularly, especially when my friend Anna was the local medical examiner, but it's almost a year since my last visit. An attempt to redecorate gives the impression of lipstick on a pig. The orange cushions, freshly painted white walls and colourful fake flowers do little to distract from the tatty carpet and cracked windowsills. At least the former aesthetic was consistent.

A compact woman with dyed red hair bustles in from somewhere and plonks herself on the chair behind the reception bench. 'Dr Mattingly will be with you in a minute,' she says, without looking at me.

'Thanks. I'm waiting for my colleagues.'

'Mmm.' The receptionist tugs her impressive mane loose from its messy topknot and holds a red plastic clip between her teeth while she rearranges it. 'Want a coffee?' she asks around the hairclip. 'Going to make myself one, so it's no trouble.'

'I'm fine, thanks.'

She turns on the radio and disappears into another room. A talkback caller is complaining about receiving coathangers as a present from her sister-in-law.

I check for new emails but I don't have any. Normally when I'm working, I'm inundated with updates and requests, along with a seemingly infinite pile of paperwork. Not having these peripheral tasks is making me feel untethered and exposed. I'm relieved when the front door pushes open, and Holdsworth and Everett walk in.

He screws up his face childishly. 'God, this place stinks. Why do they make it smell like this?'

'Better than the alternative,' I say.

'Have you seen Mattingly yet?' he asks.

'Not yet.'

He swaggers to the front desk. 'Excuse me, hello?'

The woman returns, sipping from a mug. She lifts her head and eyeballs him.

'Can you let Mattingly know we're here?'

'Please.'

'I'm sorry?' says Everett.

'Can you let Dr Mattingly know we're here, please?' the woman says as if talking to a child. 'That's what you should say.'

I smile and notice Holdsworth trying to hide her own grin.

Everett has the decency to blush. 'Is Dr Mattingly here, please?' he mumbles.

'Yes, he is. Please wait here while I get him for you.' She beams at us and disappears into another room.

'Jesus Christ,' mutters Everett.

Moments later the door to the morgue swings open. 'Good morning!' Boyd Mattingly enters the waiting room in full scrubs, brown eyes sparkling. 'Lovely weather today. A shame we're stuck inside doing god's work.' He gestures for us to enter the morgue. 'After you.'

'Hey, Boyd,' I say, 'can I grab you for a minute?'

'Sure,' he says affably. 'You two go ahead and keep our friend company.' He holds out his hand like a tour guide.

Everett glares at me and stalks into the morgue, Holdsworth trotting behind.

'You're back on the payroll now, I assume?' Boyd says. 'That was quick.'

'I'm just helping out on this one.'

'Good. Like I said, they could use your help.'

'Thank you.' I hope my tone conveys how much I appreciate his vote of confidence.

'You wanted to chat about something?'

I nod. 'I didn't get the chance to ask you yesterday.'

'Crime scenes do have a habit of getting in the way of a good old-fashioned Q&A,' Boyd quips.

I laugh. 'Especially with me being a bit out of practice. It was just about the woman that went missing from the hospital—the corpse.'

'Sadly, we never met.'

'I know. I just wanted to know what the process is. You were alerted about her on Sunday night . . . ?'

'Actually, I wasn't rostered on this weekend: Claire was. Claire Messenger is the new assistant ME. Marvellous woman! She started just after you went on leave. You'll love her.'

'So Claire got the call about the body on Sunday?'

'Yes. But I'd already heard about the accident from a friend. We were having dinner at that lovely new place, Finch, on Rawson Street near the old bakery. Have you been?'

I shake my head.

'You must! It's very good and quite reasonably priced, too—Asian, but not with all that awful sauce that's usually loaded onto everything. Anyway, my friend got a call from his brother, who'd driven past the crash on his way home, and I had a feeling someone would be turning up on my table. I get a spidey sense about these things sometimes.'

'But would you have done the autopsy on Monday morning?'

'Not unless Claire called me to assist. I wasn't scheduled to work again until yesterday.' He sneaks a glance at his watch. Morgues run on a tighter schedule than most airlines.

'Have you ever had an issue with collecting corpses from Smithson Hospital?'

'No issues.'

'Body parts haven't gone missing, or corpses, for that matter . . . ?'

Tilting his head, he asks, 'Are you thinking this isn't a one-off?'

'I've heard of people selling organs on the black market or even using them for scientific purposes, so I'm exploring possibilities.'

'A few years ago, there was a morgue assistant in Sydney who helped himself to body parts and sold them online, but I haven't come across anything suspicious here. It's all very low-key, and everyone knows everyone.' He checks the time again. 'We should join your friends and make sure they aren't getting started without us.'

I nod.

'I have to say, I felt a little guilty when I heard what had happened. I mean, it's standard for us to leave a corpse at the hospital overnight, but if Claire had collected her that evening, we'd have a chance of working out who she was.'

'Maybe,' I say noncommittally. I know better than to play the what-if game.

He asks the receptionist to hold his calls, then we enter the morgue. On the far side of the room, a white sheet is draped over a body on a metal table. There are several bare tables in a row down the centre, and on our left is a wall lined with drawers. Every surface gleams—with the exception of the glass jars containing human organs on a shelf near the sink, the room could moonlight as an industrial kitchen.

Everett and Holdsworth watch me pull on scrubs and put on a hairnet, then we form a little huddle as Boyd gives us a quick preamble. His style is inclusive—I get the sense it's for his benefit as much as ours. He likes to narrate his autopsies, and we are being treated to the prologue.

He steps his legs apart in a sporty stance and looks at each of us in turn. 'Now, even though I saw the body at the scene, I have no preconceived notions. Today I'm on a fact-finding mission to work out how and why this person has found themselves on my table. I consider likely possibilities as I go, but my mind is open. Cause of death is the key question to answer, of course, but there might be other revelations, too. He might be able to tell me what was going on in his life, in his head and within his body before he died. With any luck we'll discover all sorts of things.' Boyd sanitises his hands and pulls on some surgical gloves. 'Polly!' he calls over his shoulder. 'We're about to start.'

A young woman enters the room. Her cheeks and nose are dotted with a constellation of freckles, and her wavy blonde hair is pulled back and captured in a net. Blue eyeliner makes her hazel eyes glow. She nods politely. 'Hi, I'm Polly. Nice to meet you all.'

'Pol's the best in the business,' adds Boyd.

She grins as she places several tools on a tray and hands it to him. 'I'm learning from the best. Does anyone want a seat?'

We shake our heads.

Boyd hooks on a face mask and strides over to the table. Removing the sheet with a flick of his wrists, he reveals Roger's body. Its nakedness is jarring, and the deep wounds on the chest and torso are shocking against translucent skin. That blank stare makes me shudder. I've seen enough bodies to know we're all more similar than different in the end, and I've witnessed dozens of autopsies over the years, but the recency of seeing Roger in full flight is making his decline particularly shocking. Although I didn't know him well—and I suspect I wouldn't have liked him much—I feel sad at the waste of a life cut short.

Boyd begins the examination, murmuring observations to Polly, who studiously takes notes.

'How many stab wounds?' I ask.

'Half a dozen—and all of them penetrated the skin. There are no misses. This could indicate he knew his attacker, who was close when he was caught off guard. Or it could suggest the killer easily overpowered him. There's some bruising on his upper right arm, perhaps caused by someone grabbing him with their left hand while stabbing him with their right. The wounds indicate a solo right-handed assailant.'

'Hardly narrows things down.' Everett holds up his right hand.

'It's narrowed down to less than fifty per cent of the population, though,' I say.

He looks confused.

'The killer is unlikely to be a woman, even if they caught Kirk off guard.'

'I've already said I never thought it was a woman,' Everett says dismissively.

'We know Kirk was having marriage troubles,' I press, 'and there's a chance he was having an affair, so there might be an angry woman or two out there. But, based on the physical evidence, maybe we're looking for an angry husband.'

'I actually can't rule out a woman, but it was definitely someone quite tall,' Boyd says, examining the wound at the top of Kirk's chest. 'The weapon used was incredibly sharp, which might have compensated for physical strength, but the position of the wounds indicates the assailant was taller than the victim. See how all the cuts are above the bottom of the rib cage?'

'Are we sure we can rule out Jack Barnes?' I ask Everett. 'He's tall, and he had access and possible motive if they were working together.'

'His story checks out,' says Everett. 'And he has an alibi for earlier in the morning—several people saw him walking his dog. When you factor in the cafe visit, his movements are accounted for.'

I refrain from reacting to his patronising tone.

'What's your estimated time of death?' I ask Boyd.

'Based on his temp and the condition of the body at the scene, we're talking anywhere between six-thirty am and eight-thirty am. Once I examine the stomach contents, I'll be able to be more precise, but the cereal bowl suggests he was killed in the hour or two before he was discovered.'

'Do we know what Barnes was doing the night before?' I ask Everett and Holdsworth. 'Perhaps he argued with Kirk and arranged for someone to attack him. Him discovering the body might be part of his alibi.'

'The team are interviewing him again this morning,' says Holdsworth, 'so I'll make sure they check that.'

'Thanks. And can we confirm Roger Kirk was currently Barnes's client, and that he didn't owe him any money? We need to explore every aspect of their relationship, especially because he was trusted enough to have keys to Roger's house.'

'His teeth are in good nick,' says Boyd, his gloved fingers probing Roger's mouth. 'Consistent with being wealthy.'

Everett ignores Boyd's attempt at humour. 'We haven't got all Barnes's account info yet, but rest assured it will be covered off, Woodstock.'

'I know you checked his communication records,' I say, 'but I still think we should be digging into a possible affair. Kirk was probably used to getting whatever he wanted. Maybe he didn't want to wait to be single before he had some fun—his credit cards might provide clues. Or the affair might have ended badly, and he was paying someone off. We could ask Barnes about it. Perhaps it's the kind of thing Roger shared with a friend.'

Everett is sceptical. 'Pretty risky, someone like Kirk having a secret relationship around here. Smithson's not that big.'

I raise my eyebrows at his naivety. I know firsthand how the risk of being caught having a clandestine affair is often no match for the pull of desire. 'Hasn't stopped anyone before.'

Holdsworth pipes up. 'My neighbour is sleeping with my friend, and they don't think I know. Sometimes I see her leaving his house really early in the morning.'

We all laugh, except for Everett.

'There might be some DNA coming your way,' Boyd says, examining Roger's hands.

I remember something. 'Yesterday you mentioned his finger is damaged.'

'It is, but it's not from a knife wound. He might have tried to punch his attacker or been warding off a blow. So there might be some goodies for us under his nails.'

'How long will that take?' I ask.

'At least a few days, I'm afraid. You'd think Smithson was New York City, the way the lab carries on. Full tox reports are taking roughly seven weeks at the moment.'

I clench my jaw, even though I knew it was unlikely to be any quicker. I'm desperate to narrow things down—it all feels far too loose for my liking.

'Commencing act two, team,' says Boyd as he slices Roger's body from chest to groin, exposing his insides.

This is the moment, for me, when the dead transition into an inanimate object, their body becoming an artefact. My empathy for the loss of life is still high, but to do my job effectively I need to separate their humanness from the investigation. Emotion blurs clues and complicates theories. I need to do what the loved ones can't.

Boyd busies himself removing Roger's organs so he and Polly can measure and weigh them. I fade in and out of his narrative as I focus on forming a mental list of all the things that need to be followed up, trying to arrange them in priority order. Contrary to what the general public might think, there's no handbook for a murder investigation. There's process and precedence, and the practical realities of access and the law, but the structure of an investigation is ultimately down to the lead detective. There's a surprising amount of autonomy—on the downside, if things are missed, they are missed forever. We're all chasing the legendary breakthroughs and love hearing about the gut feeling that nailed a bad guy, but it's the grunt work that tends to pay off.

'I can confirm he died very quickly,' Boyd says, 'within five minutes of the first wound being inflicted.'

Everett's phone lights up, and he excuses himself, the door swinging shut behind him with a metallic click.

I ask, 'Can you tell us anything else about the knife?'

Boyd's eyes meet mine. 'Well, as I said, it was extremely sharp. There was zero resistance in any of these lacerations. I've seen similar on other vics, and that was from chef-grade knives. I've got a contact

I could send some photos to for an opinion. She's good with knife wounds.'

'Yes, please.'

Polly makes a note.

Everett returns, his face alert with news. He gestures to Holdsworth to go to him, then tells her quietly, 'We need to leave.'

'What's happened?' I ask, joining them in the corner.

'Dominique Kirk's at the station, demanding to speak to me. She wants to make a confession.'

CHAPTER TWENTY-ONE

'Dominique Kirk wants to confess to her husband's murder?' I'm trying to understand.

'I assume so,' says Everett. 'Not sure what else she'd be confessing to.'

My hands curl into fists. 'You didn't ask?'

'Apparently she's extremely emotional. It's just Minnie there with her, so I said to sit tight and try to keep her calm.'

'Why is Minnie at the station alone?'

'A few of the boys were called out to a workplace accident, and everyone else is working these cases. It's not like we're raining resources right now.' He jerks his head at me. 'Hence this arrangement.'

'What's that supposed to mean?'

'Desperate times.'

Above his mask, Boyd's eyes dart back and forth between me and Everett. He must be loving this insight into police politics.

'Let's all go,' I say firmly.

'I've got this, Woodstock,' Everett replies just as firmly. 'You should stay.'

Ignoring him, I thank Boyd and Polly. 'Please call us straight away if you turn up anything interesting.'

'Of course,' says Boyd. 'The draft report should be with you later today. I'll see if I can put a rush on the initial tox and DNA, too, although sometimes it's worse if you hassle—you know what it's like.'

'Thank you,' I say. 'Let's talk outside,' I mutter to Everett as I walk past.

'I'm being summoned,' he says loudly. 'And yes, *thanks* everyone, I appreciate this has been more challenging than usual.'

I stalk past the receptionist and am in my car with the engine revving when Everett and Holdsworth emerge. Winding the window down, I call out to him, 'Meet you there.'

He blocks the glare of the sun with his hand. 'Honestly, Woodstock, it makes no sense for us to double up on every task.'

I throw the car into reverse, clutching the gearstick so hard my knuckles turn white. 'I couldn't agree more. Maybe you should find something else to do.'

When I arrive, the front desk at the station is unmanned. Jonesy always says that a well-lit, organised front desk with a friendly face is critical; he thinks it's important that people are greeted calmly the moment they step into a police station. Whether it's his influence or not, I agree—and I feel irrationally irritated that no one's there now.

I knock loudly on the door to the main office, and a few seconds later I hear footsteps on the other side. Minnie's relief when she sees me is palpable.

'Hey, are you okay?' I say, careful not to take my frustration out on her.

She bites her lip. 'Is it just you?'

'Everett's on his way with Holdsworth.'

Minnie lets out a ragged breath. 'She's in the front room . . . Roger Kirk's wife. I figured that would be okay. I made her a tea. She wants to speak with Everett.'

'No worries.' I remind myself that witnesses and loved ones often feel a connection to a particular detective. 'He should only be a few minutes.'

'I tried to calm her down, but she's still very upset.'

I put a hand on Minnie's arm and look her in the eyes. In our previous interactions she has always been cool and calm, but now she seems flustered and unsure of herself. 'As soon as Everett arrives, we'll start the formal interview. I'll get her set up, then you can send him in, okay?'

She inhales deeply and forcibly relaxes. 'Okay, sure.'

'Thanks, Minnie. Have you told Jonesy about this?'

'No. Was I supposed to?'

I cock my head at her change in demeanour. 'I just thought you might contact him, seeing as there was no one else here.'

'He's unwell today and I called Everett,' Minnie says stiffly. 'He's my line manager.'

'It doesn't matter,' I say with a reassuring smile. 'I'm a bit rusty on how it all works these days.'

Leaving her at the desk, I head into the front meeting room. Dominique is standing in the corner, wringing her hands. Her wrists and fingers are painfully thin, so much so that I wonder if she suffers from disordered eating. Her diamond ring is like a boulder on her left hand.

'Dominique,' I say gently. 'Hello.'

She spins around. Her manicured eyebrows move toward each other above her sharp nose, causing faint lines to crease her pale forehead. 'Who are you?'

'A detective—my name is Gemma Woodstock.'

'I didn't meet you yesterday,' she replies robotically. 'At the house.'

Everett enters and closes the door behind him. 'No, but we met.' He flashes a smile at her. 'You did so well yesterday, Dominique. I know it was hard, but speaking to you was really helpful. I'll just get this set up, then we can talk some more.' He removes the recording equipment from a table in the corner and casually arranges it in front of Dominique. 'Here we go, I'll just plug this in . . . Yep, just like this.' Her eyes are glued to his hands. 'This little switch is a bit sensitive, so let's just all sit down. And then when we're ready, I'll hit record, so we don't miss anything. Sound like a plan?'

She nods. She appears mesmerised by him.

'I see you've got a tea there,' he says, indicating the mug clutched between her hands. 'Need anything else? Coffee? A cigarette? I can't offer you anything stronger, unfortunately.' I have to give him credit: his tone is pitch perfect, professional but warm.

A ghost of a smile plays over her features. 'This is fine, thanks.' Her voice is barely a whisper.

I pull my chair close to the table and rest my forearms on it. 'I'm very sorry about your husband's death. It must be an awful shock.'

She turns to me, her eyes brimming with tears. 'Yes,' she murmurs. 'I can't believe it.'

If she's shocked by Roger's death, then surely she can't have been responsible for it. And if she's not confessing to that, then what is this visit about?

I can't tell what Everett's thinking. Is he as confused about Dominique turning up here as I am? We're far from a point where we can anticipate each other's actions.

'Let's get started.' He clicks on the recording. 'Are you happy for us to record you, Mrs Kirk?'

'Yes, I know you need to.'

'We do if you want to make an official statement.'

A pulse throbs in her jaw as she swallows. 'Yes, that's what I want. I need to.'

'Detective Woodstock, the honours please,' Everett says.

Without missing a beat, I state our names, the date and our location, surprised at the steadiness of my voice. Before Everett has a chance to say anything, I lean forward and ask, 'Why are you here today, Mrs Kirk?'

She closes her eyes. 'We've been having some issues, Rog and I. Suddenly we couldn't seem to agree on anything. I know he was worried about his work—and there was pressure about the new centre, I do know that—but when I tried to speak with him, he shut me out.' Her voice is high-pitched and breathy, like that of an actress from an old Hollywood film. 'He shut me out of everything. I didn't know what was going on with his job or our money. I was angry. I was, but I still cared about him. He's the father of my children.'

'Of course,' I say.

As Dominique starts to cry, her eyes won't focus, and her hands shake. She reminds me of a vulnerable baby bird.

Everett's expression is sympathetic, but he doesn't say anything. I sense he wants me to play bad cop.

'How bad did things get between you?' I ask.

'It got bad, but it was never violent, if that's what you mean.'

'We just want to hear it in your words,' I say neutrally.

'Roger would never do anything to hurt me or the kids. I yelled at him sometimes, and he got annoyed with me, but it was because we couldn't get in sync. He was out much of the time, and when he was at home he was working. I felt neglected.'

'Sometimes the most acute loneliness can be when you're in a crowded room,' says Everett gently.

She fumbles for a tissue and dabs at her eyes. 'Yes, exactly,' she whispers.

I clear my throat impatiently. 'I understand it's very distressing, Mrs Kirk, but we need to find out who killed your husband. Do you have information that can help us?'

Her jaw wobbles. 'Yes, I do,' she murmurs.

'You said you had something to confess,' I urge.

She pushes her hair from her face, bunching it at the nape of her neck. I'm finding it hard to imagine her fragile energy coexisting with Roger's brash arrogance. 'I've done something very stupid.' She drops her head in her hands. 'I'm involved with someone.'

'Romantically?' I clarify.

'Yes.' She's chewing on a nail. 'I know it's wrong—and I'm sorry.' She doesn't direct this last comment to me, but rather to the ceiling as if her dead husband is there.

'When did the relationship begin?' I'm careful to keep my voice devoid of judgement.

'In January.'

'How did you meet?'

'Online. But it wasn't through one of those dating apps.'

My mind goes to some kind of scam: someone coaxing Dominique to provide her bank details or tricking her into donating to a cause or a person she believes is worthy. We come across it all the time.

'I'm confused,' Everett says. 'Was it through Facebook?'

'I'm an art dealer,' she says hollowly. 'I commission pieces and projects for a select group of buyers, and I manage a gallery in Sydney. I curate shows.'

I recall the artworks in the Kirk household and wonder if Dominique chose them. They seem incongruent with her bohemian style.

'Roger collected art, but we had very different tastes,' she continues, as if reading my mind. 'That's how we met—he was buying art when I was first dealing, and our paths crossed. I helped him out with a few pieces.'

Everett leans back in his chair. 'And is that also how you met the person you're involved with now, through the art world?'

'He contacted me about a painting, a beautiful piece, one I'd commissioned from an artist I've worked with for years. He loved it, too, and we formed a bond.'

'A bond,' repeats Everett. I sense he's starting to regret not letting me do this interview on my own.

'Did he purchase art from you?' I want to ask whether she has been cheated out of any money, but I'm mindful of not making her feel foolish. I've dealt with the victims of con artists before—it's a soul-destroying experience, and Dominique has already had a significant shock in the past twenty-four hours.

'No, it was never about business,' she replies earnestly. 'We both just love art. We've sent hundreds of emails back and forth.' Her face crumples. 'It felt like a holiday from my normal life. I became addicted to checking my messages . . . like a giddy teenager.' She seems horrified at the words coming out of her mouth.

'What's his name?' I ask.

'Dylan. Dylan Roberts.'

'Did your husband know about your affair?' Everett asks.

Colour floods her cheeks. 'It wasn't an affair,' she says sharply.

'How would you define it?' I ask.

'It was a romance. A connection.' Her chin trembles. 'An affair sounds so crass, and it wasn't at all. There was nothing sordid about it.'

My impatience is building. 'Mrs Kirk, who you choose to have a sexual relationship with is of no interest to us—unless you think it is linked to your husband's murder.'

She draws herself upright. 'I wasn't *sleeping* with Dylan.'

'You . . . didn't have sex?' I say, confused.

'No.' She's shaking her head vigorously. 'No, we never met.'

'You never *met*?' A deep line appears between Everett's eyebrows.

'It was just emails?' I'm certain now that this person is not who Dominique thinks they are—and that she has been comprehensively catfished.

'Yes, but we emailed several times a day. And we sent photos.' She grips the table, desperately holding on to her fantasy. 'We made plans to be together. I was going to leave Rog, and Dylan was going to leave his wife. But we needed to be careful, so careful.'

Everett slaps his hands on the table, making Dominique jump. 'Mrs Kirk, this is getting a little tedious. We appreciate you telling us about this relationship, but unless you have information about your husband's murder, we need to wrap this up so we can get on with our investigation.'

'That's what I'm trying to tell you! She was so jealous.'

'Who was?' Everett asks.

'Dylan's wife! She found out about us and lost her mind.' Dominique begins to weep. 'She killed my husband, and it's all my fault.'

CHAPTER TWENTY-TWO

'An affair of the mind.' Candy flicks a lighter on and off, sporadically illuminating her pretty face. 'Honestly, what's the point?' She directs the flame toward the citronella candle and waits for it to catch.

'Bring that over here,' I tell her, 'before I get eaten alive again.'

She places the candle on the table in front of me and grabs a handful of corn chips before plonking herself down on the nearby loveseat, stretching out her bare legs. Insects are never interested in Candy, whereas I already have four sizeable welts on my arms and ankles. I sit back against the cushion on my wooden deck chair, feeling the specific kind of exhaustion that comes from a long day of work.

For a moment we just munch on chips, watching the sun sink into the trees. Lola is playing contentedly on the playmat in the house, and Scarlett is asleep in her bouncer. Ben is at Jodie's so he can spend time with his other half-sister, Ruby, and Mac is in his study working.

He was on the phone when I got home, pausing long enough to mouth a hello, then point to the lasagna baking in the oven and the salad on the bench. I kissed his cheek and leaned in for a hug, close enough to feel his heartbeat and hear a female voice on the other end of the phone. He waved me away, giving me an apologetic look, but I sensed his annoyance. As I left the room, he laughed in a familiar way, and I could hear his low murmurs as I padded back down the hall. I'm used to Mac being absorbed in a case, but something about the way he's behaving still feels different. Perhaps he's been offered a job in Sydney and doesn't want to tell me out of guilt.

Candy asks me something before she pushes another handful of chips into her mouth.

'Sorry, what was that?'

She struggles to keep the chips in her mouth. 'Gemma, geez, I hope you were sharper than this at work today or they'll have you doing the traffic rounds. I asked if Dominique really never met this guy.'

'I'm just tired,' I murmur. 'And no—apparently Dominique and this man emailed each other several times a day since the start of the year but never met. She says she wasn't ever willing to physically cheat on her husband, and he was reluctant to cheat on his wife.'

'Bullshit,' Candy says cheerfully.

'It seems odd she would confess to the relationship and then lie.'

Candy eats more chips as she shakes her head. 'I do *not* see the point of going to all that effort for a penpal. I hope the messages are X-rated at least.'

'I haven't gone through them all yet, but they're fairly PG. Lots of talk about art and life, and lots of fantasy planning a future together. There's a bit of innuendo, but I don't think you'd approve of the lack of smut.'

She seems mystified. 'If I was going to cheat, I'd be minimising the emails and maximising the sex.'

Although I laugh along with her, there's a heaviness in my chest. Mac and I used to email each other when we first met, our wit bouncing back and forth until it became unbearable—or at least it did for me. Checking to see if he'd written became an addiction. The intensity has naturally subsided, but Mac still occupies the main stage of my desire. He is both my anchor and my north star—or he was until he started to feel so distant.

'I think she was lonely,' I say. 'Being married to Roger doesn't sound easy.'

'Lonely and rich as fuck,' Candy says glumly and pours herself more wine. 'I hate this type of money-doesn't-buy-happiness story. What is someone like me supposed to aspire to?'

'Moderate wealth and contentment?'

She laughs again. 'Sounds bloody awful.'

Behind the flywire door, Lola trips over a plastic toy and starts to wail.

'It's okay, overtired lady.' Candy goes inside and picks her up. The tears stop instantly.

'We'll eat soon,' I say. 'Want to stay for dinner?'

'Nah. Philip's coming over and bringing dinner, so we need to get going. I'm all set for a dull but pleasant night.'

'He's a good cook,' I say, trying to be positive.

'He does know his way around a kitchen. Shame about his other capabilities.' She shakes her hips suggestively and I laugh.

'You seem to be getting along well, though,' I venture.

Candy smiles angelically. 'No point rocking that boat. I can tolerate a weekly meal in exchange for relatively frictionless co-parenting arrangements.'

'Does he still want equal custody?'

'Probably. But he's also aware it doesn't make sense.'

Candy's ex is the head chef at a restaurant in Gowran, working six nights a week. Ever since they split, Philip has maintained he wants more time with Lola than in the arrangement Candy enforced—but she has shut him down, citing his impractical work hours while failing to acknowledge her own unorthodox schedule. The ongoing battle is mainly fought in private because Candy has made it clear that going up against her in court is something Philip would live to regret.

I like him, but he's no match for Candy. Their power imbalance was so overt that, in the end, I think she saw him as an employee not a life partner. He expressed some issues with the conditions of their relationship, and she swiftly dismissed him. A few days later she rented a one-bedroom studio and took the opportunity to buy a new couch, a bed and a TV. 'Our kid is a legend, but we were a bad match' is her overall summation of their short-lived union—along with her assessment that Philip is boring. 'That's the main reason I don't want Lola spending too much time with him,' she said to me once. 'It won't be good for her personality.'

The cynical among us might wonder if she used him to have a child. Mac says that is absolutely what happened.

Candy asks me, 'You don't really think this guy's wife had anything to do with Kirk's murder, do you?'

'I doubt it.' I picture Roger's blood-soaked body. 'Based on the forensics it seems unlikely, but we'll obviously investigate it, especially if she really has made threats.'

'Maybe it was actually Dominique's Romeo who wanted Kirk dead, and she just doesn't want to consider she was exchanging love letters with a psycho.'

'That seems more likely,' I agree, 'although Dominique was adamant. But I think it's even more likely that the person who killed

Kirk had nothing to do with his wife. As Everett keeps reminding me, Roger Kirk pissed off a lot of people.' I don't tell Candy about my other train of thought: that Dominque was being catfished.

'What was his name again?' Candy says innocently. 'The online lover?'

'Nice try,' I say, standing up to see her off. 'You're lucky I even told you about this. It's all off the record, remember. I mean it.'

She hoists a huge bag onto her shoulder and adjusts Lola on her hip. 'Gemma, you kill me.'

'I'm sorry to be such a disappointment,' I reply with mock seriousness.

She snorts. 'You are one of the only things in my life that is not disappointing.' Then she pauses, softening. 'It must feel good to be back in the thick of things.'

'Yes,' I admit. 'Of course, I was a little rusty.'

'Jonesy must have loved it.'

'He was sick today. I spent most of the time with Everett.'

'Lucky you.'

I think about Everett's odd little power play on the way back from the cafe this morning, then the unexpectedly comfortable rhythm we found ourselves in after Dominique's interview. 'I can handle Everett. He's manageable.'

'As long as he's not your boss.'

'It's my first official day back. Give me a second.'

'Sure! I'll give you a day to catch your breath before you take over the world.'

'So generous.'

Grinning at me, she puts Lola down and shepherds her to the front door. 'I hope you enjoy a perfect domestic evening after your hard day of purposeful employment.'

'I'll try.'

She calls out goodbye to Mac as she leaves.

'Bye, Candy!' he calls back.

Scarlett is still asleep in her bouncer, and aside from the soft whir of the oven, the house is quiet. Sipping my wine, I move from room to room, closing the blinds and thinking about Mac. I'm reassured by my theory that his behaviour has something to do with him feeling torn about work. We're both torn, I realise, and that's fine, expected even, but clearly we need to find time to talk properly and make some decisions about the next stage of our life together. Anxiousness rolls through me. My gut says that Ben needs to stay here in Smithson, but I'm not sure it's the right place for Mac, while Jonesy retiring complicates things for me: does it make my local career prospects better or worse?

My phone sounds with a text from Minnie.

Initial tox results are in from the crash. The woman was not recently pregnant. Everett said I could let you know straight away.

I text a thank you back and return to the kitchen, the smell of the lasagna making my mouth water. I check on Scarlett, who is stirring but content. Topping up my wine, I consider Minnie's text. While it's possible the woman was involved in an adoption or surrogacy arrangement, the tox results mean a link is unlikely. My disappointment about that is vastly outweighed by my relief that the infant's condition is stable. Earlier today, paperwork was filed for her to be placed into temporary foster care next week unless someone claims her. We owe it to her and anyone who loves her to work out what led to her abandonment at Sonny Lake. I'm still hopeful of a reunion.

I set the table on autopilot, weighing up different scenarios again. I know what it's like to struggle with an infant and can empathise with not being able to cope; I can even understand feeling like the best thing for my baby would be to get it away from me. But why leave the baby in that unsafe place?

I lift the steaming meal onto the hotplate and slice the lasagna with the spatula. It smells incredible, and I need to eat—my thoughts are becoming wilder. I keep returning to the fact that no one has reported a missing baby. Babies are occasionally kept secret, but unless her mother was living completely off-grid, someone must know she is gone.

Even though it's after seven, Mac is still in his study. Feeling something akin to nerves, I make my way down the hall and nudge open the door with my foot, revealing the dim room. 'Hey, I'm about to eat your amazing dinner now. Do you want to join me?'

His head jerks up, and I can see him transitioning from whatever world he was lost in to this one. 'Yes, of course. Sorry, I lost track of time.'

'It's fine,' I say, not wanting him to apologise because it suggests I'm annoyed. 'Is everything going well?'

He looks down at the desk, the computer screen and sprawl of papers as if he's not sure where they all came from. 'Pretty well,' he says.

Our jobs aren't like other people's: a good day can mean a horrible revelation or a gruesome find. Unfortunately some of my best days at work have been someone else's worst. 'Come on,' I say. 'Let's eat.'

Scarlett cries out when she sees us, and I settle her in the highchair. Mac feeds her yoghurt as I place a plate of lasagna in front of him and spoon some salad onto the side. He laughs at Scarlett's eagerness and smiles at me.

'This is amazing,' I say. 'Thank you for cooking.'

'You are very welcome.' Every time I try to meet his gaze, he fusses at Scarlett.

'Is everything okay?' I ask.

'Of course. Isn't it?'

'I just wanted to make sure we're good.'

He laces his fingers through mine. 'We're good. I'm excited for you, being back at work.'

'I'd be more excited if we were making more progress.'

'You will.'

The food is delicious, and it feels nice, just the two of us eating a meal together. Despite my doubts, satisfaction rushes through me.

'How's your dad?' Mac asks.

'Better. He'll probably go home tomorrow.'

'I bet Rebecca is relieved.'

'Very.'

'She's stronger than you give her credit for,' Mac says.

'Rebecca? I guess so.' I'm not entirely sure what he means. 'Strong' is not a word I associate with Rebecca, it's true, and maybe that's not fair. She has embraced life with my dad in a way that makes me wonder what she would have done if they'd never met. But perhaps the same could be said about me and Mac.

'Does your dad ever talk about your mum?'

I blink. 'Huh?'

'Your mum . . . I just wondered if your dad ever talks about her.' He busies himself extracting a plastic spoon from Scarlett's firm grip.

'Oh.' A funny sensation drapes itself over me. 'No, not lately. We've never talked about her much.'

'Really? When my mum died, Dad talked about her a lot. He was always telling me stories from when I was a kid.'

I try to remember. 'I think it just made Dad too upset.' I push my plate away, remembering how confused and angry I felt during this time. How hard I found navigating my grief alongside Dad's immense sorrow. His love for her was so strong that my sadness almost felt unworthy in comparison. 'Why the impromptu interview about my parents?'

'I'm just curious. When your dad was sick the other night, it made me think about how little I know about your childhood.' He taps Scarlett gently on the nose. 'It's fine if you don't want to talk about it.'

I take a deep breath, irrationally annoyed. 'I don't mind. I just don't know that much. Mum was always a bit of an enigma.'

Mac pushes his plate away, too. 'How do you mean?'

I'm already regretting saying that. 'I didn't mean that . . . She just wasn't very maternal.' I shake my head. 'It's hard to remember.'

'And she died when you were, what, thirteen?'

'Fourteen.' I pick at my salad, then struggle with a piece of cucumber that has gone down the wrong way.

'That must have been so tough, Gem.'

'Lots of kids have it tough. Think about Ben.' I'm dangerously close to tears.

'I suppose you—' His phone vibrates on the table; he snatches it up and swipes to answer. 'Mac speaking.' He listens for a beat, then says, 'Yes, yes. Give me a minute.' He whispers to me, 'Sorry, got to get this.' He's already on his feet and heading to the hallway. I hear the soft thud of the study door closing.

Scarlett shrieks and throws her sippy cup onto the floor. I look at the abandoned meal, at Mac's half-finished wine, and have the urge to do the same.

CHAPTER TWENTY-THREE

The morning sun hits the tin roof of the police station, the glare slicing white through my vision. I'm determined to spend at least an hour working before the day gets away from me. I left Mac in the kitchen with Scarlett, her face smeared with porridge as she sat in her highchair, kicking her bare legs and laughing exuberantly as he pretended to hide behind the bench. I have no idea how he's going to get anything done today. Ben was fast asleep, his body taking up a surprising amount of the single bed. Jodie dropped him home around nine pm, and he wasn't in much of a mood to talk. Being at her place stirs up memories of Scott, so I didn't push him, but I wish there was a way of peering inside his head and making sure he really is okay.

I nod hello to the constable on the front desk, a young man with freckles and a moustache, and use my new pass to scan through to the main office area. Bulky computer monitors sit opposite each other on the parallel rows of desks like diners with nothing to say. Notebooks, mugs and pens are scattered across the surfaces, and

a sad-looking plant in a bright blue pot is positioned precariously
on the desk closest to the window.

I pick up a pencil from the floor and place it on the corner of
my old desk, remembering when I was a cadet. I was so intimidated
coming here. The office seemed alive with the business of policing,
and everywhere I turned there was something I didn't understand:
a process, a rule, an in-joke. Everyone spoke a language that I was only
just beginning to grasp, and I constantly felt a step behind, desperately trying to keep up while not knowing how to get everything to
make sense. But after those first few weeks, the days fell into a natural
rhythm, and I started to mentally file and log information with an
ease that drifted into boredom as my mind was drawn to the more
complicated cases. I was often quicker than my peers, anticipating
what was needed and suggesting what should be done next.

Jonesy's support was unwavering. He wasn't demonstrative, but he
sought out my opinion in briefings and listened to my perspective.
He silenced the doubters and rebuked the outright bullies. Under
his watch my confidence bloomed, and I not only found my feet
but started to lead the way as well.

And now here I am again: older, wiser and undoubtedly more
cynical, but with the same hunger to solve cases and right wrongs.

I take advantage of the quiet office and get to work, mapping out
a detailed timeline of events along the spare wall in the case room.
The sequence of information is often the key to ruling suspects in
or out based on who knew what and when.

I'm halfway through Monday's points when I smell Everett,
a woody cologne that doesn't fit with the musty aroma of the office.
He stands in the doorway in an expensive suit, and not for the first
time I wonder what led him to leave Melbourne and take a role in
Smithson. It's rare that a senior detective relocates to a small town

mid-career. Smithson has become more of a drawcard in recent years, but in my experience, city cops only give up their plum metro roles when a problematic personality is being off-loaded or—like in my situation—when someone wants a fresh start due to personal reasons. Much of Everett's origin story is a mystery to me, so maybe I should make more of an effort to find out what brought him here.

'Good morning,' I say neutrally.

He scans my timeline-in-progress but doesn't say anything.

'Minnie updated me on the missing woman's initial tox report.'

'I know you were hoping for a pregnancy result, Woodstock,' he says with a hint of smugness, 'but it seems we're dealing with separate incidents after all.'

'We still need to see if the baby is linked to Roger Kirk. And I still think the car crash and missing corpse might be related, even if the woman wasn't the birth mother—we can't ignore the proximity of the events.'

He just turns and walks off. So rude.

I finish my timeline, then return to my desk. Chatter rises and falls across the office as more people arrive. I read through the incident report from the car crash. It's assumed the woman died from internal bleeding or head trauma due to the amount of blood in the car, and the comments provided by the medical team and the ambos back this theory up. The ambos' statements suggest that she most likely hit her head on the steering wheel, and that she endured chest trauma as well. They claimed that her seatbelt was undone but looped around her arm when they shifted her out of the car; the report concludes she must have been wearing it when she crashed, or she would have been killed on impact. I wonder what was going through her mind as she battled unbearable pain and the shock of the collision, undoing the seatbelt to free herself, summoning the last of her strength to survive.

The pictures show a crumpled station wagon, its bonnet wedged into an ancient gum. There's a modest spray of blood on the windscreen and the dashboard, and smears on the driver's seat and the carpeted floor, likely from a nosebleed. Considering the age of the car and the speed it left the road, it's a miracle the whole thing didn't go up in flames.

I move on to Bob Dalgliesh's witness statement, but there's nothing in it I don't already know.

The map shows the crash scene is about six kilometres from the centre of Smithson, on a section of the only road in and out of town to the west. It's a thoroughfare primarily used by farmers and truckies; locals are generally heading east toward Sydney. Unless both vehicles came from one of the farms along the highway, they had to have come via Smithson.

The town doesn't have a lot of CCTV—nothing like the amount of coverage I was used to in Sydney and Melbourne—but it's improved in recent years, and now most public spaces and main streets have cameras. I need to keep pushing for the team to work our way through the files—surely at least one of the vehicles will turn up on footage from Sunday night.

I tap a pen against my teeth, thinking. Where was this woman coming from and where was she headed? I re-examine the photos of the car's interior. The driver's side is awash with shattered glass, but the passenger seat and back seats are empty and look clean. The boot contains nothing but three empty grocery bags from the Smithson supermarket. There's no jacket, no phone, no wallet, nothing except a key on a plain leather ring in the ignition. Everything has been submitted for testing but I'm not getting my hopes up seeing as we don't have any suspects to match any evidence against.

Flicking through the file again, I wish the woman was in the photos. Trying to solve her mystery without knowing anything about her is like hunting a ghost.

I read over the initial toxicology report from the blood tests Minnie texted me about. There was no trace of alcohol or drugs, though some substances take a few weeks to show up. As far as I'm aware we haven't got word whether her DNA is on file, which is odd as this is typically faster than the initial tox reports.

I'm about to ask Everett about it when he claps his hands to round up everyone for the case meeting. 'In here please, team. Let's get this show on the road.' He stands next to the whiteboard, rubbing his hands together impatiently as we all file in and sit on the uncomfortable chairs.

Several team members look at my timeline, and one constable gets out his notebook to jot a few points down.

'As you're aware,' Everett begins, 'we have several live investigations on the go. We've got Roger's Kirk's murder, the suspected attempted murder of our Jane Doe and the theft of her body from the hospital, the abandoned infant, as well as a suspicious workplace accident and a few loose ends from the pub brawl to tie up. And I don't need to tell you that we are short on resources. Part of our task is determining whether these incidents are linked so we can be as effective as possible with our time. I can confirm the woman from Sunday evening's car crash did *not* give birth to the baby who was left at the lake, nor is the baby related to Roger. I was granted a rush job on some of the DNA tests, and the results are conclusive.'

He avoids eye contact with me. Unless he got the results about Roger and the baby in the past twenty minutes, he deliberately didn't tell me earlier. My face grows warm with frustration.

Minnie asks tentatively, 'Are we thinking these are three unrelated incidents then?'

'Not necessarily,' I reply. 'They might just be related in a different way, so—'

'It's tempting to want everything to neatly connect,' Everett cuts in, 'but it's our job to make sure we're not jumping at shadows. These results make a link a lot less likely.'

I bite my tongue to avoid making a rude comment. He's probably right but I dislike his lack of imagination. Cases require lateral thinking and he's so rigid. And his dismissive style grates as well.

'Someone took that woman's body from the hospital, And Kirk was one of the few people who might have known she was there. We can't rule out a link between the two, especially in the wake of his murder.'

'If Kirk was involved in taking the corpse,' says Everett, 'what was his motive?'

'I'm not sure. But I don't think we have a clear view on why anyone would take her, do we?' I pause, everyone's eyes on me. 'Perhaps Roger was involved with the dead woman and her body implicated him in an affair somehow. Maybe he was involved in running her off the road.'

'Happy for you to look into whatever you feel you need to, Woodstock. What we do know is that Roger's wife was involved with a person calling himself Dylan Roberts, whom we are trying to track down, so I'd prefer to focus on that.'

I disagree that Dominique's online love interest should be our priority—I've made it clear to Everett and Holdsworth that I believe she was a wealthy woman being catfished—but refrain from saying so in front of the group. 'Seeing as the DNA and tox reports aren't throwing us a bone so far, what about CCTV? Have we had new footage come in?'

'Yes, I'd like an update on the CCTV situation as well, please, Detective Everett.'

I jump at the sound of Jonesy's booming voice. He stands at the rear of the room, belly bulging against his shirt. The grey-tinted skin under his eyes is the only sign he has been unwell. He rocks on his heels and surveys the room the way I've seen him do a hundred times before.

Minnie looks terrified, and I remember Everett said she is managing the various CCTV files. But he's the one who starts talking, neatly summarising the evidence and DNA dead ends, and laying out the plan for the day—which, as far as I can tell, excludes me. He's articulate and unemotional, sticking to the facts. Despite feeling slighted, I also feel a begrudging sense of admiration. I often get tongue-tied trying to corral my thoughts into clear plans. Even thinking about all the times I've been put on the spot in front of an audience causes my cheeks to flush.

'Woodstock, what about you?' Jonesy barks, and my face grows hotter.

'I have a few things to follow up.'

'Nothing you're willing to share?'

'I'm trying to see if there are dots to connect between Roger and the missing woman.'

'Sounds like the wife was the one doing the dirty,' Jonesy says.

'Maybe they both were.'

'All the money in the world but miserable as hell.' He snorts. 'Speaking of money, where are we at with Roger's finances? Anything come up?'

'There's no sign of anything unusual at this stage,' says Everett, 'although we haven't checked the wife's accounts. We'll get to that today.'

'What about the uncle?' Jonesy asks.

Everett blinks—it's his turn to be caught off guard. 'Carlyle Kirk has an alibi, sir.'

'Check him anyway.' Jonesy runs his fingers through his sparse hair. 'They're business partners as well as family, and Carlyle was Roger's only alibi for Sunday night. And even if there is no obvious motive, he has money and the means to do whatever he likes.'

I'm a little surprised: Jonesy made it clear he is no fan of Carlyle's, but his comments border on asking for a witch-hunt.

'Where was Carlyle when Roger was murdered?' I ask.

'At home alone,' says Holdsworth. 'But we know he spoke to one of Roger's kids that morning to wish her a happy birthday. Dominique's mobile records show the call from his landline came in just after seven-thirty am and lasted for several minutes. There's no way he could have got to Roger's place and back in time—he lives on the outskirts of Gowran.'

My heart breaks for the kid whose birthday will forever be the day her dad was killed.

'Just check him,' Jonesy repeats. 'The man thinks he's above reproach, and I want it to be clear that he's not.'

'I can speak to him,' I say quickly. 'And seeing as we don't have the manpower to conduct any property searches, I'll also head to the hospital—if that's all right with you, Everett. I want to speak to some of the staff again.' I'd like to ask Sophie about Roger's potential links to the baby and the dead woman. I also want to pin Ash Amato down—I left him a message yesterday that he hasn't returned, and I'm sick of him dodging me.

'What property searches do you want to do, Woodstock?' Jonesy asks.

As calmly as possible I reiterate my theory that the woman escaped imprisonment from a farm along the highway or another property in the area. I end my spiel with, 'I know we're tight on resources but I'm worried there might be other hostages.'

Jonesy doesn't say anything for a few seconds. 'Roger's murder is the priority seeing as we have more to work with, but let's try to get a team to at least check out the properties between Smithson and the crash site over the next few days. That woman didn't just appear out of thin air, and if Woodstock is right then I don't want to risk leaving stones unturned or we'll look like fools.'

Somewhat sated, I nod. It's true that not knowing the woman's identity limits our ability to investigate her murder but from my point of view this shouldn't mean we don't do everything we can to get her justice.

Everett turns to the whiteboard, and I swear I can see the steam coming out of his ears. He starts writing up the actions. 'I'll speak with Carlyle, Woodstock. You do what you need to do. Just make sure you log everything so we can keep things in some kind of order.' The tendons in his hand strain as he grips the Sharpie.

I roll my eyes. I'm the one who documents everything meticulously.

'I'll work out who can do some farm visits tomorrow,' he adds under his breath.

I consider mentioning The Retreat but take another look at his expression and decide to leave it for now.

'Keep me posted,' Jonesy says before he's seized by a coughing fit. Once it passes, he marches to the exit and loses his footing, catching himself on the doorframe. I start toward him to check he's okay but he rights himself and shakes me off.

'Hurry up and get moving,' he orders over his shoulder. 'The lack of progress so far is unacceptable.'

The stress of his looming retirement must be getting to him; he's not usually so aggressive. Or perhaps he's still feeling ill. I can feel a tension headache coming on and take a few sips from my water bottle. As everyone starts making their way out of the room, I notice that Minnie stays in the corner, hunched over her notebook. She's probably intimidated by all the male energy in the room. She makes no effort to get up despite Jonesy's orders, and I figure she wants to get me alone so we can talk.

'Would you like to come with me today?' I call out to her. 'If it's okay with Detective Everett, of course.'

Minnie chews her lip and avoids my eyes. 'Sorry, Gemma, I have a few things to follow up. Another time?'

Everett and I exchange a glance, and I can tell he is as surprised as I am stung.

Holdsworth returns to the room, holding several pieces of paper in the air. Her eyes are shining. 'Dylan Roberts doesn't exist,' she announces. 'Detective Woodstock was right—Dominique Kirk's been catfished.'

CHAPTER TWENTY-FOUR

The hospital is abuzz with sounds. There aren't enough chairs in the waiting room to accommodate everyone, and a woman sits cross-legged on the floor and plays with her toddler while an older child tries to climb onto her back. Near the main desk, a security guard and a nurse are trying to calm an agitated elderly man who sporadically yells out, 'Rachel!' A child's high-pitched wails underpin the scene. No one looks pleased to be here.

I'm still wondering about Minnie's refusal to spend the day with me. When I was a cadet, I jumped at the chance to shadow detectives. Perhaps she thinks buddying up with the only senior female detective will raise questions of favouritism, something I'm certain she's already battled during her short career.

Resolving to speak to her about it, I focus back on the bustling reception area. In the corner, a small table is covered with an ill-fitting white cloth. Piles of flowers rest on the left-hand side, and on the other there's a glass jar containing coins and banknotes. I move closer to read the typed words on the sheet of paper stuck to the wall above the table: a longwinded request for donations to the hospital in memory of Roger Kirk. The printout features a photo of Roger with his family; his arm is hooked around Dominique's waist, and they're smiling at the camera. I wonder if when it was taken she was already exchanging bad poetry and declarations of love with her catfisher. Gently, I nudge a few of the cards open on the bouquets—generic thoughts and prayers.

After dropping a five-dollar note into the jar, I head to the ambulance headquarters. The paramedic I met at the lake on Monday tells me that Ash's shift doesn't start until twelve-thirty pm.

Sophie doesn't answer my call, so I take the lift to the third floor.

'Gemma! This is a nice surprise.' Dad is dressed and sitting in the chair next to the bed. There's an empty tray on the fold-out table.

I bend down to hug him. 'Just thought I'd pop in and say hello while you're still here.'

'Before you ask, I feel great. And yes, I ate all of my breakfast.'

'Good.'

The elderly man in the bed opposite has been replaced by a younger man with his leg in a cast. A gaudy bouquet of confectionery is on the shelf behind him, alongside a card that reads *1# Dad*. He glances up at me but keeps watching something on his phone, earbuds visible.

I turn back to Dad. 'When's Rebecca coming?'

'In about forty-five minutes.'

'And you're sure you're ready to go home?'

'I am—and even the experienced doctors think so,' he adds, teasing.

I hold up my hands in surrender. 'I must have learned how to worry so much from you.'

He laughs. 'Touché. Are you here for work again?'

'I might be,' I say coolly. 'Did Rebecca tell you?'

'Ben did, actually.'

The annoyance I felt toward Rebecca shifts to Ben before I can swat it away. 'Oh.'

'He's worried about you, Gem. We all are. As you pointed out, it runs in the family.'

'I'm not a child.'

I hate how defensive I sound but he knows this is a sore point.

'You're *my* child,' Dad replies. 'It's my job to worry about you. Anyway, just be careful, please. The attack on that Kirk man sounds awful.'

I don't reply. Although I know Dad's proud of me, he never understood my decision to become a cop, and the longer my career has gone on, the less comfortable he's become with it. Understandably his concern has amplified since the incident Ben and I were involved in last year—and Rebecca's tendency to fret about things she sees on TV doesn't make it any better.

'I'm just helping. I'm not leading the case.'

Dad removes his glasses and rubs his eyes, then puts them back on and smiles at me in a way that suggests the conversation is over. I guess he knows by now that neither of us is going to get what we want out of it.

'I better go,' I say. 'I'll see you at the house over the next few days. Promise you'll call if you need anything.' I lean forward to hug him again.

'I promise.' He squeezes me tight.

'And don't you dare touch that half-painted fence,' I add. 'Mac and I will get it sorted.'

Taking the lift back to the main reception, I try calling Sophie again—still no answer.

I recognise Jessie, the receptionist from Sunday night, and wait while she directs a distressed woman to the emergency department.

She turns to me. 'Yes? Can I help you?'

'Hi, Jessie. I need to talk to a staff member, Sophie McCallister. I'm with the police.' She clearly doesn't recognise me, so I show her my badge. 'I've been trying to call her. Is she here?'

The young woman perks up at the sight of my credentials. 'Sophie is in her office. I can show you where it is.' She pats her hair self-consciously. 'Sophie's pretty upset about what happened . . . I mean, we're all upset, obviously, but she's barely keeping it together.'

'They were colleagues for a long time,' I say neutrally.

Jessie purses her lips. 'Sure, that's true.'

'How long have you worked here?'

Her head dips to one side. 'It must be almost two years, I suppose. I'm still not sure it's for me, if I'm honest. People can be so rude when they're sick. And it's always so busy.' She shoots a disapproving look at the crowd in the waiting area. 'My friend said that two beauty salons are opening in the new estate next year, so I'm thinking I'll try my luck there. They're offering all the latest treatments straight from Hollywood. Maybe I'll keep working here as well—just hustle my arse off. I want to save up for a house.'

'How did you find working with Roger?'

'Hang on,' Jessie says under her breath as she gestures for an elderly couple behind me to come forward. She gives them some paperwork to fill out and explains the wait will be long. They trot off toward the single chair she pointed out, on the far side of the room, and her voice returns to its cynical drawl. 'So, Roger . . . I mean, I didn't know him *well.*' She seems disappointed at this admission. 'He was attractive. I could tell he thought highly of himself, though.' Her heavily made-up eyes dart sideways. 'I probably shouldn't say that after what happened to him, should I?' She makes a face, clearly not that concerned. 'He was loaded, wasn't he? Are you thinking someone killed him for money? I told my friend he seems like the kind of guy who'd be involved in a dodgy deal.'

I lean forward conspiratorially. 'What makes you say that?'

'Nothing specific—he was just always rushing around, whispering into his phone. Classic suspicious behaviour. Hey, there's Sophie now.' Jessie points behind me.

I turn to catch the back of Sophie's blonde head as she exits the hospital via the main entrance.

'Thanks for your help,' I say to Jessie.

'Want me to come?' she asks hopefully.

'No, thanks.'

I find Sophie in a nook around the side of the hospital. Her teeth protrude over her bottom lip as she scrolls on her phone.

'Sophie.'

Startled, she lifts her eyes to meet mine. Gone is the assured woman I spoke with a few days ago. She seems smaller. She's not wearing lipstick, and she manically scratches at the skin under her watchband. I spy a cigarette packet in her handbag.

'How are you?' I ask, even though it's obvious.

'There's just a lot to deal with, to manage.' Her voice is raspy as though the words are sticking in her throat. 'I'm not sure . . .' I don't think she notices herself falling into silence, her gaze fixed and glassy.

I sense she is on the brink of spilling her guts or shutting down completely so I'm going to need to tread carefully to get what I want from her. Not only is Sophie someone Roger might have openly confided in, but even if he didn't, her regular proximity to him means she might hold knowledge that not even Dominique or his uncle were privy to. I'm also mindful that his death may benefit her professionally, and I want to explore if that could justify a motive.

'You must be very upset. Roger was your colleague. Your boss.'

She jerks as if remembering I'm here. 'Yes.'

'And a friend . . . ?' I press. 'You worked closely together.'

'Mmm.' Clearing her throat, she runs her hands along her suit sleeves, brushing away imaginary lint. 'I'd better get back. I just needed some air.'

'You can smoke if you like. I'll wait.'

She blinks and blushes. 'I don't—'

'It's fine.'

She pulls out a cigarette and lights it, her cheekbones sharp as she inhales. Closing her eyes, she rests her head against the wall. 'God,' she murmurs, before taking another toke.

'I wanted to ask you a few questions.'

'Are you back from leave now?'

'I'm helping with this investigation,' I reply, and she nods. 'How did you find out about what happened to Roger the other day?'

'I was here—a staff member told me. She heard from a friend who lives on his street.'

I feel sorry for Sophie. She seems like the kind of person who would want to process what happened in private and then decide how to inform the team, not be blindsided in public.

'It must have been a massive shock.'

'Yes.' She appears to be remembering the moment and shivers. 'No one could believe it. Still doesn't seem real.' Tears glint in her eyes, and she rushes to say, 'I mean, Roger was a polarising person, but you just never think something like this will happen to anyone—and not to anyone you *know*.' Her resolve crumbles, and she tries to steady herself with another long puff.

'Polarising how?'

'He was strong-willed, impressive. He took no prisoners when he wanted something.' Smoke curls out of her mouth as her jaw trembles. There's a hint of pride in her voice when she adds, 'But in a role like that, you can't afford to be wishy-washy.'

'Did he have enemies you knew of?'

She busies herself with rifling through her bag but doesn't take anything out.

'Were *you* ever an enemy?' I ask.

'Me? No! We worked well together. Everyone said so. We had the same standards. A lot of people in the health system are lazy—they want change, but they're all talk. Roger and I got things done, and he was very proud of that. So was I.'

It's an odd little speech but seems genuine enough. I think about the two times I saw Sophie and Roger interacting. He was dominant, borderline rude, but she seemed to revel in being his right-hand person and she's certainly not offering up a counterargument to that position now. Was something going on between them in the lead-up to his murder?

I move the conversation away from the personal. 'Sophie, do you have any reason to believe that what happened to Roger is linked to the corpse disappearing? Did Roger say anything to you about it?'

'No. He was worried about it, as you know, mainly because of the impact it might have on the research centre investment. He'd only just been announced as the CEO, so it was bad timing.'

'I wasn't aware of that,' I say, mentally kicking Everett. It's the kind of information I would have put on the case board. 'When was the announcement?'

'Last week.'

'Was it a surprise?'

Her expression slides before she grits her teeth and firms her jaw. 'Most people didn't expect it. He's on the record saying he wanted to lead the hospital for at least another decade but things change.'

'Did you know about his appointment?'

'I was happy for him,' she says, avoiding the question. She forcefully flicks ash from the end of her cigarette.

Her protectiveness toward Roger is throwing me, but based on seeing them together I'm not convinced they were in a relationship. Maybe they were involved at some point and things had soured. I can imagine Roger getting what he wanted, breaking things off and expecting her to resume their professional relationship again without a fuss. Sophie might have continued to have feelings for him but I'm unclear how that links to what happened to him unless she felt jilted enough to seek revenge.

'And I guess you're also aware that he was accused of helping out mates with contracts at other medical institutions, and that they haven't always gone too well.'

'I'm sorry, no, I don't know what you're talking about.'

'Machines and equipment that don't work . . . ?'

She looks at me blankly and I get the sense she doesn't know what I'm talking about.

It's hard to know how much more to push her but she worked with Roger for years, it stands to reason she must know something that will help with the case. I try another angle. 'And Roger was heavily involved in raising capital for the research centre?'

'He was a great communicator, good at explaining the big picture and helping people understand what needed to be done to achieve it.'

'But, Sophie, my understanding is that he misled some investors—fed them bogus financial information to make the centre look more attractive.'

'Why would he lie?' She looks confused. 'Have you seen the plans for the centre? It's going to be incredible. Any investor in their right mind will want to contribute!'

Bingo, I think. Her tone is bordering on evangelical, and I wonder what her involvement with the centre is, if any. Sophie strikes me as a lifetime 2IC but maybe Roger's death means she believes she is a chance for the research centre CEO role. I go in for the kill. 'On the day Roger died, an article was published about the mismanagement of hospital funds. Do you have any idea where that information might have come from?'

'Of course not! That article was a beat-up.'

'It sounds like someone from the hospital was a source and had knowledge about the research centre as well, so—'

'It would be best if you directed these questions to Roger's lawyer, Jack Barnes.'

'Do you know him well?' I ask conversationally, trying to get her back onside.

'He's been involved in a few of the lawsuits we've had to manage.'

'When did you last speak with him?' I press.

'A few weeks ago, I think. I can get the exact date if—'

'But you weren't close?'

'No. We just worked together when we needed to.'

'Are you aware that Jack discovered Roger's body? They had arranged to meet.'

Her resolve wavers. 'Yes, I heard.'

'You didn't know they were meeting that morning?'

Little red spots appear on her neck and chin. 'I can't remember if I knew. Roger may have mentioned it, but it wasn't my business to keep track of his diary.'

Sensing she's about to snap, I decide to go for broke.

'And did Roger ever confide in you about his marriage, Sophie?'

'What? No.' She pops a mint, pulls a bottle of sanitiser from her bag, squirts some onto her hands and puts it back. Then she retrieves a tiny perfume dispenser, which she uses to efficiently spray her wrists and neck. 'We never talked about anything like that.'

She refuses to meet my gaze. I've definitely hit a nerve, but whether she simply feels loyalty toward her deceased boss or it's something more personal, I'm not sure.

'Do you have a partner?'

She shakes her head. 'I'm too busy for that. And I need to get back.' Her eyes are still red, but her expression has become steely.

'Will you become the CEO now?'

Her mouth falls open.

'Will you?' I press. 'Or maybe you will consider a role at the research centre? It was clearly important to Roger.'

Sophie sniffs and straightens her jacket, wiping non-existent lint from her pencil skirt. 'I'm acting in his role as per our business continuity plans,' she replies robotically. 'At an appropriate time, the role will be advertised, then the hospital board will decide who to appoint.'

'Will you apply?'

'I haven't even thought about it,' she says frostily. 'Detective, if there is anything else you need as part of your investigation, let me know.' She steps around me, her heels tapping against the concrete as she walks away.

I can't work out what to make of her reaction. I expected her to be upset about her boss's murder, but her emotions seem uneven and unusually intense. It's the kind of response I would expect from someone who feels guilty. None of the evidence from the crime scene points to her killing him but perhaps she was involved somehow. I make a note to check her finances so we can rule out a blackmail trail.

It's still over an hour until Ash is due to arrive, and there are no updates from Everett. I take the opportunity to time the route from the day ward to the morgue, helping to validate a few time-line scenarios. Then I get a coffee and, for the second time, read through the staff statements from Sunday night on my laptop. There was nothing out of the ordinary regarding the missing woman's medical treatment; she went into cardiac arrest seconds after she was transferred from the ambulance and, despite the collective efforts of the emergency team, she couldn't be saved. All the statements taken corroborate this and the medical staff provided each other with alibis for the rest of the evening, as did the other hospital and admin staff. It strikes me that people are rarely alone in a hospital—except for the security guards. I also wonder if it's possible that Ash Amato triggered the woman's cardiac arrest just before she was taken into the emergency department. He claims he went home after his shift but no one can confirm this. Maybe he returned to the hospital to steal the corpse? I chew my lip, thinking. It fits, especially considering his evasiveness, but he has an alibi for the crash so why would he suddenly want the woman dead? Unless he recognised her when he arrived at the scene?

Feeling overwhelmed, I finish my coffee and force my focus back to the statements. When the blackout occurred, Lenny Tisdale was on a break. He says he was in his car on the phone to a friend. His car was parked down a side street at the same end of the hospital as the morgue. He claims he returned from his break when the fire alarm was going off, and this was when he discovered the exterior morgue door was open and alerted Sophie.

My heart starts to race. I check the rest of Tisdale's case notes. His record is clean, although he's had a few close calls with the police and was suspected of being involved with a home robbery several years ago. His eldest brother is in gaol for burglary, and his other brother has been charged with a string of minor offences. I mentally review my timeline, adding in the details of Tisdale's movements. He could have staged the discovery of the open door to hide in plain sight; an accomplice could have disposed of the body while he was with Sophie.

Shoving my computer into my bag, I head out the front so I can accost Ash when he arrives. I leave a message with Everett, asking him to call me urgently about Tisdale's statement. Just as I hang up, a call from Mac comes through.

'Hey,' I answer, sinking onto a bench seat. I fish a muesli bar out of my bag. I'm not used to going so long without food. When I'm home with Scarlett I snack all day.

'Hey. How's your day going?'

I'm instantly wary—the pleasantries are clearly a precursor to the main point of the call. 'Been okay so far,' I say, hoping my chewing and swallowing isn't obvious.

'Good. That's good.'

'Is everything okay?'

'Yes, everything is fine. But, Gem, I'm sorry, I need to head off tonight, for work.' His words come out in a tumble.

'What do you mean?'

'I need to get up to Brisbane. There's a new lead on my case, and I need to be there on the ground.'

'Okay.' My insides turn to ice. When I was with Scott, this was me a million times. Mostly it was genuine, but there were times when I used work as a cover for my affair. 'When are you leaving?'

'I fly in four hours.'

I see Ash get out of a car and cut across the parking lot toward the hospital. I start to follow him, still processing Mac's news. 'You've booked your flights already?'

He pauses. 'Yes. I wouldn't go if I didn't have to, Gem.'

'I know. It's fine. I get it.'

He exhales, and his palpable relief makes me even more worried. 'I know it's not ideal.'

Ash has disappeared behind a delivery truck, and I rush to keep up. 'It's fine,' I huff. 'I'll be home soon.' Shoving my phone in my pocket, I dart from one row of cars to another. Ash is entering the hospital when he turns and sees me, his mouth twisting into an unreadable expression. He continues walking briskly in the opposite direction from me.

'Ash!' I call out as I follow him into the hospital.

He's walking very quickly now. As I cut through the waiting area, I almost trip over a runaway toddler and stop to apologise to his mother before I jog to the ambulance office. A woman at the entrance demands to see my credentials before she lets me through.

Ash's not in the tearoom. Through the windows I see him climbing into an ambulance. 'Wait!' I yell, causing several people to stare at me.

I make it to the parking bays just as he slams the door. Out of breath, I watch the ambulance peel out onto the road, sirens screaming and lights strobing.

CHAPTER TWENTY-FIVE

I drive home feeling uneasy. I check my reflection in the rear-view mirror: tired green eyes, pale freckled skin, dark hair loose and wild. Yes, I don't look my best, but that doesn't explain Ash's behaviour. First Minnie, then Ash and now Mac—people are turning off me in droves. I call Holdsworth and ask her to speak with Ash and arrange for him to brief a sketch artist. Hopefully she has better luck than me.

Roger's blood-streaked body enters my thoughts. The missing dead woman does, too. That grainy footage Minnie shared has made her feel more real despite not being able to see her face. Slender with dark hair and pale skin. Bloodstained and broken as the life left her body. Alone in the small freezer until someone took her. She deserves justice and to be returned to the people who loved her. The baby deserves that, too. And Roger's kids deserve to know what happened to their father. We need to work harder.

I park in the driveway and yank on the handbrake, taking a few steadying breaths.

I'm surprised when Everett answers my call. 'I can't make the check-in this evening,' I tell him.

'Chasing a lead, Woodstock?' he says sarcastically.

In the bedroom window, I see Mac holding Scarlett and moving from the wardrobe to the bed, where his suitcase is propped open as he packs for his trip to Queensland. 'There are just some things I need to take care of.'

'Righto,' Everett replies. 'Clearly important things.'

'I don't really need to explain myself to you.'

He sighs. 'Likewise. Although you may as well know, we still have no idea who Dominique's catfisher was. The only thing the tech team can confirm is that the emails were sent from somewhere in Australia. They reckon highly sophisticated encryption software was used.'

'And what about the fake social-media accounts?'

'Same deal. They were set up in Australia at the end of last year, but so far the tech team can't trace the account holder. We do know that all the images were ripped from real Facebook and Instagram accounts. I read more of the emails today, though, and— Jesus Christ, it's bonkers stuff. Pages and pages of poetry and declarations of love.'

'It's a lot of effort to go to. And for what?'

'It's got to be money! But Dominique swears she never transferred a cent to Dylan Roberts, and we can't find any evidence that she did.'

'Maybe the catfisher hadn't had the chance to strike yet.'

'Hell of a warm-up. Months of drivel back and forth.'

'Some people are patient if they think the reward is big enough.' This feels good, us tentatively collaborating, and I take the opportunity to ask about my call earlier. 'Did you get my message about Lenny Tisdale?'

'Yep.'

I wait for him to elaborate but he doesn't. 'And?'

'And nothing—it all plays. Tisdale was having a smoke in his car when the fire alarm went bananas. He didn't know about the blackout. He entered the hospital via the food-delivery doors to avoid being busted back late from his break, and that's when he noticed the morgue door was wide open. He bumped into Sophie at the top of the stairs, and they returned to the morgue.'

'And you're sure he checks out?' I press, unconvinced. 'There's no way he could have disposed of the body?'

'I wouldn't be hiring him any time soon, but yeah, he checks out. We have him exiting the hospital and going to his car at nine-thirty. We can place him in the food storage room at ten-fifteen, which doesn't give him enough time to dispose of the body.'

Yet again, I feel like Everett has made up his mind and isn't considering every possibility. I know it's his investigation and he's across more of the detail than I am but that doesn't mean he's not missing things. I keep pushing. 'And he didn't see a car leaving the side entrance? If he's telling the truth, he might be the only witness we have.'

'You'll be shocked to know we did ask him about that,' Everett says drily. 'And no, he says he didn't see anything.'

'So Tisdale was just minding his own business and having a smoke in his car,' I say sarcastically. 'Hang on, why *was* he smoking in his car? Surely he'd prefer to avoid stinking up his vehicle. Was he having a private conversation or something?'

'Weed, Woodstock, not cigarettes,' Everett says with mock patience.

My cheeks burn. 'I assume you're going to report him.'

Everett hesitates. 'I gave him the fright of his life instead. Don't worry, he won't be messing about on the job again.'

'He's working security at a hospital,' I retort, thinking of vulnerable patients like my dad.

'Yes, but he'll never do it again, and I think keeping a kid like Tisdale employed is a good result in the long run. He knows he's on thin ice.'

'I didn't realise you were such a Robin Hood,' I say, even though he has a point.

In our line of work we often make judgement calls, deciding what's right and wrong on the fly. Lord knows I've done it. Problem is, you don't get rewarded for making the right call, but you risk a lot by making the wrong one.

'Do you think the theft was a two-person job?' I venture.

'I'm not sure. One person implies a creep into necrophilia. Two or more people makes it feel professional. Either way, Woodstock, I have to go. I'm pretty busy, too.'

'Is Minnie around?'

'Yep.'

'She okay?'

'Everything's fine, Woodstock. It's almost as if we've survived without you this year.'

I bite back a nasty retort, disappointed at how quickly our civility has descended into rudeness. 'Will you send me the case updates after the check-in, please? Also, I assume we're still waiting on the woman's DNA report or it would be in her file. It would be helpful if there's a match in the system.'

'I'll try to remember,' he says and hangs up.

Mac meets me at the front door, looking as frazzled as I feel. 'Hi.'

Scarlett reaches out, and I take her, her shape and weight so familiar it's like I've been missing a piece of myself all day. I drop my nose to her head and breathe her in.

Returning to the bedroom, Mac talks to me over his shoulder. 'How was it today, Gem?' He shoves socks and underwear in his suitcase before disappearing into the bathroom to fetch his toiletries bag.

Normally I would tell him everything, including how frustrated I am with Everett, but he's distracted. I don't want to feel like I'm being half listened to. 'It's all going fine.'

'That's good.' He surveys the room, then holds a finger in the air. 'Runners.' He grabs them from the cupboard.

'How long are you going for?'

'Probably only two days—I'll be back by Saturday afternoon at the latest.'

'Okay.' I'm disappointed but I try not to show it. He's been so supportive about my returning to work.

'It's bad timing. I'm sorry, Gem.'

'I told you, it's fine. It's not like I'm leading the case. I can log whatever hours I like.'

He nods and zips the bag shut, the sound like a xylophone up my spine. Outside, a car pulls in behind ours. 'I booked a driver. I'd better get going.' Tugging on his jacket, he calls out goodbye to Ben. Scarlett and I walk him to the door, where he kisses her goodbye. Then he kisses me long and hard on the mouth.

'Are you sure everything's okay, Mac?'

His minty breath is warm on my face as he pulls back. 'What do you mean?'

'With us . . . I just feel like you're so distant at the moment. Maybe I'm being silly, but I think we need to talk more like we used to. I know I've been preoccupied over the past few months.'

Concern flashes across his face. 'No, it's my fault. I've been distracted by this cold case—not that it's an excuse,' he adds hurriedly.

'As long as everything really is okay,' I say, feeling a little better.

'I love you,' he says with surprising intensity. 'I'll be in touch when I know how the next couple of days are shaping up. We'll talk when I get home, I promise.'

We kiss again and then reluctantly I let him go.

As the car pulls away, he waves at us. I feel an acute sense of déjà vu from when Ben was little and I would see Scott off to work, grimly steeling myself for the long hours ahead, convinced I wasn't living the right life. This is different, I tell myself. I'm a different person now. Ben is almost a teenager, and I'm not trapped anymore. I want to be with Mac. But the memories leave me with a hollow feeling.

I roam listlessly around the house, then I wipe the kitchen bench, take out the rubbish and recycling, and tidy Scarlett's toys. The study door is shut, and I open it and step inside.

Mac's desk is neater than it's been in months, with only a modest stack of papers, a few pens and the computer monitor. I sift through the stack, but there's nothing of interest, just a few bills and printed emails of old case files. I wonder where all the papers and photographs from the other day have gone. The desk drawers are empty, but surely he hasn't taken all the files with him.

I scan the desk again. The sudden neatness seems suspicious, as does this sudden interstate trip—but I know Mac, and his words earlier were genuine. I shake my head as if to force the suspicions away. I need to stop this spiral, or I'll lose my mind.

I busy myself making dinner and talking to Ben about his day. We call Dad, who sounds delighted to be home, then I put Scarlett to bed. Mac texts to say he's arrived in Brisbane, and I reply with a photo of Scarlett asleep.

When I return to the lounge, Ben is watching TV. I make us hot chocolates and step out into the yard to call Candy.

'Hello, detective,' she answers cheerfully. 'Got some updates for me?'

I stretch out my back. 'Nothing I can share.'

'Blink twice if you have a major lead on Roger, once if you have nothing.'

I try to summon the energy to play along. 'But you can't see my eyes.'

She sighs. 'I know, it's very frustrating.'

'Very.'

'Seeing as nothing's happening on the Kirk murder front, or the other cases, we should pick up our conversation from earlier in the week.'

I sip my hot chocolate. 'Which one was that?'

'Our trip out to The Retreat,' she says. 'I'm assuming you haven't gone there yet.'

'Candy, I've hardly had time to eat let alone follow up a lead for your story.'

'What about tomorrow?'

'I can't. Mac has gone to Brisbane for work, just for a couple of days, which has derailed my plans somewhat.'

'Bad timing.'

'Yeah. Although, I don't know . . . maybe me dabbling in this case is a stupid idea.'

'That's not true, Gemma. Don't be silly.'

'I guess.' I'm annoyed at my self-pity but can't seem to shake it off.

'I've got an idea,' Candy says.

'Please, no,' I say with a laugh, trying to lighten the mood.

'Let's tag team tomorrow. We can divide and conquer. I've got Lola due to a childcare mix-up, so this works perfectly.'

'You do know I can't let you sub in for me.' I'm not sure how serious she is.

'Likewise! I wouldn't trust you to write a story if my life depended on it. But we both have stuff to do, so let's take shifts. I'll have the kids in the morning, then we'll swap.'

It's tempting. I don't want to give Everett the satisfaction of thinking I'm not up to the job, and I don't want to ask Rebecca to look after Scarlett with Dad only just home. 'You do know I won't have time to go to The Retreat tomorrow morning,' I say. 'Not with the case meeting and the leads I already have to follow up.'

'I know.'

'And I don't think you should go on your own. Will Sam go with you?'

'We'll talk about it tomorrow.'

'Candy,' I protest wearily.

'See you at seven-thirty!' she trills.

CHAPTER TWENTY-SIX

Scarlett wakes at two and screams inexplicably for over an hour, refusing to settle. She wakes again just after five. This time I don't return to bed, even though she falls asleep quickly. In the dark kitchen I flick on the kettle and make a coffee. My body feels sluggish, which is strange as my mind is as jumpy as a possum.

Sitting at the kitchen table with my coffee and my notebook, I enjoy the stillness of the house as I jot down revelations and questions. If Dominique's catfisher didn't want money, then what did they want? And is it linked to Roger's murder? I wonder if having contact with his wife was a way of tracking his movements: if the emailer knew when Dominique was out of town, then they knew when Roger was alone. Or perhaps they were hoping to blackmail her by threatening to show the emails to Roger, but to demand money or something else? Dominique probably has access to information that might be useful to Roger's business contacts. But as Everett pointed out, eight months is a long time to sustain that level of interaction; most criminals want a faster payoff.

I rub my eyes and finish my coffee, which has done nothing to make me feel more awake. Whatever led to Roger's murder, I don't think it had anything to do with his wife—or not directly, anyway. She seems genuinely thrown by both his death and the revelation that her affair was bogus.

Ben enters the kitchen, startling me. 'Morning.' He's in his pyjamas, his hair sticking out in every direction.

'Hey,' I say, 'I'm sorry if Scarlett woke you up last night.'

'It was fine. I went straight back to sleep. Did you get some sleep?'

'I did,' I say. 'Hopefully it was just a glitch—she's normally pretty good.'

He rests his head on my shoulder. 'Was I a good sleeper when I was a baby?'

'You weren't bad. I just didn't know what I was doing. I think sometimes my stress stressed you out.'

He makes himself a Milo and some cereal, and I'm overwhelmed by a rush of affection.

After spooning a mouthful of muesli into his mouth, he says, 'It's weird how you had so many years with me that I can't remember.'

'It is. My earliest memory is from when I was about four. My mum wouldn't let me wear my favourite T-shirt because we were going somewhere nice and there were holes in it. I threw a big tantrum.' I picture it: me flinging myself onto my childhood bed, tears streaming down my face; my mother, exasperated, trying to coax me into another outfit.

Ben smiles. 'I remember being on Dad's shoulders and holding on to his head. He kept giving me high fives, and I was scared I was going to fall off.' He says it casually, but his jaw clenches several times and I can tell he's fighting tears.

'Hey.' I get up and go to him, wrapping my arms around his upper body. 'I love you.'

'I know.'

'Your dad does, too.'

'I know,' he whispers.

I give him another hug. 'I'm having a shower. Will you get Scarlett if she wakes up?'

He nods and smiles shakily at me.

Ben being upset has made me upset, but I feel a little better after my shower. Scarlett cries out just as I'm finishing with the hairdryer, and I go into her room and change her.

I'm feeding her in the highchair when Candy arrives with Lola. 'Good morning!' She drops a giant tote bag on the bench. 'Hey, buddy,' she says to Ben.

'Didn't know you were coming,' he says, grinning and returning her high five.

'Your mum sucks at sharing information,' she quips. 'But here I am, ready to roll with Candy's Kinder. Off you go, Gemma. I've got everything under control here, don't you worry.'

'Do you want help putting in the extra baby seat?'

She waves my offer away. 'Already put in Lola's old one this morning. Now go! We can catch up when you get back.'

I say goodbye to the kids and blow a kiss to Candy.

When I arrive at the station, Everett is with Jonesy in his office, their heads bent close together. Jonesy sees me, says something to Everett and curls his finger, indicating I should join them.

I hover in his office doorway. 'Morning.'

He gets to his feet. 'Woodstock. I didn't expect you to be here today.'

Everett closes a file on the desk before shoving it into his satchel. 'Why not?' I ask.

'I just figured the kids might make it difficult for you to be here in the morning.'

I'm confused—does Jonesy know Mac is away? He hasn't mentioned being involved in Mac's cold case, but it's likely he's aware of it. Maybe I'm being paranoid. 'Well, obviously I managed. What's happening?'

'We might have a lead on the baby,' Jonesy says. 'A heavily pregnant white teenager from Brisbane ran away two weeks ago and hasn't been seen since. There's a history of mental health issues, and she told a friend that she wanted to give the baby up for adoption.'

'When can we get DNA to confirm?'

'We're sorting out samples with the family now,' says Everett, 'and we'll push to get results by tomorrow night. But the timeline fits. Plus, the pregnant girl visited Smithson when she was younger—her cousins lived here—so there's a connection with the area.'

'Are we planning a press conference?' I ask. 'We need to get that girl's photo out there asap. She might be in real trouble if she gave birth on her own.'

'You'll be shocked to know I've got the team checking to see if she's turned up at any hospitals or shelters.'

'We need to go broader. Why wouldn't we get the media to do the heavy lifting?'

'Because we don't even know if she's missing yet! Or if the baby is hers.'

Shooting warning looks at us, Jonesy walks around his desk and sinks heavily into his chair. 'Let's just sit tight until we have the test results and then decide on next steps.' He checks the time. 'Don't you two have a check-in to go to?'

'You're not coming?' I ask.

'I've got some calls to make.'

Holdsworth kicks off the check-in, confirming that she got on to Ash Amato, who agreed to brief a sketch artist later today. He clearly has an issue with me but I try to let it go. No one has anything new to share except for the possible baby lead, and it feels like all we're doing is validating dead ends. There's no progress on the identity of Dominique's catfisher, while Roger's finances all seem to be in order. Jobs and contracts for his mates certainly seem to be ingredients in all the pies he had fingers in, but he was never the ultimate decision-maker on those deals, merely a convincing influencer.

'Some of these emails are pretty nasty,' I say, scanning the printouts that have been added to the case board. I wonder if Sophie would defend her former boss so stridently if she read this correspondence.

'There are some very expensive noses out of joint,' Everett agrees.

'This guy might be worth following up.' Holdsworth hands me a file. 'Eddie Maher, an old uni friend of Roger's, works at a specialist clinic in Sydney. He introduced Roger to the owners, and they invested in a whole bunch of equipment owned by his other mate, Dino Fricker. There were issues with the machines, then issues with the insurance. Maher seems furious.'

I scan the printouts again, noting the emotional language and that Roger signs off by suggesting Maher get in touch with his lawyer, Jack Barnes. 'Roger fobbed his mate off to Barnes?'

'Seems Barnes has cleaned up after the Kirks for years,' says Everett. 'Roger trots him out at the first sign of things getting heated.'

'And what do we know about Barnes's business dealings? Is he clean?'

'Seems so,' replies Everett. 'He's a busy boy, but everything seems just above board. He's a master of managing the loophole. We've discovered he owns a shit-ton of land—acres of bush and farmland all around Smithson. He inherited it from his parents. He's already building a suite of offices and townhouses along the reserve, and

I assume he has more planned. He'll make a killing with the influx of people buying property here.'

'It all seems to check out. Interestingly the team have also determined that he's one of the proposed investors in Carlyle Kirk's research centre. He sold Carlyle the land that The Lyle complex was built on originally. He's set to be one of the centre's biggest local investors.'

I flick through a few land contracts and building permits. Bilson Constructions is completing the works Barnes commissioned out near the reserve; I try to remember where I've heard that name recently. A moment later, it comes to me: the men Lee Blight attacked at the pub work for Bilson. Henno didn't rate them and, despite his shortcomings, I think he's a good judge of character. I wonder what kind of employment checks Bilson is conducting and whether the company is above board. More money than ever is flowing through Smithson, and in my experience, where there is big money there is corruption.

I re-read some lines from the emails. 'Based on these, Roger Kirk doesn't seem like an investment I'd be rolling the dice on. Surely if Barnes knew about this he would be advising him to pull his head in.'

'I think Barnes just kept his mouth shut and took the pay cheques,' says Everett.

'What was your sense when you spoke with Carlyle yesterday?' I ask.

His jaw tightens. 'He's a fascinating guy, but as suspected, none of Roger's money goes to his uncle, so I don't think we'll stumble upon a smoking gun there. And Roger was his newly announced, investor-approved CEO—he needed him.'

I refrain from pointing out that it was Jonesy, not me, who asked him to follow Carlyle up and feel newly irritated that it wasn't me. After listening to all the interviews he's done I'd like to talk to him myself. I wonder if Everett probed him about the potential of Roger being involved with someone romantically. And whether he knew his incoming CEO was walking a fine ethical line by promoting his mates' products and services. I sigh, probably not. I make a note to speak to Carlyle again if nothing else turns up over the next few days. Minnie provides an update on the CCTV analysis and Everett runs through a few more leads he wants followed up before he dismisses the team. I try to catch Minnie's eye, but she's busy with her phone; I really need to find time to take her out for a drink and ask her what's going on.

'Anything you want me to do?' I say, once Everett and I are alone.

He doesn't look up from his phone. 'Whatever you like.'

I think about Ash and Sophie but don't volunteer my suspicions to Everett. My theories aren't tight yet and I don't want to give him another reason to accuse me of being flaky. Instead, I simply say, 'I might try to speak to Lenny Tisdale myself, if you don't mind. For better or worse, he is a key witness. Maybe something relevant will come to him.'

'Sounds good, Gemma,' Everett says in a tone I would use to placate a toddler.

'Great,' I reply brightly. 'I won't make it back here later today—I need to be at home this afternoon with my daughter—but I'll let you know if anything shows up.' I figure I may as well just own my caring responsibilities, rather than having him speculate about my commitment.

We walk out of the meeting room, and I pass his desk on the way to mine. There are no personal effects, nothing to hint at his life outside the force. We're probably about the same age, but I have no idea if he has children or a partner, or even a pet. I shoot a text to Nan, a detective and former colleague in Melbourne, asking her for intel on Everett. She knows everyone and is a great contact when I need a quick star rating on someone in the force.

Grabbing my bag, I turn to leave and almost walk straight into Everett, who has snuck up behind me. 'Oh! Sorry.' My hand is on my chest. 'You gave me a fright. Everything okay?'

'I just wanted to ask you a question. One of the guys mentioned he didn't think you were going to stay in Smithson after you return from parental leave. But I assume your plan has changed now . . . ?'

'I'm not sure exactly what my plan is yet.' I'm surprised at how overt he is, essentially asking me if I'm applying for Jonesy's job.

'But you grew up here, right?'

'Yep.'

'But your partner didn't?'

'No, he's from Sydney.' I'm trying to work out where this is going.

'I heard he's a detective as well.'

'He used to be—now he consults on special investigations and works with unis.'

'You went to school here?'

I raise my eyebrows. 'You want to talk about my childhood, Everett?'

He attempts a smile. 'Just trying to be friendly.'

Growing wary, I say curtly, 'I lived here until my late twenties. And now I'm back.'

'Do you have other family here?'

'Just my dad.'

'Does he—?'

'What about you? You moved here last year from Melbourne, right?'

'That's right.'

'Did you come on your own?' I press.

He steps around me, rubbing his hands together. 'I don't really have time to chat, Gemma,' he says bluntly. 'I've got to keep moving— we've got a shitload of work to do.'

I'm left standing in the middle of the office open-mouthed, staring at his retreating figure and breathing his obnoxious cologne.

CHAPTER TWENTY-SEVEN

My hands are like claws around the steering wheel, my dislike for Everett growing with every passing second. Who does he think he is, grilling me like that? And why does Jonesy seem to hold him in such high esteem?

As much as it pains me, I know the answer: Everett is an option for the top job as much as I am—and, in the eyes of many, a more suitable candidate. There's a difference between being incompetent and intolerable, and in fairness he's probably only the latter, which doesn't make him a bad cop. Jonesy is simply hoping a smooth transition to his successor will be part of his legacy. Still, Everett's attitude toward me rankles.

I check the time. Just over three and a half hours until I need to get home and look after the kids. I call Lenny's number and get no answer, so I call the hospital switchboard and ask to have him paged, only to have the receptionist inform me he's not rostered on today. I try Rufus, his boss, who confirms it's his day off. Now what? I could go to his house, but there's every chance he won't be home and then I'll have wasted my morning.

Screw Lenny Tisdale, I think, veering off the main road to head east—and screw Everett as well. He said I could do whatever I like so I'll go and speak with Carlyle Kirk myself. I'm aware that my desire to talk to him goes beyond asking questions about Roger's murder: I'm fascinated by his ethos, his ambition and his optimism for humanity. He's also highly perceptive and I'm interested in his reaction to his nephew's death. In the podcast interviews I've listened to, he said he works in his psychiatry practice seven days a week, so it's a safe bet I'll find him there. Whether he'll talk to me or not is another story.

Despite the promise of sun, the day is decidedly grey. The wind reveals the underside of the leaves as the fields of grass ripple like the sea. I call Mac on the bluetooth but get his voicemail. A light anxiety settles across me after I leave a message, and I fight the urge to call Candy for an update on Scarlett or to text Ben. Flicking on the radio, I do my best to relax into a pop song.

The news comes on, signalling it's ten am. There's only a brief mention of Roger's murder: Candy was right, the lack of new information has downgraded the story from an inferno to a grassfire. It's been replaced by the unexpected death of a high-profile rugby coach in Sydney. The attention economy theory is supported by our reactions to homicide—good luck to your dead self in getting more than a brief by-line if you're not attractive, white or wealthy. Even then, the general public is only interested for a week or so. Journos like Candy are doing everything they can to even things out when it comes to diversity in death reporting, but it will take them a while to help dismantle decades of bias, especially when the audience votes with their eyeballs.

Twenty minutes later, The Lyle complex looms before me. Its shining white walls and European-style roofs jar against the dense

Australian bushland; it looks more like a set of extravagant dollhouses than destinations for psychiatric services and aged care.

I turn off the highway and into the full car park. Cloud Consulting, Carlyle's private practice, is to the left, while the retirement village, Lyle Lodge, is on the right. Further along is Harmony, the health centre that offers Pilates, yoga and an onsite dietician. I park in one of the few spare spots, noting the fee of three dollars an hour, a concept unheard of in Smithson.

I walk back toward Lyle Lodge. It's huge: four levels high and at least twenty rooms wide. Large windows look out on lush lawns and a front yard reminiscent of pictures from Rebecca's gardening magazines. Wattle trees explode on both sides of the building, creating the impression it's backlit. I watch the groups on the lawn, mainly elderly people with their adult children and grandchildren. A few staff members mingle with them, leading the groups in simple-looking activities. Near the main entrance, a little boy performs somersaults while his father and an elderly man shower him with applause. Everything seems pleasant enough, if not slightly manufactured.

I double back and approach the psychiatric clinic. Cloud Consulting is about a quarter of the size of the retirement village. Its curved walls are paired with sharp angles, all done in a palette of cool earthy tones. I push through a mirrored door to the reception area, where an elegant East Asian woman in a fitted white dress is watering a towering fiddle-leaf fig in a shiny ivory pot. Abstract paintings matching the ones at Roger's house adorn the walls, and lifestyle magazines are spread out on the glass coffee table. A middle-aged white woman sits on one of the three chairs in the corner, so quiet and still I didn't notice her at first; she seems enthralled by whatever she's reading in her magazine, only her eyes moving.

The Asian woman places a dainty watering can on the floor and comes to the podium desk, where a lone laptop is positioned.

She asks how she can help me. After I introduce myself and explain I want to speak with Carlyle, she exits the sparse room without a word. I'm not sure if she'll return with Carlyle or security—or at all.

I wait awkwardly in the corner, trying to understand the appeal of the paintings. They look like nondescript grey blurs to me.

'Detective.'

I spin around. Carlyle Kirk is standing next to the fiddle-leaf fig. He's wearing brown slacks and a blue shirt with a charcoal cardigan, an outfit reminiscent of a college professor. Despite his age, his posture is ruler-straight, and his dark eyes are alert. He has an undeniable presence and I get the sense he doesn't miss much.

'You're welcome here, of course,' he says, 'but I wasn't expecting you.'

'It's somewhat of a surprise visit,' I acknowledge. 'We're covering a lot of ground, talking to a lot of people. I'm hoping you have some time to chat with me.'

'Mary Flynn,' announces a robotic female voice from a speaker in the ceiling.

The woman in the corner tosses her magazine on the coffee table and strides across the room. Smiling shyly at Carlyle, she pushes one of the wooden panels and disappears through it.

'I'd be happy to have a chat, detective.' He ushers me toward a hidden door on the other side of the room. 'My office is this way.'

I follow him along a sleek grey corridor until we reach a chic office where there are more vibrant plants, a tasteful lamp on a glossy wooden desk, and gauzy curtains revealing a lush green lawn in an enclosed garden. 'This is all very impressive,' I remark.

'Is this your first visit to The Lyle?' He sounds delighted, as though he's showing off his newborn baby.

I nod.

'I hope you like what you see.'

I can't help but think how young he looks: his tan skin is clear, his eyes sparkling with good health.

'Would you like some tea? I'm having some.'

'No, thank you.'

I take a seat in an extremely comfortable armchair watching as he pours a shot of tea from a teapot on his desk into a small glass and drinks it in one gulp before settling in the chair opposite, rather than the one behind his desk.

Before I can speak, he says, 'We service a large area, from Smithson to Gowran, and increasingly people are coming from Sydney, even Melbourne and Adelaide. It means their families visit less, but it's preferable to the uninspiring sardine tins on offer in the city.'

I'm not sure whether this is a generic comment or a sales pitch. I think about Dad and wonder if he would ever agree to live in a place like this. Until his heart attack he'd always been so healthy that caring for him in old age seemed a long way off. I'm certain he'd prefer to stay at home, but I suppose at some point that might not be an option.

Carlyle seems to expect a response, so I simply say, 'I've lived away from Smithson a long time and wasn't here when The Lyle was built.'

'Ah, I see.' Folding his hands together, he leans forward slightly and looks at me expectantly.

'I'm sorry about your nephew,' I begin.

'I've endured tragedy before, so there is a familiarity to this situation. But I can assure you it's not the kind of path you want to be experienced in walking. And the shock of something like this is always difficult to process.'

'Of course.' His words ring true when I think about the familiar grooves of my own grief. 'I remember Franklin. We were in primary school together.'

'It's been almost twenty years since his accident, an amount of time that seems impossible.'

'I'm sorry,' I offer again, unsure if it's the right thing to say.

He sniffs in acknowledgement. 'Thank you. At least Roger's murder doesn't involve the humiliation I experienced with my son—and the cruelty of hope.'

I feel a pulse of empathy. It must have been very difficult to be an esteemed clinician specialising in mental health and have a child with such serious mental health issues. The judgement must have been brutal, yet Carlyle persisted and succeeded.

'Is there still hope for Franklin?' I ask tentatively.

Carlyle's face softens. 'I'm not often asked about my son,' he says quietly. 'I appreciate the opportunity to talk about him. Yes, there's progress in the fields of neuroscience and stem cell research. I believe we will be able to bring Franklin back eventually.'

Part of me thinks he's crazy for keeping his son alive, but the other part knows I would probably do the same if it were Ben or Scarlett.

I ask, 'Do you get to see him often?'

'Several times a year. He is in excellent care with my friends in Switzerland.'

'Is any research you're involved in linked to Franklin's condition?'

'Not specifically, although there are adjacent benefits to all scientific developments.'

'I've been reading up on the research centre.'

'I'm glad to hear it,' he says warmly. 'The more people we have interested in science the better.'

'I do wonder about Smithson being positioned as a global scientific hotspot, though. Is that realistic?'

'Why not? I've got support from the mayor and the business community. It could increase our commercial growth by a further ten per cent per year for the next decade.'

'Because of the scientific developments . . . ?' I say, trying to understand.

'In part, yes, but also because it will help attract all kinds of critical roles to the area. The positive halo effect it will have on the community will be unprecedented. We'll run global conferences and set up various clinical trials. This kind of investment is a magnet for young professionals and their partners.'

It's a speech I'm sure he has given before, and his delivery is compelling. The family resemblance with his nephew goes beyond traditional good looks. Roger exuded the same easy charm and firm conviction, but Carlyle also has a gentleness to his demeanour, a softness. But what he's saying still doesn't quite add up to me. I get that Smithson is his home and his ambition has paid off here so far but surely it makes sense to develop the research centre in a major city.

'You didn't consider Sydney or Melbourne?'

A text lights up his phone and he grimaces gently. 'No, I only ever wanted to build my centre in Smithson. I'm sorry, detective, but will this take long? It's been lovely to meet you and have a chat—I'm just not sure how I can help you. I assume you're aware I've spoken to your colleagues.'

I scramble to catch up with his gear change. 'Yes, they were checking off your alibi and gathering basic information.'

'And you're here for something else?'

His grey eyes fix on me and I experience an odd sensation. It's as if he knows what I'm thinking. I rearrange my legs and reset my expression in an attempt to override the feeling. I came here on a whim, partly out of curiosity and partly because I wanted to speak to Carlyle myself and not be stuck with more of Everett's second-hand information. But now that I'm here I find myself wanting his professional perspective. I've worked with psychs throughout my career and I'm sure he will have formed a robust psychological profile of his nephew whether he intended to or not.

'I'd like to know what you think your nephew did—or didn't do—that led to someone wanting him out of the picture.'

'I wish I could tell you.'

'You have no opinion?'

A smile flutters across his lips. 'I always have an opinion but it's not going to give you any answers, just context, I suppose you'd call it.'

'I'm listening,' I say. I can see why he has done so well in his field; he has such a nice way of putting things.

'Well, detective, I think it's fair to say my nephew carried the Kirk curse.'

He states this so earnestly it implies I'm supposed to know what he's talking about but I haven't a clue.

I clear my throat. 'Sorry, what does that mean, exactly?'

He plucks a pen from his shirt pocket and twirls it deftly. 'Roger comes from a line of tortured geniuses—my grandfather, my great-grandmother and her mother before that; more recently, my mother, my brother and my son.' He pauses briefly and looks at the pen. His expression is sad and I'm sure he is thinking about Franklin. 'On a good day I put myself in the same category.'

'I'm sorry, but I don't really see your point.'

'We Kirks are highly intelligent and driven, but sometimes these qualities are directed toward misguided ventures. For Franklin, it was drugs and railing against authority. He suffered from manic episodes, severe highs and lows. For my mother, it was dangerous men. For my grandfather, it was gambling. Gambling is my brother's vice, too—or at least it was until he was estranged from the family.

For me it's work, and Roger was the same. We are passionate about what we do, but we can be unhealthy about it.'

'And you think this led to Roger being murdered?'

'Roger and I were close from a business point of view, but we didn't talk a great deal about personal matters. In recent years I recognised in him an obsessiveness about work that has caused me to act foolishly in the past. And with Roger there was something else, too—he was quite distracted by money and power.'

'He was trying to attract investors for the research centre,' I say. 'I assume it's hard to avoid becoming quite focused on money.'

'Yes. But Roger was on the phone to investors around the clock, chasing every deal as if his life depended on it. It was unhealthy. I was worried about him.'

I lean forward, mirroring his stance. 'I'm still not understanding why you think Roger's workaholic tendencies might have led to someone wanting him dead.'

'I'm not confident I can draw a direct line between the two for you. It's simply my observation that Roger became greedy. He had never been exposed to this level of wealth before, and he became addicted to it, calling me at all hours, wanting to discuss ideas and opportunities.' Carlyle looks away, as if he's retrieving a memory. 'Then, over the past month or so, he stopped sharing information with me . . . and Dominique, although that is another story. He withdrew. I now believe, considering what happened, that along the way he became tangled up in something, something, ah—' he looks around the room as if searching for the right words '—something that became dangerous.'

'Dangerous,' I repeat, but I'm considering his mention of Dominique. They seemed close outside the crime scene, and I don't think Carlyle is in a relationship. I wonder if he was the catfisher. I wouldn't be surprised to discover he knows how to conceal himself online; if he doesn't, he must know people who could do it on his behalf. But why? I think about the content of the emails. Maybe he has feelings for Dominique but couldn't act on them because of Roger. Or maybe it's more sinister—wooing Dominique might have been a way to exert perverse power over his nephew.

'Roger was exhibiting signs of poor decision-making,' Carlyle continues. 'He started doing foolish things, such as trying to pit investors against one another. We had a come-to-Jesus moment about a fortnight ago, and discussed whether he was the right person to be announced as CEO. He was contrite and convincing and, against my better judgement, we went ahead with the original plan.'

'Against your better judgement because you didn't believe he could change his ways?'

'I had a gut feeling. I'm sure you experience them in your line of work. They have no scientific explanation but I rarely find them to be wrong.'

'And you think Roger was involved in something dangerous? Can you be more specific?'

'I saw his body, detective.' He winces at the memory and begins spinning the pen through his fingers again. It must be a nervous tic. 'I don't think the danger is a point of contention.'

I try to clarify. 'What I mean is, do you Roger's death was linked to his business dealings or something else?'

Carlyle seems disappointed in my question. 'It stands to reason that if you gather the evidence, you will find your answers.'

I'm annoyed at his unsolicited advice and I'm starting to feel like I'm being managed. I ask him outright, switching to a direct approach. 'Do you know who killed your nephew, Dr Kirk?'

He blinks in surprise but quickly resumes his unflappable persona. 'I would obviously tell you if I did!'

'Was Dominique involved in Roger's business dealings?'

Carlyle laughs politely. 'Absolutely not. She's a sweet woman, but she does not have a mind for business. She's far more interested in spending money than making it.'

'She generates a revenue stream from selling art, surely?'

'She does well off the back of our connections.' He gestures to a canvas featuring a hazy blur of white and yellow shapes near his office door. 'But outside of the art world she would be lost.'

Maybe my theory is off, I'm not getting the sense that he has any interest in her. 'The marriage was in trouble—had they decided to separate?'

'I'd say that was the most likely path forward, although Roger was in no hurry.'

'Was he involved with someone else?'

Carlyle lifts his shoulders briefly. 'I've learned never to say never when it comes to that kind of thing, but I very much doubt it. He was simply obsessed with his work.'

'Lots of busy people manage to find time for an affair.'

'True.' Carlyle presses his lips together as he studies me intently and I fight the urge to squirm. Can he tell I'm talking from experience? I let out the breath I'd been holding as he continues.

'But Roger loved Dominique, even though he was neglecting her. He was too wrapped up in his own ventures to be worried about anyone else.'

'Do you think—'

He holds out an open hand to quieten me and stands. From someone else this might come across as rude but from him it seems gracious. 'Detective, I have enjoyed our conversation very much, but I have appointments and funeral arrangements to attend to. You know where to find me should you need to talk again.'

It feels like an invite to see him professionally and I scramble to my feet and stand as tall as I can to reassert the appropriate dynamic. 'Yes, of course. Thank you for taking the time.'

He reaches past me to his desk and picks up a brochure. 'Here, please take this.'

A full-bleed shot of The Lyle complex is on the front page with a gold-embossed headline reading *Welcome to a Healthier Life.*

'I'm happy to show you around or discuss our services if you want to make an appointment.' He presses a button on the phone on his desk.

I open the brochure and scan the copy. It does look a lot better than the other aged care facilities I've seen. Maybe I should use it to guide a discussion about the future with Dad. 'Thank you.'

The door swings open and the elegant lady from reception appears.

Carlyle smiles. 'Esme, please show the detective out. And please give her a Harmony voucher.' He places his hand on the small of my back and brings his head to mine conspiratorially as he guides me to the door. 'We offer meditation, yoga, Pilates, music therapy, nutrition plans—all wonderful for stress.'

CHAPTER TWENTY-EIGHT

As I return to the car park, the chorus of birds and insects is almost offensive in contrast with the cool stillness of Carlyle's consulting rooms. I found my conversation with him stimulating if not slightly unnerving; I can't shake the feeling he could see right through me. His response to his nephew's death intrigues me, too. It's as if the scientific world he operates in has forced him to be exceptionally pragmatic, making him almost immune to typical human emotions.

I look up at Lyle Lodge again, marvelling at its scale. Carlyle's ambition is admirable whether it's curing his son or building a world-class research centre in Smithson. I can see why he's been so successful: his quiet confidence is compelling.

'Detective, hi!'

Keys in hand, I spin around to see Boyd Mattingly standing a few metres away beside a striking auburn-haired woman. Pleasantly surprised, I shield my eyes from the glare. 'Hello! What are you doing here?'

He walks over to me, jerking a thumb toward the retirement home. 'This is my target audience. I'm here all the time.'

I frown, feeling slightly alarmed. 'To review suspicious deaths . . . ?'

He grins. 'Always assuming the worst is a terrible habit, detective! I've only had two suspicious death investigations here, and both were suspected assisted suicides that turned out to be natural. Mainly it's just cause of death stuff, but we're not fussy—we take whatever we're given. Don't we, Claire?' He turns and realises the woman hasn't joined him. 'Claire! Get over here.'

She weaves between the cars and holds out her hand, offering me a smile to rival Julia Roberts's.

'Detective Gemma Woodstock, this is Claire Messenger.'

'It's great to meet you, Claire.'

'Likewise. I've heard a lot about you. You're such a go-getter!'

I don't know how to respond to this. I'm sure she means it as a compliment, but it makes me uncomfortable, especially as I'm not sure what she's referencing.

'Thanks,' I say.

'She's so modest.' Claire directs this to Boyd, which feels patronising.

This time I don't reply but just stand awkwardly in front of them.

I study Claire. Soft tailored layers flatter her lanky figure, and a thick leather belt cinches her svelte waist. Her skin glows and her amber eyes are rimmed with a striking green liner.

She meets my gaze and smiles widely. 'You're just back from parental leave, right?'

'Only half back,' I say. 'I'm actually heading home now to look after my daughter.'

'It will be great to work with someone who knows the ropes so well.'

'I might be a bit rusty!'

'Rubbish,' Boyd says. 'Gemma knows Smithson like I know small intestines—hideously well.'

We all laugh.

Mindful I've been accused of frostiness toward female peers in the past, I ask Claire, 'Where have you found a place?'

'Over on Carlton Street, near the pool. I'm a swimmer, so it's the perfect spot for me.'

'Nice,' I say. She looks like a swimmer, tall with broad shoulders.

Boyd holds out an open biscuit tin full of shortbread. 'Want one? A resident called Maisie baked them for me—or more likely she stole them from the kitchen, seeing as she's ninety-five, but either way they're good.'

Claire nods enthusiastically and helps herself. 'This is my third,' she says proudly.

'Ah, sure.' I take a biscuit. They're right: it is delicious.

Boyd says approvingly, 'Nothing beats old people treats—they never go easy on the sugar.' Chewing, he asks, 'What about you, Gemma? What brings you here?'

'Just following up a few items in regard to the Roger Kirk investigation.'

Boyd nods. 'Can't say that one has been easy to shake from my mind.'

'I saw the photos,' says Claire soberly. 'It was brutal.'

'Has anything turned up yet?' Boyd asks. 'The scene didn't give you much to work with.'

'It's been slow going,' I admit.

Behind us, a well-dressed couple emerge from the gleaming automatic doors of Lyle Lodge. The woman is checking things off on her fingers, the veins in her neck straining as she talks, while the man walks in silence, hands in his pockets. They get into a shiny white Land Rover and peel out of the car park; I can see the woman's mouth moving through the tinted window.

I'm reminded that beyond the soft furnishings and delicious biscuits, this place is a well-oiled money-making machine. Mental health, wellness and aged care are big business, and Carlyle's vision and determination ensured he hit the jackpot with all three. Considering the full car park and research centre plans, it's clear that the lawsuit had no long-lasting impact on his reputation or success.

'How long have you been coming out here?' I ask Boyd, keen to get his take on the historical accusations.

He's licking crumbs from his fingers. 'Must be at least ten years or so now.'

'What's your take on the negligence claims from a few years back?'

He shrugs good-naturedly. 'I never saw anything that had me concerned.'

'This is heaven compared to some of the places I've had to deal with,' says Claire passionately. 'I could tell you the most *appalling* stories but I wouldn't want to say them out loud they're so awful.'

'Surely there isn't smoke without fire,' I press. 'There were multiple claims.'

'Apart from a few grumpy staff,' she replies, 'the place runs like clockwork. Even the food is good—' She laughs and lays a hand across her flat stomach as if to prove a point.

'I'm sure it's fine now, but wasn't there evidence of neglect back then?' I smile and angle my body toward Boyd, directing my question to him. Claire's earnestness is starting to grate a little. 'I read about food being withheld from patients.'

'You're challenging the old memory a bit, detective,' he says, 'but I think it all originated from a pair of wealthy sisters who got it in their heads their mother was being abused by a staff member. I believe one sister had been treated by Carlyle in his psych clinic and that hadn't gone well, so perhaps there was bad blood there. Regardless, they put their poor mother, who was in her nineties, through the ringer with all kinds of tests. They made her give several statements and rallied a few other children of patients to come forward with various complaints, and it snowballed from there.'

I feel sorry for this woman who was probably intimidated by the legal process, especially as I get the feeling Boyd thinks it was unnecessary. 'How do you know what they were claiming wasn't true?'

'I don't,' he admits, 'but I never saw anything to cause concern, and I met the sisters. I'm afraid it was a case of two people believing their own hype and others jumping on the bandwagon. I think the outcome was the right one,' he adds diplomatically.

'And do you have a lot to do with Carlyle?' I ask him.

'He's very inspiring,' Claire butts in excitedly. 'Some of his ideas are out there, but you have to admire his pioneering spirit. More people like him are needed in the science world.'

'We don't tend to deal with him directly.' Boyd wipes his mouth and puts the biscuit tin into his backpack. 'But occasionally there's an issue with an autopsy report, and he gets involved.'

'What do you make of him, Boyd?'

'Claire's right—the man is a visionary. He's extremely driven, and it's paid off. I admire his ambition. And his age doesn't seem to be slowing him down.'

'He *is* a total workaholic,' adds Claire. 'But aren't we all!' She laughs at her own joke, her eyes on her phone as she types something. Based on her comment I assume it's work-related.

'I'm not sure he thinks much of me.' Boyd smiles ruefully. 'Usually, my presence is linked to death and paperwork.'

I laugh. 'I guess I'm in the same boat.'

'But you know,' Boyd continues thoughtfully, 'I've never seen him flustered, not even after what happened this week. He is the epitome of being good in a crisis.'

Claire nods, then asks seemingly out of the blue, 'Is there any news on the Jane Doe whose body went missing?'

'We're following up several leads,' I say, feeling annoyed. 'Hopefully we can identify her soon.'

She exhales dramatically and smiles again. 'I hope so. I would hate for a relative of mine to be taken like that. It's so important for the family to get closure.'

'Yes, it is. You were scheduled to do the autopsy on Monday morning, is that right?'

'Yes.' She's playing absently with a delicate pearl ring on her middle finger, and I notice she doesn't wear a wedding ring. 'The alert came in at, what, nine pm?' She looks at Boyd for confirmation. 'It wasn't urgent, so I agreed to go get her in the morning. Obviously now I wish I'd insisted on going in straight away.'

It takes me a moment to process what she's said. 'Hang on, you agreed to come in the following morning? What do you mean?'

Claire seems puzzled. 'The hospital suggested I come in the morning. They were short-staffed and thought it might be easier to wait.'

'Who at the hospital?'

'Sophie McCallister.'

CHAPTER TWENTY-NINE

Candy is holding court with the kids. Lola and Scarlett are in their highchairs, staring at her as if she's a magical creature—and maybe she is. The house is spotless, and there are two clean plastic bowls drying in the dish rack. Scarlett squeals when I walk in but immediately returns her attention to Candy.

'Successful morning?' Candy is expertly twisting a balloon into the shape of a heart.

'It was . . . interesting.'

'Anything *I'd* find interesting?'

'Have you secretly become a kids' party host in your spare time?' I drop my bag on the table and pour a glass of water, admiring the collection of balloon shapes on the table. There's a dog, a cat and an impressive array of magenta fish.

'I just google shit I think she'll like and teach myself how to do it. A bag of these bad boys is cheaper than a Disney+ subscription.'

'Very impressive,' I say.

'So, you were telling me about your big breakthroughs.'

I pluck Scarlett from her highchair. 'Nice try.'

'Gemma, come on. You know I live vicariously and emotionally through you.'

'No big breakthroughs, unfortunately. Everett was being a dick at the case meeting.'

'Hardly a newsflash.'

'Do you know anything about him, like why he moved here?'

'I'm not sure . . . but I can find out, if you like.'

'No, it's fine. I've asked around. I just thought you might have heard something.'

'All I've heard about is his ego,' she says. 'I figured he moved here for a tree change.'

'Maybe,' I murmur. 'Also, I met the new assistant ME, Claire Messenger.'

'Classy Claire,' says Candy approvingly. 'Good to have a woman in the mix—it's been a bit of a barbecue in the dead zone since Anna left.'

'Claire seems nice,' I reply evenly. 'Enthusiastic.'

'I like her,' Candy declares. 'We've caught up a few times for a drink.'

I feel a pulse of envy. 'You have? When?'

'When she first moved here, just after you had Scarlett. I wanted to get her onside, but I ended up just digging her vibe. She's fun.'

'That's great.'

With a smirk, Candy says, 'There are rumours about her and Boyd Mattingly, you know.'

'I thought he was married?'

'His wife quietly moved back to Melbourne last year. Apparently she was sick of him being married to the job.'

I think about bumping into Boyd and Claire earlier: they were very easy with each other. 'Do *you* think they're seeing each other?'

'Well, she seemed very happy to be single after a shocker of a break-up,' Candy says. 'Maybe they're just shagging. I'll ask her when we catch up next. You should come!'

'I'm sure I'll get to know her better once I'm back in the swing of things.'

She smirks again, and I smile back: we both know I don't want to have a drink with Claire.

'I went out to see Carlyle Kirk at The Lyle,' I say, changing the subject.

'It's incredible, isn't it?'

'I had no idea it was so big. Must have cost a fortune.'

'Millions,' she says, 'but aged care is such a cash cow it's already turning a profit. Nate loves all that stuff, so I did a bunch of stories on it when I worked with him.'

'Carlyle's interesting,' I say.

'The understatement of the century.'

'He's clearly still grief-stricken about his son.' I consider that Franklin is his Achilles heel, the main focus of his emotions and the experiment he can't fully justify but will never quit.

'What are you thinking?' Candy says, hungry for any scrap of information.

'I'm just trying to consider all the angles.'

She scowls. 'I've had Australia Post deliveries ship faster than this story.'

I can't help laughing.

Her scowl turns into a smile as she wipes food from Scarlett's face. Appreciation surges through me, and I think of how important her friendship is to me.

Meanwhile, I haven't heard from Mac. I shake my head; I don't have the energy to fall into another worry spiral about our relationship.

Arching her back, Candy yawns loudly. 'Well, Gem, if it's okay with you I'll head off on my hippy adventure. My stories aren't going to write themselves.'

'I still don't think you should be going out there on your own.'

'Don't worry, I've roped Sam in to coming with me so I can get some footage in case this story pans out. He can double as a bodyguard and take on the psycho peacekeepers.'

I laugh at the thought of lanky, gentle Sam taking on anyone. Candy is far more likely than he is to get into a physical fight.

She grabs her bag and kisses Lola on the head, then Scarlett. I walk her to the door. The wind has really picked up; branches writhe chaotically, contorting like drunk dancers.

'Call me when you get out there,' I say, hugging her goodbye.

'See you later!' She gets into her car, fluffing her frizzy hair as she checks herself out in the mirror.

After I watch her drive off, I return to the kitchen. 'Right, you two,' I say, voice bright, 'what should we do now?'

Both kids stare at me blankly.

'Maybe I can read to you.' I'm already wondering how long is reasonable until I can turn on the TV. I read them a few books, and Lola jumps around repeating some of the words, making Scarlett laugh.

My thoughts wander to the case. Did Sophie deliberately delay the collection of the corpse? Could she be involved in a grave-robbing venture? Or perhaps the dead woman was a drug mule, and someone promised Sophie a cut of the profits. She seems so proper, but maybe she was sick of working hard for Roger and wanted to get rich quick.

Is Carlyle right about Roger? Had he become so obsessed with the new venture that he wasn't behaving rationally, and could that have motivated whoever killed him? It's clear he made promises he couldn't keep. But the motive isn't what's really bothering me—it's more that we need to match the motive with the brutality and professionalism of the attack. It was a clean job, like a hit, and it gives credit to Everett's theory that someone might have paid to have him killed.

Without taking in any details, I've been reading book after book to the kids. I'm interrupted by a sharp bang outside. It sounds like a branch has fallen against the shed.

'Read!' Lola yells. 'Read more!'

'I will in a minute, Lols. I'm just not sure what that sound was.' As the trees continue to shake wildly, the sky is transitioning to a dark indigo. I hope Candy will be okay—tough as she is, she's at her best when she is well groomed.

I try to keep reading in a cheerful voice but am too unnerved by the erratic weather.

'Intermission!' I announce. I change their nappies and make Scarlett a bottle. I secure her in her bouncer, and she gurgles the milk greedily while I heat up some porridge and stir pureed apple through it. I feed Lola in her highchair, readjusting Scarlett's bottle every few minutes. I'm proud that so far everything is under control.

My thoughts drift again, this time to the stolen corpse. We need her DNA report in case she's a match with a missing person or a crime scene; we need a lead to follow, a thread to pull. Maybe I should just call the lab—I'm sick of having to ask Everett for things.

A text from my old colleague Nan appears on my phone:

Hi Gemma, nice to hear from you. Yes, I know Julian Everett a little, but I never worked closely with him. Overconfident and smug is my take. I don't know what happened, but he left in a hurry. I think he pissed off some big-wig. Good luck with that. Cheers, Nan

After I clean up the food, I burp Scarlett while walking her around the kitchen. What did Everett do in his old role? People clash in the force all the time, but it sounds like a specific incident prompted his move. I could always ask Jonesy, but I don't want to seem petty. I settle Scarlett back in her bouncer and jiggle it until her eyes glaze over, then I give Lola a sippy cup of water and wolf down a piece of toast.

Mac finally texts me, asking how my day is. I reply with a photo of Lola and Scarlett, not bothered if it makes him feel guilty.

There's another bang outside, louder this time, and then another. A branch must be hitting the shed roof now. 'It's crazy out there,' I murmur.

Lola is wiping water on the highchair tray, and Scarlett is close to sleep.

'It's time for a nap, Lola. What do you think? Scarlett's asleep—'

'No!' she roars. 'Not me!'

A gust of wind sends the branches skyward again. It takes me a moment to realise that the knocking is coming from the front door. 'I'd better see who that is.'

'Ding-dong!' Lola calls out in her high-pitched voice.

I pause in the doorway and make a silly face at her. She squeals and slams the sippy cup on the table. I put my finger to my mouth. 'Shhhh.'

In the hallway I close my left eye and look through the peephole. No one's there. The hedge that borders the porch blocks off the view to the street, but there's no car in the driveway. Maybe it's a delivery—something for Mac.

I open the door. Nothing. I step out, stand on my tiptoes and crane my neck. No one is parked in the street. Lola yells out again, and I step inside. I pull the door shut and head toward the kitchen.

A chill slices through me as the door I just closed swings open.

Arms circle me roughly and push me forward against the wall. A hand clamps across my nose and mouth. I'm lifted off the ground, a knee digging into my spine. Then there's a sharp sting in my neck, as I try but fail to scream.

CHAPTER THIRTY

Everything hurts. I'm face down on concrete, my left cheek pressing against the cold surface. My arms and legs are bound behind me. My eyes won't open, and I yell but no sound comes. Is there something in my mouth, or is it that my mouth won't move? I can't feel most of my face.

Where am I? How long have I been here? Sobs ricochet silently around my numb body. My god, what if the girls have been attacked, too, or abducted, or worse? Why can't I open my eyes? I strain to hear anything that will help me orientate myself, but a monotonous roar is pulsing through my ears—the wind outside, or perhaps just my own blood pumping.

I can't cry; I can't move. I lie in the darkness, praying, *pleading* that Scarlett and Lola are safe. But I'm imagining the worst.

Mac—why isn't he here? The girls need him. *I* need him. I remember the soul-shattering pain as I pushed Scarlett out of my body, the hollowness afterwards, the utter depletion and almost intolerable fulfilment when I held her slimy body against mine. Mac gazed adoringly at her, completely besotted. Where is Scarlett? And Ben—where is Ben? I will die if something happens to Ben.

My thoughts jump to Scott, sick in the hospital, then my dad pasty-white after his heart attack. Roger's bloody corpse against the stark white of the rug. The abandoned baby in the hospital crib; the mothers at the lake with their cool curiosity. Jonesy telling me he's leaving. Everett mocking me. 'Did you grow up in Smithson?' he yells at me. 'Did you?' I recoil and back into a corner, away from him, and find myself at one of the counselling sessions I had in Sydney years ago—but Carlyle Kirk is the counsellor. 'Why do you do this, detective? Why do you always sabotage your own happiness?' His bony fingers steeple at his chest. 'Don't you think you deserve to be happy?'

A sliver of real vision. My left eye is open.

I try to make sense of my surroundings. Mac's bike. Storage boxes. An unfamiliar blue rug and a bedside table I bought in Sydney that has a broken drawer.

I'm in our shed—I haven't been out here since we moved in. Past my feet I can see all the way into the empty carport at the back of the garage door. Closer to me there's a stack of archive boxes I've never seen before. They must be Mac's. But then I notice one of them has *Smithson 1978–79 Braybrook* scrawled on its side, so perhaps they are mine. I try to clear the grainy film across my vision. No, I'm sure I've never seen them before.

I can hear crying. I don't move. I don't breathe. There it is again—I'm sure of it. Is it Lola? Scarlett? Is it me? I try to lift my head, but after a few attempts the floor disappears. I'm plummeting through the darkness once more.

CHAPTER THIRTY-ONE

Someone is calling my name.

I shift to the right and wince as pain darts down my arm. My muscles ache, and my mouth tastes stale. I'm freezing—my top has ridden up and exposed my midriff, which scrapes against the rough concrete, but I can't move my hands to pull it down. I strain against whatever is holding my limbs behind me, but I can't break free.

'In here,' I whisper hoarsely.

Tears stream from my eyes. I picture Scarlett and Lola in the house alone and helpless with the person who attacked me. Oh god, please, *please* let them be okay.

My name again, louder this time. Then a rattling that isn't the wind.

With a protracted groan, the side door to the shed heaves open. A gust of cold air hits my bare stomach. I hear a sharp intake of breath and feel footsteps vibrate through the floor. 'Gemma! Gemma? Oh my god.' It's Candy. 'Call them again,' she hisses. 'Tell them it's an emergency and then go back inside.' I feel warmth on my face. 'Hey, hey, you're okay. Gemma, holy fuck. Who did this? What happened?'

'The kids,' I murmur through cracked lips.

'They're okay.'

She exhales around a shaky sob, and something inside me breaks. In all our years of friendship, I've never seen Candy cry.

'Gemma, can you open your eyes, tell me what happened?'

'I don't know, I—' I keep picturing Ben and Scarlett being taken from me.

'It's okay. Here.' Candy lifts my head and slides something soft underneath it. She strokes my face, and I try to keep my breath even, try to feel my toes and fingers. 'I'm not sure if I should move you. Fuck, I should have done that bloody first-aid course Philip is always pestering me about. Are you hurt?'

I moan but manage to say, 'Where are the kids?'

'Gemma, they're fine, I promise. Sam's inside with them now. He's called for help.'

She runs her fingers through my hair as she keeps talking. I'm aware she's trying to stop me from losing my mind, to assure me that everything is going to be okay.

'We went out to The Retreat. What a fizzer. Just a bunch of families planting vegetables and singing "Kumbaya". To be honest it was kind of nice in its own weird way, very peaceful. They could make a fortune renting it out as a bed and breakfast. There must be at least two dozen families living out there. And the vegie garden is ridiculous! Everything is double the size you get in the supermarket— god knows what they put in that dirt. I don't know, maybe it's not such a bad idea, raising kids like that. You know, everyone chipping in and twenty-four seven built-in babysitting. I can see the benefits, even if those people are all completely nuts.'

She's babbling, but I'm thankful: trying to follow her narrative helps me stay focused.

'We found a guy who seems to be in charge—like the head dad guy or something—and asked him about Lee Blight. But he had no idea who we were talking about. And, honestly, I'm not sure it makes sense that Lee was there, because it's only families and young couples wanting to start a family. Maybe he stayed somewhere else, and Henno was confused. There are probably a bunch of wellbeing places that people can go to and disappear for a while.'

I hear a car door slam, and Candy scrambles to her feet. I peel open my eyes and see her shoe, then have to close them.

'In here!' The relief in her voice is palpable.

More footsteps. 'Jesus. Is she all right?' It's Everett, or at least I think it is—a nasty headache has latched on to my skull with a vice-like grip.

I can't make out Candy's response, her voice echoing around me.

A scraping sound is followed by the snipping of scissors. My limbs are free, and I gasp, the pain momentarily worse as my muscles tense before the release comes. Firm hands grip my shoulders, then make their way along my body. My eyelids are pulled open, a bright light blasted into each pupil. 'Gemma, Gemma, can you hear me?'

'Mmm.'

'I don't think anything is broken,' a man says. 'Let's load her up.'

I'm rolled on my back, lifted sideways and secured at the middle before I'm suspended in mid-air. I cough and try to talk, but my tongue feels thick, and I can't get it into the right position.

'We think you've been drugged, Gemma,' Everett says with uncharacteristic kindness. 'Don't worry, I'm making sure you're being looked after.'

My eyes flutter open, and I see an unfamiliar ambulance officer. His name badge reads *Fred*: Ash Amato's partner. I try to ask for Ash, but Fred hushes me.

I'm wheeled into the driveway. The streetlights are on; I must have been out of it for hours. My entire body is aching, and a fuzziness hums across my scalp. Thoughts circle my head at a dizzying speed. 'Scarlett?' I whisper. 'Ben?'

'Your kids are fine.' Everett's voice comes from above me. 'Your son is with his stepmother, and Scarlett is with our officers. We haven't told your son that anything is wrong.'

I'm grateful for Everett's bluntness. But when I moisten my lips to say thank you, I can't get the words out.

The sky shakes and then disappears as I'm loaded into an ambulance. Its door closes with a crunch and the engine rumbles. Capable hands fuss over me, and an oxygen mask is fixed over my nose and mouth.

The last thing I see, before I drift away, is Ash's worried face staring down at me.

CHAPTER THIRTY-TWO

Scarlett is asleep in the crook of Mac's arm, the light from his phone illuminating his face. He looks exhausted. Panic seizes my chest but then I remember that the kids are okay. I let out a long shaky breath, relief coursing through me.

'Hi,' I say huskily, after a few moments.

Mac lurches forward, startling Scarlett. 'Gemma! Oh, thank god. How are you feeling? Hang on, the doctor just left. I'll grab her.'

I don't protest as he leaves the hospital room. As I push myself up, I wince at the pain in my wrist and shoulder. I feel weak but alert, my mind blissfully sharp again. The events of the day flood back—the attack, the shed, my fears for the kids—and I focus on my surroundings to distract myself. The décor is the same as in Dad's room, but there are no flowers or cards, just medical equipment and one of Scarlett's bottles on the table next to my bed.

Mac returns with a doctor.

'What time is it?' I ask.

'It's good to see you awake, Detective Woodstock.' She checks my blood pressure and asks me a few questions while Mac holds

259

Scarlett, looking worried. 'Right.' The doctor sounds satisfied. 'Aside from a few bruises, you're doing very well. Unless anything changes, we'll be sending you home tomorrow morning. You should feel a lot better over the next few hours.'

'What time is it?' I repeat.

'Almost midnight,' the doctor replies. 'You've been asleep for a few hours.'

'I was drugged . . . ?'

Her mouth forms a thin line. 'We believe you were knocked out with Propofol. It's an anaesthetic mainly used in surgical procedures, so there's no long-term damage—although you were given a dangerously high dose. Anyway—' her voice lifts again, and she smiles '—you should be almost back to normal tomorrow, but sing out if you need anything, okay?'

I nod.

'I'll leave you to it.'

'Where's Ben?' I ask Mac the second she leaves.

'Staying with Jodie—she's going to take him and Ruby to see her parents at their farm tomorrow, so we don't need to worry about him. Jodie knows something is up. Someone at the restaurant told her you're back at work, so she was asking me questions.'

I sigh. Jodie has never been shy when it comes to expressing her uneasiness about my job. Our relationship has always been polite but strained, although it's got worse since Scott died. We're civil for Ben's sake, and I don't ever question the time he spends with her—mainly because I want him to have a relationship with his half-sister. Jodie is a decent person, but I can't shake the feeling she's bitter that I got so much more time with Scott than she did. I find her painfully judgemental, and Scott told me she thinks I'm deliberately intimidating. Maybe we'll never be on the same page.

'I'll talk to her,' I tell Mac.

He nods, sitting on the edge of the bed and gently taking my hand. 'God, Gemma, I'm so glad you're okay.' Squeezing his eyes shut, he holds my hand to his lips. 'I was beside myself when Candy called.'

'I'm sorry. It happened so fast, I couldn't . . . I should have—'

'Don't.' He shakes his head, eyes shining in the dim light. '*I'm* sorry. I should have been there.'

My vision blurs as I stroke Scarlett's face. 'If anything happened to her or Lola, I don't think I could keep going.'

'She's fine,' murmurs Mac, but I can tell his mind has gone to the same dark places mine has.

'Excuse us.' Everett is at the door with Jonesy.

'Jesus, Woodstock, you don't bloody do things by halves.' Jonesy's tone is light, but his face is etched with concern.

'Are you up to answering a few questions?' Everett asks. 'We're obviously keen to speak with you as soon as possible.'

'Yes, of course.' I know how important it is for a victim or witness to recount the details before they fade and morph.

'Let me know when you're done,' Mac says to them, squeezing my hand again.

I squeeze back, feeling uncharacteristically needy. His blue irises glow with concern.

After he has gone, I tell Everett and Jonesy what I remember. It feels like we're doing role-play, an exercise we might do for training purposes, although the underlying panic that flares as I recall the attack makes me know it's real. Everett frowns while taking notes. Jonesy balls his fists when I describe being grabbed at the front door.

'And after the check-in this morning, you went to The Lyle, right?' Everett says, once I've told them everything I can think of about the attack.

'That's right,' I say, trying to recall if I told him I was going there.

'I spoke to Carlyle this afternoon,' Everett elaborates, sensing my uncertainty. 'He mentioned your visit.'

I can't tell if Everett is annoyed.

'Carlyle had some interesting things to say about Roger's recent behaviour,' I say. 'Did he tell you that Roger was almost ditched from the CEO role at the research centre? He was saved by a last-minute board vote. Also, I met Claire Messenger, who was visiting Lyle Lodge with Boyd. Did you know that Sophie McCallister told her to hold off on picking up the woman's body on Sunday night?'

'She included that in her statement,' Everett replies. 'I'm not sure it means anything. It followed procedure.'

'It wasn't in the file,' I say.

Now Everett looks annoyed. 'I remember her telling Holdsworth, perhaps it got missed but either way there was no reason to rush the autopsy, so I really don't think it's incriminating.'

Frustratingly, Jonesy doesn't seem bothered by the missing info or Sophie's instructions.

'I think it's worth revisiting with her,' I insist.

'Everett can follow this up with her tomorrow,' says Jonesy, drawing a line under the topic. 'Now Woodstock, did you go anywhere after you saw Carlyle?'

'No, I went straight home. I needed to watch the kids.'

'Because your *journo mate* wanted to do recon at The Retreat,' Everett says. 'Her idea entirely, I'm sure.'

'You obviously spoke to Candy.'

'Yes, at the scene,' Everett says.

'At your house,' Jonesy clarifies. 'She was extremely worried about you. We all were.'

'She must have completely freaked out when she found the kids alone—she knows I would never leave them unless something happened to me.'

'The kids are fine,' Everett says firmly. 'Whoever attacked you didn't touch them, and luckily you had them safely strapped in the highchair and the bouncer. They won't remember a thing.'

My eyes well with tears as all the what-ifs force their way into my imagination again.

'They're fine, Gemma,' Everett reiterates.

I nod, grateful again for his blunt assurance.

'Did the person who attacked you say anything?' Jonesy asks.

'Not a word.'

'And nothing has happened at your house in the lead-up to this?' Everett asks. 'No break-in or prowler, no drive-by, no hang-ups?'

'Not as far as I know. We don't even have a landline connected.'

'Mac doesn't think anything is missing,' he says, 'but we'll need you to check as well. Jewellery, cash, electronics, documents—you know the drill.'

'Do you think it was an attempted robbery?'

'Not really,' he says, 'but it's always a possibility.'

I remember waking up in the shed, seeing the furniture—and the storage boxes.

'Was anything taken from the shed?' I ask.

'Mac doesn't think so,' Everett says.

We lock eyes before he looks away. His dismissiveness feels loaded, but maybe that's just because I'm tired. I'll ask Mac about the boxes later.

'The perpetrator knew what they were doing,' I say. 'It was very well timed, ringing the doorbell and waiting out of sight before they attacked me. And they're sure of themselves, especially seeing as it was the middle of the day. They're tall and strong. They probably have a medical background, considering they drugged me with a non-lethal but powerful dose of anaesthetic. It might be someone who works here at the hospital. We also need to consider if they were after Candy, not me—she was at the house all morning, and they might not have realised we switched.'

Jonesy grunts in agreement. 'I think you're the more likely target, Woodstock, but it's something we'll look into.'

'Hopefully the forensics team can give us a lead,' says Everett, 'but no doubt the perpetrator was careful, so I'm not holding my breath. We've arranged for security to be outside your room all night. Ms Fyfe's ex is staying at her house tonight, as a precaution.'

Thinking how much Candy will hate that, I almost smile.

He adds, 'We can arrange to have a car at your house this week if you like, too.'

The three of us fall quiet. I wonder if they're thinking what I am, that it might have been someone in emergency services or the military—or even the police force.

'Were there any other case developments today?' I ask, breaking the silence.

'Nothing,' Everett replies, 'unless we count what happened to you.'

'You think it's linked to Roger's murder?' I ask, already knowing the answer.

'I'd bloody say so, Woodstock,' says Jonesy. 'Unless you're involved in something else we don't know about.'

'Of course not,' I mutter. I let my weight sink into the pillow. I know what this means: my role on the investigation is going to be reviewed.

'We've actually been investigating The Retreat as well,' Everett says. 'I was out there today. I must have missed your friend and her sidekick by about an hour.'

I jerk my head in surprise. 'You were looking into The Retreat as part of this case?'

He nods.

'Great minds,' I say sarcastically.

He chuckles. 'At least yours still seems sharp. Clearly there's no permanent damage from today's events.'

'You should be so lucky,' I reply, smiling in spite of myself. 'What were your theories about The Retreat?'

He sniffs and scuffs his shoe on the floor. 'Your property-search theory inspired me actually and I decided to take a look in case our lead on the runaway doesn't pan out. There's been rumours of kids being born out there and never registered, so I wondered if a pregnant teenage resident wanted to get rid of a baby.'

'That was what I wondered, too. I also thought there was a chance the woman from the car crash had been living there and fled—it helped explain her not wearing shoes.'

'Candy said she was looking into someone who'd been staying out there, but that's all she would tell us because she has to protect her sources.'

I'm impressed by Candy's stubbornness even in the face of a police grilling. I wonder how much I can trust Everett, but Jonesy is also waiting for a response, so I say, 'I can leave her sources out of it, but she heard Lee Blight might have been staying there and wanted to confirm if it was true.'

'The kid from the pub fight?' Everett looks confused. 'Why are you interested in him?'

'Marty's kid?' Jonesy says at the same time.

'The circumstances of the fight seem slightly odd, so we were following it up to see if anyone out there had any context,' I reply, reluctant to reveal everything just yet. 'And Candy was planning a story on The Retreat anyway.'

'You think that fight had something to do with The Retreat?' Everett asks.

Before I can answer, Jonesy groans and staggers forward. I strain to sit up and help him but don't have the energy. For an awful second I think he's going to hit the floor but Everett grips his upper arm, pulling him upright. 'You okay, boss?'

Jonesy bats him away, sinking into a chair. 'Just bloody vertigo. I've only had two coffees and some god-awful fruit salad all day. This diet is going to kill me.'

Mac appears in the doorway, dark shadows under his eyes, holding a sleeping Scarlett. He mouths, 'Are you okay?'

Jonesy's breathing remains ragged despite his insistence he's fine. Everett's usually tan complexion is sallow, and god knows what I look like.

I'm suddenly desperate to be alone. 'Let's call it a night,' I say firmly. 'You all look like shit, and I've got some drugs to sleep off.'

CHAPTER THIRTY-THREE

I wake up feeling well enough to eat my cereal and drink my juice. In fact, I feel fine except for my aching shoulder.

After my shower, I dress in the mismatched clothes Mac hurriedly brought last night. Today the attack feels like a dream—I can barely believe it happened. But then my phone pings with an email from New South Wales Police reminding me to access their complimentary psychology services. I'm all for talking about what happened, but right now I'm itching to get out of here and back to working the cases.

The doctor gives me the all-clear to go home. While I wait for Mac in my room, I text Ben and then Jodie, thanking her for having him and saying I'll call her to catch up soon.

I switch on the TV. On the news there's a vaguely insensitive story about the sombre preparations for Roger Kirk's funeral. It features footage of Dominque driving her Porsche out of a funeral home car park while navigating a horde of journos and camera operators who seem to be trying to get run over—I'm glad I don't see Candy or Sam among them. A news anchor says that tomorrow the hospital will hold a minute's silence and a public memorial in Roger's honour. The program jumps to a reporter interviewing Sophie and a man in a dark grey suit outside the main entrance yesterday afternoon, wind tousling their hair. That clip ends with a soundbite from Carlyle declaring that while now is the time to mourn, he understands people want assurance about the research-centre plans. He confirms nothing will change except for the name: it will now be known as the Roger Kirk Research Centre. He adds that it will be operational by October next year.

Next is a story on the missing corpse, even though there are no updates. A popular reporter, dressed in a black shirt and a white pencil skirt, walks in front of a virtual map of New South Wales as photos of missing women appear all around her like letters on *Wheel of Fortune*. She holds out her hands as if offering a bowl of chips at a party. 'It could have been any one of these women's bodies that was stolen from Smithson Hospital last week, denying a family the chance to lay their loved one to rest.'

I refrain from shouting at the TV. DNA results will confirm if the missing body matches any of these lost women. In the meantime, giving any skerrick of false belief to their grieving families is appalling. The photos of the missing women fly into a conga line, each one enlarging when it gets to the left of the reporter's head. She recites their names, ages and home towns in a monotone before concluding with the fact that the local police have no leads and are struggling under the weight of competing investigations.

'Great,' I mutter, feeling the familiar pressure that mounts when a case refuses to break. It's not just the family members and close friends who want closure: except for true-crime podcasters, no one likes an unsolved mystery.

My mobile rings: Everett.

'Good morning,' I say. 'How's Jonesy?'

'Fine. I dropped him home last night. I think he was just spent.'

I'm sure Everett's right, and Jonesy is hardly a healthy specimen, but in all the years we've worked together I've never known him to call in sick or be obviously unwell. In light of Dad's heart attack, it's making me uneasy.

'Anyway, I was just calling to see how you're doing today,' Everett says.

'I'm fine,' I reply quickly. 'About to head home, actually.'

'That's great.'

'Yep. Will you speak to Sophie today?'

'I told Jonesy I would,' he says stiffly.

'Okay, good. And any updates on the runaway teenager?'

'We should get the DNA results any minute to know if we have a match.'

'I hope she's all right.'

He doesn't reply, and I refuse to help him out by filling the awkward silence. While he seemed genuinely concerned about me at the house yesterday, I still have no idea where I stand with him.

'In other news,' he says, surprising me by speaking as though I'm a close confidante, 'Dominique has hired a private investigator to track down her online lover who—surprise, surprise—has stopped responding.'

'She clearly has no faith in the New South Wales Police,' I comment wryly.

'Evidently not.'

'I hope she's ready for whatever she might find. She knows that Dylan Roberts doesn't exist, right?'

'Yes, but I get the feeling she thinks there's still a chance for her and lover boy.'

'Doesn't she realise the catfisher might be a creepy guy with a woman problem or a group of professionals trying to rip her off?'

'I reckon it's an AI chatbot,' says Everett, 'or a teenage boy.'

Encouraged by our banter I say, 'I did wonder if it might have been Carlyle.'

'Why would it be him?'

'I don't know, it was just a thought.'

'I doubt it. He seems above that kind of thing.'

I think about Carlyle's meticulously controlled demeanour. 'Yes, I know what you mean.'

'Anyway, what is certain is that Dominique is very intense. She called five times yesterday requesting information to give to her private investigator.'

'Maybe she and Roger were a better match than she knew,' I say, recalling Roger's intensity. A thought strikes me. 'Do you think there's any chance it was Roger himself?'

'Sending her the emails, you mean?'

'Think about it—if they were having marriage trouble and she was poised to take him to the cleaners, her having an affair would give him some good ammunition and it would explain why they never met.'

'It's possible,' Everett admits. 'And the emails have stopped.'

'True, although that's most likely linked to the nationwide coverage of her husband's murder. But the Roger theory does make sense if we consider—'

'Gemma.' His voice is suddenly serious.

'What?'

'Are you sure it's a good idea for you to keep working this case?'

My pulse quickens. 'What do you mean?'

'After what happened yesterday—'

Disappointment courses through me. Following the roll we were on just now, this feels particularly cruel. 'I told you I'm fine.'

'Gemma, come on. You could have died.'

'It was bad, I know that, and I'm lucky it wasn't worse. But I think it was designed to scare me off. Like you said, they could have killed me if they'd wanted to—' I swallow '—and hurt the kids . . . yet they didn't.'

'I don't think just because whoever attacked you didn't murder you or abduct your kid that everything goes back to normal. You need to lay low for a while. And you know you would advise a victim to do the same if you were in my position.'

My face grows hot. 'You don't get to decide if I work this case.'

'Gemma.' He exhales into the phone. 'I appreciate it's clear I haven't loved having you around, but I respect you as a detective and think we're finding a groove. Anyway, that's all beside the point, because I'm not sure it's safe.'

'You need my help,' I say, trying to keep the desperation out of my voice.

There's a pause.

'Maybe you can just step back a bit,' he concedes. 'Work in the background.'

'You'd love that, wouldn't you?'

'I'm just trying to be reasonable—and responsible. My priority is ensuring your safety.'

'No doubt.'

'Gemma.'

'I've got to go,' I say, ending the call.

Seething, I sit in the uncomfortable chair beside the bed. How dare Everett use what happened to stand me down. My mind strays to the panic I felt when I was attacked, and I dig my heels into the floor, knowing that he's right to be worried. Underneath my frustration *I'm* worried, especially about the kids.

I sense eyes on me.

Mac has arrived with Scarlett. 'Hey. How are you feeling?'

'I'm fine.'

He hesitates at my tone but enters and sits on the edge of the bed opposite my chair.

I sigh. 'Sorry. I'm just . . . Can I hold her?'

He places Scarlett on my lap. 'You've got her?' he says, seemingly reluctant to let go.

'Mac, I *am* fine. The doctor gave me the all-clear.' I don't mention my bruised shoulder. When I kiss Scarlett, I once again thank the universe that she wasn't harmed. 'Apart from this terrible outfit you tricked me into wearing, I feel completely normal.'

'Good.' But the smile doesn't reach his eyes.

'Are *you* okay?'

'Of course. I just feel awful I was away.'

'That's silly.' I reach out to him. 'There's no way you could have known something like this would happen.'

'I still feel bad.'

I lift my hand to his face and trace my fingers along his unshaven jawline. We lock eyes and he breaks away. I move his face, trying to get him to look at me again, but his gaze remains on Scarlett.

'Mac, in the shed when I woke up yesterday, there were a bunch of filing boxes.'

A nurse walks past, pushing medical equipment, and his eyes follow her. 'I put all my case files out there because I didn't want to clutter up the study. But I'm done with most of them now, so I'll send them back.'

'One of them had *Smithson* written on it—and something about Braybrook in the seventies?'

He stands up and brushes down his jeans at the thighs. 'I was sent a lot of info for the cold case I'm working on. Nothing that turned out to be useful, unfortunately.' He smiles at me and Scarlett. 'Should we get going, ladies?'

I decide to leave it alone for now. I just want to get moving.

As we walk through the foyer, we pass Sophie McCallister. *She's setting up for Roger's memorial*, I think, remembering the news report. Her usually neat hair hangs limply around her face, and her eyes dart from left to right as she types on her mobile.

In the car, Mac is quiet. I let my eyes fall out of focus and blur the familiar landmarks, while Scarlett babbles happily in her seat.

Mac pulls into our driveway, and the sun streams through the windscreen, heating my clasped hands. Trees and flowers flutter in the light breeze. He sighs heavily.

'What's up?' I'm annoyed he won't just say whatever's on his mind.

He rubs his eyes before turning to me.

'What?'

'Yesterday really scared me, Gem.'

I soften slightly. 'I know.' Taking his hand, I lace my fingers through his. 'Me too.'

He curls his hand around mine. 'You're deep in these cases,' he says tentatively, 'and I want you to be, I really do, but now I wonder if maybe you should ease off.'

'Oh god, not you, too.' I pull my hand from his grasp. 'Mac, come on! You know it doesn't work like that.'

He presses the skin between his eyes. 'It feels dangerous, Gem. I would never tell you what to do, but you were attacked in our home. Our daughter's life was at risk.'

'*You* would never let a case go,' I snap. I get out of the car and open the back door to retrieve Scarlett. I march up to the house—then realise I don't have my keys so have to wait for Mac to let us in. I scan the neat kitchen and let my gaze go to the backyard, to the shed door. Everything looks the same as always, which is somehow unsettling.

'You're right, in most circumstances I wouldn't,' Mac says. 'But if my family were in danger, I think that would change things.'

I whirl around to face him. 'That's not fair.'

'I'm sorry, Gemma. I am. But the safety of my family and friends is my priority.' He paces, combing his hands through his hair in time with his steps.

'I'll be more careful.' I sit down at the kitchen table. 'And I know how to protect myself.'

'Yesterday could have gone very differently, and that's no reflection on you.'

'Our jobs are dangerous. You know that better than anyone.'

He sits next to me and kisses the side of my face.

'I get it,' I say. 'But I can't just walk away.'

'Maybe you can, though, Gem. Maybe we should stay somewhere else for a while.'

'You want to leave Smithson?' I feel desperate now. It feels like everything is sliding out of my control.

'We could go away for a while. Go to Sydney.'

I can't work out if he's serious or just throwing around options to make himself feel better. 'Ben has school. And you're in the middle of a job. Don't you need to be here?'

He shakes his head. 'It's not important.'

I understand he feels guilty for not being here yesterday and I was frustrated at his last-minute trip but he must know that I don't blame him for what happened. 'That's not true.'

'It's not as important as *this*,' he says, holding out his hands expansively.

'Everett mentioned arranging some security for our home,' I say, picking up my phone from the table. 'So why don't we let him sort that, then we can talk about this later . . . ?'

'What are you doing?' Mac asks, glancing at my phone.

'It's nine. I'm calling into the case meeting.'

Mac grips the back of one of the dining chairs so hard his knuckles go white.

Trying to ignore him, I focus on my call. Minnie answers with a gasp. 'Gemma? Oh my god, I'm so glad you're okay.'

'Thanks, Minnie, I'm fine. I'm hoping you can keep me dialled into the case meeting. Hopefully I'll be back at the office tomorrow.'

'Ah . . . I guess so, sure.'

Minnie must have put her hand over the speaker because I can hear her talking but can't make out the words.

'Woodstock.' Everett comes on the line, his voice restrained. 'What's going on?'

'I just want the latest updates. I don't want to miss anything again, like your theory about The Retreat.'

'I really don't think—'

'There's no harm in me doing this, surely.'

He doesn't reply, but Minnie says, 'We're all heading into the briefing now, Gemma. I'll keep you on speaker.'

Mac glowers at me as I move to the couch and settle Scarlett on my lap while keeping the phone to my ear. I can't hear much as everyone files into the case room, but once Everett starts talking it's not too bad. There are bits and pieces on Roger's business dealings, but none of the major investors have criminal records and there's no evidence to suggest any of them orchestrated his murder. Minnie provides details of the new CCTV footage—supplied by the council—of the streets around the hospital as well as the roads in and out of town, along with private footage from Roger's neighbours.

So far, all of this has turned up nothing, but I shoot a text to Minnie, asking her to send me the files anyway.

Everett shares the update about Dominique hiring a private investigator, and he uses it to put pressure on our team. Then he reveals that the lead on the baby hasn't taken us anywhere: the runaway and her newborn have been found—they were holed up with a friend. 'So, we're back to square one on the baby,' he says defensively.

The team run through their updates, and I strain to hear.

When they're done, Everett speaks again, sounding impatient. 'Great, everyone, solid plans. In addition to working with Constable Holdsworth on the last of the investor interviews, I'll be reviewing the incident that occurred at Detective Sergeant Gemma Woodstock's house yesterday. We believe there's a strong chance the attack on Gemma is linked to her involvement in Roger Kirk's murder investigation. So while it's a priority to get Gemma justice, it's also an opportunity to pick up a lead. Keep your minds open and come to me with anything you think you have, big or small. Minnie, can you see if there is any CCTV in the surrounding streets near Gemma's place please, and let me know if you get any hits? Okay, great. You're dismissed. Thanks, team.'

There's a few seconds of chatter, followed by Minnie's voice. 'Got to go, Gemma, but I'll speak to you soon.'

The call disconnects. I stay sitting on the couch with Scarlett, feeling absolutely enraged. How dare Everett paint me as a victim in front of the team.

I feel Mac's eyes on me and ask, 'Don't you have work to do?'

'Unlike you, I'm not prioritising work right now.'

We glare at each other from opposite sides of the room.

Then he sighs and walks over to me. 'Come on, Gemma, I don't want to argue with you. Why don't you go and lie down? I'll bring you a hot drink.'

'I feel completely fine.'

He takes my hands and rests his head against the couch, then adjusts Scarlett so she's propped up between us. I don't want to fight with him either. After feeling so disconnected from him, it's nice to have him so attentive, to feel like we're a strong unit.

I am scared—more scared than I want to admit—but not enough to give up working these cases. The thought of being benched is making me crazy.

'Yesterday's attack is under investigation,' I say, 'and I'm sure they'll find the perpetrator—but until they do, I'll make sure I'm armed at all times and that the kids are safe. I don't want to freak Ben out, though, because he worries enough as it is.'

Mac kisses my cheek. 'We'll both keep them safe. I'll work from home from now on. And you need to promise me you'll be careful, Gem. No risks.'

'No risks.'

He returns to the kitchen table, flips open a folder and starts reviewing a file. Still frustrated, I pick up Scarlett and fetch an apple from the fruit bowl. I make her a bottle and get some snacks, and we sit together eating and drinking until my phone rings: Jonesy.

'Hey,' I say perkily as I answer the call. I'm keen to convey that I am up to the task. I step out onto the back porch and slide the door shut so Mac can't hear.

'Woodstock. You sound cheerful. Is everything okay?'

'Yep. I'm home already and just wrapped up the case meeting over the phone.'

'Right.'

I cross the lawn and go to the shed. Tentatively I push its door open to reveal the small enclosed space. Our old furniture is still there, but the storage boxes are gone. Perhaps Mac's moved them into the garage or the study in anticipation of getting rid of them.

'What about you?' I ask Jonesy. 'Are you feeling okay today?'

'As right as rain.'

'Sounds like everyone is firing on all cylinders then,' I plough on before he can reply. 'I'm hoping to get my hands on the DNA report from the car crash. I've asked Everett but I got nowhere. Can you chase that up? I don't know why it's taking so long and it's critical we know if the woman has any matches in the system.'

'Woodstock, listen.' Jonesy's voice is no-nonsense. 'I know you're going to hate this, but we need to reconsider our arrangement—just for now, until we know what we're dealing with. Everett agrees. And I've arranged a unit to set up camp at your place over the next few days just as a precaution.'

'I shouldn't have to stop doing my job because of this.'

'The attack was personal, Woodstock. I don't like it.'

'Jonesy, come on. I really don't think that—'

'Woodstock, I mean it. Back off for a few days and let the team do their job. It's not personal—I just need to ensure you stay out of trouble.'

It's all I can do not to scream. 'You just said it *is* personal.'

'You know what I mean.' He's clearly annoyed now. 'Everett will keep you updated on anything significant. Once we think you're good to go, we'll let you know.'

His tone leaves little room for argument. 'Okay,' I mutter, ringing off.

'Who was that?' Mac asks when I return to the kitchen.

'Just Jonesy.' I don't want him to know how upset I am.

'Any updates on what happened yesterday?'

'Not yet.'

The ticking of my mother's cuckoo clock echoes through the quiet house until I feel like my head is going to explode.

'I don't want to be cooped up here all day,' I say abruptly. 'I'm heading out for a walk. I'll take Scarlett, if you like.'

'Gem—'

'I'll walk along the main road. And I'll take my gun.'

CHAPTER THIRTY-FOUR

Under Mac's watchful eye, I load Scarlett into her pusher and wheel it down the driveway. I stomp along the street, conversations playing on repeat in my mind. After a few minutes, the tension still hasn't left my body. I check my email: nothing except a routine note about a fire drill. Has Everett already taken me off the case distribution list? I make a frustrated sound, and Scarlett turns her head toward me. 'It's bullshit, isn't it?'

At the corner of an intersection, I stop, unsure what to do next. Several cars pass by.

I squint into the sun, trying to think. The doubts I had about returning to work have evaporated now it's been taken away from me. And it's all just so convenient for Everett. He even gets to flex his faux empathy and play hero; worse, he now has an excuse to trawl through my personal life.

A car slows, the driver gesturing for me to cross at the intersection. But I wave him along, jerk the pram to the right and continue along the footpath.

Maybe none of the cases are linked, maybe I'm looking at this all wrong, but there's no doubt someone wants to scare me. Have I got closer to the answers than I realise?

My phone buzzes with a text from Nan in Melbourne.

> My turn to ask you a question. You have a constable in your squad.
> Mina. What's she like? I've heard she'll be transferring here at the
> end of the year.

A funny feeling zaps through me. So, Minnie wants to leave Smithson for a metro role. It sounds like she's made up her mind and set the wheels in motion. Part of me isn't surprised: I've sensed something not quite right with her all week.

I carefully consider my message back to Nan.

> She's great. Young and full of potential. I didn't know she was plan-
> ning a move. Any idea why?

Three dots indicate Nan is replying. I walk the pram in a wide circle on someone's driveway.

> My friend said she's just not liking the small-town vibe and wants a
> change. Reading between the lines I think she was going to file a
> complaint against someone up there and a city move was flagged
> as a sweetener. Her dad wouldn't want her caught up in any internal
> politics, I know that for a fact.

I remember that Nan worked in Brisbane before she was in Melbourne. She must have crossed paths with Minnie's police commissioner father—I've heard he's notoriously old school.

I like Nan's message, then do a few more circles with the pram, my mind travelling at breakneck speed. Minnie's behaviour suddenly makes total sense: she was going to complain about Everett, then decided not to. She's miserable but figures it's better and easier to leave than to put her head above the pulpit.

I wonder what he's done—if it's low-grade sexism and bullying or more sinister. A few years ago a colleague assaulted me, and I remember how much that ate away at me and made me question everything. It took me a lot longer than I expected to feel like myself again. I have an urge to call Minnie and demand she tell me everything, but I need to tread very carefully.

Fed up with my thoughts, I call Candy. 'Gemma,' she breathes. 'How are you? I just texted Mac because I didn't want to disturb you if you were resting.'

'I'm fine. Are you working today? Any chance you want some company?'

'Of course! Philip has Lola. Where are you?'

'On the side of the road near my house, with Scarlett.'

'That sounds smart after what happened. I'll come get you.'

I text Mac that Candy is picking us up. His reply asks me to be extra vigilant and to let him know where we go. I quell my frustration. It's reasonable that in light of what happened he's worried.

Once Scarlett is buckled safely into Lola's seat, I fill Candy in on my conversation with Everett and Jonesy about The Retreat.

'Glad to know I was barking up the right tree.' She beams like a child given a gold star.

'Same tree, different dog. You were looking into Lee Blight's year of rest and relaxation. They're trying to find out if the woman from the crash or the mother of the baby lived there.'

'Details.' Candy dismisses my point with a polite snort.

'Regardless, Everett seemed to think it was a dead end. Maybe it's just a nice place for people to power down and avoid the relentless pressure of living in a capitalist society.'

'Maybe,' she says diplomatically, 'but Lee went *somewhere*. There's probably a bunch of places like it out there.'

'Have you heard of any others?'

'No,' she admits, 'but I haven't done much digging yet. I did speak to one of Lee's old mates yesterday, when we drove back from The Retreat. He helpfully informed me that he'd heard Lee went somewhere to sort out his fucked-up head.'

'But this friend didn't say where?'

'I don't think he knows. They were drug friends, didn't keep in touch after he left town.'

'Well, Everett's right about one thing: we don't have the manpower to search random properties. Not now.' I lean my head against the palm of my hand, feeling tired.

'You sure you're okay, Gem?'

'If you ask me that one more time it's you who will be in a bad way. Concentrate on the road.'

She makes a face. 'Well, you certainly have your attitude back. I haven't seen you like this in a while.'

'I'm pretty pissed.'

'You'll be pleased to know that is coming across loud and clear. Can I ask why?'

'I've been taken off the case.'

'You serious?'

'Everett's thrilled about it. But at the end of the day, it's Jonesy's call—he's spooked by what happened yesterday. Mac wants me to ease off as well, which feels a bit hypocritical considering the way he is with his work.'

Candy doesn't reply. Her silence is loaded.

'What?' I ask.

We turn into the main street and pause at the crossing. A steady flow of people make their way along the sun-dappled path, pausing to peer into shops or accommodate bathroom breaks for their dogs.

Candy looks at me, her face serious.

'What is it?'

'Should we get a coffee?' she says too brightly.

'No coffee until you tell me what's going on.'

With a groan, she massages her temples with her manicured fingers. 'I thought about this all night and this morning, and maybe it's nothing or there's a good reason.'

'What is it?' Panic gathers in my stomach.

She spreads her hands on the steering wheel. 'Yesterday I called Mac straight after we called triple zero . . .'

'Yes, and?'

'He was obviously really worried about you and the kids. He was beside himself.'

I raise my eyebrows, implying she should get to the point.

'I reassured him that you and Scarlett were fine and said I'd wait at the house with the kids until he got home from Brisbane—which I did.' She finally looks at me again. 'I called him at five pm. He got to the house just before eight pm.'

My stomach starts to churn as I do some quick calculations.

'I didn't think anything of it at the time. I was relieved to see him and still reeling from everything that had happened, but later I—'

'Realised there's no way he could have got from Brisbane to Smithson in three hours.' Vomit surges in my throat and I swallow it down. I was right, something is up with Mac.

'Yeah,' she says miserably. 'I'm sorry, Gem. I wasn't sure if I should tell you. But, fuck, you're my priority.'

I take a deep breath. 'I'm glad you told me.'

'We don't know what it means,' she says hopefully.

'No, we don't.'

She bites her lip, uncharacteristically unsure. 'Should we actually get a coffee? You may as well enjoy your forced hiatus, and I might even let you help me draft my story.'

'I've got a better idea. Let's pay Lee Blight a visit.'

CHAPTER THIRTY-FIVE

SATURDAY, 24 SEPTEMBER, 12.40 PM

Smithson doesn't have a gaol, just four holding cells attached to the police station. These are predominantly reserved for the drunk and disorderly, hence the power hose on the wall next to them. A small facility with twenty permanent cells and plans for more down the track has been proposed for Smithson to accommodate the forecast population growth, but its future depends on the outcome of the next state election. For now, anyone charged with an offence in Smithson is sent to the prison in Gowran.

As Candy's car zips along the highway, she turns up the music. I'm grateful—it seems she can tell I want some time to think. She embraced my suggestion to speak with Lee, simply remarking, 'I guess no one said anything about you not being allowed to do work experience with me,' before throwing the car into reverse.

Her revelation about Mac has joined the chaos in my brain that was already trying to work out what to do about Minnie. I push the thoughts into a corner, letting them run like a software program completing an update, churning through the possibilities.

An hour later we arrive in Gowran. After finding a spot in the busy prison car park, we step into the visitor checkpoint. The walls are beige and adorned with posters about family support programs. The sky-blue paint on the concrete floor is chipped, revealing the dull grey underneath. The sole skylight is thick with grime and the artificial lights either aren't turned on or don't work.

'Glam,' Candy comments, taking it in.

We make an odd trio: Candy in her white bejewelled T-shirt and denim jacket, me with my messy ponytail and Scarlett strapped to my front. No doubt everyone will assume we're family members visiting an imprisoned loved one—and sure enough, when I show my credentials to the guard and explain who I am, she cocks a shaggy eyebrow. 'Bring your kid to work day, is it?' Her name tag reads *Janice*.

'Something like that,' I say.

'And your name?' The guard eyeballs Candy.

'Hi, Janice,' she says, lifting her chin. 'I'm Candy Fyfe. Media.'

Janice taps her name into the register. 'I hope youse aren't making a true-crime podcast. I've had a bloody gutful of them.'

Candy, who yearns to launch a crime podcast, opens her mouth.

I quickly interject. 'We just want to see Lee Blight, an old friend.'

Janice looks at us doubtfully, folding her lips into themselves until they disappear. 'Up to him if he wants to speak with you.'

'Of course,' I say.

She gets to her feet, and we both wince as her hip cracks. 'Wait here.'

We don't talk. Candy scrolls on her phone, and I sway Scarlett gently, watching as she slips into sleep.

Janice reappears. 'You've been given the green light, ladies. This way.'

She lets us into the complex and leads us along a corridor, past several closed doors and into a large sterile room with linoleum on the floor and halfway up the walls. I detect top notes of cleaning products that mask a base of sweat, urine and stodgy food. Three guards stand near a kitchenette, talking loudly about the latest release of a computer game. At a table in the corner, an older man is sitting across from a woman our age, his hands in cuffs.

Janice gestures to a table and chairs. 'Blight'll be brought here.'

We sit and wait again. I arch my back to prevent Scarlett digging into my pelvis.

Lee enters the room with a guard who guides him toward us. He looks nothing like his dad, Marty, a huge ox of a man whose grey hair was once dark. Lee's features are finer, and his hair is blond. He has a nasty split lip, and there's a scab on the left side of his chin. His sallow skin hangs from his cheekbones. A large bruise purples his left eye socket, and a row of stitches travels from his temple to his left sideburn. At odds with his rough appearance are clear blue eyes.

They widen at the sight of me, and he stops a metre short of the table. 'Did my dad send you?' His voice is much softer than I expected: Marty's timbre is low and gruff, while Lee's is light and tentative. Old track marks are obvious in the inner creases of his elbows.

'No, and I'm not here in an official capacity. We just want to ask you some questions.'

'I don't know.' He casts his eyes to the floor and mumbles to himself. Then he says, 'I should check with Dad.' Looking up, he seems to notice Scarlett for the first time. 'You have a baby.'

'Yes, this is Scarlett,' I say softly. 'Please, Lee, sit down.'

He gingerly takes a seat, and the bored guard walks off to join his peers.

'I'm Candy. I know your dad, too. I'm a journalist.' She pats his cuffed hand, but he keeps looking at Scarlett. 'Can we ask you a few questions, Lee?'

'I dunno.' His sapphire eyes are mesmerising; if he put on some muscle and made a barber appointment, his fortunes might be halfway to turning around. He's scratching at a scab on his elbow. 'Like what?'

'I'm doing a story on The Retreat, and we were told you spent some time there. True or false?'

'False,' he says.

'You've never been there?' Candy asks. I can feel her disappointment.

'I don't need to talk to you.' When he's defensive, his gentle lisp makes me think of a young child saying no to his parents. 'I don't need to talk to anyone.'

'But what have you got to lose?' says Candy. She gestures to our depressing surrounds.

'You don't know anything about me,' he mutters.

'We know you got into a pub brawl on Sunday night,' I say, 'and are facing a bunch of charges. We know that before that you had a rough few years, and that you were trying to turn things around.'

His response is a grunt, but something flashes in his eyes.

Candy drums her fake nails on the table, plastic on plastic. 'It's a simple question. Have you ever been to The Retreat?'

He shifts in his chair. 'Years ago.'

'What for?' I ask.

'Just delivering stuff—when I worked at the supermarket, I did deliveries sometimes.'

I picture the grocery bags in the boot of the car from the crash and wonder if there is any chance of a link.

'What kind of stuff?' I press.

'I just delivered whatever groceries I was told to.'

'But you didn't stay out there?' I ask.

'Of course not.'

'How do you know the guys you fought with?' I ask, trying to break him down from a different angle.

He presses his lips together before saying, 'I don't.'

'Are you in the habit of punching on with complete strangers?' Candy asks.

'No,' he says sullenly.

'So what happened?' she says.

'They were just dickheads,' he mumbles.

'Lots of people are dickheads,' she points out. 'Do you punch all of them?'

'They were talking shit about someone, all right.' He's still speaking quietly but with a menace that wasn't there before.

I ask, 'About someone you know . . . ?'

'Fuck off!' he spits, drawing the attention of the guards.

Bingo, I think. 'Where have you been these past few years, Lee?'

'Out bush.'

'That's not very specific.'

'Nope.'

'Is there a reason you can't tell us where you were?'

'Fuck off,' he mutters. The scab on his hand is bleeding now, dripping onto the table.

Candy and I recoil.

Leaning forward, Lee smears the blood with his forearms. 'I said, fuck off!'

Scarlett wakes up and starts to cry. I get to my feet, keen to be away from him. I pull Candy up and make eye contact with one of the guards who is apparently concerned enough to be making his way toward us. Quickly I say, 'I'm sorry we upset you, Lee. We just wanted to talk.' I hiss, 'Come on,' to Candy while I try to soothe Scarlett.

As we leave, I glance over my shoulder at Lee. He looks terrified.

CHAPTER THIRTY-SIX

'He's lying,' Candy says, typing furiously on the laptop wedged between her thighs and the steering wheel.

I lay Scarlett on a plastic bag in the boot and change her nappy. 'You can't lie if you barely say anything,' I point out.

'You know what I mean. Maybe there really is something going on at The Retreat.'

'You said it was just a bunch of people homeschooling their kids.'

'Maybe that's all for show,' she says darkly. 'It *was* creepy, all that wholesomeness.'

I mix Scarlett a bottle and sit in the front seat holding her while she drinks. 'Whether he's lying or not I don't think he's very well. I hope he's getting some support in there.'

'Unlikely,' Candy replies. 'Those guards could barely be bothered to scratch their arses.'

'True.' I nudge the bottle into Scarlett's mouth again, encouraging her to finish it. 'It's lucky your piece on The Retreat doesn't depend on Lee having lived there. You can still unpack why people choose to live off the grid and the merit of that lifestyle, right?'

'Seriously, what if Lee is lying about not living at The Retreat?' Candy says as if I haven't spoken.

'Why lie?'

She types on her laptop as she talks. 'Maybe he's embarrassed. He thinks it makes him seem weird—which it does.'

'I feel like he's past the point of worrying about his reputation. Why else?'

'Because he promised someone he wouldn't say anything,' she guesses.

'That's the only thing that I think makes sense if he is lying. He's promised someone or he's been threatened by someone to stay quiet. Don't you think he seemed jumpy?'

'Which brings us back to your question. Why would he need to keep quiet about The Retreat?'

'I don't know—they're cooking meth, organ harvesting, human trafficking?'

'Jesus, Gemma.'

'You're the one who pushed to investigate the place. And there *is* a stolen corpse somewhere out there.'

'I thought I might do a nice story about people marrying their cousins,' says Candy, 'not black-market kidneys!'

'I was joking, but maybe there's something in it,' I muse. 'I've thought for a while that someone might have wanted the corpse for a medical reason.'

Candy wrinkles her nose. 'Don't you have to be alive to have your organs harvested?'

I quickly google it. 'Apparently, eyes and some tissue can be used after death, but all the major organs need to be used virtually straight away and removed from a body on a ventilator.'

'Maybe they wanted her *eyes*,' says Candy in a creepy voice.

'Don't be gross.' I jiggle the bottle to entice Scarlett to keep feeding.

'Lee isn't much like his dad,' Candy observes.

'No. And along that same line of thinking, I wouldn't have picked him to start a brawl. He's erratic but he doesn't come across as an alpha.'

'I wonder who the guys at the pub were talking about to set him off?'

'Must have been a mutual friend.'

'But I thought the cops found no link between him and the guys at the pub.'

'Maybe the guys don't know there's a link, and Lee kept his mouth shut. In their statements they said they didn't know why Lee lashed out.'

'Mmm.' Candy is distracted by something on her phone. 'God, they're really milking this memorial thing for Roger Kirk. It looks like the premier is coming! Shit, I'd better update the website and the socials.' She's typing madly.

I sink into theorising about Lee Blight, feeling out the possibilities. Does he have a romantic interest that the guys at the pub knew? Or was he defending a friend? Maybe one of his brothers? His dad?

I google other retreats in the area, but all I get is an ad for Harmony, Carlyle's wellness business, and suggestions for romantic bush getaways. That makes me think about where Mac might have been yesterday and who he might have been with, and I feel ill.

To distract myself, I access my emails. Minnie still hasn't sent me the newly available CCTV footage. And when I log on to the system I'm unsurprised to find that the dead woman's DNA report still hasn't come through. I decide to call Minnie; it might be good for me to build some rapport before I bring up her transfer to Melbourne—and I really want to get the report. I can't understand why Everett isn't prioritising it as well. I try Minnie's number, but it goes to voicemail. Everett doesn't answer either.

'Dammit,' I mutter.

'What?' Candy says, her eyes glued to her screen.

'No one will answer my calls.'

'Burn.'

'Yeah.' I strap Scarlett back into her car seat and ward off a tantrum with a dummy.

My anger is building again. I can't believe I've been shut out like this. At the very least, Everett owes me an update on my attack.

Candy answers a call from Sam and launches into a comprehensive to-do list, barking orders at him. I can't help but smile. She's not everyone's cup of tea, and poor Sam should be knighted for putting up with her, but her abrasiveness is one of the things I love about her: she's unashamedly bossy and determined to make shit happen. The world could do with more of her energy.

On a whim, while she natters away next to me, I call the lab and am passed from person to person. Finally I reach a woman who can help me. Shaking out a cramp, I exit the car and take a few steps, scuffing my sneaker against the lip of the gutter. Into the phone, I explain who I am and what I'm after.

'Okay, darl, just give me a second.' There's typing and clicking, and faint conversation in the background. 'Found it. This report has already been sent, darl—two days ago, to the requesting officer, a Detective Sergeant Everett.'

My heart pounds in my ears. Everett lied to me: he's had the report for two days.

I manage to say, 'Thank you, yes, I know, but I'm out of the office and can't get on to anyone. I urgently need to crosscheck a piece of evidence. Can I please trouble you to send the report to me now?' I give her my email address and hear more typing sounds.

'With you now, darl.'

I thank her, end the call and return to the front seat, fighting waves of impotent energy. I feel like punching something. I look at Scarlett, who has her eyes shut, dummy bobbing frenetically, and try to calm down.

'Ready?' Candy drops her phone in the console and guns the engine. 'I need to get back—can't leave the site content up to Sam, or god knows what will end up on there.'

Without thinking I retort, 'He's not an idiot. You shouldn't be so mean to him.'

She lets my comment slide, turning her head to reverse out of the car park. 'Everything okay, Gem?' she asks lightly.

I already regret my outburst. It's not Candy I'm mad at. 'Things are just great.'

'Convincing!'

We drive through Gowran, navigating the moderate traffic, then I watch the businesses and houses give way to thick bush. I spot an echidna fossicking at the edge of the road.

Candy doesn't say anything but suddenly dials Henno on her car's Bluetooth. He answers, sounding like he's just woken from a nap.

'It's Candy. Who told you Lee Blight was living at The Retreat?'

'Oh. Hey, babe.'

'Lee. The Retreat. Who told you?'

'I love when you go slow,' he jokes. 'Why don't you let me take you out for a drink and we can chat about it.'

'No way. Tell me now or I delete your number from my phone.'

Henno makes a sound that indicates he's stretching and Candy taps the steering wheel impatiently. 'I can't remember but it was a while ago, after he first left town. I think one of the young guys who used to work here mentioned it. He knew him.'

'Did he actually say he was living at The Retreat?'

'Seeing as I didn't know this morsel of information was going to be the key to your heart I wasn't taking notes but I think so. I remember being told he'd gone to live off the land, organic food, no internet . . . all that good god-awful stuff. Maybe I just assumed it was The Retreat he went to because it's the only place around here that I know like that.'

'Okay. Thanks.' She cuts off the call and asks me, 'What do you think?'

I'm trying to remain invested in Lee's mystery destination but with everything else going on it's a challenge. I try to sound engaged and say, 'Who knows? Right now, we need to find out if the tradies or the other kids Henno mentioned from the pub fight have links to The Retreat.'

'Good idea.' She calls Sam again.

He sounds stressed, and this doesn't lessen when she asks him to track down the guys from the pub. 'I thought you wanted me to focus on the content updates,' he grumbles.

'I do! But you can multitask, Sam. I've seen you shoot film and play online poker at the same time, so I know you can do it.' She hangs up to him muttering something.

In an attempt to apologise for my earlier comment, I say, 'I was being a dick before but he will leave if you're not nicer to him.'

'He'll never leave me,' she says dramatically.

I give her an exasperated look and settle into the drive.

Half an hour later we enter Smithson and immediately hit traffic. When we finally pull up outside my place, I lean over to hug Candy, eyeballing the patrol car parked across the street. 'Thanks for today. And be careful, okay.'

'Right back at you. I'm covering the memorial tomorrow, but I'll call you when I can.'

She drives off, and I position Scarlett on my hip and steer the pusher with my other hand. The day is fading, leaving traces of rose in the sky. Dusk light casts long shadows across the front lawn.

Before I make it to the porch, Mac opens the door.

'Hey.' He takes Scarlett from me and hugs her to his chest. I watch him hold her, feeling heartbroken that I can't trust him anymore.

'Is Ben here?' A sudden urge to hug my son overwhelms me.

'In his room.' Mac drops his voice. 'I didn't tell him anything. I wasn't sure how much detail you want to give him.'

'Thanks.' Doubt swirls through me again. He's been so supportive of me and my family. There must be a logical explanation for him lying to me. I can feel myself daring to hope this is all a silly misunderstanding, and without Scarlett to hold as a comfort I cross my arms and sway gently from side to side.

Mac kisses Scarlett on her head. 'Did you have a good day?'

It's a loaded question, but I let it skim past. 'Yes, it was nice hanging out with Candy. I was helping her with a few work things.'

'That's good. I'm just about to start preparing dinner. I'm thinking I'll make a roast.'

'Sounds great.'

I take Scarlett and he flicks on some music, a band he likes from Nashville, and pulls items from the pantry. His mannerisms are so familiar, and I love all the funny little contradictions that make him unique, the quirks that we share. Him risking it all doesn't make sense. I need to confront him about his trip, but I'd prefer to know what the answer is going to be before I ask him. I want to be able to prepare myself.

I rush along the hall to Ben's room and interrupt his video game. He tolerates my hug and then he holds Scarlett while we talk. He seems more reserved than normal, but perhaps he's just tired after his day at the farm with Jodie's parents and his half-sister. I decide not to tell him exactly what happened but I tell him that someone is trying to scare me off a job, and that while I'm completely fine, we all need to be extra vigilant. His green eyes lock with mine and he nods. His resigned expression makes him look so much like his father it takes my breath away.

Settling down on the couch, with Scarlett on her playmat at my feet, I load the news and see the same headlines I saw this morning. I google Franklin Kirk and read up about the search for him all those years ago, struck by the extent to which the reporting of suicide has changed over the past decade. A younger Carlyle Kirk is pictured at Tyson Falls, watching as emergency service workers comb the area for his son. I read about the flight to Switzerland and the plan to mend Franklin's brain with experimental treatments. In several articles, Carlyle is quoted on scientific breakthroughs and his confidence that he can bring his son back.

I click on related links, skimming through old articles about the Kirks. Eventually I read about Roger's appointment to the position of hospital CEO: he was hailed as a modern, dynamic leader.

After that, I come across a lengthy *Science Today* profile of Carlyle from four years ago. As a young boy, he was interested in biology and physics, and especially fascinated with plants. He was always collecting data and doing experiments with the science kit his mother bought him for his sixth birthday.

All The Lyle businesses are owned by a holding company, Life Matters, which Carlyle describes as a *progressive organisation looking to better the human experience here on Earth*. Life Matters has been involved in launching pharmaceutical products, as well as architecting cutting-edge psychological treatments proven to fight depression and anxiety and to assist in the management of illnesses such as

Parkinson's disease and multiple sclerosis. Carlyle has shares in Life Matters, but it's owned by a Chinese company.

'Dinner will be about an hour,' Mac says. 'Would you like a drink?'

'Sure, thanks.'

Red wine in hand, I download the CCTV files Minnie sent me via Dropbox, load the ones she said haven't been reviewed yet, and start to watch. This lot of footage captures the streets around the south of the hospital and various angles of the car park. I fast-forward through patients coming and going, then pause as a camera captures Sophie sneaking into the alcove at around seven pm; I watch her type on her phone and smoke two cigarettes. An ambulance leaves the holding bay just before seven forty-five pm, followed by another one a few minutes later. The pub fight and the car crash.

Outside the lounge-room window, the glow of the sunset creates dramatic silhouettes of the gum trees. Adjusting my position, I refocus and zoom through two more files. Halfway into the next one, my body jerks as I recognise Ash coming out of the main entrance and walking over—at the edge of the screen—to talk to another man.

I scramble to pause the tape. It's from a camera at the front of the hospital, most likely fixed to a streetlight in the car park. The time stamp reads *7.09 pm*. I press play again, and the pair of men walk together off screen, in the direction of the side street.

I rewind and zoom in on the other man. His face isn't visible, but his uniform is, and his height and hair make him easy to recognise: Lenny Tisdale, the security guard.

I replay the footage, my mind racing. It's not surprising that Lenny and Ash are friends—they're around the same age—but there's something suspicious about the way they're walking, the forced nonchalance and covert glances. They're heading toward

Lenny's car. Are they just going for a smoke together? Maybe they're hooking up as well. Or is Ash buying drugs? A lot of paramedics struggle with addiction.

I exhale and sit back against the couch. So, this is why Ash has been avoiding me: he was stoned while working on Sunday night, and he thinks I know. Well, now I do. I remember he said that he and Fred had finished their shift but were called back to attend the crash scene. Rubbing my eyes, I try to work out how best to approach him with my suspicions.

Scarlett starts to fuss, so I pick her up and hold her on my lap. I pull up my work emails and check the ones from today: no case update. Everett really has removed me from the group.

I click on the email from the lab and open the DNA report.

'Five minutes until dinner, team!' Mac calls out.

'Yep,' I mumble, adjusting Scarlett so she's looking over my shoulder. I pat her on the back and scroll through the report to the results.

My heart stops when I see the dead woman has a match in the system. But it's not with missing persons or from a crime scene: it's a police officer match. The woman shares DNA with me.

CHAPTER THIRTY-SEVEN

As I emerge into consciousness the next morning, my DNA link with the dead woman hits me like a ton of bricks all over again. My brain shovels everything else on top: Minnie's transfer, Ash and Lenny, the attack on me, Mac.

Last night I bumbled my way through dinner, trying to engage with Mac and Ben, trying to seem normal, but all I could think about was how the woman is related to me. My dad has cousins in the local area who he isn't close with and who I've never met, so that's the most likely explanation; I need to speak to him and see if he can help me figure out who the woman is. Everett's strange line of questioning the other morning suddenly makes sense—he's known about this since Thursday. Jonesy must know as well, and his betrayal needles at me. I should feel pleased by this tangible lead, but instead I feel violated and exposed.

With a grim determination to face the day, I ease myself out of bed and get ready. Mac is in the shower. Scarlett only woke once during the night and blissfully is still asleep. Ben is on the couch, watching someone give a blow-by-blow account of how to unlock a level in a computer game. I hug him, smoothing his hair until he bats me away.

After checking the shower is still running, I go to the garage. The storage boxes aren't there, and they're not in the boot of the car either. Returning to the house, I head straight to the study. Papers and notebooks are spread out across the desk, along with three used coffee cups, but there's no sign of the boxes here either. Mac's phone sits in front of the laptop; I pick it up, waking the screen. It's locked, but I can see news alerts, a text alert from a number he doesn't have in his contacts, and a missed call from Julian Everett.

Breath catches in my throat. Why the hell is Everett calling Mac?

My body turns to ice. I have an impulse to throw the phone against the wall.

A text arrives from Everett, its preview showing briefly.

Call me back, we need to talk.

The shower has stopped. I quickly try to log in using Mac's password—the date we met—but I'm served an error message: he's changed it.

I can hear him opening and closing dresser drawers, so I place his phone back on the desk and return to the kitchen. A few minutes later, Mac enters dressed in jeans and a T-shirt, his hair damp. He's holding his phone, and I wonder if he's replied to Everett's text yet. He hasn't called him—I would have overheard.

Without speaking, I hand him a bowl of muesli.

'Thanks,' he says, leaning in to kiss me. 'Sleep okay?'

'Very well.' I duck out of his hug, hoping I come across as flirty not dismissive. 'You?'

'Can't complain.' His forehead wrinkles as he types on his phone.

I find myself holding my breath.

Sitting in silence, we eat our breakfast. I half listen to the radio, which drones on against the backdrop of Ben's weird computer-game narration.

'I haven't had any updates from Everett and Jonesy on my attacker,' I say quietly.

'Maybe they don't have any yet.'

'I guess not.'

I remember how Mac left the room when Jonesy and Everett arrived at the hospital. I thought he was giving me space and wanted to let me talk freely to my colleagues, but maybe it was something else. Was that when the contact started? Did Mac and Everett exchange numbers that night, deciding I needed looking after? Did Mac ask to be provided with information directly?

'Do you have much work to do on your case today?' I ask.

He swallows and pushes the bowl away. 'Not really—I've hit a lull. I might just hand the info back to the local team and focus on my upcoming lectures.'

I raise my eyebrows in surprise. It's unlike him to give up on a job and I wonder what's prompted it. 'Are you serious?'

'Yes. I'm enjoying the teaching more these days anyway.'

'You must be disappointed . . . ?'

He gathers our dishes. 'Not really. Cold cases are always challenging. Plus, it frees me up a bit—I'd probably taken on too much.'

Scarlett cries out, and Mac moves to get her. 'No, let me,' I say. She's in a happy mood, kicking her legs and laughing as I change her nappy and wrestle her into a fresh outfit.

'What about you?' Mac asks as I return to the kitchen. 'What are your plans today?' His tone is neutral, my removal from the case an elephant on the table between us.

'I might see how Dad is going at home, and I'm thinking I'll go to Roger's memorial.'

Mac frowns.

'What? It's a public event, and I did know him.' The bloody mess of Roger's corpse and his pale skin at the autopsy work their way into my mind.

Although Mac exhales loudly, he seems to decide he doesn't want to argue. 'Do you want me to take Scarlett?'

'I don't mind.'

'You had her yesterday—I'll take her. I was thinking of heading to the hardware store to buy a few bits and pieces. Ben and I are talking about building a vegie garden. Scarlett can help me choose some things.' He tickles her cheek. 'Won't you, little green thumb?' He seems calm and content, not like someone on the cusp of blowing everything up.

'Sounds great,' I manage.

Moments like this make me feel like I'm overreacting, but then I remember Everett's text, the storage boxes, the handwritten letter, and the fact I don't know where Mac was on Friday. My stomach is choppy with doubt and fear.

Mac heads off with the kids, and I keep moving, aware that if I'm occupied, I'm less likely to catastrophise. I tidy the kitchen, wipe the bench and rearrange the fruit bowl. When I can't bear it any longer, I leave. The memorial is starting soon.

Jodie calls while I'm in the car on the way to the hospital. Sighing, I answer via the bluetooth. Her voice fills the car. 'Gemma.'

'Hey, Jodie.'

'I've been waiting for you to call me.'

'Yes, sorry.' Immediately I feel defensive. 'It's been a crazy few days.'

'I didn't know you were planning to go back to work early.'

'I didn't feel the need to broadcast it.'

She sighs, which irks me. Jodie often treats me like an unruly teenager she's forced to negotiate with. 'A heads-up would have been good, so I could be prepared to speak to Ben about it.'

'I don't think you need to speak to Ben about my job.'

'It stresses him out, Gemma. You know that. And I think he has pretty good reason to be stressed. Something happened at your place the other day, didn't it? Was it a burglary?'

'It's all under control. Mac and I are being extra cautious, and my colleagues are managing it with me.'

Her silence suggests my assurances are far from reassuring.

I approach the hospital and edge along the road in a long chain of cars. The parking lot is almost full, so I head straight to the back row, toward the spaces that look out across the empty block where the research centre was originally going to be built.

'Jodie, I'm happy to chat to you properly, but I'm kind of in the middle of something. Can I call you back?'

'Gemma, Ben's been vaping.'

'What?' I narrowly avoid running into a car that brakes suddenly in front of me.

'He's been vaping,' she repeats.

I almost laugh at the thought. 'Don't be ridiculous,' I say. 'He's twelve.'

'I drove past the school the other day around lunchtime, and I saw him with some friends down the side of the oval. I spoke to him about it yesterday.'

My incredulity shifts into irritation. 'Fuck, Jodie, why didn't you talk to me?' But I'm already wondering why Ben didn't mention this last night. It was the perfect opportunity to bring it up and he didn't.

'Because I was the one who saw him—and because I didn't think I needed to check with you to have a conversation with my stepson.'

'Whatever,' I mumble.

'Anyway, I don't think it's a massive deal. He's obviously going to experiment with things, and we had a good chat about why he wanted to try it . . . But I wanted to let you know. I think you should talk to him as well. I'm worried he seems a little lost sometimes.'

'Of course he's bloody lost. His dad died.'

Jodie's breathing sharpens. 'It's great he's seeing the counsellor, but all of us need to be in lock step. You need to talk to him about your plans, make sure he feels secure. Your work bothers him, whether you like it or not.'

'Jesus, Jodie, I don't need you to give me parenting tips, okay?' I can hear Scott's voice in my head, telling me to cool it.

I slide the car into a spot at the furthest corner.

'Gemma, will you just talk to him?'

'Yes, of course. I speak to him all the time—he is my kid.'

The call disconnects.

'Fuck!' I slam my forearms against the steering wheel, then drop my head to rest against it. Even though Ben vaping isn't the end of the world, it feels like another breach of trust. Something else I have let get out of control. I'm tempted to burst into tears but feel too drained.

Exhaling in a huff, I straighten up, grab my bag and hurry out of the car park. I join the crowd of people making their way to the hospital entrance. Frazzled staff usher everyone through the reception area.

I keep my eyes peeled for Ash but can't see him. Instead I spot Jessie on the phone, with Everett a few metres to her right, talking to Sophie and a familiar man in a suit. Everett gives me an exasperated look, and I give him a stony smile back as I continue to move with the group into the large enclosed courtyard at the centre of the hospital. White chairs stand in rows, and there's a trestle table with a donation box and glossy brochures fanned out for people to take.

It feels like a wedding, especially seeing as I'm certain the chairs were hired by a close friend of Candy's for her nuptials last year.

The media has turned out in full force, cameras aimed at a huge glossy photo of Roger on a stand next to the podium at the front of the courtyard. His teeth are blindingly white, and there's a notable difference between the skin tones of his face and hands. I grab a brochure, find a spot opposite the media scrum and have a read. Roger's professional achievements are listed alongside cheesy shots of him at various Smithson Hospital events. I use the brochure to fan my face.

After a few minutes, people start shushing each other and taking their seats. Soft orchestral music plays as Dominique arrives, her thin arms herding her three children toward the front row and into reserved seats. The kids are in stylish black outfits, their faces solemn. Dominique's navy dress has intricate pearl beading along the collar, and her strawberry-blonde hair hangs down her back. She sits without acknowledging any other guest and tucks her hands around her two younger children, hugging them close before gripping the shoulder of her eldest son.

Carlyle appears at the entrance and scans the courtyard, looking puzzled. He drifts to the far-left corner, behind the media scrum, folds his hands and glances expectantly at the empty podium.

A little further along, Rufus the head security guard talks into his mobile. On the opposite side of the room, Lenny Tisdale towers over an elderly couple and makes eye contact with Rufus, his phone against his ear.

The suited man I saw talking to Everett walks with Sophie to the front. Her black outfit follows the lines of her small frame, and her blonde hair is twisted into an elegant knot at the nape of her neck. She grips several A4 pages.

Standing at the podium, the man introduces himself as the Health Minister of New South Wales and thanks everyone for coming. He talks about the success of the hospital and the tragedy of Roger's death, listing his many achievements. The minister then launches into an enthusiastic promotion of the research centre, which he says will form part of Roger's legacy.

I notice Carlyle listening intently. Sophie is at the foot of the podium, her expression polite, her eyes flitting across the crowd until they come to rest on Dominique.

The minister finishes his speech. Sophie composes herself, self-consciously squaring her shoulders. They exchange places, and she adjusts the microphone to her height, attempting a smile. 'Thank you,' she says, her timid voice amplified.

Once everyone quietens, she explains she is the acting CEO and launches into an overwritten speech about Roger's career. It's peppered with personal anecdotes from their time working together in Smithson and earlier, when Roger was involved in various health ventures.

Several nurses in the front rows dab at their eyes with tissues.

'This is not a funeral,' Sophie says, her voice shaking. 'This is something we wanted to do as colleagues to pay tribute to Roger. He loved his work so much, and we were lucky to work with him. Please join me in remembering him with a minute's silence.'

Her voice breaks on the last word. She seems to freeze.

I glance at Dominique, who is staring at Sophie with her arms still around her children.

I'm scanning the rest of the room when I realise that a minute is surely over. Sophie makes a strangled cry before descending into a flood of gulping tears.

CHAPTER THIRTY-EIGHT

Sophie clutches the podium and cries while everyone watches on, unsure what to do. The public display of raw emotion feels obscene, and people busy themselves with fishing tissues out of handbags and murmuring to each other.

The minister turns in a panicked circle, gesturing at staff to comfort Sophie. Eventually two nurses jump up and lead her off into a room at the side of the courtyard.

A woman in a fitted grey dress and bright red lipstick takes the mic. 'Thank you everyone for your generous donations to the hospital today,' she says, in what's obviously a request for more.

The string quartet plays a familiar tune. Once it becomes clear that no one is going to formally wrap things up, most of the crowd starts to jostle for a spot in the exit queue.

Dominique hasn't moved, her profile rigid as she watches everyone leave, her jaw clenching sporadically. I wonder what she's thinking. Losing a husband and a soulmate in less than a week is a lot to deal with, but she seems remarkably stoic.

Carlyle has disappeared. Why wasn't he seated with Roger's immediate family?

As I move with the throng, I play the scene back over. It's tempting to view Sophie's grief as disproportionate—or inappropriate, considering her professional relationship to Roger—but I've learned to be careful when judging emotions. It's part of my job to assess people's reactions, to consider their behaviour and identify anomalies, but there is no right way to grieve. Any loss can stir up a cocktail of feelings, dredge up past traumas and guilt, and trigger discomfort about our own mortality. It's clear Sophie is in the kind of pain typically associated with losing a loved one. Were they more than colleagues? I still want to probe why she advised Claire to hold off on picking up the corpse. Maybe Roger's death is linked to that incident, and Sophie knows how.

I keep moving, careful not to knock a middle-aged woman on crutches who is talking loudly on her mobile. It's a relief to exit the courtyard into the relative calm of the foyer. I break away from the crowd and look around for Candy.

Everett and Holdsworth stalk past, both talking into their mobiles, and I feel the same inferiority I felt when they showed up that first night at the hospital. I badly want to march up to Everett and give him orders. It rankles that he is the one Jonesy has sided with, and it feels ominous in light of decisions that will need to be made over the next few months.

A familiar dark head comes into view—Ash has just entered the hospital.

I rush through the crowd, pushing past people to get to him. 'Sorry, sorry, excuse me.' I lose sight of him, but he must have gone into the ambulance headquarters.

As I step into the tearoom, Fred Katz appears with a mug and a sad-looking cinnamon donut.

'I need to speak to Ash Amato!' I practically shout at him, then take a deep breath. 'Please, Mr Katz, I'm a detective investigating the crash you attended last weekend.'

He raises his eyebrows at me. 'Okay, sure, but he's in the gents.'

I hover beside the door to the toilets, catching snatches of muffled conversation.

Fred reappears and gives me a curious look. 'He'll just be a sec.'

'Thanks.'

'I see his point,' Fred says, walking off before I can ask what he means.

Ash emerges, looking terrified.

'We need to talk.' I hold out my hands as if to prove I come in peace. 'And I need you to tell me the truth. Do you understand?'

He nods slowly. 'I briefed the sketch artist. Is that why you're here?'

I point to a table and chairs in the corner of the empty tearoom. 'Over there.'

I shepherd him across the room and take the seat that means my back is to the wall. 'Sit.'

He obeys.

'You were with Lenny Tisdale in his car last Sunday night. Were you smoking?'

His shoulders are hunched in defeat. 'Yes,' he whispers. 'My shift was finished. I have trouble sleeping, so sometimes I buy weed from Tisdale to help me rest.'

'But then you got called back to attend the crash scene, is that right?'

'Yeah. I was back here grabbing my stuff when our boss asked me to head out with Fred. Ro and Charlie had gone to the pub, and the crash was urgent. I could hardly say I'd been smoking, and I felt okay, so I went.' He drops his head into his hands. 'It was stupid, but once we were in the bus I just tried to concentrate and get through it.'

'And that's why you've been avoiding me? Because you thought I'd figured it out.'

He lifts his head and stares at me. 'Sort of.'

'What do you mean?' I'm breathing hard and talking too fast, so I inhale deeply and try to slow down. 'Sorry, Ash, but I need you to tell me what the hell is going on.'

He eyes the door as if he's going to make a run for it. Then he nods to himself, his lips moving without sound, before he stares at me again, an odd expression settling over his features. He clears his throat. 'This is going to sound so stupid, and maybe my head was a mess from the weed, but it's just that to me you look exactly like her. It freaked me out.'

There's a funny feeling in my chest, as though someone is stroking my rib cage from the inside. 'Who do I look like?'

'The dead woman.'

CHAPTER THIRTY-NINE

I feel ridiculously conspicuous. It's like I'm wearing a silly costume in a roomful of people in normal clothes. My instinct is to laugh off Ash's comment but I'm struggling to keep my emotions under control. All I can see is my name on the DNA report sheet.

'How similar are we talking?' I ask lightly.

He moistens his lips, eyes darting to the side. 'Identical . . . I mean, that's how I remember it, but—'

'They say everyone has a twin.' The desire to end this conversation is overwhelming—I think I might be sick. 'I need to report you about the weed. I'm not sure what will happen.'

'Yeah.' He shoves his hands into his pockets. 'I figured.'

'I'm sorry. Good on you for coming clean. I've got to go.'

My vision blurs as I stand and turn on my heel, unable to take in his response. The world around me lurches. I hope my disorientation isn't obvious as I head to the disabled toilet I used to change Scarlett after the alarm went off.

I lock the door and stand in front of the mirror, hands gripping either side of the sink. I stare at my reflection. Is this the face Ash

314

saw in the crumpled car that night? Was she still alive when I was here visiting Dad? I was here when her body was removed from the icy drawer and taken into the night. I picture my own body, cold under a morgue sheet, and dry-retch into the sink.

I allow myself to process the possibility that my dad fathered a child after my mum died.

There's a knock on the door. I hastily wipe my mouth and exit, muttering profuse apologies to the woman on crutches waiting outside.

The reception area is still full of people who attended the service, talking in small groups, interspersed with patients waiting to be treated.

Panic grabs at me. As I rush to the exit, my lungs feel like they're about to burst. Outside I hold on to the railing along the entrance ramp, trying to calm my breathing.

'Gemma! Fancy seeing you here.'

Candy and Sam are standing a few metres away. Sam is vaping, and I realise we're in the designated smoking area. I remember my phone call with Jodie about Ben, and my legs start to shake. I walk a few steps to the left and sit on a park bench, letting the sun warm my face.

'You look like you've seen a ghost, Gemma.' Candy comes over and peers into my eyes. 'Are you okay?'

'You're even paler than usual,' Sam adds helpfully.

'I just got a bit claustrophobic in there. I'm fine now.'

'What a circus,' says Candy, 'including that bonus performance from the new CEO! But we have other things to fill you in on, Gemma—Lee Blight.'

What's she talking about? I try to focus. 'What about him?'

'Sam spoke to the guys from the pub. The Bilson tradies.'

Sam puffs on his vape, which smells like apples. 'Last night I tracked them down at another pub and buddied up with them. They can certainly put the beers away! I didn't get home until midnight. Paying for it now.'

Candy beams at him. 'You did good, Sam.'

'Thanks. Can I charge the beers back to you?'

'We'll discuss that later . . .'

'What did they say?' I ask.

'I pretended I was new in town and keen for a labouring job with Bilson. We got chatting, then I mentioned hearing about the pub fight. They admitted they were giving Blight shit last Sunday.'

'Did they say why?'

Sam gives me a sombre look. 'They said he'd been with an underage girl.'

I exchange a look with Candy and ask, 'Why do they think that?'

'I couldn't get them to tell me without it being obvious I was grilling them, but I think it had something to do with their work. They've only been living in Smithson for the past couple of months, so it has to be recent. Anyway, that's what they said they hassled him about. I don't think they expected him to lose it like that, though. A bunch of times they referred to him as a "stoned loser"—that's a direct quote.'

I try to remember what Henno said about bumping into Lee the night before the fight. 'Was it possible Lee was working for Bilson as well?'

'I didn't get that impression,' says Sam. 'I think they saw him with this young girl somewhere. They kept calling him a "paedo".'

'Not an accusation to be tossed around lightly,' I say.

I shouldn't be surprised but I am. Lee came across as damaged and scared but he didn't strike me as a predator. If this is true I hope that the girl is okay.

'Right?' says Candy, who despite the seriousness of the claims can't contain her excitement. 'We need to put all this to Lee and see what he has to say about it. We can head back to Gowran . . .'

'Let's call him,' I say hastily. The thought of being stuck on a long drive fills me with dread. I add, 'But I think it's unlikely he'll talk to us.'

'We can call from my car,' Candy offers. 'It's just over there.' She turns to Sam. 'I'll speak to you later. Make sure you get those pics up on the site asap. Come on, Gemma.'

I can tell Sam is crushed at being cut loose after his stellar investigative work.

'Great job, Sam,' I say, my mind swarming with thoughts as I follow Candy.

While I'm curious about what Lee has to say, I'm distracted by the likelihood that Dad has been lying to me. I think back to the awful few years after my mother died. As far as I know, Dad was grief-stricken and spent most of his time working or at home staring into space. I have no knowledge of him being in any kind of romantic or sexual relationship, but I suppose it's not necessarily something he would have shared with me, especially if it wasn't serious. *Maybe he doesn't know he had another child*, I think. As awful as that would still be, at least it would mean he hasn't betrayed me.

After we get into Candy's car, she takes a call from someone who claims to have a tip-off about the missing baby.

Half listening, I connect to my hotspot and pull up Lee's file. He was first arrested at sixteen for damaging a car and stealing. A series of minor offences followed, ranging from possession of drugs to shoplifting, graffitiing and drink-driving. At twenty he did a short stint in rehab, but a year later he was arrested for possession again. After that there's nothing on his record until the pub fight

last week, a break of almost two and a half years. I skim through
the rest of the notes. Lee could have been released on Wednesday
while awaiting formal charges, but he has declined bail, opting to
stay behind bars.

Candy ends her call about the baby, which she says was bogus,
then connects to bluetooth and calls the prison. She speaks to
a guard, then we're put on hold.

I tell her about Lee's record and the declined bail. 'Knowing
Marty he probably wanted to teach Lee a lesson. He must have been
furious about his behaviour.'

'You'd think his mother might have advocated for him?' Candy
muses.

'Marty is very traditional. I'm not sure she would have had a say.'

While we wait, I think about how to manage this with Lee.
Not only is he delicate, he's unlikely to want to talk to a cop or a
journo about being accused of paedophilia unless he thinks we're
open to hearing his version of events. I'm going to need to be direct
but careful.

After a few minutes, Lee's reedy voice comes on the line. 'Hello.'

'Lee, it's Candy Fyfe, the journalist from yesterday. I'm here
with Detective Woodstock. We have some more questions for you.'

Lee makes a noncommittal sound.

I jump in, wanting to control the conversation. 'We heard you
got into that fight because those guys were giving you shit about
a girl you were involved with. She must be important to you, Lee.'

'I don't want to talk about it.'

'The thing is, we're really worried about her, Lee,' I say. 'We
want to help her and that's where you come in.'

He draws a sharp breath and says, 'Why? Has something
happened?' I'm encouraged by his response but I wonder again
about his mental state—he seems a lot younger than twenty-three.

I hold up my hand to quiet Candy and lean closer to the car speaker. 'Do you think she might be in danger, Lee?'

'No. I don't know.' His voice has dropped to a whisper.

'Can you tell us where she might be?'

He doesn't reply but I can hear his ragged breathing.

'We can help her,' I say, 'but we need you to tell us whatever you can. Can you do that?'

Silence.

'We really need to know where she is, Lee. Like I said, we're really worried about her.'

'Who knows you're talking to me?'

'No one,' I reply.

'Not my dad?' He sounds terrified.

'Not your dad. We wanted to speak with you first and try to sort this out without it becoming a big deal.'

There's a long pause and then Lee's breath grows loud again. 'Will you do something for me?' he says abruptly.

Candy and I both sit up straighter, sensing a breakthrough. 'We'll try,' I say.

'The baby . . .' he trails off. 'The one they found at the lake . . . ?'

Candy clamps a hand over her mouth to suppress an outburst.

'Yes, what about it?' I say as calmly as possible.

'Is she okay? There's nothing in the news about her anymore.'

I'm sure the surprise on Candy's face mirrors mine.

'Why are you interested in the baby?' she asks.

'Why, Lee?' I press. 'We can't tell you anything unless you talk to us.'

His breath catches in his throat as he chokes out, 'She's mine.'

CHAPTER FORTY

Candy weaves in between vehicles as she marches toward the hospital, narrowly avoiding side mirrors.

I run to keep up with her. 'Candy, wait! You can't just storm in there.'

'Why the hell not?'

'Candy, seriously, stop. What are you going to do, front up to the maternity ward and demand a paternity test?'

She spins around, her multicoloured earrings swinging against her jaw. 'I don't see why not. I mean, what if it's *true*, Gemma?'

Lee refused to tell us anything else—he just wanted our word that the child is safe. His concern seemed genuine, but it's hard to know whether to take him seriously, given his erratic behaviour and mental health issues. Does he really believe he's the father—and is it even possible?

Candy and I are in a stand-off, her toned arms crossed, her stance wide.

'I don't think the baby can be Lee's,' I say. 'If his DNA was a match, I'd know.'

'How?'

'Because Marty Blight is in the system—all cops are—and would have registered as a familial match if she's his grandchild.'

Candy chews her lip. 'So, Lee's lying?'

'Not unless Marty isn't Lee's biological father.' *Or unless the information has been kept from me*, I think.

'And Lee has a record anyway,' Candy says glumly, the wind rushing from her sails. 'So it would have linked to him, too.'

'Well, his prints will be in the system but probably not his DNA. I'll speak to Jonesy, see what I can find out.'

At the entrance, we step out of the way when the automatic doors open. An anxious-looking man pushes an elderly woman in a wheelchair, a younger woman following them. She attempts to participate in a conference call about the stock market as she fishes keys out of her handbag and presses the unlock button randomly at the rows of cars.

The doors open again to reveal Everett deep in conversation with an exhausted-looking Sophie McCallister. He stops short when he sees me, and Sophie's gaze flits nervously between the two of us. The sight of him makes my blood run hot.

He asks, 'You're still here, Woodstock?'

'We're admiring one of our favourite public spaces,' Candy says with an exaggerated smile. 'I was just saying to Gemma that I like what they've done with my taxes.'

Sophie seems to take this as her cue to leave and heads to her smoking nook. I gesture at her retreating figure and say to Everett, 'Have you asked her why she delayed the corpse collection yet?'

He glares at me. 'I'm not answering that in front of the media.'

I roll my eyes, chastised.

He folds his arms. 'I'm not getting the impression you're taking it easy, Gemma.'

'I'm fine.'

'I'm leaving now, and I think it's best if both of you ladies clear off as well.'

Candy puffs her chest indignantly, preparing for a fight, and I jump in before she gets herself arrested. 'I have a question. When you ran the abandoned baby through the system, was there a match?'

'It's not Roger's child, Gemma.' He speaks slowly, as if I'm thick.

'Yeah, I got that,' I snap. 'I just want to confirm there were no hits in the system at all?'

'No. Why?'

'Just double-checking, seeing as some DNA reports have been kept from me lately.'

He narrows his eyes, and I think in that moment he must really hate me.

'Do you have any updates on my attack? I'm not being kept informed.'

'You'll be the first to know the second there's something worth sharing, Gemma.'

'I highly doubt that.'

Candy watches our back-and-forth conversation as though it's a tennis tournament.

With a dismissive grunt, Everett turns to leave.

I ask, 'Have you checked with your friend Sophie whether any Propofol has gone missing from the hospital? That seems like an easy place to start, if you're looking for some direction.'

He reels around so fast, I step back in surprise. 'Jesus, Gemma, just back off. This is *not* your case. When are you going to get that?' Saliva flies from his lips, and he rakes a hand through his hair.

My mouth falls open in shock. I quickly close it: I don't want to give him the satisfaction of knowing how shaken I am by his outburst, let alone how I feel about him hiding things from me and talking to Mac behind my back.

'Lose your cool much?' Candy attempts to defuse the tension, but I just want to get away from him.

'Whatever,' I say, then start walking back toward the car, tears burning my eyes.

The clip of Candy's high heels is not too far behind. 'Jeez, what is his problem?'

'I'm not sure,' I say, trying to keep my voice steady.

'Gemma? Talk to me.'

'I'm fine. Just frustrated.'

'Fuck them and especially Everett. That was totally uncalled for. And I got the distinct impression we interrupted something, don't you?'

'What, Sophie and Everett? I don't think so.'

'Stranger things have happened.' I can tell she's pumped up from the run-in with him—she's bouncing around, excess energy radiating from her body.

In contrast I feel raw and wrecked. 'I don't know what Everett's playing at. Anyway, I should go. Let me see what I can find out about the baby. I'll share what I can with you but you know it's likely to be off the record.'

'If it is his baby we can go and visit him again,' she says unperturbed. 'Push him for more info.'

'I'll let you know. I need to speak to Mac.'

Her hands twist together. 'How is that going, Gemma?'

I smile tightly. 'Everything is fine.'

I get in my car and sit there while the aircon kicks in. What I said to Candy is true: I can't work Everett out. While there's politics at every level of the force, as a unit we generally present a united front. But he seems unwilling to work with me.

A thought shudders into my brain. Everett knew I was home the other afternoon, and he probably knew Mac was away. He said he went to The Retreat, but what if he lied?

No, no, no. Surely not. That line of thinking is paranoid. He might be competitive, he might not like me much, but he didn't attack me. He wouldn't risk going to gaol just to take me out of the running for Jonesy's role. Plus, there was no guarantee I would be removed from the case.

Swallowing, I picture Scarlett and Lola alone in the house again. Anything could have happened to them, and I just can't believe Everett could have done that out of petty spite.

But who else knew I was at the house alone? Mac? Candy? Jonesy? Did Carlyle follow me from The Lyle or send someone after me?

'Stop it,' I say out loud, shaking the suspicion from my head. 'Stop it.'

I release the handbrake and flick on the indicator, turning out of the car park. The sun has dipped, and I flip down the visor.

Smithson is alive with shoppers gathering in small groups to talk. At the lights I scan the window of a real estate agent; every second ad is promoting property on the new estate, the promise of a dream home with easy access to everything you could ever want.

The town is bursting at the seams—I can suddenly sense it, as if there's pressure building, about to pop. I feel it in my limbs, a nervous restlessness. For another fifteen minutes I drive aimlessly, problems grinding through my brain. After my third lap of the main street, I know where I want to go. I turn left at the roundabout and head out of town.

CHAPTER FORTY-ONE

Several kilometres along the highway, I spy a blue-and-white checked ribbon against the natural hues of the landscape. I pull over. Aside from the crime-scene tape, there's nothing to suggest what happened here.

I exhale a long shaky breath. Stepping off the road, I wade into the grass and walk toward the huge gum tree I recognise from the case-file photographs. In my mind's eye I imagine a dark four-wheel drive running the woman off the road, her station wagon flying through the air. It passes over my head. When the impact comes, everything stops.

I'm unsteady on my feet. For a moment I just stand still, feeling the solidity of the ground. Shards of glass glint in the sun, tiny jewels buried in the dirt. I circle the tree, the outside layers of bark peeling back like there's a gaping wound. Closing my eyes, I see the crumpled car, imagine the woman inside.

'Who the hell were you?' I whisper.

My skin crawls when I think of the three men talking about the DNA report, discussing me, deciding what to tell me, protecting me: Jonesy, Everett and Mac. It wasn't the attack they were worried about—it was this.

Fuck, Mac knew about this and has been keeping it from me. I march in a circle, rage building with every step. The betrayal hits me physically, a cramp deep in my body. I start to cry, but anger wins out, my muscles hardening until I feel like my insides will burst. My teeth clench painfully as I call him.

'You knew,' I hiss when he answers.

'Gemma, what?'

'You knew about the woman's DNA match with me and didn't say anything. You've been talking to Everett behind my back.'

'Where are you?' He sounds worried but also scared—and this, more than anything, lets me know I'm right.

'I'm on the highway at the crash site.'

'I'll come and meet you.'

'No. I don't want to see you. I—' Emotion bubbles from my throat. 'What the *fuck* is going on, Mac?'

He doesn't say anything. All I can hear are the shrill cries of insects in the surrounding paddocks.

'Okay, fine. I'll explain, shall I? You've been lying to me.'

'I didn't mean to find out,' he says softly.

'Everett told you?'

He hesitates. 'Jonesy.'

That name is a knife to my gut. 'Why wouldn't he just talk to me? Why wouldn't *you*?'

But I know why: it's the same reason I would have been wary to speak to Mac if the same thing had happened in reverse. I'd want to know what I was dealing with first; I'd want to know what I was going to say, how I thought he would respond. I look over at the tree and feel an acute sadness. Whoever she was, we might never find her.

'You don't talk to me anymore!' I'm unable to keep the emotion out of my voice. 'You're shutting me out. Why?'

'Gemma, I'm sorry.' I'm sure he's pacing now. His hand will be in his hair as he tries to choose the right words—I've seen him do it a hundred times. 'This isn't sinister. Everyone just wanted to understand the situation before getting you involved.' He pauses. 'Especially after the attack.'

'It's all so convenient, isn't it? Everyone felt justified in making plans about me without consulting me, as if I'm just a victim.'

'It's not like that.'

'What is it like, then?' My voice wobbles.

'Jonesy called me because he knew about the cold case I was working on. I'd emailed him to request gaining access to some old files.'

I think about the boxes in the shed. 'Jonesy was helping you on the cold case . . . ?'

'Sort of. The original investigation is decades old, and I got stuck—the new lead I had, it fizzled out. Jonesy was a junior cop here back then, and I knew he was across the case, so I asked him a few questions.'

'I don't understand how any of this is relevant to keeping information from me.'

'Once the DNA match with you was clear, he figured it was linked.'

'Linked to what?' I'm on the brink of a full-blown explosion.

Nearby, a horse kicks and whinnies softly, flicking flies from his tail.

'Gemma, this is a lot. I've wanted to talk to you about it—of course I have—but I wanted to be sure before I said anything.'

'Fuck, Mac, this talking-in-riddles bullshit is getting beyond tedious. The woman is related to me, that much is clear, so just fucking tell me what you think you know.'

'It's about your mother.'

My neck snaps back and catches a nerve ending. 'My mother?' I knead the sore spot with my thumb.

'Yes. Before you were born, she . . .' He trails off, then simply breathes, 'Gem.'

'She *what*?' I roar.

'She was involved in an extreme religious group,' he says quietly. 'The Braybrook cult. She ran away from home and disappeared for several years. No one in her family had contact with her.'

'The Retreat,' I whisper.

'Yes.'

'What else?'

He swallows. 'In her early twenties, she moved to Queensland. By all accounts she was building a new life.'

I want to grab him by the shoulders and shake the words out of him. 'And then?'

'She was accused of a serious crime.'

Puzzle pieces click together in my head. 'The murdered priest . . . My mother was accused of killing him.'

Mac makes a small affirmative noise.

My throat contracts, and I gulp for air. 'That's insane,' I manage. I feel faint and wait a few seconds for the feeling to pass before I ask, 'What about the woman from the car crash? Who is she?'

'That is not my news to tell, Gem.' Mac's voice cracks. 'You'd better speak to your dad.'

CHAPTER FORTY-TWO

I hang up on Mac and stumble back to the car. My legs feel weak and unreliable, and I fall into the seat, my breathing ragged as I try to think what to do. Mac calls repeatedly, the bleat of the phone an assault on my tranquil surrounds, and I put it on silent.

I turn the key in the ignition, but I don't drive. I sit there, scouring the internet for information. I read about a woman I thought I knew, but her name is unfamiliar. Old news articles tell me that when she was twenty-two, my mother was investigated for the suspected murder of a former cult leader. She was released under a cloud of suspicion only three years before she gave birth to me.

As I drive to Dad's house, I don't think about what I'm going to say to him or what he is going to say to me. Mac's name flashes on the phone screen, over and over. I hold the steering wheel tighter and tighter. It's easier to think about Mac than my dad right now, so I focus my anger on him. How dare he sneak around behind my back and make me feel like I was going crazy? How could he speak to Everett and Jonesy about me like that? I think back to all the promises we made and feel so bitterly disappointed in him—and in myself for letting it get to this point. The moment I sensed something was wrong, I should have confronted him.

Childhood memories fill my mind, as if the articles have opened a floodgate. I fix on an image of my mother, with her dark hair, neater and straighter than mine, gathered in a ponytail as she surveyed the pantry, hands on her slim hips; a nothing moment, but so vivid she could be in front of me now. She moves her head up, then down. 'Casserole,' she decides. She rarely sought permission and wasn't especially collaborative—she wasn't seeking validation from anyone. All my life Dad has described her as a doer, a go-getter: 'Your mother gets things done, Gem. I'm just there to assist and marvel.'

His voice echoes in my head as I pull up outside his house and stalk up the driveway. It's all I can do not to kick the half-painted fence.

I'm already pulling out my spare key when I pound my fist against the front door—once, twice, a third time. Too impatient to wait, I jam the key in the lock and enter. Music is playing, a sparse flute solo I recognise as being part of Rebecca's yoga playlist. I storm down the hallway, dread filling me with every step, and burst into the lounge room.

Dad is attempting to get up from the couch, where he is propped up against Rebecca's bright yellow cushions and covered with one of her patchwork blankets. He's holding a pencil in his right hand, today's crossword on the coffee table next to him. His smile turns to a look of alarm. 'God, Gemma, what is it?'

I find myself holding on to the wall, overwhelmed by what I'm about to ask him. There will be no coming back from this. I have an urge to drive as far from Smithson as possible so I never have to deal with it.

'Gemma?'

I go to the sound system and flick off the music.

'Gemma,' Dad says, 'you're scaring me. What is it? Are the kids okay?'

I appraise him more coolly and try to channel my work mode, knowing that if my emotions break free they will derail me. 'Dad, I need to know about Mum.'

His mouth drops open, panic flaring in his eyes.

'You need to tell me everything. Right now.'

He falls back against the cushions like a deflated balloon. 'I'm not sure that—'

'What? That now is a good time to talk about it?' My hands ball into fists. 'You're right. It's not a good time, a good time would have been—oh, I don't know, Dad—about thirty fucking years ago.' My voice is like gravel, the words landing like blows.

'Gemma!' he protests feebly.

I fight the impulse to go to him, conscious of his heart but also that if we don't do this now, I will implode. 'Tell me what she did. Who she was. Who you were. What you've done.' I whisper the last few words, aware that my world is about to spiral.

'Gemma, please. Please, calm down.'

Rebecca slides open the rear glass door and steps inside, dressed in exercise clothes, a quizzical expression on her flushed face.

'I thought that "tell the truth" was one of your rules,' I say to Dad. 'You drilled that into me enough times.'

'It is! Of course it is. But this was different.'

'What on earth is going on?' Rebecca says, but we ignore her.

'How is this different?' I ask.

'Sometimes you have to weigh up the pain of telling the truth, consider the hurt it might cause and make the best decision you can for your family.'

I think about the woman from the crash, my look-alike. 'There's so much you haven't told me.'

He presses his lips together. 'Yes. I'm sorry, Gemma.'

I fight a wave of nausea. Dad seems so frail, so old. Tears run down my face as I recall moments we've spent together flailing in grief, moments that now somehow feel like a lie. I have always been his daughter, his only child. Our bond isn't showy, but it's deep and real. As desperate as I am to know the truth, my heart breaks at the thought of the trust between us being so comprehensively shattered.

I tense my muscles and summon the grim determination that has brought me this far. 'Tell me the fucking truth, Dad, or I won't speak to you ever again.'

CHAPTER FORTY-THREE

Rebecca is asked to leave the house in a rare display of assertiveness from my father, who still hasn't moved from the couch. 'I need to talk to Gemma on my own. I'll let you know when we're done.'

Clearly stung, Rebecca hovers in the kitchen doorway, wringing her hands. 'Perhaps you should discuss whatever this is later, Ned. You're still not one hundred per cent.'

'Please, love, this is important.'

After shooting a bewildered look at me, she snorts gently and throws her hands in the air. She gathers her things and marches to the front door. A few moments later, she reverses her car down the driveway.

Dad takes a big drink of water and several steadying breaths. He looks utterly broken, but I refuse to soften. I'm owed this and need to hear it now, whether he is ready or not.

'I'm waiting, Dad.'

'It's complicated, Gemma. You have to understand that it's complicated.'

'Just tell me,' I whisper.

And he does. In his familiar, steady voice he tells me that he knew my mother when they were young teenagers, that they met on a camp and stayed in touch even though they had gone to different schools. He knew she was having trouble at home with her parents, who were strict and seemed to favour their son. After a few years, he lost contact with her, and eventually he heard she'd run away to join a fast-growing religious group on the outskirts of Smithson. She essentially disappeared, but Dad never forgot about her.

Then the cult leader died performing a ceremony in the dam on the property. His death was treated as suspicious, but no charges were laid; it was ruled an accidental drowning. This caused rifts to form among the senior members, and after a few months the property was abandoned. Little offshoots popped up in Queensland and the Blue Mountains, but they never reached the scale of The Retreat.

One of the senior leaders returned to the Catholic Church and became a priest in Brisbane. A few years after the cult fell apart, he died at a private dinner at his home and his autopsy revealed traces of bleach and ammonia. His murder was briefly a national news story, but the Church, not wanting his link to The Retreat to become widely known, successfully restricted the media coverage with threats of defamation lawsuits. My mother was charged with murder, her tumultuous past with the priest cited as a motive. But the evidence was weak, and there were other suspects. She was released without charge.

Dad wrote to her during this time, and they corresponded for several months. By then her parents had moved to Perth, and he encouraged her to come home, where he'd opened his small maintenance business. When she was twenty-three, she moved back to Gowran with a new name and a new look, determined to start over.

'She rarely spoke about The Retreat,' Dad says. 'Occasionally something would come up and she'd mention a person or one of the pets, but she was badly affected by her time there. I tried to get her to see someone about it, but she didn't want to dredge it up—she wanted to move on. And because she seemed happy, I didn't push it.'

'And no one here knew who she was?'

'Don't think so. She'd gone to a tiny country school with only a handful of kids, and she looked completely different from when she was a teenager. She stopped bleaching her hair and wearing heavy make-up and she was a lot thinner. She hadn't had any contact with her family since she was sixteen, and all the cult members were gone. In many ways her life started when she moved back here. I'm sorry for always telling you that she was an only child and an orphan, but I didn't know how to tell you the truth about that either. I have no idea where her parents are now or if they're alive. By the time we had you, we never spoke about her past. It was clear she didn't want to.'

'Were her parents abusive? Is that why she ran away?'

Dad falters. 'I'm not . . . sure. I got the feeling her father was, but she never said so, and I didn't ask her outright. You must understand that things were different then, Gemma. There was so much that was never talked about.'

'And you thought I wouldn't be able to handle it?' I can't hide my hurt at the knowledge that so much of my mother and her family was kept from me. There was a distance, and a coolness about her, and knowing all of this would have helped me make sense of her.

'It wasn't like that. We just blocked it out—truly, it was like it had never happened. Then she died, and I was a mess. It never occurred to me to tell you. I think it would have seemed like a betrayal.'

As angry as I am, I understand at some level. Since Scott died, I've negotiated the delicate dance of what information is mine to tell and, if I do share something, how he would have wanted me to frame it. The inability of the dead to defend themselves—to correct, to comment and to explain—makes it very hard to present any detail about them without feeling as if it needs to be followed with a raft of caveats.

I ask, 'Dad, what happened after she died, when you were a mess?'

Rubbing his eyes, he adjusts his position. 'I'm not sure what you mean.'

'The car crash,' I say, 'the one last Sunday—there was a match, a DNA match in our system, with me.'

He stares at me incredulously.

'She looked like me, the crash victim, and we were related. Soon after mum died, did you have another child? Or could you have and not known?'

Dad breathes out. 'Oh, Gemma, no—no, of course I didn't. Really, until Rebecca there wasn't anyone for me. I missed your mother so intensely I couldn't even think about anyone else. All I focused on was you.'

Relief runs through me. Then a new wave of anxiety rises. 'I don't understand. Why is she a match with me? Is she one of your cousins?'

Dad looks at the ground, his jaw shaking uncontrollably.

That's when I know. My knees buckle, and I think for the millionth time about how corrosive secrets are, how destructive. How what we don't say can prove just as dangerous as what we do. 'Say it! You have to say it.'

Dad closes his eyes, pauses, then opens them. 'You have a sister—a half-sister. Your mother had a baby before we were together. I'm sorry.' Tears are running down his cheeks.

I can't believe it was only two weeks ago that I was driving to the hospital, praying he would be okay. Intense exhaustion overwhelms me. My childhood feels like it belongs to someone else. My father is a stranger.

'Your mother only spoke about it once, and she was adamant it was better for everyone that the baby was kept a secret. After she died, I wasn't sure what to do. She'd never wanted you to know, and I worried you would become obsessive about it. I—'

'Enough,' I whisper. 'That's enough.' I press my hands to my face, dig my fingers into my temples and emit an anguished scream. I need to get out of here. I spin around and head for the door.

'Gemma!'

'It doesn't matter,' I cry. 'My sister's dead now anyway, so it doesn't matter.'

CHAPTER FORTY-FOUR

A few hours later, I wake up feeling awful on my couch. A dream lingers: I was in a car crash, and when the movement stopped, glass covered me like rain. I turned toward the driver and discovered it was me, bleeding from the temple, lifeless eyes staring.

'Ugh.' I pull myself upright. In my mind's eye I still see my half-sister, my look-alike, bleeding and lifeless.

The house was empty when I came here from Dad's, and I was relieved. Still feeling shattered, I sank onto the couch, where I looked up more stories about my mother and The Retreat.

When that became unbearable, I delved into Lee Blight's social-media footprint. He hasn't posted anything in just over two years, but prior to that there are dozens of images of him fishing and going on road trips with mates. I clicked through his publicly available Facebook friends and comments, trying to find anything that might lead us to the mystery girl. At some point I fell asleep.

Now Scarlett is on the playmat in front of me, clicking her tongue as she whacks a plush koala against the ground. I stroke her cheek, and she responds with a huge smile.

'You all right, Mum?'

I startle—I hadn't noticed Ben at the kitchen table, drinking a Milo and reading a book. I gesture for him to come closer, then pull him into a hug.

'Where's Mac?' I ask.

'He's on the phone.' Ben points at the window to the backyard. 'I said I'd watch Scarlett because you were sleeping. Do you want me to make you a hot chocolate or a coffee?'

'No, thanks. But I do want to talk to you.'

He bites his lip and nods.

I pull Scarlett onto my lap and kiss her head, studying Mac through the window. He appears deep in conversation, a worry line etched between his brows. I wonder who he's talking to, yet again feeling a distance between us.

Gently, I ask Ben about the vaping. He stumbles through an answer, his hands fidgeting in his lap. Listening to him, I'm taken back to my teenage years; I recall the yearning I felt for a life that wasn't my own, the ferocious curiosity I had about everything and how badly I wanted freedom. Both confident and apprehensive, I felt constant pressure to make the right choices, even though I had no idea who I was trying to impress.

'I need to be able to trust you,' I say softly. 'You're going to try things, and that's fine, but I need to know you're making good decisions. Vaping is not a good decision, because it's bad for your health.'

'I'm sorry,' he says, embarrassed, as he pushes his hair away from his face 'I didn't like it much anyway.'

I ask him to give me all the vaping paraphernalia, and he says he already threw it out.

The conversation with my dad rings in my ears as I take a deep breath and explain to Ben why I wanted to go back to work early. I acknowledge that I can't guarantee it will be safe but that I want to do it anyway. We talk about Scott and about the events in Fairhaven last year. Ben tells me he thinks about it sometimes, that he's still scared to walk anywhere alone in case someone scary comes up behind him. I hug him and am honest about what I can and can't control and the fact that I don't know exactly what our future holds.

When Scarlett starts crying, Ben reaches down and picks her up, stroking her hair and jiggling her on his lap. My chest tightens. He is so good with her.

Behind us the door opens, and Mac comes inside. His movements are jerky, showing me he's unsure of my mood. Then he notices our tear-stained faces. 'Is everything okay?'

'Everything is fine,' I say, although I'm avoiding his eyes. 'It's getting late—let's get dinner sorted.'

As we prepare the meal, we don't speak but move in an easy flow, our bodies in sync.

'Would you like a glass of wine?' I ask him stiffly.

'Please.'

I pour him a glass of his favourite shiraz. Our eyes lock, and his expression is pleading, but I'm not ready to talk yet. To let him off the hook.

We sit down to eat. Ben inhales his meal and excuses himself to have a shower.

'Did you speak to your dad?' Mac asks as soon as Ben leaves the room.

I keep my tone neutral. 'I did.'

'How did that go?'

'I don't want to discuss it.' I clean Scarlett's face and hands, remove the remnants of dinner from her highchair and replace them with a tube of yoghurt.

Mac reaches out to take my hand, but I pull away. 'We have to talk about this, Gemma.'

Darts of anger shoot through my body. 'Just like you've been talking to me, you mean?'

'I've been an idiot. I'm sorry.'

'Who were you speaking to on the phone before?'

'Molly. I thought about what you said the other day, and you were right. I haven't been keeping in touch with the kids like I should, so I called her.'

'And where did you really go the other day? I know you weren't in Brisbane.'

He sighs. 'Victoria, just over the border.'

'What's there?'

'Your half-sister's foster parents and her closest friend from school.' Mac seems nervous. 'They were reluctant to speak with me over the phone, and I wanted to be available for a few days if they took a while to warm up, so I booked a room so I could be close by.'

'Why didn't they want to speak with you?'

'They knew about your mother's past, and I think they were scared of getting caught up in a criminal case.'

I'm irrationally annoyed at these strangers for not doing everything in their power to help my sister. 'Why didn't they report her missing?'

'They didn't know she was. They haven't seen her in almost twenty-five years.'

My anger morphs into a crushing sadness. 'Why didn't you just tell me where you were going?' I whisper.

'I didn't want to completely lie to you about what I was doing, and I'd mentioned the case involved Brisbane. It was stupid.'

Looking at him, I wish so badly he had just talked to me. 'I can't believe all of this.'

'I know. I'm so sorry. This isn't us, Gemma, and it's all my fault. Once I realised your mother was involved in the cold case, I didn't know what to do. But I shouldn't have gone behind your back.'

'No, you shouldn't have.'

'How do I fix it?'

'I don't know if you can,' I say honestly. 'For now, I just need some space.'

Mac swallows but doesn't challenge me. 'What did your dad say?'

I remember walking out on Dad, how small and hopeless he looked on the couch. As I drove home, Rebecca sent pleading voicemails for me to come back and talk to him. I didn't listen to them all.

Sobs threaten to take over, but I'm determined not to keep crying. 'Mac, I'm sorry . . . I can't talk about this with you yet. I need to get my head around it first.' I run my fingers along the skin under my eyes, cleaning away the tears and remnants of make-up. 'And I'm finding it hard to trust you.'

He looks crestfallen, but he nods. 'I'm worried about you. This is a lot to deal with.'

'Yeah, well, I don't have much choice, do I?'

'Do you want me to tell you what I know about her, your half-sister? It's not much yet, but I'm here for you whenever you're ready to talk. Her family sent me a few things.'

'Not now, Mac,' I say wearily. 'I just want you to leave me alone.'

Feeling beyond drained, I go into the lounge room and settle Scarlett in her bouncer. Then, on the couch with my laptop, I google the contact details for Ash's boss so that tomorrow I can make a formal complaint about his drug-taking and ask that he be given the support he needs. I'll tell Everett that he needs to report Lenny Tinsdale as well.

I pull up Lee's file and go back over his long list of misdemeanours, some of which I skimmed earlier, but some I didn't, searching for anything that might make sense of the claim he has committed statutory rape. I feel a jolt of empathy for Marty Blight, even though I always found him to be a bit of an arsehole. I know how damaging an addict can be to the family unit.

I read through some of the court orders. Lee's drug possession saw him serve thirty days in prison before he was ordered to complete six months of community service. He attended compulsory rehab and was treated for depression and paranoia. Carlyle Kirk is listed as his psychiatrist.

CHAPTER FORTY-FIVE

MONDAY, 26 SEPTEMBER, 10.02 AM

The air is thick with the minty tang of eucalyptus. I'm driving to Gowran after a cafe breakfast with Ben before I dropped him at school. I left Scarlett with Mac without asking about his plans for the day; I just told him I was meeting with Candy and Sam. I felt guilty about lying to him but then rationalised it by assuring myself that this is what happens when someone crosses the line the way he has. The centre of gravity is off balance in our relationship, and the old rules no longer apply.

We'll get it back, I tell myself. Once things have settled down, we'll go back to how we were.

I probably should have asked Candy to come with me, but I know she'd sense something is wrong and crack me open. I don't want to talk about it all yet. Plus, none of this could be on the record anyway and I can't risk her breaking a story and jeopardising the investigation. I'm flip-flopping between eerie calm and panic, like a dam is about to break around me and there's nothing I can do but wait to be slammed by the water.

Anxious about wasting time in the car, I call the manager of the ambulance station and tell her about Ash. She assures me that she'll address the matter with him straight away. I call Everett, ostensibly to ask for an update on my attacker, but he doesn't answer. Then, heart thumping like crazy, I call Jonesy.

'Woodstock, I'm going to need to call you back. I'm in the middle of something that can't wait.'

'I need to talk to you,' I say, but he's already gone. Maybe it's a good thing he hung up on me: I want to confront him in person so he can't dismiss me. Plus, I want him to see how upset he's made me.

I call Minnie as I turn off the highway.

'Sorry, Gemma, I'm not sure of any updates,' she says, when I ask her about the investigation on my attack.

'How's everything else going?' I want her to see me as an ally, someone she can open up to.

She hesitates. 'We've identified another teenage runaway from Sydney who was pregnant when she left her home and has turned up with no sign of the baby, so we're looking into that. Not sure about anything else.'

'It's okay, Minnie,' I say. 'You can talk to me. I'm still a cop.'

'I know—I just don't want to get in trouble.'

Uneasiness flares in my gut. 'What do you mean?'

'I just want to focus on doing my job.'

I think of myself at her age, flush with ambition, so intent on winning. At work I spent every moment pushing the envelope, being obnoxious and making myself known. I was embarrassingly overconfident, Jonesy's early support providing me with a safety net. In contrast, Minnie sounds timid and scared—and it makes my blood boil that someone has diminished her and made her feel small.

'You know you can talk to me, Minnie.'

'Sorry, Gemma, I have to go. Roger's funeral starts at eleven.'

'Dammit,' I say to the silent car, feeling acutely lonely. 'Get a grip,' I murmur. 'Get it together.'

At the gaol I move through the initial security checkpoint. When I reach the second station, I provide my name and ask to see Lee. After staring at my chest inappropriately, the burly guard shakes his head and walks off, leaving me standing there, wondering what the hell is going on. He returns a few minutes later, stroking his auburn beard. 'Sorry, you can't see him.'

While I knew this trip might be a waste of time, I can't help feeling let down. 'Why not?'

'He's not well.' The guard sticks his lower lip out in a pout. 'Not suitable for visitors.'

I'm instantly on alert. 'What's wrong with him?'

'Sorry, love, can't talk about it.' He hooks his thick thumbs into his pockets and appraises me again. 'We need to protect the privacy of our boys here. You understand.'

The way he says this makes me assume Lee's had some kind of mental health episode.

'I'm sure you can speak to your boss, see if he'll tell you more.' Irritated by his patronising tone, I thank him and head back the way I came.

As I round the corner to the car park, I almost collide with Marty Blight. 'Gemma.' He looks a lot older than I remember; he's put on weight and seems to slope to one side. 'Gemma,' he repeats. He's on edge, his eyes darting behind me as if he's worried someone will see us. 'How are you?'

'Hi, Marty. You're here to see Lee?'

'Yes.' He grabs my arm and hustles me over to the side of the building.

'What are you doing?' I cry, pulling away from him.

His face flushes red and his eyes shift back to the direction of the gaol entrance. 'Sorry, I need to lean against something—my damn hip is playing up again.'

Marty and I never really got along but, after a few years of working together, I did manage to gain his respect. And while I didn't like his style, he always had an impressive presence. But not now. Now he looks like a confused elderly man. I decide to be upfront about why I'm here and see if I can get him to tell me what's happened. 'I wanted to speak to Lee as well. Is he all right? They told me he's sick.'

'Just leave it alone, Gemma, will you?' Marty snaps, some of his trademark arrogance rising to the surface. He runs a hand over his face, pulling at his generous jowls. Little beads of perspiration are forming in his widow's peak.

I don't let his tone deter me; he's obviously stressed about Lee. 'What's going on, Marty?'

He focuses on me briefly and then seems to get distracted by something else in the car park. He digs his hand into his hip and looks pained. 'I mean it, Gemma. Just go home. You should be worried about your own family.'

My heartbeat quickens. 'What's that supposed to mean?'

'It means you don't need to get involved in this.'

Does his comment mean he knows who attacked me the other day? Emboldened, I go for the jugular. 'Lee told me the baby abandoned at the lake is his.'

Marty slumps against the wall, his hand curling into a fist. 'God, he's an idiot.'

'Is it true?'

'Of course it isn't bloody true. He's not well! Doesn't know what he's saying.'

'He seemed pretty certain.'

Marty grunts dismissively but there's genuine panic in his eyes. I don't relent. 'Where has he been, Marty?'

'Gemma,' he groans, but some of the fight seems to have gone out of him.

'Marty, you know me. You can tell me what's going on. Was he at The Retreat?'

For a minute I think he's going to talk but then he mutters, 'I don't have time for this.' He tries to sidestep me but loses his balance, and I steady him with my hands on his shoulders.

'Please,' I say more gently, 'I want to help, Marty. Lee seems scared. He was worried about the baby. I'm worried about you. Let me help.'

'He has no idea. None.' Marty's broad nose reddens as he tries not to cry. 'The boy needs to keep his mouth shut and focus on getting better. I don't see how that's so bloody hard.'

'Is Carlyle Kirk treating him again?'

Marty's head whips up. 'What?'

Heart racing, I say, 'Dr Kirk treated him after his last arrest. Do you know Dr Kirk?'

Marty blinks a few times, wringing his hands. 'All I've ever tried to do is help my kids.'

'Of course you have,' I say with feeling. 'But I also know how hard it is to care for someone with an addiction.'

'It's fucking impossible.' Tears fill his eyes. 'I didn't know what to do with him. We couldn't help him on our own—we needed to get him out of here.'

I'm not sure what he means but I'm breaking him down. It's like he's been craving someone to talk to about his son; it's probably not something he wanted to share with his old police buddies and I don't imagine his relationship with his wife is built on great communication. 'Where has Lee been, Marty? Did he go and get help somewhere?'

He wipes his nose and pushes against the wall to right himself. 'I need to go and be with my son.'

I nod. 'Tell me what's wrong with him.'

Spittle hits me in the face as he hisses, 'He was attacked last night, okay?'

I recoil, my mind grappling with this revelation. 'Who attacked him? Was it another inmate?'

Marty turns away from me. He seems to decide he's said too much.

'Why didn't you post bail for him? Did you leave him in gaol on purpose? Come on, Marty, you know me, talk to me.'

He leans so close that I can smell the stale cigarette smoke on his breath. 'Gemma, listen to me. You need to drop this. I mean it.'

The fear in his eyes scares me. For better or worse, Marty never seemed scared of anything when we worked together. This isn't some standard gaol brawl; he's too spooked for that.

'Is Lee okay, Marty? What aren't you telling me?'

He checks his phone, wiping the sweat from his head with a handkerchief. 'He was beaten up pretty badly, okay? I'm waiting to hear if they're moving him to the hospital.'

'This is linked to the baby, isn't it? Lee was scared something like this would happen, wasn't he? You both were.'

Marty's expression darkens again. 'Seriously, Gemma, for once in your life, just do what you're told and fuck off!'

CHAPTER FORTY-SIX

The drive back to Smithson feels long, as unresolved threads of information dance around in my head. Someone hurt Lee. Surely it's a warning, a move to stop him from talking. But what does he know? From what his dad was saying, it sounds as though Lee has been in rehab. There isn't a live-in centre at The Lyle, but maybe Carlyle referred him somewhere else as part of his treatment.

A thought creeps around the edges of my mind. Jonesy and Marty are close. Jonesy has already concealed one set of DNA results this week—what if he's kept the baby's DNA secret as well? And if what the Bilson workers at the pub said is true, then that would mean Marty knows his son had a child with an underage girl and is protecting him, a thought that makes me feel sick. The problem is, I don't even know if she exists.

I let out a groan. I should tell Everett about Lee and the potential link to the baby, but I have no idea if I can trust him either. He lied to me, and I can't shake the idea that he's the reason Minnie wants to leave.

The breeze has settled; the sun wrestling with a slight chill. A seed of an idea quickly becomes a plan: I want to see The Retreat for myself. If Lee really is being warned not to speak about it, I want to know why. I pass the turn-off to Smithson, and before long I'm flying along the highway, being ignored by herds of horses and cows in lush paddocks. Despite everything, I start to feel calmer.

As I veer off the highway, the old homestead is visible through the wall of acacias and gums. It's bigger than I expected, single storey with a large veranda and bay windows. The exterior looks freshly painted and the terracotta tiles on the roof are in good condition. I arrive at the end of the long dirt driveway and turn off the engine, thinking about my mother leaving her family to live here but struggling to picture her as a wayward, bleach-blonde teen runaway. She was always so serious and sensible. There don't seem to be any other cars, but there's a tractor in the open carport ahead and several other pieces of farm machinery in a makeshift annex to the right of the house. On the other side there are flowerbeds full of blooms and trees heavy with fruit. Several bikes are scattered on the lawn, and boots are lined up on the front porch. Further along, close to the house, are six campervans that, judging by the gardens growing around them, are being used as permanent dwellings. On the opposite side of the homestead is a large shed, a huge pile of firewood and the biggest vegetable garden I've ever seen. *Braybrook* is carved into a wooden sign above the front door of the house. I feel like I've stepped back in time.

After I get out of the car, I turn around to find a young woman staring at me. 'Hello.' I shield my eyes from the sun. 'Do you live here?'

'Are you a journalist?' She seems even younger than I first thought, although perhaps it's her outfit giving that impression:

a brown smock dress and boots. Her tawny hair hangs loose to her waist. She isn't wearing make-up, and her skin glows with health. Her wide-brimmed hat is at least two sizes too big.

'I'm a police detective,' I say, showing her my badge. 'My name is Gemma Woodstock. Did you meet the other detective who came here the other day?'

'Cops have no reason to come here,' she says robotically.

'But didn't you see another cop here the other day?'

'No.'

There's ice at the base of my spine. Did Everett lie about coming here? I think of the needle in my neck and shiver. 'Who else lives here?' I ask the girl.

'My family.' She doesn't break eye contact, and it's unnerving.

'Can I meet them?'

She walks across the lawn to the shed, pulls open the door and disappears inside. Unsure of my welcome, I follow her.

A man emerges from the shed, followed by three women, and three dogs that race toward me. 'Hey, hey.' I put out my hands, even though they can't protect me if the dogs attack.

'They won't hurt you,' the man calls out. Faded jeans hang from his lean frame, and his dark hair is past his shoulders. The dogs circle me, sniffing my shoes. The man stops about a metre away, the gaggle of women pausing behind him. They all stare at me.

'I just wanted to come out and see this place,' I offer, after realising they were waiting for me to speak first. 'I've been hearing about it since I was a little kid.'

The man's fingers move so quickly, I can't make out what he's doing. There's a click that I think comes from his mouth, and the dogs run off, fast as rabbits. He looks at me expectantly—I'm certain the dogs will be back and far more aggressive if he doesn't like what I have to say.

I introduce myself and ask, 'Did you meet with another detective a few days ago?'

'Julian. Yes, we spoke.'

I'm almost winded with relief: Everett wasn't lying.

The man sucks air through his teeth. 'I can show you the animals, if you like.'

'That would be great.' I'm happy to take his lead.

I fall into step with the other women, who continue to stare at me, and we follow the man past the row of campervans. As we walk, he answers my questions. His name is Myron, and he's lived here for almost twenty years. New members don't turn up often but are welcome; there are only seventy-three people living at The Retreat, and a lot of them are related to one another—siblings or cousins—but he insists there's nothing untoward. No, he's not in charge: everyone who lives here is equal.

Myron points out the cows and sheep, the chickens and the pigsty. He casually puts his arm around one of the women as he explains the way they manage the land, rotate the animals, and plant the crops based on weather patterns. A lot of the farming practices are Indigenous, Myron says, and don't cause any long-term damage.

I ask where the others are, and he says the children are in lessons and the babies are with their mothers. Some of the men have gone down to fish in the creek.

He's apparently never heard of Lee Blight, and when I show him the young man's photo on my phone, he says he doesn't recognise him.

'Lee used to deliver food out here,' I say.

'We ask delivery people to leave goods in the shed—we try to avoid contact with the outside world as much possible.' Myron says this matter-of-factly, with no awareness of how paranoid it makes him seem.

I ask him if he spoke to the journalist who visited the other day. 'Yes. The tall lady and the man. I told them no photos,' he adds, 'but I think he took a few with his phone.'

I hide a smile. I have no doubt Candy told Sam to snap as many surreptitious shots as possible.

I put my hands on my hips and take a deep breath, enjoying the feeling of fresh air in my lungs. It *is* a beautiful spot. I can see how it would be easy to forget the rest of the world exists if you lived here. 'Aren't you scared something might happen?' I ask. 'What if one of you needs to go to hospital?'

'We try not to expect the worst, Gemma.' He says my name carefully, turning it upward like a tick. 'In my experience, things tend to work out how they're supposed to.'

'But surely if a child was unwell, you would want them treated?' I can't understand his fatalistic logic when we have access to the benefits of modern medicine.

'It's a choice for the parents,' Myron says. 'They decide. God takes care of us.'

'It's actually a choice made by the legal system,' I retort, making a mental note to follow up on the wellbeing of the women and children who live here.

He keeps walking, unfazed. The women walk behind us in unnatural silence and I wonder what they are thinking.

I admire the plump brown and white cows in one of the paddocks, their hides glossy in the afternoon sun. We head back toward the homestead, along a wooden fence lined with buttercups.

Stopping in front of the house I ask Myron, 'Can people leave The Retreat?'

'Of course. Everyone can do as they please.'

'But does anyone leave?'

One of the women briefly locks eyes with me and I smile, trying to make a connection but she immediately looks away.

'A few have moved on over the years,' he admits. 'But once people experience how much better things are here, they generally want to stay.'

I survey the campervans, the washing lines threaded between them, the pots full of herbs, and the children playing on the grass. 'Thanks for showing me around, Myron.'

'Being here is good for the soul. Hopefully, you will leave a little lighter.'

I lift my shoulders feeling self-conscious. A floaty feeling *has* settled over my body but so much of what Myron said set off alarm bells. 'Maybe.' I wave to the group and walk to my car. Opening the door, I pause. He's watching me; they all are. 'Myron, was there ever a woman living here who looked like me?'

He studies my face and shakes his head. 'No.'

Behind him, all the women shake their heads.

The bright sunshine streams through the windscreen as I put the car in reverse. I manoeuvre into a three-point turn—there's no way I'm going to reverse all the way down the fifty-metre driveway with an audience.

About twenty metres along I notice a faded dirt road through the trees, leading in the opposite direction to the highway. Without turning the car off, I come to a stop and get out, cutting across a stretch of bushland to access the alternate track. It doesn't look like it's in use; it's littered with sticks and stones, and blocked by a large fallen branch.

Myron appears from behind my car. 'What are you doing?'

I point to the dirt road. 'Where does that lead?'

'It's the old driveway to the main house, when it led around the back. Hasn't been used in years.'

'Right.' A cigarette butt has caught my eye, a few metres along the dirt road. It's not worn—someone dropped it recently. The branch is positioned very neatly, and the sections around it look clear, as if it has been moved and the debris cleared away. I scan the surrounding trees and can't see where the branch originated. 'When did that fall?'

'A few months ago, maybe.' He makes his way around my car and stands next to me. Then his elbow brushes my left arm, and his hot breath is on my ear.

The three dogs appear and start circling us, yelping sporadically. My body is screaming to get away from them and I put my hand on my gun, poised to use it if I have to.

'When the weather is bad,' Myron says ominously, 'you have to be careful out here. Branches come down and can do some real damage. It's not safe to be on your own.'

The dogs stop their manic loop and sit in front of me. The one on the left growls, and all three bare their teeth.

'Go in peace,' whispers Myron.

I throw a final glance at the dirt road and get back into my car. He slams the door shut and taps the roof, holding his hand up in a silent farewell, his features serious.

I'm relieved when I break out onto the highway. Adrenaline pumps through my body and in the rear-view mirror my eyes are wild and I realise my hair has come loose from its ponytail. 'God,' I mutter, pushing the strands behind my ears. My phone beeps several times. The Retreat is obviously out of mobile range, and I wonder if there's a landline on the property—there must be.

I pull over and load Google Maps, trying to zoom in on The Retreat and the dirt road. I locate the beginning of the track, but it seems to peter out after about a hundred metres, fading into acres of bushland. I'll need to find another way to work out where it leads.

Connecting to the car speaker, I play my voicemail recordings. There's an update about Scarlett's childcare placement. Then there's one from Jodie, asking me to call her back.

Another message loads: a photo from Mac of a teenage girl.

This is a photo of her when she was 17. I thought you might like to see it.

She's holding a dog and smiling at the camera, her bare legs stretched out in front of her. She looks so much like me.

CHAPTER FORTY-SEVEN

MONDAY, 26 SEPTEMBER, 5.19 PM

Tears spill down my cheeks as I stare at the picture. I've lost something I didn't even know I had: a sister. There's a deep well of sadness inside me. I ache for the chance to meet her, to know her. My limbs feel heavy and loose; even holding my hands to the steering wheel is an effort. I crave the numbing effect of several drinks in quick succession, but I know from experience that this wouldn't help and would make tomorrow more unpleasant than it's already certain to be.

For the second time in as many days, I feel like I have nowhere to go. I don't want to talk to Mac or Jonesy, and I'm not ready to share this with Candy and face her supportive but relentless analysis. Dad was always my last-resort safe place.

In the end I text Mac, thanking him for the photo and letting him know I'm going out for dinner with a friend, that I'll be careful and not to wait up for me. Then I drive to my childhood home and park out the front, staring at the familiar yard with the wonky gum tree, memories dancing through my mind. I lived here with my parents, then with Scott when Ben was a baby.

My mother lived a whole life before my birth, something I knew subconsciously but never thought to probe. She broke away from her birth family and stepped into the fold of a cult. What was she running from, and what was she looking for? Whatever it was, she didn't find it there, running from that life, too. I can't help wondering if that's where I get my restlessness from. It never made sense to me before; now it seems it might be in my genes. And like me, my mum ended up back in the place where she started, making a life in Smithson. But not before she had a child, my sister.

Did my sister know about me? I play with the question, unsure what I want the answer to be. The thought that she knew about me but never sought me out is devastating. I imagine us as two pins on a map and wonder how close we got to each other.

I moan, the agony of so many unanswerable questions stirring the meagre contents of my stomach. A car approaches, and I'm surprised to see that the headlights are on, that it's dark now. The female passenger cranes her neck to look at me before the car turns into a driveway a few metres from where I'm parked. Time to go.

The streets are almost empty. At first I think only the supermarket shows signs of life, but then I drive past the pub with muted light in its windows, the silhouettes of patrons talking and laughing. I loop back to Sonny Lake, driving past the body of water that can be seen from the road, the trees rustling gently in the breeze.

In the town centre I fill up the car with petrol and buy a chocolate bar and an energy drink, then consume both as I drive, feeling simultaneously tired and restless.

Minnie, I think. I'll go and see Minnie. I dropped her off at home a couple of times last year when I first worked with her. As far as I know, she still lives in the small brick block of flats a few streets back from the main shopping strip.

I drive there and knock on the door of the second unit, hoping she's home. It swings open to reveal Minnie in a fuzzy apricot bathrobe, her long hair wet and combed, a pair of bright blue Crocs on her feet. A skinny guy in gym gear peers out of a doorway further along the hallway behind her.

'Minnie, hi.' I force a smile. 'I'm sorry to call past so late.'

'That's okay,' she says, but her eyes are wary. 'Is everything all right?'

'Everything is fine. I just wanted to talk to you, away from the office. Can I come in?'

She hesitates, pulling the tie of the robe tighter.

'Please.'

Her housemate exchanges a look with her, then goes back into his room.

'Sure,' she says with false cheerfulness. 'Come in. I'll just throw on a jumper.'

I follow her into the narrow hallway and through to a cosy lounge room, where I take a seat on a battered navy couch.

'Would you like a drink?' Minnie asks, returning dressed in light grey sweats that accentuate her long limbs.

'I'm fine, thanks.'

She perches on a retro mustard armchair next to a cluster of indoor plants.

'This is a great little place,' I say.

'We like it. Gavin is a furniture maker.' She points to a TV cabinet and a beautiful wooden bookshelf along the wall. 'He made those.'

'They're great. Is Gavin your—?'

'Just a friend,' she says quickly.

We fall into silence and I try to read her. I would have been beside myself if a senior detective visited me at home when I was a junior constable, but if anything, she seems disinterested.

I relax my posture, trying to put her at ease. 'Is everything going okay at work?'

'I think so.'

'This must be one of the biggest investigations you've been involved with, right? I can't think of anything like this happening since I've been on leave.'

'It's big,' she agrees. 'I'm learning a lot.'

'Cases like this are more common in the city,' I muse. 'Do you think you'll eventually want to move?'

She doesn't reply, just fiddles with her watch.

'Minnie?'

'What?'

I look at her. So capable but still so young. I want her to tell me what's on her mind without having to ask her but I can tell she's not going to do that. 'What's wrong? You know you can talk to me.'

'I can't,' she murmurs.

I hold my hands out, as if to show her she can trust me. 'Yes, you can. And if there's something you need help with, you should tell me.'

'I'm fine, Gemma, honestly.'

'You've requested a transfer to Melbourne.'

She inhales sharply.

I plough on, determined to have this conversation. 'And I think you're planning to leave because of someone else.'

Suddenly she's angry. 'I can't talk to you about this,' she hisses. 'Please, leave me alone.'

I feel stung but say, 'No way, Minnie. This is too important to just sweep under the carpet.'

'Please.' She lets her long hair hang in front of her face.

'Why won't you talk to me?'

'I just can't. I don't want to involve you.'

'Don't worry about me. It's you I'm worried about.' I lean forward, elbows on my knees. 'I'm not leaving until you talk to me.'

Her voice is faint. 'It's just that you're so close to him.'

My suspicion solidifies. Gone is the confident woman I met last year; she's nervous and hesitant, deliberately flying under the radar—telltale signs of abuse.

'Who hurt you, Minnie?'

'Please,' she mumbles, her face in her hands. 'I just want to start over. It's been less than a year, so it's not a huge deal. It will be better for everyone.'

'No, Minnie, don't ever think like that.' My jaw aches as I grit my teeth. 'This is a tough gig, we both know that, but we need people like you in the force now more than ever, so don't you dare let anyone make you feel like you shouldn't be here. You do not need to leave.'

'It's like they say, though—who's going to believe me? Or do anything about it even if they do believe me.' She sounds so young, and I'm furious that someone has made her feel so small. 'The thing is, he's a great cop and a good guy. Everyone likes him. *I* like him.'

'Everett,' I whisper, my skin on fire. 'What did he do to you?'

'Not Everett.' Her voice is quiet but firm. 'It was Jonesy. He assaulted me, Gemma.'

CHAPTER FORTY-EIGHT

I reel off options and answer her questions as best I can. I don't dwell on what she's said, I just try to make sure Minnie knows I believe her. 'It's going to be okay,' I repeat a few times. *It's going to be okay,* I tell myself.

I leave Minnie's flat, letting the shock I've been keeping at bay flow through my system. I'm struggling to come to terms with what she told me. A hundred moments bubble up in my mind: a reassuring palm on my shoulder, a pat on the back, an encouraging nod.

Jonesy has always been supportive of me. There's never been anything sinister about it, and I've never seen him be inappropriate with anyone. I've heard rumours about other cops, stories of drinks that got out of hand and senior sergeants manipulating the roster to give themselves access to female team members; I've witnessed tawdry jokes and unwelcome physical contact dressed up as paternal concern. In every station I've worked at, the female staff know who to tolerate during the day and give a wide berth to at drinks. But to my knowledge there have never been rumours about Jonesy. He's old-fashioned, sure, and not always the most tactful when it comes to using the right terms or language, but he is always kind. Something I learned from him is that no matter our personal views, every colleague, suspect and victim deserves our time, attention and respect.

And yet I have no doubt Minnie is telling the truth. Her fear and frustration are so pure, her anger at having to deal with the inconvenience of what he's done so real, that there is no doubt in my mind.

One-offs are rare. Has this been happening the whole time? Did no one tell me because they know Jonesy and I are close? I can't bear the thought that my trust has been used as a cover, that my status as a female ally might have acted as an insurance policy for him.

I do another lap of the circuit I've established, driving past Minnie's apartment block again. I process the details she provided like I would a case. It happened at the end of a night out, when everyone was celebrating a solve. She'd only had one drink when she offered to drive Jonesy home, noticing he was leaving at the same time and didn't have his car. Drunk and creepy, he laid it on thick in the car park, grabbing at her like they were in a playbook sexual harassment training scenario. She laughed it off and went back inside, staying at the pub for another hour just to be sure he'd gone.

So where does that leave me and my relationship with my boss and mentor? Years of loyalty are torn apart. The sense of loss is unfathomable. I'm aware I need to stand up for Minnie, that I need to help her deal with this, but the thought of confronting him feels impossible.

It's as if my insides are straining against my skin. I don't know where to begin, what horrible thing to deal with first. I think I'm going to be sick.

Before I have a chance to pull over, a dog walking on the footpath darts out in front of my car, its teenage owner screaming and chasing after it. I calmly pump the brakes, years of training taking over. A driver diagonally opposite blasts his horn as he flies across the intersection, unable to stop. The dog miraculously evades being hit and bounds back to its owner, tongue flying. 'Thank you,' the teenager mouths in my direction before he scolds the dog, looping the leash around his wrist. The other driver screams abuse out the window and disappears down the road.

The blare of the horn lingers in the air as the tension drains from my jaw and limbs. My monkey mind has been jolted into focus. Only one thought remains: I need to find my sister's body. I can't stand the thought of her discarded and lost forever.

I'll go to the police station. Hardly anyone is likely to be there at this time of night, or at least no senior staff, and I always liked working there on my own after hours.

I check my phone. Mac has called twice, and texted me, but there are no calls from Dad or Rebecca. I wonder if they've all spoken, and if Mac has suggested they leave me alone for a while.

When I arrive at the station I pretend to talk on my mobile, flashing a quick smile at the constables on the front desk before confidently scanning into the main office. The only sound is the unhealthy hum of the ancient fridge in the kitchen. The rows of shadowy desks look oddly beautiful, but the truth is revealed when I flick on the lights, illuminating the years of wear and tear.

I go to my old spot, where I used to sit when I was a cadet. The view of the room from this angle jolts me backwards in time, and I recall the daily anticipation of the unknown, the constant fear I would make a mistake despite my bravado. I wasn't happy back then, the trauma of Mum's and Jacob's deaths never far from my mind, but the job gave me something I'd never had before: a sense of purpose. And policework has been the one constant in my life ever since. It's still my North Star, I realise—it's still the thing that gives me my bearings.

Jonesy's ghost lingers here, too, his unwavering support as I forged my path, but I don't let it haunt me right now.

My laptop whirs to life, and I log on to the network. My mother's maiden name was Cullen, so I start my search with that and find nothing. Next, I search the name used in the articles about the trial: Morrow, Justine Morrow, a name I'd never heard before.

As I click through the dead ends, I think about the boxes in the garage. Did they hold clues as to who my sister was? Maybe I should just call Mac. I know he'll tell me everything he can, but something bristles in me. I don't want his help—it feels important that I do this by myself.

Finally I come across a short article about my maternal grandparents that someone uploaded from the local paper onto an archive about Gowran's history. My mother rarely spoke of her parents, people I was told were long dead. I never questioned this; I suppose I wasn't interested in people I'd never met. My grandfather was Tobias, my grandmother Florence. The information about them is scant: the article includes only brief references to their sheep farm and the prizes my grandmother used to win at the local show for her pumpkins. There's nothing further, except for some patchy coverage about the trial in Queensland fifteen years later.

Through these pieces I learn more about the Braybrook homestead and its transition to The Retreat. My mother was engaged in daily animal sacrifices and violent 'exorcisms', and she was allegedly submitted to ritualistic abuse at the hands of senior members. These middle-aged men, rejected from senior roles in business or the Church, had regained their power within this new belief system, its rules giving them back what they felt they were owed.

Despite making several attempts, my mother's parents claimed they had no contact with her until the trial—and, even then, she refused to acknowledge their relationship. She also rejected the claim she had murdered Quinn Parker, the priest found poisoned in his Brisbane home years after The Retreat had disbanded. Parker, the only senior cult member to escape charges and rebuild his life, had hosted an extravagant gathering in his home on the night of his murder. My mother was one of many guests. While she admitted to not being invited, it seems many attendees had a motive to murder Parker, so her presence alone wasn't deemed to be damning. In the end the case against her was dismissed because of flimsy circumstantial evidence involving unreliable witness statements and Parker's history of consuming dangerous substances. After the finding, she reasserted her innocence but said she was glad Parker was dead after being subjected to years of his abuse at The Retreat.

One article mentions that my mother was rumoured to have given birth during her time with the cult, but there are no further details.

I enlarge the only two pictures of my mother that my search has turned up and stare at the grainy pixels, wishing that seeing her young face might help me understand. After the trial, she disappeared from the internet until she turned up in the Smithson paper in my birth announcement with a new name. Sitting back against the chair, I try to think. Was my sister the product of rape? Was my mother forced to give her up or did she do so willingly? Whatever the case, there must be paperwork, a trail.

I'm listing other names mentioned in the articles so I can start a new search, when I register the electronic beep. Shit, someone's scanning into the office. I have a fleeting impulse to turn off the lights and hide, but I force myself to stay seated and calm. I'm not doing anything wrong—not strictly, anyway.

Muted voices, male. The side door clicks open, and their conversation rolls into the main room. 'That's because you're so important!' A man with dark blond hair and a round face enters the room. 'Show me your office and your fancy detective things.' His tone is teasing, his broad shoulders straining against his fitted white T-shirt.

Everett walks in after him, smiling and rolling his eyes. 'I don't have an office. This isn't like when I worked in—Gemma.' He stops dead in his tracks.

I stand, and the two of them look at me, none of us speaking. The shock of seeing him unexpectedly dilutes the anger I've felt toward him all day.

'I'm just doing some research,' I say finally. 'It's quiet here.'

Everett clears his throat. 'I've just come to grab a few things.' He walks purposefully to his desk.

'Cool, great.' Relieved he isn't berating me, I turn to the other man. 'Nice to meet you. I'm Detective Sergeant Gemma Woodstock. I work with Julian.'

'Gemma!' he says knowingly. 'I'm Jarrod.' He lunges at me with enthusiasm and reaches out to shake my hand. 'Great to meet you, too.' Then his eyes dart to Everett, who is flipping frantically through a notebook.

They are a couple, I realise, all my assumptions about Everett evaporating.

We make eye contact, and I nod slightly, understanding why he's kept this part of his life a secret. Smithson has come a long way over the past few years, but it's still a country town where tradition is favoured over any desire to join the twenty-first century—except when it comes to the introduction of Asian cuisine and faster internet. While diversity has improved slightly at the police station when it comes to female representation, it's no secret that most of the old boys tolerate rather than celebrate challenges to the status quo.

I sit down at my old desk and wait to see what Everett will do next.

Jarrod hovers near the door. 'This place could use some greenery, babe,' he comments, 'and a throw rug.'

Over by his computer, Everett glares at Jarrod as he uses his mouse to click on a file, dragging something to save on a thumb drive.

Jarrod winks at me and makes a face.

'Anything I can help with?' I ask Everett, smothering a smile.

'I'm good, thanks.' He clears his throat, making way for the standard bravado to return. 'In fact, explain to me again why you're here. As far as I'm aware, you shouldn't be working on anything right now.'

'Someone needs to investigate my sister's death. It may as well be me.'

Jarrod's eyebrows shoot skyward, and he lifts his hands in the air. 'I'll wait out front and leave you two to talk.'

Neither of us acknowledges him as he backs out of the room.

'I can't believe you didn't tell me,' I say.

Everett merely grunts.

'Jarrod seems nice.'

He scowls. 'Leave it, Woodstock.'

I laugh cruelly. 'I see. My private life is for everyone to trawl through, while yours is sacred.'

He closes his eyes and takes a deep breath. 'For what it's worth, I said we should tell you straight away.'

'I highly doubt that.'

'Well, it's true. And I'm sorry. I wouldn't have wanted something like that to be kept from me, even if it was with good intentions. It was shitty.'

To my horror, tears well in my eyes and spill over.

'Gemma.' He takes half a step toward me.

'No, don't.' I hold up my hands, openly crying and unable to stop.

Clearly unsure what to do, Everett asks, 'Do you want me to get you a glass of water?'

'Isn't it tea you're supposed to offer me? The universal cop comfort drink.'

'Yeah, but I happen to know the office is out of milk,' he says, 'and tea bags.'

I laugh through my tears and wipe them from my face.

'Breathe,' he orders.

I do as he says, and he sits opposite me.

'I really am sorry,' he says seriously. 'The situation snowballed quickly and I'm still getting my head around the politics. There was a lot Jonesy wanted to manage himself, then things got messy when we found out Mac was already working the cold case and you had such a strong link to it all. Even though you and I haven't exactly been working in lock step, it still felt off, keeping information from you. I told Jonesy it made me uncomfortable.'

'I had no idea about any of it.' I feel like an idiot but also want him to know how utterly blindsided I've been. 'I didn't even know about my mother and The Retreat.'

He nods. 'It's a lot, especially on top of the attack.' Then he pauses. 'Do you want me to call someone? Mac? That journo?'

I appreciate him trying to make me feel better. Suddenly I feel a primal urge to share the load with him. To present all of the theories flailing around in my head and get him to help me sort through them. I'm so tired of trying to deal with it all on my own and feeling like I can't fully trust anyone. 'No, I'm okay. But while we're making confessions, I should tell you . . . There are some things I've been keeping from you as well, about the case.'

It's his turn to take a deep breath. 'Jesus, Gemma.'

The office lights tint his tan skin a sickly grey, and thick stubble peppers his chin and jawline. He needs a haircut. We both do.

'I'm sorry,' I say. 'But I can take you through them now.'

'Not here.' An energy enters his eyes. He returns to his computer, ejects the thumb drive and logs out of the system. After pulling another notebook from his desk drawer, he slams it shut and locks it. 'Come on, let's go.' He cocks his head toward the exit.

'Where are we going?' I ask, grabbing my laptop.

'It's a Monday night in a backwater town. I guess we're going to my place.'

CHAPTER FORTY-NINE

Jarrod is thrilled about my impromptu visit and maintains a steady stream of chatter, asking me about my work history and life in Smithson. I'm sitting in the back of the Land Rover, copping the full force of the pineapple-scented car freshener that dangles from the rear-view mirror.

I text Mac that I'll be late and that we'll talk tomorrow. My chest aches with a feeble surge of milk, and I realise I've unintentionally weaned Scarlett off her remaining daily feed. I try to assuage my guilt by reminding myself that I breastfed her for longer than I did Ben, but it feels clumsy—I think it should have been a conscious decision, not the collateral damage of a chaotic week.

We reach a part of town I've never been to, one of the new estates that Scott's company built just before he got sick. Jarrod turns into a driveway and fumbles in the centre console for the garage remote, all while cheerfully highlighting the neighbour's terrible taste in outdoor furniture. 'Home sweet home!' he chirps.

Everett is silent as he gets out of the car. He didn't say a word the whole way here, and I get the feeling he's regretting his impulsive invitation.

'Through there, Gemma.' Jarrod points to an internal door just as Everett steps through it.

'Thanks for the lift,' I say.

'My pleasure.' Conspiratorially, he adds, 'I think he's in a mood. Lucky us.'

'I think he's annoyed at me,' I say, feeling the need to explain.

'I think he's *jealous* of you.'

I don't know what to say to this, so I look around the spacious garage instead. The walls are lined with identical boxes stacked all the way to the ceiling. 'What's all this?' I ask Jarrod.

'Pyjamas,' he replies.

'Pyjamas,' I repeat.

'Yep!' He goes to an open box in the corner and pulls out a garment, holding it against his chest. 'See?' It's a fitted black pyjama shirt with tiny dachshunds printed all over it. 'I own a company called The Sleep Solution—we manufacture custom pyjamas, robes, slippers, and we've just expanded into bedding. I've tried to get Jules to model for me, but he says he has a reputation to uphold.'

I laugh at the thought of Everett modelling anything, let alone pyjamas.

Jarrod does a little spin and winks at me over his shoulder. 'It's doing very well. Next year I'm going global.' Rocking back on his heels, he surveys the boxes proudly. 'I'll give you some to take home. I've got kids' stuff as well. Anyway, come on, we don't want to keep Princess waiting.'

Princess?

I follow him into the beautifully furnished house, with soft textures complemented by striking artworks. It doesn't have the jumble of life with young kids, but unlike the Kirks' impersonal mansion, it feels warm and welcoming.

Everett is getting glasses out of a kitchen cupboard. His tie is on the bench, and he has kicked off his shoes. 'Wine?' he offers as we enter the room. 'Red or white? Or we have whisky if you prefer?'

'Red, please. I've just been hearing about your budding modelling career.' I fail to keep a straight face.

Everett scowls at Jarrod, who pretends not to notice, humming under his breath as he connects his phone to a set of speakers. A light electronic melody plays, and Everett hands me a wineglass. Despite the events of the past two days, I begin to relax.

'So,' Everett says.

'So.' Now that we're here I feel unsure where to start. I'm also not sure if I'm ready to share the news about Jonesy yet. I don't know quite how to frame it.

'Don't mind me,' says Jarrod. 'I'm going to occupy myself with non-policey things while you two talk shop.' He picks up an iPad and leaves the room.

'Let's sit at the table.' Everett places his wine and satchel on a stunning oak table positioned between the kitchen and the lounge and gets out his computer.

'What were you doing at the station?' I ask him.

'I requested a bunch of information about Carlyle Kirk's investments that I left to download while we were at dinner. And some new CCTV footage has come in.'

'What footage?'

He clears his throat. 'The footage you suggested we get from Roger's neighbour.'

'I thought you already had that?' I say, remembering the case meeting from days earlier.

'Not all of it,' he says sheepishly. 'Not the footage you suggested we track down leading in and out of the street. There were some issues getting our hands on it.'

'I won't remind anyone it was my idea,' I say, and he gives me a quick smile.

He clicks open a bunch of files on his desktop.

'Carlyle's not in financial trouble, is he?' I ask. 'I assume he's made millions from all the drug trials he invested in. And I thought The Lyle businesses all turn a profit . . .'

'That's not what I was looking at.' Everett frowns in concentration as he stares at his laptop.

'What do you mean?'

'It's like he can predict the future. Everything he touches turns to gold. His investment portfolio is huge, and he doesn't put a foot wrong. I spoke to a contact of mine, a guy in the same field. He says this kind of strike rate is unheard of. Dr Kirk is considered a freak of nature in the big pharma world. He quoted some numbers the other day that I wrote down but maybe it's online.'

I'm enjoying the fluidity the wine is giving my thoughts. 'Well, he started his career in research, right? And he's obsessed with data—it sounds like he always has been—so I guess he does his research on the research.'

'Yeah, maybe,' Everett mutters.

'I guess that's why he's pushing the research centre so hard. He's already seen such success in investing, it makes sense he wants to initiate some studies of his own, considering that's his area of expertise.'

'I've been thinking about that, too,' says Everett. 'Apparently the centre will focus on neurological treatments—he wants to develop anxiety and depression treatments for people of all ages, but especially the elderly, as well as treatments for drug addiction.'

'Yes, that's what he told me. It's obviously an area he's passionate about. Makes sense, seeing as there's a history of addiction in his family.'

Everett massages his temples and says, 'One of Roger's confidants told me he was considering pulling out of the CEO role at the centre.'

'But it was only announced last week?'

'Apparently he decided he didn't want to give up his position at the hospital—and he couldn't do both. There was already an online backlash about his conflict of interest during the transition. People were worried about the CEO of a public hospital being so tied to a private enterprise.'

'That was what Roger planned to discuss with Jack Barnes the morning of his murder,' I guess.

Everett nods. 'Barnes was going over his options. I'm not sure what Carlyle or the other investors knew, but from what Barnes says it sounds like Roger had lost perspective and was not behaving rationally.'

'He was already lying to investors about the exclusivity of the deals.'

'Exactly. And we know Carlyle didn't want to risk a backflip shaking investor confidence. Apart from the wobble out at Lyle Lodge a few years back, he's always been squeaky clean.'

I think about this. 'Carlyle said he had doubts about Roger anyway, so he might have been happy if Roger was having second thoughts. But surely you're not suggesting that Carlyle killed him because he was getting cold feet?'

'I don't know what I'm suggesting,' Everett says wearily. 'I guess I'm wondering what it all means. I don't understand what Carlyle

Kirk's motivation is. He's mind-bogglingly wealthy and in his seventies, so why establish something like this now?'

'For the same reason all wealthy, powerful men do anything: to get more wealthy and powerful, and to leave a giant fuck-off legacy.'

'I suppose.' Everett is loading video files on his computer.

'Is that the footage from Roger's place?'

'From the opposite neighbour's exterior camera and from a phone booth around the corner. If anyone came and left that morning, they should be on this tape. There's no other way to access the property unless the person who killed him lived in his street.'

I watch Everett watching the video for a few moments before asking, 'Who told you about Roger having doubts about the new CEO role?'

'Sophie McCallister.'

'And you believe her?'

With a yawn, he stretches his arms above his head. 'I think so. I've been working her pretty hard. I don't get the feeling she wants the top job—I think she was hoping Roger would stay at the hospital and things would remain the same.'

'She really doesn't want to be CEO . . . ?'

'Don't think so. I don't think Sophie is a fan of change.'

'Roger was incredibly dominant. I wonder if deep down she resented him. She might be reinventing history to suit her narrative. And she might not want to come across as too aggressive.'

'Yep.' He draws the word out. 'That's possible. But she isn't faking her devastation. She seems lost without him, even though I get the feeling she carried him professionally.'

'Do you think they were involved romantically?'

'It sounds like he confided in her, but there's zero evidence of an affair.'

Our discussion hits a lull. I sip my wine, synapses buzzing. This camaraderie is what I've been craving; the back-and-forth dance of an investigation is always so much better when done with a partner.

I brace to ask him a difficult question, hoping it doesn't break the spell but wanting his opinion. 'Do you have any idea if what happened to my sister is linked to Roger's murder?'

'No, Gemma, and no one else does either. At this stage the two crimes aren't linked.'

'Not officially,' I say.

He nods. 'Not officially.'

'At the hospital the other night, Roger looked at me funny. I thought it was because he recognised me—and maybe he did—but now I can't help thinking that perhaps he knew her, my sister.'

'I'm not saying it's not possible,' Everett concedes, 'but we haven't found anything to suggest that's the case.'

'Is there any link to anyone we've been speaking to?'

'The only link she has to Smithson is you,' he says gently. 'And your mother, of course.'

'Is that the real reason you went out to The Retreat?'

'Partly—and, like I told you, it was also to follow up about the baby.'

Lee Blight pleading me to give him an update about the baby interrupts my thoughts. I need to tell Everett everything. I need his help to work out if Lee did assault a minor and make sure she's safe but first I want to understand everything he knows about my sister.

'And you really didn't find anything?'

Everett shakes his head. 'There's no suggestion your sister was ever there. And there's no evidence that anyone living there gave birth recently. All of the residents match our records, so short of conducting a full search of the place, it's a dead end.'

'My sister would have been at least forty-three, I think.'

Everett nods. 'Forty-four, we believe.'

I exhale, the air coming out of me in a whoosh.

'Would you like to talk about her?' he asks softly.

Anger rolls through me followed by sadness at the fact I will never meet her. 'What was her name?' I manage to ask.

'Sandra Cullen.'

I mouth the unfamiliar name and take a deep breath. 'Thanks.'

He looks pained. 'Least I could do.'

After a minute more of silence, he quirks his mouth and says, 'Is it time for your confessional yet?'

I draw a breath, relieved to change the subject. 'Lee Blight thinks that baby is his.'

Everett cocks his head. 'The cop's son from the pub fight?'

'Yep.'

'Did you work with his dad?'

'Yes. He's kind of an arsehole—not sure if that's relevant.'

'And what, Lee just reached out to you about the baby . . . ?'

'Not exactly. Candy got a tip-off that Lee was living at The Retreat and has been following it up for one of her stories. I went with her to the gaol after you cut me loose the other day.' Everett frowns and I quickly continue, 'He asked us about the baby and told us it was his, but I figure that can't be true or it would have come up on the system as a familial match with Marty.'

Everett still looks annoyed. 'Not necessarily. When did Marty retire?'

'About nine years ago.'

'He might have been missed off the register.'

'It's possible that Jonesy redacted the results,' I say quietly.

Everett is surprised. 'Are you serious? Why?'

'Because he is mates with Marty. And because he's already done it once this week.'

'That was to protect you! Come on, Gemma, you know how straight down the line Jonesy is.'

I mumble a neutral reply, thinking about what Minnie told me.

'Either way, we should get Lee tested asap.' Everett straightens in his chair, energised by the lead. 'Did he say anything else?'

'He didn't confirm this, but I'm worried the mother is an underage girl. Candy got some intel from the men he attacked at the pub who claim he was involved with a minor. We really need to find out where he's been these past few years.'

'Okay.' Everett is all business now. 'I'll speak to him again in the morning. Maybe he'll talk when we apply a bit of legal pressure.'

'We can try . . . but he was beaten up in prison last night.'

'By an inmate?'

'No one would tell me anything, but I found out that Lee didn't post bail last week, and I think this is why. He thought it would be safer in prison.'

'Fucking hell.'

'Yeah. Marty was there today, and he spoke to me. He seemed spooked and told me to back off. He knows Lee is mixed up in something bad.'

I can tell Everett is doing the same as me: trying to work out what move to make next.

'Anything else?'

Despite how well we're getting along, and as much as I want to, I can't share what Minnie told me about Jonesy without her consent. And it's not fair on Everett if I talk in the abstract about it either.

'I think that's enough for now.' I add, 'There might be something I want to run by you but it's not about the case.'

He nods, yawning again.

It's past midnight, but I sense our truce will end when this conversation does; despite my exhaustion, I'm keen to prolong it. 'How long have you been with Jarrod?'

He gets to his feet and grabs his glass. 'Want some water?' he calls over his shoulder.

'Sure.'

'Beep, beep,' says Jarrod, smiling as he enters the room. 'I'm not eavesdropping, I'm just grabbing a charger.'

'I was just asking Everett how long you two have been together.'

'We've been lovers for almost eight years,' Jarrod replies. 'We're so happy together—aren't we, babe?'

Everett places a glass of water in front of me, his jaw like stone. 'It's late. I think it's bedtime.'

I stand, suddenly embarrassed to be in their home at this hour. 'Of course, I'll call a cab.'

'Don't be ridiculous, Woodstock. We're in Smithson—a cab could take months. Jarrod can drive you or you can sleep on the couch.' His tone is gruff but friendly.

Jarrod nods. 'I'll get you something to sleep in. And you can try some of my new bedding!' He darts out of the room before I can protest.

'Are you sure?' I ask Everett.

'Please, don't argue.' He snaps off the kitchen light. 'I'll be up early and can drop you home, or Jarrod can drop you later. There's a spare toothbrush in the main bathroom off the hall, top drawer.'

I'm tempted to say, 'Yes, sir,' but settle on, 'Thank you.'

As Jarrod showers me with sleepwear options, Everett stands watching. He's probably scared to leave Jarrod alone with me in case he gossips about their relationship again.

'Good night,' I say. 'Hopefully all the answers will come to us in our dreams.'

'As Bob Dylan said, they're probably blowing in the wind,' Jarrod says dreamily, unfolding a chic-looking pyjama set.

His words stir something lodged in my mind. 'Hang on.' I lift my eyes to Everett's, unable to hide my excitement. 'Yes, yes,' I say, trying to make the pieces click together.

'What is it?' He can recognise that a thought has landed, that there's a connection I'm trying to reel in before it loosens and frees itself from my grasp.

'I think that . . .' I picture a framed quote propped on a shelf. 'Oh my god.' I lock eyes with Everett. 'Sophie McCallister is Dominique Kirk's catfisher.'

CHAPTER FIFTY

I wake up in a cocoon. I don't know what Jarrod's pyjamas are made of, but the material is impossibly soft against my skin. My cheek slides along the pillowcase he insisted I use. Reluctantly I wriggle out of the warmth and locate my phone. I write a quick message to Ben, letting him know I had to go away for work but I'll see him later today. He writes back straight away, and I feel relieved, reading his message several times. The kids are okay, I tell myself—everything else is a mess, but they're okay, and that's what really matters.

'Sandra Cullen,' I whisper. I roll onto my back and stare at the ceiling. I want to believe my mother was forced to give her up, or felt she had to, because the thought of her willingly abandoning her baby further messes with the understanding I have of her. Childhood vignettes flit through my mind, all tainted now. I don't know who she was, and now I wonder if that means I don't know who I am.

But isn't that what you *did? You left Ben here and moved to Melbourne.* The intrusive thoughts keep thundering in, and I toss my head to make them go away.

There's enough morning light creeping into the room that I can take in the impressive vinyl collection next to an expensive record player and the cluster of framed photos on the mantelpiece. They're mainly shots of Jarrod and Everett in exotic locations, some as a couple and others with groups of happy-looking bronzed people. I'm not quite willing to believe that I read Everett all wrong, but he's obviously a lot more layered than I thought.

Through the walls I hear the muted flush of a toilet and the swish of a shower being turned on. I don the fluffy robe Jarrod left on the armchair and make sure my clothes are in a neat pile, my underwear wedged between my jeans and jumper, before I go to the kitchen and fetch a glass of water. Chugging it down, I review the array of magnets on the fridge, mainly inspirational quotes that might or might not be ironic depending on whether they are Jarrod's or Everett's.

After I announced my theory that Sophie is Dominque's catfisher, Jarrod went to bed while Everett and I stayed up for another hour, trawling over the emails Dominique and Dylan exchanged. We're convinced I'm right. Now we're looking for it, the catfisher had an obvious interest in Dominique's marriage, carefully probing for information. It's possible that Sophie was privy to all kinds of intimate details about Roger via Dominique.

'Morning.' Everett enters the kitchen dressed in a tailored suit, hair slicked back. He points to a coffee machine that has more buttons and levers than my washing machine. 'Want me to make you one?'

'Yes, please.' I'm craving the clarity of a caffeine hit. I need to eat, too—I've existed solely on fluids and a chocolate bar for the past twenty-four hours.

'Help yourself to some fruit as well,' says Everett, as if he's reading my mind. 'And cereal. We have everything.'

I bite into an apple and polish it off as he places a cafe-quality latte in front of me. I'm relieved things still seem relaxed between us—last night wasn't a one-off.

'We should confront Sophie about the emails today,' I say. 'See if she comes clean.'

He pinches the skin between his eyes. 'I think we need more than what we have. I'll get the tech guys onto it, see if they can link her to the accounts and the emails.'

'She mentioned her brother is a tech genius,' I say, remembering her talking to Rufus, the head security guard at the hospital. 'Perhaps he helped her set up the accounts.'

Everett peels a banana and looks thoughtful as he eats it, a hand on one hip.

'Does she have an alibi for the night before he was killed? If they were involved, maybe she was with him. What if she was already in the house the day before and stayed there?'

'Good point. We only confirmed her alibi for the morning. She said she was home alone the night prior and got to the hospital just before seven-thirty am. As far as we can tell, Roger was by himself at his place. He sent some emails at around seven pm, and it looks like he heated up a frozen meal. We're waiting on phone data to confirm his location. But, Gemma, without wanting to dredge up an old argument, I really don't think Sophie is our killer. She's not physically strong enough.'

'If Sophie was there the night before, she could have left a door open for someone. Maybe she's in on it with her brother. Or maybe Roger *was* killed by a smaller woman—assuming he trusted Sophie, he would have let his guard down around her.'

'Maybe . . .' Everett sounds far from convinced.

'Send me the CCTV footage you have from around Roger's place. I can look at it today while you're at work.'

'Her prints didn't show up anywhere in his house,' Everett reminds me. 'And there's no evidence she was involved with him.'

'It's still worth checking.'

He pulls out his laptop and starts zipping up the CCTV files to transfer. 'What if Sophie was the one who attacked you, or organised the attack with an accomplice?'

Surprised, I place the coffee down with a clack. 'But why?'

'Because you questioned her, and she wanted you to back off.'

'And?'

He looks at me blankly. 'Isn't that enough?'

'Maybe. But could it be linked to my sister? Sophie was at the hospital that night—she knows how that place works better than anyone. I still think the fact she delayed the pick-up of the body is suspicious.'

'Jesus, I don't know. I guess it's possible.' He yawns and settles his gaze on me, his mouth turning down.

'What?'

'Woodstock, I'm happy to speak to Jonesy about you working the case again.'

A rush of pleasure courses through me, but all I say is, 'I'd appreciate that.'

'But—' he holds up a hand '—I need to make sure it's a good idea.'

'It is,' I say quickly.

'Simple as that.' His smile is wry.

'Please, Everett. I need to do this.'

'As long as you're sure. I am genuinely worried about you.'

'I'm sure. And thank you.' I'm grateful for his kindness, both now and last night. It's pulled me out of my slump and given me a burst of energy just when I need it.

He knocks back a shot of a mysterious dark green liquid. 'I have to get going.'

My phone beeps: Mac is asking if I'm okay and wanting to know when we can talk.

'All good?' Everett asks.

'Yep. I should get going soon, too.' An intense desire to have it out with Mac overwhelms me. It's time.

'Trouble in paradise?' Everett doesn't say it meanly, but it's enough to reinstate some of the tension between us. I remember that parking everything else, we're still competing for Jonesy's job.

'I just need to sort out the kids.'

He nods. 'I can take you, if you can be ready in the next few minutes.'

'Absolutely not,' Jarrod trills, entering the kitchen. 'She's mine.' He points to Everett. 'You need to get to work, and I'm not sending our guest on her way without a luxury spa experience.'

I open my mouth to protest, but Jarrod flicks his hand out. 'I'm allergic to the word "no", so keep it to yourself, Ms Detective.'

Everett frowns.

'Go.' Jarrod is insistent. 'You can take the Land Rover.'

'I'll try not to grill him about you too much,' I say sweetly.

CHAPTER FIFTY-ONE

Showered, smelling of frangipani and sporting a salon-style blow-wave, I get into Jarrod's black Volkswagen.

'Feel better?' he asks.

'I feel amazing.'

He beams. 'Good. And you have everything I gave you?'

I pat the calico tote bag. 'Yep.' Inside are four sets of pyjamas and a silk pillowcase, plus a brochure featuring his upcoming range.

'Perfect for Christmas presents,' he says.

'You should get Everett to take some of these brochures to work. You'd clean up at Mother's Day.'

Jarrod sighs dramatically as he turns onto the road. 'Julian isn't at that point yet.'

'They *are* a rather conservative bunch,' I say diplomatically.

'His party line is that private lives are best kept private. To be fair, he's a rather reserved person in general. But in this case, the real story is that he's scared.'

'Scared of what, exactly?'

Jarrod's eyes shift to the left, and he twists his mouth in the same direction before they centre again. 'He won't want me to say anything, but I can tell you're okay. There was an incident at his previous workplace. Things got a little nasty.'

'Because his colleagues found out he was gay?'

'It was a suspect, someone he knew from uni, actually—someone he dated before he was a cop. It's a long story, but his supervisor didn't handle it well, and honestly neither did Jules. There was a detective he worked with who saw the situation as an opportunity to make a career move, and the whole thing got very political. It rocked Jules's confidence. He's convinced it's why he was passed over for a promotion.'

I nod. A lot about Everett is making sense now.

'It's made him tougher,' Jarrod muses. 'He wasn't exactly sunshine and rainbows before, but now he has a sharper edge. I'm hoping he'll snap out of it and relax.'

I remember the handshake Everett gave me when we met: it was unnecessarily aggressive, and his disregard for me was obvious. I wrote him off as an arrogant jerk, but perhaps that was his intention—he was asserting his tough-guy persona.

We reach the police station.

'It was a joy to meet you, Gemma,' he says. 'We've kept to ourselves since we moved here, and I'm bored out of my mind. Maybe you and your handsome partner can come over for dinner sometime.'

'How do you know I have a handsome partner?'

'Jules may have mentioned you're shacked up with Harrison Ford's twin.' He grins, and it's impossible not to smile back.

'I'll eagerly await my invitation.'

Jarrod plucks a neon-pink business card out of the coffee-cup holder and gives it to me. 'Let's you and I manage the logistics.'

'Deal.' I tuck the card in my pocket with another smile. Then I grow serious. 'Thanks, Jarrod.'

'Anytime.' He toots the horn as he drives off.

I drive home and let myself into the empty house. Sitting on the couch, the calm I felt in the car turns to gut-churning anxiety.

I'm greeted by a scatter of breakfast and lunchbox debris on the bench, but no one's home. Mac must be dropping Ben at school. I move through the house, putting things away, running my hands over the photo frames on the mantelpiece. I pause in Ben's doorway and smile at his shambolic bed-making attempts. Going to his desk, I pick up a discarded chip packet and neaten the leaning tower of books. There's a silver lighter in the small space behind the books.

I frown. Ben said he got rid of his vaping paraphernalia, and I believed him. So what's he doing with a lighter? Trying not to be obvious, I hunt around but can't find anything else. I feel like crying—the last thing I need right now is Ben lying to me.

Dad's car turns into the driveway, and I shove the lighter in my pocket and go back to the lounge. Mac must have borrowed it when I didn't come home. I listen for Mac's footsteps, his key in the door, the click of the lock. Everything is familiar, but it feels different today. He's been my anchor since the moment we met, my biggest cheerleader and confidant. He's pushed me and believed in me. I think that's what burns the most, that for whatever reason he didn't believe I was strong enough to handle this.

He steps inside, holding Scarlett. He's wearing a baseball cap and needs a shave. 'Hi.' After placing the keys on the table, he comes to stand in front of me. 'I'm glad you're here. I was worried about you.'

My mother's cuckoo clock ticks loudly in the quiet around us. She told me it was a gift on her twenty-first birthday from a special friend. Now I wonder if that's true.

Heart thumping, I reach out to take Scarlett from him. I stroke her downy head as she burrows into my chest.

'Gemma—'

I square my shoulders and lift my chin. It's important I make it clear just how much he's hurt me. 'You lied to me, Mac.'

'I—'

'You did. You lied. And it broke my heart.'

He holds out a hand to me, but I wave it away—I'm not finished.

'On top of everything else, you lying to me hurt the most. You're supposed to be my person.'

He looks at the floor, ashamed. 'I'm sorry. I'm so sorry. I'm still your person, Gemma, I promise.'

Emotion makes my voice uneven, but I plough on. 'I know about my mother—about her joining the cult and the murder charge. But I need to know what you know about my . . . my sister. Her name was Sandra.' A sob escapes my mouth. 'But I need to know all of it.'

'Yes,' he says. We lock eyes. 'I'll tell you what I know.'

He makes us tea, and we sit at the table, taking turns to hold Scarlett.

Born three months before the leader of The Retreat drowned, Sandra lived with my mother and the other members until his death. After the cult broke up, my mother disappeared; Sandra went to live with a foster family in a farming community in regional Victoria. When it was clear my mother wasn't coming back, they adopted her. She had an unremarkable childhood, attending school and playing sport. After high school she moved to Sydney and worked as a receptionist in a vet clinic. She loved animals and enrolled in a veterinary science degree. But two years later, when she was twenty-two, she vanished.

Until now, there has been no trace of her. There was nothing to suggest foul play, but equally there was nothing to suggest she'd planned to start a new life.

Over the past few days, Mac has been trying to trace her whereabouts during that time. 'There was speculation she joined a fringe group. Her foster family claimed she suffered from depression, withdrawing from them and her friends in the months before she disappeared, but they were convinced she would never take her own life. Although the police search was extensive, nothing ever turned up.'

'And there's no suggestion she came to Smithson?'

'Her foster family told the police that it was a possibility, seeing as your mother had lived here, but there were never any leads. The DNA match from the crash is the first time Sandra registered on any system—and that was only due to you. There's nothing on official records, no Medicare, bank accounts, social media, nothing. She didn't have a car when she disappeared, and her flatmates didn't believe any of her things were missing. At least now we know she was alive all of that time.'

'Where the hell was she?'

Mac lifts his shoulders. 'I've tried to run facial-recognition technology across social media but haven't made any progress. My best guess is that she was living off the grid, alone or in a rural community—possibly overseas, although that would have required false documents, so it's less likely. My worst guess is that she was abducted and held somewhere against her will.'

My mind is racing. My mother and her first daughter both ran away and tried to become other people. The uncomfortable knowledge settles in the pit of my stomach. Can such a trait be inherited? I don't know the answer, but I can't spend time thinking about it now: the priority needs to be finding my sister.

'None of this explains why someone would want to steal her body.'

Mac shakes his head. 'No, it doesn't. But I do wonder if someone is trying to conceal something—that her body is evidence of something that happened to her while she was missing.'

We sit in silence for a few moments. While it's going to take some time for Mac and me to fix our broken bond, it feels good to be talking like we used to. I think about what he said. I'm now convinced someone took my sister's body because they felt she belonged to them, and I feel devastated that she might have been trapped in an abusive relationship.

'I can show you some of her things,' Mac says softly. 'Photos and school reports, notes she wrote. But I'm not sure if you want to see them.'

'Not yet.' I don't know how to explain it to him, but I want to wait until we've found her to go through her things. Before I try to understand her, I need to lay her to rest.

Mac nods. 'What do you want to do now?' he asks tentatively.

'Everett sent me some footage I want to look at. We're trying to verify if anyone was at Roger's house the night before he died.'

'Tell me how I can help.'

I hand him Scarlett. 'Give me a few more days to do everything I can to solve these cases and find my sister.'

'Take as long as you need.' He hesitates. 'Are you going to talk to your dad again?'

'Eventually. He lied to me for so long.' Saying it makes me upset.

'He might not have made the best choices, Gem, but he loves you.'

I sigh, feeling tired deep in my bones. 'I know.'

'I love you.'

Tears well in my eyes. 'I know that, too.'

He puts his hands on my shoulders and looks into my eyes before softly kissing my forehead. I lean against him, wishing we could go back in time before he hurt me so badly.

I go to the bedroom, put on a new shirt and some make-up. For once my hair is neat and glossy, and I give myself a once-over in the mirror, feeling better than I have in days. As I gather the pile of papers and notebooks next to our bed, I remember something.

'Hey, there *is* something you can do,' I tell Mac as I return to the kitchen.

Scarlett's in her highchair, and he's feeding her mashed banana. 'Hit me.'

'I need to work out who owns the land The Retreat is on. I want anything you can find on the titles and any businesses associated with it.'

'Sure.'

'And I want to know who arranges for groceries to be delivered from town and who pays for that service.'

'Leave it with me.'

We stand facing each other.

'Thank you.' I kiss Scarlett and let Mac put his arms around me. She lets out a squeal, making us smile.

'You smell amazing. Is this Candy's doing?'

'No—a pyjama entrepreneur called Jarrod, actually. It's a long story.'

'Should I be worried?'

'No,' I murmur, enjoying the feel of his arms around me. 'Tell me, what triggered the reopening of the priest's murder investigation?'

His body tenses. 'An ex-member came forward and said the drowning of the leader on the Braybrook property wasn't an accident, that it was murder.'

Static crackles in my ears. 'Do you think it was?'

'It's possible. It seems there had been a bit of an uprising—some of the members had grown unhappy and started to challenge his rules. The lady who came forward said there had been several violent altercations in the weeks before he died, and he'd started to lock everyone up overnight because he was scared of being ambushed.'

There's an aching in my chest. 'My mother . . . ?'

He looks pained as he continues, 'The lady said your mother was one of the main instigators.'

'Do you think she killed the leader?'

'Honestly, Gemma, I'm not sure. If she did, she didn't do it alone.'

The tightness in my chest becomes worse, and I press my fingers into my skin where I imagine my heart to be. 'What about the priest? Do you think she killed him?'

'I don't know that either. But the DNA report shows he was your sister's father.'

The room starts to spin again. Both men were undoubtedly awful, controlling and abusive, but the thought of my mother murdering them is unfathomable. 'I have to go.'

'Gemma—' His voice catches. 'There's something else.'

I'm scared to look at him, not sure how much more I can deal with. 'What is it?'

He grips my elbows and looks me in the eye. Scarlett bangs the tray of her highchair, but he doesn't turn to her. 'You should know that Jonesy knew about your mother. He's known the whole time.'

An icy feeling skitters around my body. 'How long?'

'He vouched for you back then, when you applied to be a cop.' His Adam's apple bobs. 'I just figured that with all of this—' he holds out a hand, as if gesturing to the decades of secrets '—you should know.'

CHAPTER FIFTY-TWO

I'm still feeling shaky as I fast-forward through one of the CCTV footage files Everett sent me, stopping it every time a vehicle or a person appears in frame. I'm at Reggie's, my laptop plugged into the power bank near the register and angled away from the prying eyes of fellow patrons. I couldn't bear to face Jonesy, but I wanted to be close to the station.

Nostalgia washes over me as I sip my coffee and watch the footage provided by the neighbour whose house is positioned on the corner of Emerald Drive. I've sat in this cafe so many times, trawling over the details of a case, trying to match disparate pieces of information together—and all that time I was being lied to, that Dad and Jonesy were keeping secrets from me. It feels like the tectonic plates of my life have shifted and my pillars of trust have crumbled.

I keep watching. It's past ten pm on the tape now, and the Monday night traffic has decreased to a solo vehicle every few minutes. I pause on each one, zooming in on the driver and noting down the make, model and rego, then doing a quick search of the owner.

Twenty minutes later I'm ordering another coffee and a blueberry muffin when Everett calls. 'Sophie's cracked,' he says excitedly. 'You were right.'

Validation charges through me. 'She's the catfisher?'

'Yep. She orchestrated the whole thing. It started when she contacted Dominique anonymously about one of her paintings. Sophie even went to the effort of buying an artwork and having it shipped to a warehouse in Sydney.'

'Because she wanted to get information about Roger?'

'Gemma, it's wild. She has photos of him all over her house and on her computer. I don't know how she's sourced half of them, but she hunted some down from when he was a kid. From the way she talks, it's clear she's delusional about their relationship status.'

I recall Sophie's grief at Roger's memorial. 'And being in contact with Dominique like that was another way to be close to him.'

'Exactly! She thinks Dominique didn't deserve him. There's a lot of anger there.'

'But do you think Sophie had anything to do with his death?'

'There's no indication of that. I don't think she would have hurt him and as you know the physical evidence doesn't support it.' He pauses. 'God, it's so creepy. I can't get my head around it—up each night messaging his wife, while working with him every day.'

'She was obsessed with him.'

'Completely. As soon as I confronted her about it she fell apart, but I think she was already on the brink. Anyway, we've brought her in. Her lawyer is with her, and we'll get her in front of a psych later today.'

'What about her potential involvement in stealing my sister's body?'

'She maintains there was no reason to have the body collected that evening. I checked with one of her colleagues—they were short-staffed, so she was telling Claire the truth.'

'But maybe Roger asked her to help him steal the body, and she was trying to impress him? I just want to make sure we're covering every angle, especially now that we can assume Sophie would have done anything Roger asked.'

'I'll look into it,' Everett says with apparent sincerity, but I sense he's humouring me. 'So have you gone through the CCTV yet?'

'Doing it right now. I've made a bunch of notes on vehicles, but there's nothing worth following up yet.'

'Okay, keep me posted.'

'Is Minnie in today?' I want to make sure she's okay after our conversation, but I'm mindful of giving her space.

'Yeah.'

'Does she seem okay?'

'Yeah, why?' Everett is distracted now—probably reading emails.

'Just wondering.'

'Gem, I've got to go, okay? Oh, one last thing—Lee Blight was moved to the hospital yesterday. He's stable. He has broken ribs, a cracked eye socket and concussion, but he's going to be okay. I tried to speak to him earlier—Jonesy was keen for me to hold off and stay focused on the other cases. I guess his dad complicates things.'

My stomach sinks. 'I don't give a shit who Lee's father is, if he knows something that will help us solve this case.'

'Leave it with me, okay? I'm managing it.' His tone is slightly patronising. 'Talk to you later.' He rings off.

I put the phone down, annoyed. He's the case lead and can make the calls, while I'm on the sidelines taking orders like a junior. And what he said about Jonesy rankles. Marty must be in our boss's ear, preventing Everett from talking to Lee.

My order arrives. I return my focus to the screen, stopping and starting the footage, wiping crumbs from the keyboard as I eat.

I finish watching the CCTV file that Kirk's neighbour supplied and then download the street footage. The camera faces toward the intersection leading to Emerald Drive. Three cars drive past, and a few possums jump from tree to tree. Just before midnight, a car comes into frame. The car is black, some kind of four-wheel drive—a *Toyota*, I think. It pulls up outside a house between the glow of the streetlights, next to a large tree. A hedge provides no contrast, but I can make out a tall, hooded figure getting out of the car and crossing the road to walk along Emerald Drive.

I pause the footage and zoom in. Even though they're in bulky clothing, it's clear the person is tall and slim. That's all I can gather from the angle of the shot.

I click onto the other open tab and run the licence plate through the system. My spine jerks into a straight line when the results load: the car is registered to Claire Messenger.

CHAPTER FIFTY-THREE

Every hair on my body stands on end. I scrub through the footage until the hooded figure reappears two hours later and drives away with the headlights off.

I don't wait for change from the girl behind the counter and run to my car, thinking back to my encounter with Claire Messenger outside The Lyle. She said she lives on Carlton Street, at the other side of town to the Kirks. I can't think of any legitimate reason for her to be near Emerald Drive at midnight on a Monday night.

Claire is tall and athletic. She knows anatomy, how to inflict a fatal wound, and how to stage a crime scene. She also knows how to manipulate the autopsy findings to make it look like a victim was killed hours later than they were.

But why would Claire kill Roger? As far as I'm aware, she has no connection with the Kirks beyond the proximity of their professions. There must be something we've missed. Were they sleeping together? Maybe the lovers argued, and it became violent. Or maybe it was a professional dispute. Claire's skills would be useful at the new research centre, so it's feasible Roger asked her to be involved, then they had a falling-out.

As I start the engine, another thought occurs to me: Claire knew about my sister's body being in the hospital. She's familiar with the morgue there, and how the transfer of a corpse typically happens. She and Roger might have been working together. Maybe he was having dinner with Claire that night, and he asked his uncle to give him an alibi. Roger might have set off the fire alarm and helped her with the body. Or maybe she was working with someone else, and Roger found out and tried to blackmail her.

I dare to hope that this is the break I need to find my sister.

I grab my phone to call Everett back—then I pause. He'll demand to be involved and inevitably take over. He'll tell Jonesy, and I'm not sure our boss can be trusted with this.

I access Claire's number on the system and call her. It goes to voicemail. I'm not sure what her schedule is, but knowing how hard MEs tend to work it's a safe bet she'll be at the morgue. I drive the short distance, my heart going a million miles an hour. Underneath my desire to confront Claire over Roger's murder is the idea she might know where my sister is. I feel a mixture of relief and apprehension when I see the black Toyota four-wheel drive in the staff parking bay. Shutting off the engine, I call Candy.

'Gemma, I was starting to worry you were pissed at me. Everything okay?'

'Sorry, I've just had a few things going on.'

'Juicy things?'

'Maybe.'

'Shareable?'

'Not yet.'

'Well, don't keep me hanging,' she says ominously. 'Or I'll have to find another favourite detective.'

'A terrible thought.' Bantering with her is calming me down.

'How are things with Mac?' she ventures.

'Good,' I say with feeling. 'I spoke to him, and you were right: he had a good explanation.'

'Thank god. Your relationship is the only reason I'm still on the apps.'

I laugh. 'Glad to be of service.'

'But for the record, if he messes you around, I'll kick him in the balls, write a highly embarrassing reputation-damaging story about him, publish it on my website and boost the living shit out of it via Facebook ads.'

'I'll let him know,' I say, laughing again.

'And what about our friend Lee? Any updates?'

'He was attacked in prison, Candy. He's in the hospital.'

'Holy shit. Who did it?'

'We don't know.'

'Is he going to be okay?'

'I think so. Everett is trying to find out if the baby is Lee's.'

Candy clicks her tongue disapprovingly. 'Sounds like you're talking to Evil Everett again.'

I can't wait to tell her about my sleepover when the time is right, but all I say is, 'We've called a truce.'

Candy grunts. 'I don't trust the smarmy prick. Watch your back.'

'I'll be sure to keep it against the wall.'

'You can be way too trusting,' she says mock seriously.

Even though she's being sarcastic, it stings a little.

'What are you doing now?' she asks.

'I'm at the town morgue.'

'Fun! Fresh meat for me?'

'No. I'm hoping to find Claire—I need to speak with her about some evidence.'

'Tell her to call me after you talk so she can let me know what you spoke about.'

'Unlikely,' I reply, my jaw set in a hard line as I look over at the entrance and start to prepare for my confrontation with Claire.

'Seriously, though, why are you speaking to her? Do you have something?'

I hesitate. 'Off the record, she turned up somewhere she shouldn't have been, so I'm going to ask her to explain.'

'Intriguing. Please immediately elaborate.'

'Nice try—and no chance.' I laugh, but my apprehension spikes again. 'Hey, are you free tonight? I'd love to catch up with you properly.'

'Sure. I want to show you my new website designs. I'll come over to yours . . .'

'Perfect.'

'Let me know what to bring. I'll aim for around six-thirty. Have fun at the morgue!'

I get out of the car and enter the reception area. This time the woman at the desk is dressed in a blood-red jumpsuit. 'Welcome back,' she says flatly.

'Hi. I need to speak to Claire Messenger. I believe she's in today.'

'I'll let her know you're here.' The receptionist makes a call to announce my arrival as I pace the small waiting area. 'She's running behind today, so can't take a break, but she's happy for you to go in if you'd like.'

I hesitate. When I met Claire at The Lyle, I mentioned I was going home to take care of Scarlett. Could she be my attacker? Just how dangerous is she?

The receptionist arches an eyebrow. 'Or you can speak to her another time.'

'No, it's fine. I'll speak to her now, thanks.'

I go into the cold room. Claire is leaning over a corpse, her thick hair bundled in a net. Her amber eyes sparkle above her face mask. Blood covers her gloved hands and smears across her top. She hits a button on her voice recorder. 'Gemma, hi! How are you? Sorry, I can't stop. I'm up against it today.'

'No worries. Do you need me to put on scrubs?'

'If you don't mind.' She laughs, and I picture her giant smile underneath her mask.

I pull on the gauzy outfit, careful to keep my back to the wall. I leave the ties loose at the back and rest my hand on top of my gun underneath the material. 'Did you know Roger?'

She pauses, her scalpel hovering over the body. It's an elderly male, his pale skin folded back like flower petals, revealing an array of organs. 'I met him at the hospital a few times. Why?'

I clear my throat, 'Because it seems you were in the vicinity of his house just before he was murdered.'

Claire soundlessly places the scalpel onto a metal tray and gives me her full attention. 'What are you talking about?'

'I have footage of your car on Monday, 19 September, parked in a street parallel with Roger Kirk's house.'

She shakes her head resolutely. 'That's not possible.'

'The black four-wheel drive in the car park—that's yours, right?'

'Yes.' She pushes her mask down, then comes around to my side of the table, pulling off the bloodstained gloves and tossing them into a bin. 'Where do you think my car was?' Faint lines appear on her creamy forehead.

'Where were you last Monday night?' I counter.

She looks startled. 'At home.'

'At your house on Carlton Street?'

She nods.

'Can you explain why your car was on the other side of town?'

'But it wasn't,' she says, her voice more curious than defensive.

'We have footage of someone getting out of your car around midnight, then returning and driving off about two hours later—an individual with your height and build.'

'Gemma, this is crazy. If what you're saying is true then someone must have taken my car.'

I experience the slightest hint of unease. She seems so sure of herself. 'Where is it normally parked overnight? Do you have a garage?'

She blinks, then a spark comes into her eyes. 'It was here that night. I've started leaving it overnight when I have an early corpse collection and take the work car. It's just easier than messing around in the morning.' Despite her confidence, her fingers curl at her sides, and she won't look me in the eye.

'You're sure your car was here last Monday night?'

'Yes. The next morning I collected a body from the Gowran hospice. I wanted to beat the traffic, so I left before seven am.'

'Can you check, please?'

'Here, it's in my calendar.' She pulls her phone from her pocket and flicks her manicured finger across the screen.

'So you're saying someone took your car from the car park here that night?'

'They must have. I was nowhere near Roger's house that night—or any night since I moved here.' She keeps moving her thumb across her phone.

'What about when the body was stolen from the hospital? Where were you then?'

Claire steps toward me, and I tighten my fingers around my gun and shoot her a warning glare. She pauses uncertainly, the warmth gone from her eyes.

'Where were you?' I repeat.

'I was here. I got the alert about the car-crash victim at the hospital and thought about picking her up, but Sophie said there was no rush, and I was exhausted, so I decided to go in the morning. I left my car here that night, too.'

I stare at her, recalling the conversation we had at The Lyle. 'How do you get alerted about a job?'

'Generally we get a call, then the email alert.'

'You and Boyd?'

She nods. 'And the admin team. Sometimes he gets called directly because everyone knows him, but nursing homes, the hospital and gaols have to send notifications to our central address.'

'Did you speak to him that night about the car-crash victim?'

'He called me. He knew I was working late, and I think he wanted to make sure I went home.' She gestures to the table. 'He's always saying that our patients are patient and that we need to prioritise our own health. He was fine with me doing the pick-up the next day.'

A seed of doubt plants itself in my mind. 'I need you to do something for me.'

Claire bites her lip. 'Gemma, what's going on? This is all very strange.'

I'm buzzing now, little sparks firing off in my mind. 'I need you to pull up Roger's autopsy results. I want you to check something.'

She takes a deep breath but goes to a bench on the side of the room and opens her laptop. 'What am I looking for?'

'Roger's time of death was listed in the morning after dawn.'

'That's right—estimated to be between seven and eight am.'

'And this is worked out from what, stomach contents, rigor mortis, the condition of the blood?'

Claire nods slowly. 'Yes, all those things, plus bacteria, insects and the scene itself.'

'Can you check all of that on his file?' I say impatiently.

'What do you mean?'

My voice rises in volume when I say, 'I need you to tell me if you would come to the same conclusion as Boyd about the time of death.'

She removes her mask entirely and tosses it in the bin before returning her focus to the computer. 'Okay.' She talks quietly to herself as she clicks the mouse and types.

My hand still on my gun, I check my phone. Mac has texted me.

I'm pretty sure the Braybrook homestead is on land owned by a parent company that has sites here and all over the world. I'm trying to work out who the owners are. Can't find any businesses linked to The Retreat either, except this.

He attaches an image of a building permit.

I scan it, one name standing out: Jack Barnes, Roger's lawyer, acting on behalf of Bilson Constructions—the company those guys at the pub work for.

Bilson did some building work onsite about a year ago.

Mac sends through another image, this time of land plans. The large rectangle of The Retreat is there, as is the river and several lots of land further past the homestead, hundreds of acres.

This is all owned by the same mob. I'll keep digging when Scarlett has her nap.

I reply.

Thanks, see if you can link anything to do with Bilson back to Roger.

I think about the dirt road through the trees next to The Retreat. Pulling up Mac's text again, I zoom in on the land plans. The old homestead is marked on the map, as well as some of the sheds and a few smaller structures, but there are no visible properties on the surrounding land. I load Google Earth and do the same—there are just acres and acres of bush. I wonder if it's slated for development: I expect there would be a decent market for wealthy city types wanting a tree change or a holiday house. I shoot Mac another text.

Can you check if there are any development plans for the land around The Retreat? There's a dirt road next to it that might lead to something. Can you find out?

Claire says, 'Oh,' and I look up to see her expression shifting from concentration to confusion.

'What is it?' I ask, my body on high alert.

'Based on the photos of stomach contents, the time of death might have been earlier.'

I try to remain calm. 'How much earlier?'

'Up to seven hours,' she says slowly. 'Possibly more.'

My pulse quickens, and I angle my body toward the door. 'Anything else?'

She gestures to the screen. 'See here—the colour of his skin suggests he was there for several hours. It's difficult for me to assess other factors without examining the body.'

'Jesus,' I murmur, the seed of doubt now fully fledged dread.

She starts to panic. She brings her hands to her mouth, her eyes huge. 'None of the notes match the photos. I don't understand! What's going on, Gemma?'

I hold up my hands, trying to keep her calm while my brain works through the possibilities. 'Claire, since you started working here, have you been pressured to alter an autopsy, to misreport details? Maybe you were offered money and figured it wouldn't really matter, that the family would never know.'

Her pretty face drains of colour. 'No! No one has ever asked me to do anything like that, not here or anywhere else. And if someone did ask, I would never do it.'

'Who knew your car was here last Monday night?'

'The staff.'

Boyd Mattingly knew, I think. I remember what Candy said about Claire being involved with him. Fuck, we have to get out of here. I need to call Everett.

'Okay, listen, Claire, I need you to come with me to the station.'

She points at the mutilated body. 'I can't just leave him. And I need to call Boyd so he can explain what's going on with the file.'

'No. No calls.' I keep my eyes trained on the main door, one hand on my gun, the other still gripping my phone. 'You can cover the body, then we need to go. We need to get the receptionist, too. Hopefully I can get you back here in a few hours.'

Her hands are shaking, her eyes wide.

I unlock my phone to call Everett, but she still doesn't move. I turn to face her. 'Claire? Are you okay?'

A whimper escapes her lips as her gaze shifts behind me.

Instinct takes over. I spin around, pulling out my gun.

Something hard presses into the side of my head before I can make a full rotation.

I freeze.

'Sorry, Gemma, but I need to take that.' Boyd Mattingly's familiar voice curls into my ear, and my knees buckle. He traces his gun along my head until he's standing in front of me, the metallic butt digging in between my eyebrows. 'Give it to me now or I will shoot you.' Cortisol floods my system, and I want to scream at him. He extracts my gun using his other gloved hand and aims it behind me at Claire.

CHAPTER FIFTY-FOUR

I can hear Claire's breath coming out in little huffs.

'Told you I'd be quick,' Boyd says to her.

She doesn't respond, but I can smell her perfume, her fear propelling the scent into the air.

Inside, I deflate. She must have texted him, summoning him for support before she noticed the errors with Roger's autopsy.

'Boyd,' she murmurs, 'I don't understand.'

He adjusts his gloved grip on the gun. 'Maybe Gemma wants to explain.'

I don't say anything—I'm trying to work out how to get away from him. He must have come in via a back entrance, and he must have driven here. Surely someone knows he's here. I think about screaming for help but worry I'd just put Claire in further danger, along with the receptionist. I wonder if the woman would even hear me scream—morgues are soundproofed to mute the horror of skulls and chest plates being sawn open.

'Claire, come here,' says Boyd.

She cries and shakes her head, frozen in place.

411

He sighs. 'High maintenance as always.'

She just keeps crying.

'Stop that, please,' he says politely.

With a ragged gulp, she quietens.

He smiles at me as if everything is normal. 'Of course you're not crying, Gemma. You're notoriously tough. I was telling Claire all about you last week, giving her the lowdown on your colourful history.'

I muster as much confidence as I can. 'You killed Roger.'

'Is that your latest theory? Moments ago you had your hopes pinned on poor Claire.'

She emits another shaky sob.

Boyd slides his backpack off his shoulders, keeping his gun to my head. Then he points my gun at Claire again. He drops the backpack onto the floor. 'Open this for me, please, Claire, and get everything out. Now.'

She scrambles across the floor to him, coming up alongside me, and pulls items out onto the floor.

'Why did you kill Roger?' I ask.

Boyd winks at me and grins. 'Always trying to work out a motive, detective—why, why, why. I mean, don't get me wrong, I admire that about you. You're not lazy like a lot of your fat-arsed colleagues, who parade around town like they're god's gift to policing. But it's still very tedious.'

I push the fear down, trying to ignore the guns and focus on his face. 'What did he have on you? Did he try to blackmail you?'

'Wrong!' he says in a cheesy game-show voice. 'She's got it wrong, folks.' He walks in a circle around me, sliding the gun to the small of my back. 'Hands where I can see them, ladies.'

Still on her knees parallel to me, Claire sniffs and lifts her hands to the back of her head.

'Detective, you too.' Boyd nudges the gun into my skull again, and I lift my hands as well—just as my phone lights up with a call. 'I'll get that,' he says cheerfully.

From the sound, I think he jams his gun into his waistband but keeps mine pressed into my scalp as he takes my phone from my hand. I slide my eyes to Claire, hoping she might use the distraction of my phone as a chance to overpower him, but she looks like she's in shock.

'Ah, how sweet,' says Boyd. 'Detective Everett checking up on you, no doubt.'

Lee, I think. *Maybe Everett has an update on Lee and the baby.*

'Lee Blight,' I blurt out.

'Lee Blight,' Boyd repeats, his voice close and low behind my left ear. 'Name rings a bell. A messed-up no-hoper, if I'm thinking of the right person.'

His own mobile rings. A thought snags in my mind—could that be Everett calling him? Boyd surely isn't doing all this on his own. He might have killed Roger on his own, but if he was involved in running my sister off the road or stealing her body he had help, because his alibi is airtight.

He checks his phone but doesn't answer, the shrill ringtone needling my addled brain. I feel hot, like I might pass out. I close my eyes, trying to think; I don't know who to trust.

I hate that I can't see him and try to keep him talking so I can get a sense of what he's doing behind me. 'What about my sister? Where is she?'

'Shut up.' He jams the gun into the rear of my neck. 'Just shut the fuck up.'

I feel the same terror as when I was attacked at my home. It must have been him. He knew I was heading home, and he wanted me so scared I'd drop the case. But what did he think I knew? I'd asked him about Carlyle, about his business, about the negligence claims made against Lyle Lodge. Does Boyd have a stake in Carlyle's business? Were he and Roger involved in some kind of scheme and had a falling-out?

Suddenly the pressure of the gun recedes. I consider trying to get him in a headlock, but it feels too risky, and the moment passes. Then Claire starts crying again, but as far as I can see without moving my head, he's not hurting her. I tense, preparing to pounce.

'This is not the time for heroics, detective,' Boyd says, apparently picking up on my body language. 'There's no need to make things worse.'

His serenity is very concerning: he clearly has a plan. 'This doesn't make sense,' I say. 'People know we're here and will come looking for us. Our cars are here.'

'It's not ideal,' he replies agreeably, 'but I'm a solutions-orientated person. Even my ex-wife would acknowledge that—and it can be hard to get a compliment out of her, let me tell you. Remember, no one knows *I'm* here. My bike is stashed next door, and I came in through the back. I even called my assistant Polly on my way here to tell her I'd be hiking this afternoon and uncontactable for a few hours.'

'The receptionist—'

'Has been taken care of,' he finishes. 'Thought of everything.'

Claire whimpers like a dog.

I try to keep my breathing steady. Has he killed the receptionist? If not, what has he done with her? I try to think of what to say, something to unsettle him, so I can attack.

'There's evidence tracing Roger's murder to you.'

'Nope, that's incorrect. All roads lead to poor old Claire, I'm afraid. Of course, I'll help piece together how she fooled everyone, including me, when I do her autopsy.'

'No,' she whispers. 'Please.'

He returns the gun to my neck, where I can feel a bruise has formed, and nudges me to move closer to Claire. I shuffle along until I'm less than a metre from her. I'm about to kick behind me, praying I get him in the kneecap so I can spin around and fight for the gun, when Claire lets out a cry. She falls forward, lying limp on the floor.

Boyd bearhugs me from behind, forcing the air from my lungs. His cheek is hard against my face. 'Your turn.'

This time I'm anticipating the needle, but there's nothing I can do to stop it. I feel it enter my shoulder, and the numbness radiates down my arm and across my chest. Then I'm fighting the inevitable fall, faintly aware of strong arms guiding me to the ground.

CHAPTER FIFTY-FIVE

Wherever I am, whatever I'm lying on, it's vibrating. It must be a vehicle. But am I on a table? I picture a conveyor belt ferrying me into a furnace.

Then I realise it's the morgue car. The hearse.

I'm alive but it feels like I'm en route to death. My body is shutting down, my spirit fading.

I scream, but there's a soft mass in my mouth, some kind of material, so the sound just reverberates through my body, a low growl. My ankles and wrists ache—whatever they're bound with is cutting into my skin. There's pressure against my eyes. And I can hear birds singing.

———

I dream about Boyd Mattingly at Roger Kirk's house, on the phone talking about teeth. Images of teeth decaying and coming loose fill my mind. They fall from the open mouths of corpses and form little piles on the ground. I shift to the side, trying to make the images go away.

Someone is coming. Footsteps on gravel.

A low murmur.

The roll of a door. Fresh air.

Then the smell of petrol. The stink of bleach.

Hands on my legs and under my arms. I'm airborne.

CHAPTER FIFTY-SIX

White noise—a soft, steady hum that becomes louder and louder until my brain vibrates against my skull. It's a strange sensation, but it means I'm alive. This fact alone is enough to make me want to sob with gratitude.

After some time, the buzzing fades away. Everything is completely still. I exist in a bizarre nothingness. I can feel every nerve so acutely that my skin aches. My feet are free now, no longer bound, but my hands are still tied at my sacrum, and my chest muscles strain in protest. I'm lying on something soft—a bed?

My saliva is like syrup in my mouth. 'Help,' I say around the thickness of my tongue, but there's no reply. I'm pretty sure I'm alone.

I wonder where Claire and the morgue receptionist are, where Boyd is. I remember the vileness of his hot breath on my face, the hardness of the gun against the back of my head. My teeth start to chatter uncontrollably.

I try to roll further onto my side and push myself up but can't get the traction I need. With a frustrated cry, I give up. It's hopeless. *I'm* hopeless. My jaw shakes, and I struggle to breathe as I push my head against the material underneath me.

I wake up again. This time I manage to open each eye. My vision is cloudy, and everything blurs around the edges as if I'm looking through a dirty porthole.

I'm not in my shed this time—I'm in a small room that has the chemical smell of a morgue. I must be in the hospital, and I feel weak with relief. Until I realise that doesn't seem right either. There's nothing in the room except the single bed I'm lying on and a white plastic bedside table. There are no windows, but there is a glass panel on the door. It's not a hospital; it's more like a gaol cell.

I'm going to die here. The thought grips me and won't let go. I'm choking on it.

The fight goes out of me. I lie as still as I can on the bed, just listening to my heartbeat.

I'm going to die here.

'Please,' I whisper to the empty room, 'please, help me.' But I already know that no one will come to my aid.

Maybe I deserve this. I've let so many people down. I think of Mac and the kids. *I'm sorry*, I think, squeezing my eyes shut. *I'm so sorry.* I think about Dad and how angry I was, but none of it seems to matter now. Maybe I deserve this. There are so many things I regret, so many things I should have done differently.

My foot spasms, and I stretch out my legs, flexing and pointing my toes. My shoes and socks are gone, chipped red polish on my toenails. I imagine my sister's scratched and broken feet, identical to mine, and wonder if she's here—if we will finally be reunited. At least I'm still wearing my own clothes.

Am I being watched? I scan the room for cameras. There's one in the corner to the left of the door, and I stare at it. Is Boyd watching me? I don't want to give him the satisfaction of seeing me like this, but I can't stop tears from falling down my face.

No one knows I'm here. No one suspects Boyd of anything.

I wonder if Mac and Candy are looking for me, if Ben is already worried that something terrible has happened. The thought flares again—*I'm going to die here*—but this time something deep within me hardens, a tiny feeling of resolve. I don't like my chances of getting out of here, but I have to try. I owe it to my kids to try.

Shifting my weight from my chest, I do a quick inventory of my body. I don't think I'm hurt, just stiff. With some effort, I shift to the side of the bed. Bracing myself for the impact, I roll onto the floor. I land with a grunt, then manoeuvre myself onto my knees, pushing my right leg into a lunge and leaning forward so I can bring my left foot onto the floor. Slowly I straighten my knees, careful to keep my weight distributed as evenly as possible.

Once I have my balance, I go to the door and look through the glass. I see a sink, metal tables, stainless-steel doors that I think belong to a fridge—no people, no windows. Another morgue? Or perhaps it's part of the Smithson Morgue that I've never seen. But I was in a vehicle earlier, so I must be somewhere else. I move to each corner of the door, getting as wide a view as possible.

I must be somewhere at The Lyle. It's big enough to accommodate a space like this, and Boyd knows his way around the place. I think about his face at the morgue and the callous way he talked about Roger's murder. I can't work out what motivates him. He doesn't seem materialistic—I've always found him curious, passionate and, if anything, a bit of a nerd. How could I have gotten him so wrong? What does he want?

Starting to tire, I shuffle backwards to the bed and lower myself onto the edge. My wrists ache as they strain against the bindings. Nausea takes over my stomach. I whimper and battle a surge of vomit, swallowing it down. When I spit on the floor, my puffy lips mean most of it just runs down my chin.

Hunched forward, I stare at my feet, trying to think. I stretch my fingers into my back pockets. They're empty.

I take deep breaths, trying to make the horrible feeling go away. Blood rushes in my ears.

There's movement outside my cell. I brace myself, but no one enters.

With great effort, I stagger to my feet again. I make my way along the edges of the room to the door and peer through the corner of the glass panel. A man is standing a few metres away, his back to me. He has pale skin and dark hair; he's wearing a lab coat. Like me, he's barefoot. I push my face to the window, straining to get a proper look.

He shifts his head, and I gasp. It's Roger Kirk.

CHAPTER FIFTY-SEVEN

It's impossible to process what I'm seeing. *Roger? It can't be.* But it is. He's standing less than ten metres from me, alive and well.

I'm mesmerised, my face still pressed against the glass. He is tapping away on a laptop and sipping from a mug.

He must feel my eyes on him, because after a few moments he turns. We lock eyes. My certainty wavers. He looks like Roger, but the planes of his face are thinner, as if he hasn't eaten for a few days. Maybe he hasn't. *He's dead!* screams the voice in my head.

He walks out of the room, leaving me alone again. What the hell is going on? I saw Roger's body. Could Boyd have somehow procured another body to perform the autopsy on? Even though it defies all logic, I experience a flare of hope: maybe there's a chance my sister is alive.

I wait for what feels like an hour, but the man doesn't return. Too tired to stand, I return to the bed and perch on the edge. As I look down, I notice a gentle rise in the coin pocket of my jeans. The lighter I took from Ben's room is still there. It was behind the business card Jarrod gave me—whoever searched me must have missed it.

I start to cry. *Oh god, please.*

Careful not to make any obvious movements in case I'm being monitored, I pull my wrists apart from each other as far as I can. What are the bindings made of? It doesn't feel like plastic: it's some kind of fabric. Pretending to retch with nausea, I position myself next to the bedside table and squat against the corner, forcing the lighter out of the pocket. My thighs ache with the effort.

After several minutes, I hear the blessed sound of the lighter bouncing against the concrete floor.

Exhausted, I sink to the ground, letting my head sag, my eyes close. I feel around for the lighter, cautious not to push it under the bed. Once I have it safely in my right hand, I sit still, trying to picture my hands behind my back, mapping out what I need to do.

Eyes on the door, I take a deep breath and flick the lighter, willing it to work. Heat flares against my skin. I hold the position until I can't bear the pain any longer. I can smell burnt material, or maybe it's the fine hairs on my arms. Lighting the flame again, I grit my teeth as the insides of my wrists scream under the white heat.

After a few seconds, the ties fall away. I can move my hands again.

Tears run down my cheeks. Still facing the door, I drop the lighter to the concrete and kick it under the bed, using my feet to smudge the traces of ash.

I hope the burning smell fades and doesn't give me away.

I hope no one watching through the camera could tell what I was doing.

I hope.

After wrapping the loose ends of the ties around each wrist, I tuck them in as best I can. I clasp my hands together, haul myself up to the bed with a groan directed toward the camera, and wriggle backwards until I'm positioned in the corner. Then I wait.

CHAPTER FIFTY-EIGHT

Without warning, the door to my room unlocks and swings open. I don't move as the man in the lab coat enters, Boyd following him closely. Gripping my hands together behind me, I bend at the waist like an ice-skater, my legs splayed on either side.

Now I can see the man isn't Roger. The likeness is uncanny, but his expression is different, the mannerisms not those of the confident CEO. This man is taller and much paler, with silvery scars on his left temple. His movements are awkward. Compared to Boyd's healthy frame, his thinness is pronounced.

'Hi, Gemma.' Boyd is still wearing scrubs and sneakers. A gun protrudes from his waistband.

'Where's Claire?' The acoustics make my voice sound far away.

'Claire is fine. No need to worry about her.'

'What about the receptionist?'

Boyd doesn't reply, and the other man remains silent.

They both seem calm and in control, which makes me even more uneasy. 'Where am I? Is this The Lyle?'

Boyd smiles. 'A good guess. But you're at a facility we refer to as The Frontier.'

I have no idea what he's talking about. 'What kind of facility?'

He steeples his fingers. 'You could say it's the beta version of the new research centre.'

'Who runs it?'

The other man straightens. 'I do,' he says softly.

'Who are you?' I say, but I know the answer: Franklin Kirk, presumed incapacitated, is standing in front of me.

Questions are piling up in my addled mind. I think about my conversation with Carlyle. Was Franklin ever in Europe? Was he injured at Tyson Falls? Does Carlyle know he's here? I stare at him, and he stares back. His expression has an unnatural flatness to it, and I break away first.

'Have you been here the whole time?' I ask.

He pushes his glasses up his nose and seems to ponder my question.

Boyd steps forward, and I start to shake uncontrollably. My hands are clasped behind me so tightly, they're going numb. 'You killed Roger,' I murmur. 'Why?'

Franklin's expression doesn't change. 'I didn't kill him.'

'We didn't have a choice.' Boyd scowls. 'Rog was a liability.'

Franklin seems oblivious to our conversation. I wonder if he's medicated. Boyd, on the other hand, radiates aggression, his responses impatient. Both men seem unconcerned about me, certain they have the upper hand.

My panic spikes. Boyd has a gun and surely knows his way around this place—all I have is the element of surprise. He killed Roger. I need to get out of here, or I will die.

This time I can't stop the vomit. I fight to keep my hands behind my back as the contents of my stomach pool on the floor. The stench makes my eyes water.

Furious, Boyd steps back. 'For fuck's sake! Try to control yourself, detective.'

Franklin looks at the mess without reacting.

With his gloved hands, Boyd grabs me roughly by the shoulders and steers me out of the room. My feet can't move quickly enough; I stumble in the doorway. 'Keep moving,' he says, pulling me up and pushing me along. My fingers ache from the strain of holding on to each other against the force of his grip.

We pass steel autopsy tables and fridges. A large whiteboard is adhered to one of the walls, covered in neat writing. It looks like a food diary, with dates recorded next to short descriptions.

I try to look in the other direction, but Boyd shoves me roughly against a wall, winding me. I wince and double over as a jet of cold water hits me in the face. He hoses me down like a dog, leaving me spluttering and gasping for air on my knees.

'Please!' I'm dripping wet and freezing, my hair hanging in my eyes.

Franklin seems immune to my pleas, pushing his glasses up his nose and watching me curiously.

'Everett knows I went to the morgue today,' I say desperately. 'So does my partner. They'll know you attacked me.'

'That's the thing about being so trustworthy,' says Boyd, hanging up the hose. 'People believe you.'

Strands of hair are caught in my mouth, and I retch again. 'It doesn't mean you can get away with murder.'

'No,' he agrees. 'But Claire might. She's left quite a bit of helpful evidence here and there over the past week or so—and she has been going through *such* a tough time. Mental health issues. Luckily, she confided in me over email and text.'

My stomach drops. He seems so sure of himself. Even if people figure it out, it will be too late.

'And, Gemma, you let your boss know you were concerned about Claire's possible involvement in Roger's murder and that she was flustered when you met her today.'

Confused, I try to understand what he's saying. 'What?'

'I took the liberty of sending good old Jonesy a text before your phone was turned off.' He smiles. 'Used your face to unlock your phone when you were resting.'

'He won't believe it. He'll work it out.'

Boyd looks doubtful. 'I don't think so. In my experience when you plant a few seeds, people grow trees. Especially cops—they hate loose ends.'

Jonesy will probably share my text with Everett, who'll be pissed I went over his head and contacted our boss. He probably won't try to contact me again today. Even me telling Candy I was meeting with Claire to follow up a case inconsistency won't help if Boyd has set the woman up to be the scapegoat.

Candy was going to come by at six-thirty pm. Do she and Mac know something is wrong yet?

'But my car is there,' I say, 'and Claire's—'

'This isn't a case you need to solve, detective,' Boyd says. 'You'll just have to trust that I've paid attention over the years.'

'But what is all this for?' I'm yelling, my voice rasping, pieces of hair in my mouth. I glance at the stainless-steel table and shiver, fear curdling my insides. I'd give anything to have Ben and Scarlett in my arms. I start to cry again, snot and tears in my mouth. 'Why are you doing this?'

Franklin finally speaks. 'It's for our project, to understand the brain like never before.'

His words echo those from articles I've read about his father. A few more things slot together: the accusations about Lyle Lodge, and Carlyle's bizarre record when it comes to backing investments. *It's like he has a crystal ball.* Lee Blight was Carlyle's patient. Here, I realise—Lee was here, wherever we are.

'You're conducting illegal experiments. On *people*.'

'We're helping people,' says Franklin. 'People all over the world benefit from our work.'

My kneecaps dig into the unforgiving surface, and I sob openly, unable to stop. This isn't a gaol or a hospital: it's a lab. I look up at them in horror. 'You're monsters,' I choke out. 'Nothing you're doing is safe.'

'That's not true.' Carlyle Kirk steps into the room, his thick grey hair turning white under the harsh lights. 'I oversee everything.'

CHAPTER FIFTY-NINE

Carlyle places a hand on his son's shoulder and stares down at me, his gaze thoughtful. He's wearing a blue bow tie and brown suit with leather loafers. 'It's nice to see you, detective.'

'You're a psychopath.'

'Yes, well, I like to think we're all a bit crazy. And, of course, science isn't perfect. Our experiments are complex.'

'What you're doing is dangerous!'

'It's actually very important work. It might even be ground-breaking, but I never like to get ahead of myself.'

I ask, my voice pleading, 'Is my sister here?'

He gives a curt little nod. 'She was.'

My left knee rolls. I lose my balance and pitch forward, falling hard onto my chest and forehead against the wet concrete. My hands are still behind me, fingers interwoven.

'I don't know why we're all huddled around, watching Gemma shower,' Carlyle says.

'She was sick all over herself,' says Boyd.

'A normal response.' The sound of footsteps. Carlyle's voice fades. 'Bring her in here.'

'No!' I scream as Boyd picks me up and carries me. I feel like I'm going to be sick again. 'Put me down!'

He ignores me, and we follow Carlyle into another large room, a living area. There are couches with plush cushions, a tennis table, shelves full of books and board games, a kitchenette. It's homely in a sterile way, like a furniture showroom. The chemical smell is gone, replaced with the scent of fresh laundry. The room feels sunlit, but there are no windows. I study the unusual light globes and wonder how they work.

Carlyle settles into one of the armchairs, his back ramrod straight, as Boyd deposits me onto an adjacent couch. He wrestles me into an upright position, then takes a seat next to me, his fingers digging into my upper arm. Franklin sits on the other side of me, his gaze fixed on his father.

Through the pain, I focus on making sure my hands stay fused together.

'Was Lee Blight here, too?' I ask.

No one answers.

I look around at each of them. 'Whose baby was it?'

'You are *very* like her,' Carlyle says, studying me again. 'It's remarkable. Genetics never cease to fascinate me.'

'What have you done with her?' I say.

'Your sister was part of our work. She assisted us from the beginning.'

'No,' I say, not wanting to believe it.

'It's true.'

My head is throbbing so badly now that I'm struggling to keep my eyes open. I slump back against the couch. There's no way I can overpower Boyd. Even if I did, Carlyle and Franklin are unknown quantities. But I might as well keep trying to find out more. I say softly, 'How did she start working with you?'

'She was interested in our philosophy.'

'You tricked her.' I let my eyelids close.

'No—and I take offence at the suggestion,' Carlyle says. 'She was a smart girl.'

I can feel myself giving up, energy draining from my limbs, yet I can't stop asking questions. 'How did you know her?'

'We met when my dog was ill. She worked at a vet. It was clear she was depressed, so I offered to treat her.'

'That's how it works, isn't it?' I say listlessly. 'You prey on young people, trick them into being your *patients* and recruit them into your experiments.' My thoughts are woolly; I'm having trouble linking them together. 'Lee Blight?'

'He needed my help, too.'

My upper body is heavy. I feel myself sliding to the right, and Boyd grabs me. He tries to wrestle me upright, but I'm floppy. He pushes me roughly into the couch.

Wet strands of hair stretch across my face. 'Why take my sister's body?'

'We needed to bring her home,' Franklin murmurs.

'If Claire hadn't insisted on doing the autopsy,' says Boyd, 'I could have completed a bogus post-mortem and filed your sister away as a Jane Doe. Case closed.'

'What was Claire going to find? What had you done to her?'

Unruffled, Carlyle continues. 'It's not what *we* wanted, Gemma. Your sister understood what we're trying to do. She was proud of our work and embraced the concept of sacrifice for the greater good. But after that girl became pregnant, your sister started to question our decisions. Then she put everything here at risk, so we had little choice but to stop her.'

His tone is evangelical; he believes what he's saying. They all do.

The baby dumped at the lake on the night my sister died—it was linked. I was right all along. 'That baby was born here, and you were going to experiment on it. My sister wanted to protect it.'

'An infant presented a significant opportunity.' Carlyle's eyes glitter. 'Last time we had access to one, the learnings were critical.'

I think of Scarlett and Ben. My hands separate behind me, and I can't summon the strength to bring them together.

When I open my eyes, Carlyle is still seated calmly on his armchair, a serene expression on his face.

'You killed your own *nephew*?'

Boyd's breath tickles my ear. 'Don't feel too sorry for Roger. He was the one who killed your sister.'

My face contorts as I begin to sob again. 'Please, I want to see my babies. Let me see them.'

'That's enough.' Carlyle pulls out a phone. 'I have to go shortly. There's a fundraiser I need to attend.'

'What are you going to do to me?' I think about the autopsy room, wondering if they plan to kill me and take me apart piece by piece—or worse, use me as a live experiment.

As Carlyle gets to his feet, his knees crack loudly. 'It should be clear to you by now that we're not in the business of waste. Rest assured, you will be useful in myriad ways.' He bows his head to me as if giving thanks.

CHAPTER SIXTY

Carlyle doesn't look back when he leaves the room.

Boyd grabs my shoulders and yanks me toward him. I see his gun in his waistband, then he forces my head up. He sneers into my face and shakes me, jerking my neck so that I cry out. There's cruelty in his eyes—I can tell he gets pleasure from inflicting pain. He's wired wrong, missing a critical component of humanity. 'You smug cow,' he hisses. 'And look where it got you.'

My children's faces flash through my mind, and a latent instinct awakens in me. I'm not in control of my body as I lunge for Boyd's gun, curling my fingers around it and yanking it from his waistband. With as much force as I can muster, I bring my knee to his groin and jab my left elbow sideways, feeling it connect with Franklin's cheekbone.

Two yelps are followed by Boyd swearing as he paws wildly at me.

I scramble backwards along the floor, holding the gun in front of me, pointed at his head. When I reach the armchair Carlyle vacated, I shift my aim between the two men. Boyd is fuming, teeth bared.

Franklin remains on the couch, his expression blank; he touches his broken cheek uncertainly.

Letting out a primal yell, Boyd leaps at me. I don't have time to pull the trigger before his fist connects with my stomach, pushing the air out of me. I retaliate by jabbing the butt of the gun into his head. He cries out. Blood drips onto my neck.

I make myself small and wriggle away from him. Grabbing my face, he pins me down. Our limbs are tangled, his mouth near mine, and he spits into my eyes, his blood smearing over our skin. I flinch. He grunts and moves his hand along my body toward the gun.

I don't think—I fire once, twice, hoping the bullets hit him and not me.

He screams and clutches at his thigh.

I roll sideways. I can't feel my fingers as I grip the gun.

Franklin and I watch blood seep through Boyd's scrubs and pool in his lap. 'Help me!' He presses his hands into the bloody mess.

I taste bile. I'm still holding the gun in front of me, my arms shuddering. I want him dead; I want to shoot him point-blank in the head and watch the life leave his body. I think I'm going to do it. I picture it, the shot ringing out and his body slumping to the floor.

I'm underwater. Sounds are blurry shapes around me. I keep my hands on the gun and try to think.

'Franklin!' Boyd's shout pierces the fog. 'Help me.' His voice is shrill now.

Franklin doesn't move. He doesn't seem to be registering Boyd's distress, nor does he seem concerned about my gun.

Carlyle re-enters the room. 'What in god's name—'

I shift the gun toward him and fire. He cries out and doubles over.

Boyd moans. His face is losing colour.

I turn to Franklin and scream, 'Get up!'

From the floor, Carlyle wheezes, 'Franklin, don't you dare.'

'Franklin, I need you to get me out of here. If you don't help me, I'll shoot you, too. Do you understand?'

'Yes,' he says solemnly.

'Can we lock this room from the outside?'

'Yes. But we need the key.'

'Where's the—?'

He points to Carlyle.

'Get it.'

I nose the gun against the back of his neck as he approaches his father and removes the lanyard. Carlyle's eyes are closed; he's talking to himself while he presses his hands to his wound.

'Walk in front of me,' I say to Franklin.

Again he obeys.

Once we're through the door, I say, 'Pull it shut and lock it.'

He flips the metal latch to the locked position, and I check it's secure. We're in a narrow space at the foot of a flight of stairs.

I face him. 'Is my sister in here?'

'Yes.'

My knees start to give way, so I tense my legs. I have to keep going. 'Was she . . . ?' I don't know what I'm trying to ask him.

'We have preserved her. There are things we can learn from her, even now. It's what she would want.'

Fighting the urge to hit him, I ask, 'Do you have a phone?'

He nods. 'But it only works in the exercise area. It's only for calling my father.'

'Unlock it and give it to me.'

After he hands me an old Nokia, I punch in Jonesy's number. Franklin's right—there's no reception. 'We need to get out of here.' I prod him with the gun. 'Take me to the exercise area.'

'This way.'

Can I trust him? He's the only chance I have.

I follow him up the stairs. My legs burn, and my lungs feel like they're about to explode. I'm daring to hope I will hold my children again, put my arms around Mac, get the chance to talk to Dad.

We reach a landing with closed doors along each side. Like the room downstairs, it's spacious and well furnished with comfortable-looking couches, a bookshelf and indoor plants. The paintings on the wall match the ones at Roger's house and in Carlyle's consulting rooms. The Frontier reminds me of an unhinged reality TV show.

'Where are the people?' I ask, nudging Franklin along to the next set of stairs.

'In their rooms—there are two wings, male and female.'

'How many people are being kept here?'

'Fifty-seven,' he says. 'And they've agreed to live here. They aren't prisoners.'

'Jesus,' I whisper.

'It's a small sample,' he adds, in his odd monotone, 'but it's indicative. And the research centre will be much larger, so there will be more opportunity to scale our work.'

I don't have time to process what he means. 'Do we go through there?' I say, pointing at the furthest door.

'Yes.'

I push the gun against his back. 'That gets us out of here . . . ?'

'Yes.'

I look at his pale skin and thin frame, his bare feet. He's a prisoner here, too, I realise. He was nursed back from the brink of death only to be trapped in a soulless life under the guise of a misguided commitment to the betterment of humanity.

At the top of the stairs, Franklin uses Carlyle's pass to open the door. Cool air hits my face. I keep the gun firm against his shoulder blades as we step outside. I move us in a slow spin, surveying our surroundings. The moonlight illuminates four exercise stations arranged in a row. The door we just came through is wooden and fits snugly into the side of a hill. The whole structure is camouflaged, this entrance hidden by a trio of trees. It's incredible, the scale of it.

'What the hell is this place?' I murmur.

'We're in the midst of a large study,' Franklin says, 'on mental health. We've developed a drug that we believe overrides the symptoms of schizophrenia. The sample is small, as I said, but so far, the results are conclusive—with minimal side effects. It will be the first trial we run when we open the centre, but we already have significant knowledge.'

His phone comes to life in my hand, and I hit redial. It rings. I cry out with relief.

'Ken Jones.' I detect the desperation in Jonesy's voice despite the loud whirring in the background.

'Jonesy.' I'm unable to hold back my tears—of relief this time.

'Woodstock. Oh, thank god.' His thick voice cracks. 'Are you safe?'

'I'm okay,' I choke.

'Hang tight—we're coming to get you. I've got Fyfe with me. She figured out where you are.'

'But I don't know where I am!'

'Stay on the line, okay? Don't worry, we're close.'

I hear Candy's voice. 'Gemma, this wasn't what I meant when I said I wanted you to give me a lead.'

Now I'm laughing and crying.

Careful to keep the gun to Franklin's spine, I step us forward, then realise we're standing on the edge of a creek. I picture my sister clutching a newborn baby, her bare feet sore and bleeding as she made her way across the water—finally trying to do the right thing while being hunted down by people she'd trusted.

A slow buzz turns into an oppressive hum. Two searing white spotlights draw circles on the ground around us. Franklin squints up at the helicopter, his mouth open in wonder. I frantically wave before collapsing onto my knees, tears streaming down my face.

CHAPTER SIXTY-ONE

After I'm rescued and transported back to Smithson in the helicopter, all I want is to be with my family. I get checked over at the hospital but insist on being allowed to go home. The doctor who treated me after my attack agrees I can go if I promise to return for another check-up tomorrow and make an appointment with a trauma psychologist.

'I was going to make her do that anyway,' says Candy. I'd let her stay while the doctor examined me and she has delighted in answering questions about my ordeal.

'She's got some serious shit to unpack, and it goes well beyond the stuff you know about,' Candy adds helpfully.

The doctor seems unsure how to respond to this but smiles and tells me she'll see me tomorrow. I let Candy help me to her car. I'm nervous about seeing Mac and the kids. After being convinced I was going to die in Carlyle's underground lab, I'm desperate to hold them in my arms.

When we finally arrive home, it's lit up like a Christmas tree.

'For the love of Elon, I hope you've got energy-efficient globes,' Candy says.

I laugh, more grateful for her friendship than ever before.

We make our way gingerly up the driveway, her arm around my waist. Before we have the chance to knock, Everett opens the door and holds out his arms, his eyes a question. I step inside and let him hug me. 'Thank god you're okay, Gemma.'

Surprised, I say, 'What are you doing here?'

'I was at the hospital interviewing Lee Blight, then I stayed to try to speak with Carlyle after they brought him in. I thought you might be staying there, too, but I should have known better. Mac said I could come over. Hope you don't mind.'

'Gemma.' Mac moves past Everett and stands in front of me. 'Can I hold you?'

I nod, the sight of him making me dissolve into tears.

Candy and Everett go to the kitchen, leaving us alone in the hallway. He takes me in his arms and rubs my back, kissing my forehead.

'I'm so sorry,' I whisper. 'I thought I was never going to see you again.'

'I'm here,' he says. 'You're safe now.'

My sobs start to subside. 'Where are the kids?'

'In bed. They're fine.'

'I killed him, Mac.' I exhale the words.

Boyd Mattingly is dead. I heard one of the paramedics say that he bled out on the floor after I shot him.

'Don't worry about that right now.' He holds my head against the steady beat of his heart. 'The only thing that matters is that you're all right.'

I open my eyes, not wanting to think about Boyd's body on one of his own steel tables.

We join the others in the kitchen where they are talking and making hot chocolates. 'Did you manage to speak to Carlyle?' I ask Everett.

'Briefly. He seems unperturbed by his injury, even though he might need surgery. He doesn't think he's done anything wrong.'

Anger writhes up past the painkillers the doctor gave me. I hate Carlyle and his evil plans. I hate that my sister spent so much time with him. 'And did you find my sister's body?'

'Not yet,' says Everett, 'But we've just sent three fresh teams out there, along with forensics.'

Someone knocks on the door and I tense, not relaxing until Mac returns with Jonesy.

'There you bloody are, Woodstock. How are you feeling?' He stands opposite me, his doughy face lined with worry.

'I'm okay.'

'Atta girl,' he says, chin wobbling. 'Give me one of those quick,' he says to Candy, who hands him a mug of steaming cocoa.

'Boyd said it was Roger who ran her off the road,' I tell them.

Candy steers me toward the lounge. 'Let's all sit down and have a nice hot drink.' She clicks her fingers at Mac, who obediently goes to the kitchen and fetches two steaming mugs from the bench.

'Mum?' Ben appears at the end of the hallway, hair on end, blinking into the light.

'Ben!' I run to him and drop to my knees, wrapping my arms around his upper body. I try not to scare him with the intensity of my feelings.

'What's going on?' he asks as I cry into his pyjama shirt.

He sits on the couch next to me, and I alternate between running my fingers through his hair and holding his head in my hands. The others talk on the other side of the room. Everett gives Candy a withering look, which she pretends not to notice. Jonesy dribbles chocolate on his shirt, tries to wipe it off and makes it worse. Mac is listening to Everett but keeps his gaze fixed on me. I thank my lucky stars that I'm here. 'We figured out how to solve the case I've been working on, but I got into a fight.'

Pulling away from me, he surveys my legs and arms. 'Are you hurt?'

'Just my wrists.' I hold them up so he can see the bandages. 'And I was very scared.' I know I need to be honest with him—he's not a little kid anymore. Plus, this will all be on the news tomorrow.

Careful not to apply pressure, he traces a finger along the bandages. 'But is the case done now?'

I think about the fallout from Carlyle's plans, all the lives lost and impacted. 'Almost done,' I say.

Ben looks over at the others and yawns.

'Your lighter was my lucky charm at work today,' I say quietly. 'But we need to talk about why you didn't get rid of it like you told me you did.'

He sits up, indignant, and I recognise my own stubbornness in his features. 'Yes, I did! You can ask Jodie—I gave her the vape, I swear.'

'But you kept the lighter? Come on, Ben.'

'I honestly don't know what you're talking about.'

'The silver lighter in your room, behind the books on your desk.'

He looks confused. 'That lighter came with the candle Rebecca gave me for Christmas. You know, the one you said I wasn't allowed to have in my room. I didn't know where the lighter went, but I've never even used it.'

My laughter quickly turns to tears. I ruffle his hair. 'I love you, kiddo.'

Mac sidles up to us, handing me a mug of cocoa. 'Ben, you should go back to bed. It's late.'

I give him another hug, and Mac herds him down the hall.

Everyone settles on the couches. I'm tempted to go and give Ben another hug. Or wake up Scarlett so I can hold her. I think about the way Carlyle spoke about Franklin at The Lyle. I felt so much empathy for him but the reality of their relationship was so much sadder. 'I can't believe Franklin Kirk had been living there this whole time,' I say.

'It's so wild,' says Candy. 'What a bloody bizarre story.'

'This is all off the record, Fyfe, or you'll hear about it,' Jonesy warns.

She ignores him, going on her phone and murmuring something about headlines.

'I spoke to the hospital staff in charge of his care,' says Everett. 'They think he was subjected to a type of electroshock therapy.'

'Whatever they did to him, it didn't fry his brain,' says Jonesy. 'You should have seen the room in that place.'

'What room?' Candy and I ask simultaneously.

'An underground lab. There were drawers full of files and books where Franklin recorded Carlyle's experiments—hundreds of the bloody things.' Jonesy gives us all a significant look. 'I always knew Carlyle was off. Sniffed it out years ago.'

I try to remember what I saw down there. The lab room with the tables, where Boyd blasted me with the hose, and then the lounge room. But Franklin said there were over fifty people there. Ethics aside, Carlyle's audacity in setting up such a system is staggering, his lawlessness shocking. I ask Jonesy, 'How long do you think The Frontier had been operating for?'

'At least fifteen years, maybe more. We're still going through the files, but there are detailed records of experiments conducted on Lyle residents and people Carlyle treated at his psych practice, as well as prisoners they kept in the facility.'

'Did Carlyle build it?' I ask.

'It was originally an old doomsday shelter that we think Randall Goggin dug out when he set up The Retreat. When the cult fell apart, there were claims he used to lock members up underground when they disobeyed him. But nothing like that was ever found on the Braybrook homestead. At the time, the cops assumed the ex-members were confused and had just been locked in one of the outhouses.'

'How did Carlyle start using it?' Candy asks.

'Jack Barnes owns the land,' Everett says. 'We assume Carlyle paid him—or bribed him—to provide access to it. And Carlyle must have commissioned builders when he first set it up, because there's no way he constructed that facility on his own.'

'We're looking into Barnes,' says Everett, glancing up from his phone, dark rings under his eyes.

'Franklin told me that over fifty people were living down there,' I say softly.

'We're in the process of getting everyone out,' Jonesy says, shooting another warning look at Candy. 'Some don't want to leave.'

I start to shake again. I can't imagine living in that underground place and being submitted to Carlyle's bizarre tests. 'Thank god Franklin got us out of there and that you knew where to come.'

'Fyfe was the one who pointed us in the right direction,' says Jonesy.

Candy looks at her feet with false modesty. 'Mac called me looking for you, Gemma, and you'd said you were about to speak with Claire.'

I half heard this story in the helicopter but indulge her. 'But how did you know where we'd been taken?'

'I told Everett you'd said Claire was somewhere she shouldn't have been. So we got your laptop and found the last file you'd looked at. We saw the footage of her car and knew you'd assumed it was her, but I remembered her telling me that she leaves her car at the morgue sometimes so she can head straight to a job. I got Polly to check her diary and told Everett I was sure it was someone else on the tape. Then Polly mentioned that Boyd had gone hiking and was uncontactable for a few days. We were suss, especially once we went to the morgue and there was no one there.'

Mac cuts in. 'Candy called me, and I said you'd asked me to investigate a dirt road out past The Retreat.'

'And I just knew that's where you were. Thank fuck I was right.'

'Detective Fyfe,' I say, and she beams.

'You said before that the receptionist is fine.'

'Raylene,' says Jonesy. 'We found her at that place in a holding cell but she's fine.'

'What about Claire?' I ask.

Everett and Jonesy exchange a glance.

'She's been flown to Sydney, Woodstock.' A pulse in Jonesy's jaw tics. 'We're not sure she's going to make it. Her head was banged up pretty bad.'

'What happened to her?'

'We found her unconscious, tied up in one of the rooms. She may have injured herself trying to escape, or she may have been attacked.'

Everett's mobile rings, and he lets himself out onto my back porch to take the call.

Candy squeezes my hand.

'I should have tried to find her,' I say. 'I shouldn't have gone to the morgue, I didn't even think—'

Jonesy cuts me off. 'Stop it, Woodstock. It's not your fault. Let's just hope Claire pulls through.'

The sliding door opens, and Everett steps inside, his face pale.

'What is it?' I ask.

'Lee Blight is dead.'

CHAPTER SIXTY-TWO

In the Gowran funeral home, I run a hand along Sandra's cheek, careful to avoid the purple bruise on her temple that the make-up hasn't managed to cover. The lump in my throat swells, and I take a few deep breaths to centre myself. I look down at the familiar stranger, her features so like mine, and wish things could have been different.

Sandra's autopsy revealed two major surgeries on her brain and one on her stomach. She is missing a kidney and her uterus. Two microchips were embedded in her skin, one behind her ear and one in her shoulder. Like the others at The Frontier, she was a walking dataset, her life meticulously planned so that variables could be tested. Diet, medication, music, exercise—everything she did was monitored and recorded by Franklin, making her both the foundation and the inspiration for future clinical trials.

By testing his theories directly on people, Carlyle avoided expensive trials on animals and years of ethical hoop jumping. He used this data to influence legal clinical trials, investing with confidence because he already knew the answers. No wonder it seemed he had a crystal ball.

By losing his cool and running my sister off the road, Roger unwittingly created a smoking gun: her corpse was evidence of the work being done at The Frontier. They couldn't risk her body being autopsied by Claire, so a hasty plan was hatched to remove it from the hospital.

Sandra was discovered metres from where I'd been held hostage, preserved in a cryogenic chamber. It's unclear whether Carlyle found someone to build this chamber in Australia or had it imported, but he had plans to extend his life well beyond what nature intended; we found detailed instructions for Franklin to preserve his body after his death in the hope that technology would advance enough to bring him back.

My sister's foster family are coming here tomorrow to see her before she is cremated. They plan to scatter her ashes near her childhood home. I'm happy about this: I don't think she'd want Smithson to be her final resting place. I've spoken to her foster mother on the phone, but I've decided not to meet with them—maybe someday.

Leaving the funeral home, I step into the sunshine. Claire's life support is being turned off today; her parents arrived from Scotland yesterday to say goodbye. Candy and I went to see her at the hospital last night. I told her I felt terrible that I never got to know her and that my actions put her directly in danger. I asked her to forgive me and I hope that she would. Somewhat ironically, she wanted to donate her body to science, so I assume it will be sent to the University of Sydney in the next few days.

On the drive back to Smithson I wind the windows down, letting the warm spring air roll through the car. Through bluetooth, I return a call I missed from Everett.

He doesn't even say hello. 'The baby wasn't Lee's.'

'It was Boyd's?'

'Yep.'

'Jesus.'

'I know.'

Lee Blight was shot dead at the hospital after he snuck into the maternity ward and tried to steal the baby, insisting she was his child. Security was called, and after a brief altercation—Lee allegedly threatened staff with a metal IV pole—Rufus shot him.

The mother is a sixteen-year-old kicked out of home by her abusive stepfather when she was thirteen. She was homeless and addicted to drugs when Carlyle brought her to The Frontier, promising her a better life. Instead she was subjected to a raft of experimental drugs that have robbed her of the ability to taste and smell.

In her police interview this week, she told Everett and Holdsworth that she never slept with Lee, but that Boyd raped her on multiple occasions over the past two years.

'Does Marty know about the baby?' I ask Everett.

'Jonesy's telling him now.'

'Okay, good. Will the baby stay in foster care?'

'For at the least the next few months. The mum is in no state to look after her daughter.' His voice is gravelly from lack of sleep. 'She's a mess, Gemma. They all are.'

The New South Wales Police have established a taskforce to manage the people imprisoned at The Frontier. Several were missing persons, lured off the street with drugs, and many had been treated by Carlyle in his clinic. The majority were battling some form of addiction. Most of them signed contracts giving Carlyle permission to conduct medical procedures and drug trials on them, and most claim they were at The Frontier voluntarily. Their statements will play a role in court proceedings, but I suspect many of them won't be deemed fit to take the stand, and their contracts will be ruled null and void. Many have been hospitalised or placed in psychiatric care since the raid. I don't know where they will end up.

Except for the sixteen-year-old, all the females were subjected to hysterectomies.

I arrive at Dad's and sit in the car, looking at the half-painted fence. We've only spoken twice since I confronted him about Mum, and both conversations centred around my rescue from The Frontier, but I texted him last night and offered to come over to help finish the fence today. I draw a deep breath and get out, fetching the tools and equipment from the boot. Arms full, and with the handle of a paintbrush wedged between my teeth, I manage to slam the boot shut before Rebecca appears next to my car.

Startled, I drop everything. 'Jesus, Rebecca, you frightened me.'

'Gemma, you listen to me, all right?' Her nostrils flare, and she takes little steps back and forth.

I hold up my hands in surrender. 'Listening.'

'I know you think the world revolves around you, but it doesn't. And Ned has been beside himself.'

'Rebecca, I—'

'No, you let me finish.'

'Okay.'

'I've been worried about you, too, you silly girl.'

I nod. 'I'm sorry.'

'But your dad, god love him, actually does think the world revolves around you! That's something I just have to accept, but it doesn't mean you can act like a spoilt brat.'

I let her words hit me, let them hurt me, knowing this is long overdue.

'I understand you're upset about your mother, but she's not here, so you're just going to have to grow up and work through things like an adult.'

'I know.' I'm contrite because it's true. As much as I hate what's happened, it's done now, so do I really want to let it change everything?

'He had a heart attack three weeks ago.' Her eyes brim with tears. 'And I thought I was going to lose him!' Rebecca starts to sob, and I step toward her, but she pushes me away. 'I'll be damned if I let you do anything else to hurt him.'

'I don't want to hurt him,' I say. And I realise it's true—over the past few days, my anger has faded away. Everyone made choices: some were good and some were bad, but we're here now, in this moment, and it's up to me to decide what happens next. 'I'm sorry, Rebecca.' I'm not just apologising for arguing with Dad: I'm apologising for never letting her get close, for expecting more from her than I ever attempted to offer myself.

This time I don't let her push me away. I hug her as she fumbles for a tissue and dabs her eyes.

Looking up, I see Dad standing at the front door. Through my tears I smile at him, and he tentatively smiles back.

CHAPTER SIXTY-THREE

I told Jonesy to meet me at Reggie's. I want to be somewhere loud, with lots of people. We've only spoken once since he was at my house after we left The Frontier. I'm not sure if I've been avoiding him or vice versa, but when he reached out yesterday and asked if we could catch up, I didn't hesitate despite my nerves. I want to get this over with.

I arrive at the cafe first, order a flat white and take a seat at a corner table. A few minutes later, Jonesy bustles in and makes a fuss ordering his coffee, complaining about being offered almond milk.

'Milk out of a nut, for Christ's sake,' he grumbles, sitting opposite me. 'Anyway, how was it in Gowran? Did you get to see her?'

'It was surreal. But I'm glad I went.'

He nods. 'And you're feeling okay?'

'I'm fine. Apart from a few bruises and my wrist wounds, I wasn't hurt.' My burnt skin is badly blistered, but my dermatologist doesn't think there will be permanent damage. I add, 'I had a counselling session yesterday, and I'm going again on Friday.'

451

'Important you keep that up, Woodstock.'

'I will.'

'You heard about the baby?' he asks.

'Everett told me.'

'Marty's a mess about it,' he says. 'He'd latched on to that kid being Lee's.'

My interest in Marty is limited, particularly in light of his behaviour, but Jonesy cares about him so I ask, 'How is he doing?'

'Not good. But he only has himself to blame. I still can't bloody believe it.'

It turns out Marty took a substantial payment from Carlyle in exchange for handing his troubled son over to what he believed was a boot-camp drug-rehab facility. Everett thinks Marty also delivered other addicts to The Frontier in exchange for money, young men who could easily disappear without a trace.

It's not clear if Lee slept with Layla, the sixteen-year-old. She continues to maintain they never had sex despite her feelings for him, and there's nothing in Franklin's meticulous notes to suggest sexual activity between them was facilitated. Layla has confirmed she was raped by Boyd several times after she first arrived at The Frontier and that it was soon after that she realised she was pregnant. I believe that Boyd convinced Lee the baby was his, manipulating him to believe he'd been with Layla to prevent the Kirks discovering Boyd had raped the girl, but we'll never know for sure.

Lee was undeniably obsessed with Layla. Notebooks were located under his bed at The Frontier, filled with his poetry and declarations of love. When Everett hauled the tradesmen from the pub into the station for questioning, they admitted they'd seen Lee spying on Layla and masturbating when she was in the exercise yard, an enclosed open space in the middle of the complex.

I say, 'Everett told me they've found documents relating to the construction work done at The Frontier.'

'Some,' Jonesy says, 'but we think a lot of the initial work was done by migrant workers that Barnes shipped in.'

Initially the facility was basic, using the old bomb shelter footprint. Simple building work was done to create separate rooms and a lab as well as plumbing. In recent years, Barnes arranged for Bilson to expand the facility in order to accommodate the growing number of people there. After being forced to sign strict NDAs, groups of builders were transported there each night. They were only given glimpses of the whole.

'How is Layla?' I ask.

'She's going okay,' says Jonesy. 'She's named the baby Alice.'

My heart aches for Layla whose quiet strength is an inspiration. 'For a sixteen-year-old, she's been through a lot.'

'Too much. We learned that Boyd was the one with her when she gave birth. Her rapist performed her caesarean. Can you imagine it? The poor bloody kid. But she wants to keep the baby, and the foster family are committed to looking after them both, so there's a chance at a normal life.'

Neatly recorded in Franklin's notes are several experiments that Carlyle planned to conduct on Layla's baby. He was corresponding with a lab in China that had procured three orphan infants; they were planning to test medication Carlyle had developed to control parts of the brain, ultimately looking to treat conditions like schizophrenia.

There had once been another baby living in The Frontier, the son of a teenager Carlyle had treated at Cloud Consulting. Both of them died several years ago, after the pregnant girl was given experimental drugs Carlyle had developed to attempt to treat bipolar. He wanted to see if it was safe for expectant mothers. The baby was born early and unwell, and died within a few weeks. Not long after that the woman committed suicide.

'Your sister did a brave thing,' Jonesy says. 'She must have known the chances of her rescuing that kid and surviving were slim.'

He doesn't mention the abuse my sister willingly inflicted, for years, on vulnerable people under Carlyle's influence, and I'm glad. I'm still grappling with what she did, even though she was a victim, too.

'Thank you. It's hard to know how to think of her. Did Layla know my sister was going to take the baby?' I ask.

'Yes, she told us she wanted Sandra to take her.'

'Do you know where my sister got the car from yet?'

'We think it was from The Retreat,' he says. 'We've found three other stolen vehicles on the property and don't think she could have made it much further than that on foot.'

Our teams discovered two cars on the other side of The Frontier complex from the creek, vehicles that only Carlyle, Roger and Boyd had access to. One is the car we believe ran my sister off the road.

'Franklin must have helped her,' I say, echoing something Everett told me yesterday. He's been keeping me updated on developments, granting me a daily one-on-one check-in.

'We think so. From the lab records we know they were close, and she got a phone from somewhere and had Lee's number.'

I've already thought about speaking to Franklin again and asking him to tell me about my sister. Like his father, he's been charged with myriad crimes but it remains unclear whether he'll argue he suffers from a mental impairment as part of his defence. He's currently residing in a mental health facility in Sydney.

'But we didn't find a phone in the crash.'

'No,' he says. 'Still, we've uncovered the message she left on Lee's burner phone.'

I try to imagine her voice, wondering if it sounds like mine. 'He must have told her to leave the baby at the lake.'

'We assume so. Marty said he used to go there as a kid all the time.'

I remember the graffiti on the tree. 'But he was arrested before he could get the baby.'

'We think he tried to make a call from the hotel room. He was paranoid about Carlyle, and we assume he didn't want to tell the cops about the baby because he knew his dad would find out. A cleaner found the burner on top of the cupboard in the hotel room.'

'Did Sandra know about the microchips?'

'We don't know.'

'I don't understand why Lee was allowed to leave The Frontier.'

'His mother, Erin, found out that Marty had taken money in exchange for Lee and demanded her husband get him back. She'd been beside herself thinking Lee had left Smithson and was living rough somewhere. Carlyle refused to release him, but then Marty threatened to tell me everything he knew if Lee wasn't released. In the end they let him leave, making it clear that if either father or son spoke to anyone about The Frontier, they'd be in serious danger. We still don't know how Carlyle organised the hit on Lee in gaol—we assume a guard was paid off, seeing as the attack happened off camera.'

'So many secrets.'

With a cough, Jonesy looks down at the table, his pudgy hands around his coffee.

Pushing my feet against the floor, I steady myself with a deep breath. I'm so nervous that he's going to say something that means our bond will sever and that I'll have to walk away for good. But my fear doesn't overpower my desire to know the truth. 'You know we need to talk,' I say.

'I'm sorry I never told you about your mother, Gemma. Your dad was worried it would put you off joining the force . . . and, well, I thought he was right.'

'Tell me everything.'

Jonesy picks up a spoon and tries to twirl it between his fingers before it falls noisily to the floor. 'Your dad came to see me after you'd put in your application. We'd already met, remember?'

I nod.

'He told me about your mum's background—he wanted to know if it would hinder your chances. He was worried it would mean you wouldn't get accepted.'

'I think he was more concerned I would find out,' I say, the betrayal still stinging.

'I think he just knew how important being a cop was to you, though he worried it wasn't safe.'

'Did you manipulate my security checks?' I ask, my cheeks growing hot.

'I didn't have to. She was never charged, so the link was never made between you and your mum. But I'm not going to promise I wouldn't have! I thought you deserved a chance.'

'Did it—' I pause, not sure how to phrase the question. 'Did it mean you treated me differently?'

'No,' he says firmly. 'I gave you the same chance as any other rookie recruit, but I knew pretty quickly that you were a smart kid. You had something special.'

'But—'

'Woodstock, it was all you. Nothing that's happened to you has anything to do with who your mum was or wasn't and what I knew about it. You can put that rubbish right out of your mind. Hey, I mean it. There was no special treatment.'

'Thank you.'

'Don't bloody thank me,' he mumbles.

Around us patrons come and go, exclaiming at new haircuts and photos of children, complaining about the mild spring, and encouraging each other to order cake with their coffee.

'There's something else.' I'm reluctant to ruin the moment but determined to see this through.

He exhales forcefully. 'Minnie spoke to me yesterday.'

'She did?'

'I think talking to you gave her some confidence.' Our eyes meet before he looks away.

I can't keep the despair from my voice. 'Jonesy, what the hell happened?'

He closes his eyes, puffing his cheeks before slowly exhaling. 'I want to be clear,' he begins, 'this is not an excuse. I've apologised to Minnie and reported myself to Superintendent O'Connell. I'm pretty sure there will be an investigation.'

Even though I'm glad he's done the right thing, I feel sad. 'Tell me what happened. I want to hear it from you.'

'Truthfully, I don't remember exactly what I did, but I believe what Minnie told me, what she told you. She has no reason to lie.' I open my mouth, and he holds up a hand. 'I also want to be clear that it's not because I was drunk, or at least not strictly anyway. Gemma, I have Parkinson's.'

My mouth remains open and I reach out my hand to grip the side of the table. 'What?' I heard him correctly but the words don't compute.

'I'm on meds for Parkinson's disease. I've been a stubborn bugger about it, refusing to accept it and generally being a pain in the arse. I shouldn't have been drinking that night, but I wanted to go out with everyone, and I knew I'd get ribbed if I didn't drink. So I had a few beers—and, unsurprisingly, they didn't agree with the medication.'

He pauses. 'I knew something had happened. I remember being out front with Minnie and her going back inside. When she avoided me the next day, I knew I'd done something, but I was too much of a coward to ask her about it.'

I stare at him as if I'll be able to see the disease. 'I don't know what to say.' All I can think is that I'm really going to lose him this time and it's so much worse than before.

'I do. I'm an idiot. I prioritised myself over the wellbeing of a young woman and behaved like a selfish pig. I should suffer the consequences. I told Lucy straight away. She was furious—still is.' He looks up at me ruefully. 'Actually, she's disappointed, which of course is worse.'

'How sick are you?' I whisper. My nostrils flare as I try to get a handle on my emotions.

'I've found meds that agree with me, so things have settled a bit. But, Woodstock, this thing only goes one way.'

'Is this why you're retiring?'

'Yes and no. It was a catalyst, but I think it's the right time, regardless. We need new faces around here—and I need a break. O'Connell has been surprisingly supportive, in her own intense way.'

'Why didn't you tell me you were sick?' I say, fighting back tears.

'Because it's a shitty thing to talk about.'

I let out a shaky breath. 'How is Minnie?'

'She's okay, I think. I made it clear that what happened is all on me and that she did nothing wrong. O'Connell is going to speak to her tomorrow and offer her counselling if she wants it. Minnie's a bloody good cop—I told her that, too.'

He looks at me and it's a question. He wants a sense of what this is going to mean for our relationship. I look him in the eye and say, 'I agree with what you said before. There's no excuse for what you did. None. I'm angry and disappointed in you, too, but I want

us to be able to get past this. And I'm glad you talked to Minnie.'
I hope their conversation helped her feel like she can move forward.

We finish our coffees, and I try to avoid thinking about his inevitable decline.

'What about you?' he asks tentatively. 'Have you decided to stay in Smithson?'

The events of the past few weeks are weighing down my limbs, and I'm not sleeping well, but I know that Mac and I need to decide what we'll do next year. Applications close for Jonesy's job in less than a week, and we need to make plans for Ben's schooling if we're enrolling him somewhere else.

Still feeling rattled by his news, I say, 'I'm not sure yet. There's a lot to think about.'

Our table is cleared and I check my watch, realising we've been talking for over an hour. 'You probably need to get back, you must be busy.' I get to my feet.

Jonesy pats the table and gestures for me to sit down again. 'Will you stay for a bit, Woodstock? I'll shout you another coffee. You're right, they're much better here. And I have my eye on some of that.' He slides his eyes to the carrot cake on an adjacent table.

I check my watch, even though I have nowhere to be. 'Well—'

'Gemma, come on, just half an hour. Please?'

I sit.

EPILOGUE

Scarlett giggles delightedly as Mac carries her up Jonesy's gravel driveway, exaggerating his steps and making silly noises. I follow them, holding a tray of sandwiches, with a cooler full of wine and soft drink smacking against my hip. Scarlett is shedding the last of her baby features; her hair is darkening and thickening at the crown, and her thighs are losing their pillowy softness.

Mac reaches the front door, which is adorned with silver streamers, *Congratulations!* spelled out in gold across the top. He pauses to wait for me before he knocks on it sharply.

Lucy opens the door with a wide smile. She's stunning in a tailored blush-pink suit, her fair hair arranged in a classic chignon. 'Gemma, Mac. It's wonderful to see you. And especially you, princess.' Lucy puts her hands on either side of Scarlett's face. 'Gosh, she's big now. I can't believe she's almost a year old. No Ben?'

'He's with some friends,' I tell her.

'Goodness, he'll be driving soon.'

Mac laughs. 'He's already talking about saving for a car.'

461

Lucy makes a mock horrified face as she kisses me on the cheek, ushering us past the huge Christmas tree in the lounge room and into the kitchen. 'I'm glad you're here for this, Gemma. It hasn't been an easy year, as you know, so we are especially grateful for our wonderful friends. I want to thank you for being there for him after the incident with your colleague and for being a support to her, too. That was important to both of us.'

'Of course,' I say, adding our contribution to the impressive display of food. 'How is he today?'

'He's doing well.' Lucy hands each of us a flute of champagne, then picks up a half-finished glass from the bench and takes a neat sip. 'He obviously has mixed feelings, but he's in good spirits.'

'Mixed feelings,' I say, 'as in, he's threatening not to retire?'

Her lips twitch. 'Lucky we're flying to Fiji tomorrow, or he'd probably find an excuse to come into the office.'

'I'm glad you're getting some time away.' Scarlett reaches for me, and Mac hands her over. 'Whoa, whoa,' I say as she tries to grab my champagne flute.

Lucy watches us with a pensive look, and I know she has mixed feelings, too. While she has frequently resented Jonesy's career over the past four decades, it's been a big part of their lives. Most of her friends are married to cops; they're all used to fitting things around the highs and lows of cases, the unpredictability of law and order. Now she's staring down the barrel of another set of unknowns: the random nature of his illness. His retirement will be a gear change for them both.

'Should we head out back?' I ask.

Her eyes return to focus. 'Yes, please do. Ken will be thrilled to see you. Make sure he's going easy on the drinks—and the food.'

Mac hangs back in the kitchen, asking Lucy if she made the four-tiered sponge cake.

As we step outside, Scarlett squints and buries her head in my shoulder. Jonesy's backyard is a huge square of lovingly tended lawn bordered by Lucy's impressive gardening efforts. Wattle trees create golden fireworks along the back fence, and a tangle of native grasses and shrubs runs along the left. Rows of vegetables run parallel to the right fence, and a beautiful ghost gum provides shade over an outdoor dining area.

There are people everywhere. Smithson locals—cops and civilians—are talking and laughing, holding champagne flutes and beer cans snug in coolers featuring the local sports team logos. A trio of children run in between the groups, shouting to each other, and I recognise two of the staff from the cafe Jonesy has frequented for years, the place that makes the awful coffee.

I spy Jonesy, who is debuting some new clothes. He's standing with a few of the guys from the station, and I hold up a hand in greeting.

'Woodstock.' He ambles over, beaming at Scarlett. 'Hello, sweetheart,' he says, patting her head.

'Nice shirt.' I take in the lightly patterned green fabric, the fold lines not quite ironed out.

'Don't start, Woodstock.'

'I'll try to be nice, seeing as it's your special day. Congratulations.'

He clears his throat. 'Thank you. I told Lucy not to go to any trouble, but she wouldn't bloody listen.'

'I'm glad she didn't. This is perfect.' I place my hand on his arm. 'How are you travelling?'

'I'm okay. But I don't feel like I've eased into retirement—it's been a crazy time.'

'It really has.'

Carlyle Kirk was discharged from hospital last week and taken straight to prison, where he'll stay for the rest of his life. He's been charged with several counts of murder, manslaughter and human trafficking, as well as abduction, fraud, tax evasion and a raft of other offences. We know at least eight people died at The Frontier, while nine historical deaths at the nursing home are being investigated. His trial is scheduled for August next year and set to be a worldwide media circus. They've dubbed him 'Professor Kill' and can't get enough of him, with all the big networks offering hundreds of thousands for an exclusive interview. A million-dollar book deal has been proposed, and there are rumours a HBO miniseries is underway.

Carlyle, seemingly unfazed, spends his days corresponding with scientists from all over the world about his work. He insists he's on the brink of several breakthroughs and must continue. Many of his peers agree, with several labs planning to pick up his experiments and conduct their own clinical trials.

He refuses to talk about his son, his dead nephew, Boyd Mattingly, or anyone else involved in The Frontier or The Lyle. He has simply stated he always expected there would be collateral damage if genuine scientific progress was to be made.

'I don't know what I'd do if I saw Carlyle again,' I say. 'His evil is so insidious, dressed up as morality, like he thinks he's doing some kind of higher order work when really he's a cold-blooded murderer.' I don't tell Jonesy but at night I've been wishing I killed Carlyle in the underground room. When I can't sleep I picture shooting him in the heart and watching the life seep out of his body.

'I still feel bad about lying to you, Woodstock,' Jonesy says.

'We've been through all that,' I say. 'We don't need to rehash it. You're forgiven with a serious warning.'

He tugs the underarms of his shirt, where sweat patches are forming. 'I feel awful about Minnie, too.'

'I spoke to her yesterday. She's in a good place, excited about moving to Melbourne.' I went over to visit her and we sat among packing boxes, drinking coffee. She talked about the short-stay accommodation she's arranged and where she might live after that.

'I don't know why she doesn't stay—it's not like she has to see me at work anymore.'

'I don't think it's about you,' I tell him honestly. 'She wants to live in the city and make new friends. She's thinking about studying part-time.'

'And quit being a cop?' He looks pained.

'Maybe. I'm not convinced she ever wanted to join the force. She wanted to be a lawyer, but her dad liked the idea of having his daughter follow in his footsteps.' We spoke about that, too, and Minnie confided that she wants to use the move to make some big decisions about her future career. She's keen to give policing a second chance, but only one. 'Anyway, she's going to be great no matter what she does. And you are going to focus on all kinds of things you haven't had time to think about for years.'

He pats me awkwardly on the arm. 'You know you could have done my job, Woodstock. I would have backed you.'

'I know.'

'I hope you do it when you're ready. You'll be great.' He sniffs. 'You're one of a bloody kind.'

'Sorry, I didn't quite catch that. Can you say it again?'

'Don't push your luck,' he says. 'Just promise me you'll never settle.'

'I won't. But this is what's right for me right now.'

'And you get to report to Everett.'

I punch him lightly on the arm. 'Stop stirring up trouble. Everett and I are in a good place—and even if we weren't, it's not your problem anymore.'

We fall into a companionable silence as we sip our drinks.

'Are you feeling okay about retiring?' I ask.

'It depends on your definition of okay,' he says wryly. 'I'm about to eat my body weight in pineapples and coconuts. We're staying at a health retreat, if you can believe it. I have to keep a bloody food diary.'

I laugh, and Scarlett strains to be put down. When I place her on the grass, she crawls off to inspect a patch of daisies.

'I'm going to miss you,' I say, struggling to keep the emotion from my voice.

'You'll be fine,' he mutters. 'You've always been fine.'

'I'm proud of you.'

'Come off it, Woodstock,' he says gruffly.

We watch Scarlett for a few moments.

'Are things okay with your dad?' he asks.

'We're getting there.'

'You just need some time.' Jonesy pauses to give a thumbs-up to an older couple entering the yard. 'He cares about you, Woodstock.'

'I know.'

Lucy joins us. 'Sorry to steal him, Gemma, but it's time for a toast.'

'Already?' Jonesy grumbles.

Lucy hooks her arm through his elbow and pulls him to the middle of the yard. She taps a spoon against her glass. 'Attention, everyone! It's time for a toast. Make sure you have a glass of something fancy!'

I scoop Scarlett up and pry open her hands. All the plucked grass flutters to the ground.

'Hey.' Mac appears behind me and massages my shoulders.

'Hi.' I turn and smile at him, enjoying the feeling of his thumbs kneading my muscles.

'Ready, everyone?' Lucy plays with her necklace self-consciously and smiles up at Jonesy. She is tiny next to his towering frame. After taking a nervous breath, she reads out a sweet tribute. It references his first day on the job, when he unknowingly pulled over an off-duty senior officer for speeding.

Jonesy turns bright red, and everyone laughs. 'When he told me his name and his title, I almost died,' he admits. 'He hated me until the day he retired.'

Next, Superintendent Melissa O'Connell gives a short speech thanking Jonesy for his service and the support he's given her. It's heartfelt without being over the top, and I can tell he's pleased.

I catch Everett's eye through the crowd, knowing he'll be taking the opportunity to assess his new boss. He's here solo, but he and Jarrod are coming over to our place for dinner again next week. I smile at him, and he nods good-naturedly.

'I'm making him put a photo of me on his new desk,' Jarrod said when we caught up for coffee last week. 'I need you to tell me if he does it, Gemma. It's all part of Operation Big Man Baby Steps.'

'Speech! Speech!' The guys from work are calling for Jonesy to speak.

Although he shushes them, I can tell he's pleased. 'Just a few words.' His eyes shine as he talks about what the job has meant to him. He finishes by thanking the team that he has always considered family. He thanks the town of Smithson. He mentions a few of the old crew. He calls me out as someone he has enjoyed watching grow from a cadet into a detective, and says it's been one of the most rewarding parts of his career. He thanks Lucy for her patience and support, and then he falters, lost for words.

Lucy takes over, her easy charm putting everyone at ease. 'Thank you all for coming today. I think this is the most amount of social-ising that Ken has done in the past few decades, unless you count those awful cops-and-robbers trivia nights he used to organise.'

Everyone laughs again. Scarlett starts to fidget, and I pass her to Mac, who puts her on his shoulders.

Lucy lifts her champagne flute to the blue sky. 'Please raise your glass to my wonderful life partner, who has served his time and is finally free to travel the world with me.'

Jonesy makes a tortured face but bends down to kiss the tears shining on her cheeks.

'Cheers!' Glasses are raised, twinkling in the sun.

I put my arm around Mac's waist, smile up at Scarlett, and raise a toast to my former boss and to whatever the world has in store for me next.

ACKNOWLEDGEMENTS

Thanks and appreciation go to my agent, Lyn Tranter, and my publisher, Jane Palfreyman. I am so encouraged by your ongoing belief and support. And to my editor, Kate Goldsworthy, a huge thank you for pushing me (and Gemma) so hard on this one. You are undoubtedly the co-parent of this book baby. Thanks also to the team at Allen & Unwin for the attention and care they take in polishing and promoting my books. Special mention to Christa Munns and Bella Breden. I love being a part of the A&U family.

Thanks to the generous people in law, order, science and medicine who answered questions and provided a perspective on my requests for 'feasibility with some stretch'. Any mistakes you come across are mine.

My family see the very unglamorous side of writing life, and I want to thank them for putting up with me during all the weird and wonderful publication stages. I love talking to my kids about my book ideas and hope it's something we will continue to do for years to come. Thanks to my dad for being the first reader of *Body of Lies*. It was nice to have you know what happened to Gemma before anyone else did. Thanks to my parents, Kate Jay and Kate Symons, for looking after Ripley so I could finish my structural edit.

Shout out to Ripley for sleeping a reasonable number of hours each day, making it possible to finish this book.

And to Nick, thank you for always making me 'go do my writing'. I'm very glad our first date wasn't a bin fire.

Thanks also to Dani Vee for capturing the process of writing this book on her *Words and Nerds* podcast.

The idea for this book started as a 'what if'. *What if... a body was stolen from a morgue.* Intrigued by my own premise, I played around with the concept, and after a conversation with my mum (who knows lots of things about hospitals), it started to take shape. It wasn't initially going to be a Gemma book but she does have a tendency to insert herself into these kinds of situations, and of course now that's it's done, I can't imagine it without her. Gemma has been a hot, messy joy to write. I hope you liked this final chapter of her story.